MW01199252

BROKEN WORLDS:
THE REVENANTS
(1st Edition)

by Jasper T. Scott

JasperTscott.com

@JasperTscott
Copyright © 2018

Cover Art by Tom Edwards
TomEdwardsDesign.com

CONTENT RATING: PG-13

Swearing: PG-13, made-up euphemisms
Sex: mild and implied references
Violence: moderate

Author's Guarantee: If you find anything you consider inappropriate for this rating, please e-mail me at JasperTscott@gmail.com and I will either remove the content or change the rating accordingly.

TABLE OF CONTENTS

ACKNOWLEDGEMENTS

This book comes to you just two months after the last one, thanks in part to my wife's support. A good woman is worth her weight in gold. I also owe a big thanks to my editor, Dave P. Cantrell. A good editor is also a good writer, and Dave is a master of both crafts.

Finally, I owe a big thank you to my advance readers. These people never cease to amaze me. They somehow manage to wade through rough drafts of my work and still have nice things to say at the end! My heartfelt thanks goes out to B. Allen Thobois, Bill Schmidt, Chase Hanes, Dave Topan, Davis Shellabarger, Donna Bennet, Earl Hall, Erik Smith, Gary Matthews, Gary Watts, Gregg Cordell, Harry Huyler, Ian Jedlica, Ian Seccombe, Jacqueline Gartside, Jeff Morris, Jim Owen, John Nash, John Parker, Jonathan Hagee, Karol Ross, Kenny Harvey, Lisa Garber, Mary Kastle, Mary Whitehead, Michael Madsen, Paul Burch, Raymond Burt, Rob Dobozy, Rose Getch, Shane Haylock, Tim Runyan, Tom Spille, and William Dellaway—it's been a pleasure to have you all reading for me again!

To those who dare,
And to those who dream.
To everyone who's stronger than they seem.
—Jasper Scott

"Believe in me / I know you've waited for so long / Believe in me / Sometimes the weak become the strong."
—STAIND, Believe

DRAMATIS PERSONAE

Main Characters

Darius Drake "Spaceman"
Human male.
Cassandra Drake "Cass", "Cassy"
Human female. 12 years old.
Tanik Gurhain
Human male.
Dyara "Dya"
Human female.
Acolytes
Thessalus "Arok" Ubaris
Lassarian male.
Flitter
Murciago male.
Seelka
Vixxon female.
Gakram
Banshee male.

Secondary Characters

Trista Leandra
Human female.
Buddy

Togran male.
Gatticus Thedroux "Slick", "Metal Head"
Male android.
Admiral Ventaris
Human male.
Blake Nelson
Human male.
Samara Gurhain
Human female.
Nova
Human female.
Jaxxon Ricks
Human male.
Yuri Mathos
Lassarian male.

Minor Characters

Lora Addison
Human female.
Asha Wilks
Human female.
Elder Arathos
Male Ghoul.
Primus Kathari "Ra" Sievros
Lassarian male.
Ectos
Sicarian male.

Veekara
Vixxon female.
The Augur
Human male.
Feyra

PREVIOUSLY IN THE BROKEN WORLDS SERIES

WARNING: The following description contains spoilers for *Broken Worlds (Book 1): The Awakening.* If you haven't read that book, you can get it from Amazon here: http://smarturl.it/brokenworlds1

In the year 2045 AD, Darius Drake and his daughter, Cassandra, went into cryo-sleep to await a cure for Cass's cancer. They expected to sleep for fifty years, maybe a hundred, but instead awoke fourteen centuries later, and not on Earth.

They found themselves aboard a giant spaceship, the *Deliverance,* with hundreds of other cryo-sleepers, and in orbit around an unfamiliar planet, Hades.

The ship's biological crew were all dead, ripped apart by vicious alien predators called *Phantoms.* Only Gatticus, an android, survived the slaughter but with most of his memory corrupted.

Gatticus helped Darius and the others solve the mystery of where they are and why. They learned that Hades is a hunting ground of the Cygnians, A.K.A. the Phantoms.

Cygnians hunt humans and other species for sport, and they do it with the approval of the Union, an interstellar government formed to keep peace with the Cygnians. The Union sends criminals and innocent children to designated hunting grounds.

Children from every species are sent to the Crucible when they come of age. They have no memory of the experience but each receives a mark on the underside of their right wrists: the seal of life, or the seal of death. Those with the seal of death are sent to designated hunting grounds, such as Hades, while the ones with the seal of life are returned to their parents. A small percentage of children never return and are presumed dead — they are known as Revenants.

Hades is populated with those sentenced to be hunted. A society has formed on the planet and does its best to defend against Cygnian hunting parties. Darius and some other cryo patients went down to the planet to find fuel for the *Deliverance* in the hope of escaping the system before the Cygnians showed up again.

But they were too late. The Cygnians arrived. Cassandra was captured, and presumed dead, while Darius and the others were forced to flee with the help of a man named Tanik Gurhain — an exiled war criminal with mysterious powers.

After leaving Hades, Tanik assumed leadership of the band of survivors and revealed his plan to use the *Deliverance* and its frozen cargo of patients to fight a war against the Cygnians and their empire—The United Star Systems of Orion (USO). He woke all of the cryo patients and cured them of their various diseases using nanites.

Darius was surprised when the entire group agreed to go along with Tanik's plans. He learned from Dyara Eraya, Tanik's right-hand, that she had misgivings about him, and that Tanik might be controlling the recently-awoken crew by supernatural means.

Dyara and Darius seemed to be the only ones able to resist Tanik, so they plotted to overthrow him. The coup failed, and Dyara was arrested.

Gatticus learned that Tanik had a role in the death of the *Deliverance's* original crew, but before he could warn the others, Tanik disabled him and sent him into deep space on a transport ship to cover up his actions.

Tanik didn't arrest Darius for plotting against him, because he believes Darius is the key to defeating the Cygnians.

Believing his daughter to be dead, Darius only cared about revenge and wanted no part of Tanik's war. He changed his mind when Tanik told him the Cygnians actually took Cassandra to the

Crucible to be tested and marked like all of the other children.

Clinging to hope, Darius joined forces with Tanik to find and rescue his daughter from the Crucible. They succeeded, and managed to rescue a handful of other children as well, none of which had been marked. The Crucible was heavily defended and the *Deliverance* was forced to flee. Tanik took them to an abandoned world to hide and revealed the true purpose of the Crucible. It was part of a eugenics program, designed to breed more Revenants for a war against an enemy called the Keth. The children returned to their parents showed signs of being able to breed new Revenants; the ones marked for death were sent to designated hunting grounds to prevent them from propagating; and the ones who never returned were conscripted and trained to become Revenants.

Tanik revealed he's going to train Darius, Cassandra, and all of the children they rescued to become Revenants, but not to join the war against the Keth. They're going to fight the Cygnians instead.

Darius isn't pleased about joining a war with his twelve-year-old daughter, no matter how good the cause, but with no fuel and the way back to Union space blocked by Cygnian patrols, he has little choice but to go along with Tanik's plans.

PART 1 - VISIONS

CHAPTER 1

Disgusted with himself, Darius watched the scene before him unfold. Tanik Gurhain was officiating the funeral of thirty-two Vulture pilots lost in the Crucible battle. He pointed out that fourteen of them had died heroically to save Darius's life after he'd recklessly charged in to save his daughter, Cassandra. Tanik didn't say "reckless," but everyone knew he meant that. Darius hadn't asked to be rescued, yet Tanik had ordered it because of some crazy idea that Darius is the *key to everything*—that the future somehow depended on him. Still, most of the crew blamed him for the deaths. Maybe they were right. If Dyara Eraya hadn't piloted an RR-3 Eagle to save him, and those pilots hadn't been forced to protect her, he'd have died a slow death drifting in the starlit void around the Crucible, and those fourteen pilots might have lived.

Darius's gaze found the ceremonial casket floating in front of the airlock doors. The casket was actually a cryo-pod like the ones that had stored him and his daughter, Cassandra, for the past thousand years. His eyes swam out of focus and burned with the threat of tears. This should have been *his* funeral, and everyone here knew it.

Tanik stood beside the casket, giving his speech. His bald head gleamed in the bright lights of the *Deliverance's* corridors. The long, parallel scars on his face stood out in sharp relief. "Do not mourn because they are dead. Rejoice because they are finally alive! It is from the light we come when we are born, and it is to the light we go when we die. Their bodies may be dead, but their spirits live on, undying and undiminished."

With that, Tanik waved a hand over the airlock controls and the inner doors swished open. He pushed the floating casket inside and shut the doors.

"May their spirits find rest. We commit these souls to the divine light: Lisa Davies, Ectos Fisk, Ikatosh Karosik, David Hunter, Kyle Turner, Ashley Palin...." The list went on and on, and Darius began to attract angry looks from the surviving pilots. He'd become a convenient scapegoat for all of the dead, not just the fourteen pilots who'd died to save him.

Dyara flashed a particularly dark look at him, but he pretended to ignore it. She wasn't just angry about the dead pilots. She felt betrayed that he'd refused to go through with their planned coup to overthrow Tanik. Not that he'd had a choice— Tanik had promised to rescue Cassandra, and he'd delivered on that promise.

It turned out that it didn't matter, anyway. An election had been held, and the vote had come out overwhelmingly in Tanik's favor. He'd gone from military dictator to democratically-elected dictator, which was different in theory but not in practice.

There was also good reason to doubt the legitimacy of the vote. Tanik was a Revenant, and he'd already shown Darius what that meant. It meant he could tap into the zero point energy field that permeated the entire universe in order to do seemingly impossible things. Among others, he could control the minds of the people around him. He'd done that with the crew of the *Deliverance* once before already, to convince them to join his war against the Union. He'd downloaded military skills directly to their brains with something called a neural mapper, but that didn't make them soldiers. They were medical refugees who'd gone into cryo to wait for cures to their illnesses. It made no sense that *all* of them would decide to join Tanik in his war against the Union.

As far as Darius was concerned, Tanik was definitely messing with everyone's heads—or *almost* everyone's. He, Cassandra, and Dyara were all immune to his mysterious abilities because they supposedly had the same potential to use the zero point field—the ZPF for short, or *source field*, as Tanik sometimes called it. That immunity put them in a unique position to oppose Tanik, but Darius owed him. Tanik had saved both his and his daughter's lives, and out of respect for that debt, he'd agreed to set the matter aside.

Tanik was definitely up to something, but it wasn't Darius's job to stop him. At least not yet. Besides, whatever his methods, Tanik seemed to be on the right side. He was fighting against the Cygnians and the USO. That had to count for something.

Darius shook his head to clear it and swallowed past a knot of guilt in his throat. His chest ached with grief. Tanik continued rattling off a list of the dead. There'd been a few dozen casualties on board the *Deliverance*, too. Tanik didn't have a physical list of names to consult, but he didn't need to; he had perfect recall thanks to his extra-sensory chip (ESC).

Ra, the black-furred Lassarian pilot, bared his teeth at Darius and his pointed ears twitched. "Skarvot," he growled.

Darius didn't understand the word, but Ra's tone made it perfectly clear.

"I'm sorry," Darius whispered, but Ra had already looked away.

"You shouldn't have come," Cassandra whispered, as she laced her fingers through his hand and gave it a reassuring squeeze.

Darius glanced down at his daughter and shook his head. "I had to," he whispered back. "It's the least I could do."

"It's not your fault," she said. "You didn't kill them."

"Now that's a load of krak," Blake put in, and flicked a scowl in their direction. His eyes were dry, but red and puffy as if he'd been crying before he'd arrived at the funeral.

Darius frowned. Blake had his own cross of guilt to bear for a friendly-fire incident he'd caused on the Crucible, accidentally killing dozens of innocent children by firing one too many missiles at the ring-shaped station, and yet even he was piling accusations on Darius.

"Shhh!" someone said before Darius could point out Blake's hypocrisy.

Tanik finished reciting his names and then nodded once to the crowd before turning to the airlock controls to open the outer doors. A warning chime sounded, and Darius watched through windows in the top of the inner doors as crimson lights flashed inside the airlock. The outer doors parted, and a gust of escaping air carried the ceremonial casket out into space.

Turning back to the group, Tanik said, "You have the next two hours to reflect and grieve. After that, report to Ready Room One at sixteen thirty for your next mission. Dismissed."

The crowd dispersed quietly, and Darius caught a few more accusing looks as the pilots left. He decided to wait for them to go first, and Tanik's eyes met his through the thinning crowd.

"Darius, Cassandra, Dyara—" Tanik's yellow-green eyes flicked to each of them in turn. "—don't go anywhere yet. I need to talk to you about your training."

Darius narrowed his eyes at that. The three of them were supposedly all capable of becoming Revenants, just like Tanik, but so far none of them had displayed any unusual abilities—not even Cassandra who had already been *activated* during her time aboard the Crucible.

Darius favored his daughter with a worried frown. He hoped they hadn't done anything to harm her. What did *activation* entail?

As the last of the pilots left the corridor, Tanik came over with a twisted smile. Darius wondered if that expression was just a product of the scars running across the man's face, or if there was something more intentional behind it.

"You look afraid," Tanik said, still smiling. His eyes glittered with amusement.

Dyara drew herself up. "Well, I'm not."

"*Should* we be afraid?" Darius asked.

Tanik held his gaze for a long moment, then said, "We need to activate you and Dyara before we start your training."

"That wasn't an answer," Darius replied.

"It wasn't intended to be," Tanik replied.

"What does activation entail?"

Tanik shrugged. "Nothing elaborate. You have to drink the living water."

"The what?" Darius asked.

"It's water filled with little sparkly things," Cassandra said.

Darius glanced at her and saw she was making a face. "You had to drink it?"

She nodded, and Darius shot a worried look at

Tanik. "Is it safe?"

He spread his arms. "Look at me, I am alive, am I not?"

"Again, that's not an answer."

Tanik's smile broadened. "It is perfectly safe. Now come. Follow me." Tanik turned and strode down the corridor.

Darius hesitated, but Cassandra followed and tugged him along by his arm. As they went, Darius quietly regarded his daughter. "Do you feel any different, Cass?"

"I don't know. Not really. Your body goes kind of tingly after you drink the water, and then the feeling fades. Other than that I feel the same. Mostly."

"Mostly?"

"Well, it might be nothing...."

"Tell me," Darius pressed.

"Well, it's like, you know that flutter in the pit of your stomach just before a roller-coaster dives down?" Darius nodded. "Or how you feel when you're standing on the edge of a cliff, looking down?"

"Yeah..."

"It's like that, only more... I don't know. It's like I'm exposed, like I'm not entirely inside my body anymore. Like..."

"Like you're part of something bigger than yourself," Tanik supplied. "Something powerful."

Cassandra nodded. "Yes."

Darius's brow tensed into a hard knot between his eyes. "You feel all of that?"

"Yeah."

"It doesn't sound safe to me," Dyara said.

"It doesn't *feel* safe," Cassandra replied.

Up ahead, Tanik reached a bank of elevators and hit the call button. Now that power was on and the maintenance bots had fixed all the broken doors throughout the *Deliverance*, the access chutes with their ladders had become a secondary means of travel between decks.

As they reached Tanik's side, the doors of the nearest elevator swished open and they followed him in.

"So, Tanik," Darius began as the man selected level *18* from the control panel. "What makes you think we *want* to become Revenants?"

Tanik arched an eyebrow at him. "Does a blind man want to see?"

Darius frowned. "I don't think—"

"No, you're right," Tanik cut him off. "How can you want something that you can't even imagine? You'll just have to trust me—this is not a gift you should refuse."

"Some gifts can be curses," Dyara pointed out.

"This is not one of them," Tanik replied.

The elevator arrived on level 18 and the doors parted into a broad corridor with bold white letters that read: *COMMAND DECK (18)*.

They followed Tanik out and down the corridor, joining a trickling stream of other officers in matching black, form-hugging uniforms.

"You said that I'm the key to everything," Darius said in a hushed voice. "You want to explain what that means?"

"It means that without you, the cause is lost. You are key to defeating the USO and the Cygnians."

"How can you possibly know that?" Dyara asked.

"Because I have foreseen it," Tanik replied.

They reached a door with a golden plate on it and glowing white letters that read: *Captain's Quarters.*

Tanik waved his hand in front of the door, and it swished open. The room was dark, but the lights swelled to a dim setting as they walked in. Tanik waved the door shut behind them, and then walked over to a locker along the side of the room. Darius followed him there, peering over his shoulder as he opened the locker.

Tanik withdrew a silver flask as well as a large metal and glass tank. Through the glass, Darius saw what Cassandra had described—water with luminous sparkles inside. Those sparkles appeared to be the source of the radiance, and they were flitting about inside the container, bouncing from one side to another, as if trying to get out.

"What are those things?" Darius whispered.

"Sprites," Tanik replied.

"They're alive?" Dyara asked.

"They're symbionts with a natural affinity for the divine light. These are anaerobic, so they can live inside of us, but the aerobic version is more common."

"Anaerobic? You mean like bacteria?" Darius asked.

"More like fungi," Tanik replied. "Who's going first?"

Darius regarded the sparkling water in the cylinder warily. "How do we know you're not trying to poison us?"

"To what end?" Tanik asked.

"To get rid of us? You said we're immune to your abilities. That means we're the only ones whose minds you can't control."

Tanik smiled thinly. "There are other ways of controlling people, Darius, but perhaps this will help settle your doubts."

Tanik screwed the flask into an attachment at the top of the tank and then depressed a button. The living water surged up as a metal pusher plate rose from the bottom of the tank. Unscrewing the flask, Tanik depressed a button in the top of it, and radiant water came streaming out in a snaking line. He held out a hand to that stream of water, and it coalesced into a perfectly round jewel, about the size of a golf ball. With that perfectly smooth marble of water gleaming before him, Tanik crooked his finger toward it and opened his mouth. The shining ball of water floated past his lips. He clamped his mouth shut and swallowed.

"There, you see? Perfectly safe," Tanik said.

Darius still didn't like it. He felt like he was about to join a cult and this was his initiation ceremony. Suppressing a shiver, he shook his head and asked, "What if we don't want to become Revenants?"

"It is your birthright. Besides, your daughter has already been activated. Don't you want to know what she is experiencing so that you can help her through it?"

"What's in it for you?" Dyara asked. "Why are you so interested in us becoming like you?"

"Because I can't fight a war on my own. And as

I said, Darius is integral to our victory."

"Assuming your visions of the future are accurate," Darius said.

"They are," Tanik replied. He held out the flask to Darius. "This is your destiny. I suggest you embrace it."

Darius hesitated, but Cassandra gave his hand a reassuring squeeze. "They don't mean you any harm."

Darius blinked at her. "They?"

"The sparklers."

"*Sprites,*" Tanik corrected.

"How do you know that?" Dyara asked, a frown dimpling her cheeks.

"I..." Cassandra trailed off, shaking her head. "I just know."

"Yes," Tanik replied with a knowing grin.

Darius accepted the flask and studied it, turning it over and over in his hands.

"Your daughter will need your help, Darius," Tanik urged. "It will be very hard for her to go through this on her own."

"Stop manipulating me," Darius snapped.

Tanik scowled. "Then stop wasting my time. You and I both know you're going to drink it anyway."

Darius was about to object, but he realized

Tanik was right. He needed to understand what Cassandra was going through.

Darius raised the flask to his lips and pressed the button at the top. Cold water automatically streamed into his mouth. His tongue tingled, and then his throat, as he gulped down two mouthfuls of the so-called living water. Releasing the button, he lowered the flask and nodded to Tanik. "How much do I need to have?" His whole body was tingling now, and his head felt strange—like the seat of his consciousness, the thinking part of him, was everywhere and nowhere at the same time.

"Empty it. There's enough to go around, and we can cultivate more later."

Dyara gave him a dubious look, but Darius was already in too deep to worry about consequences. He raised the flask to his lips and depressed the button once more. This time he held the button and gulped until the flask was empty.

Every nerve in his body was singing by the time he lowered the flask once more. Unintelligible whispers crowded in at the edges of his hearing, their number and volume increased with every passing second. His head was spinning, and his eyes were blurry and unfocused. He blinked to focus them, but it didn't work.

"Wha..." He shook his head in an effort to clear

it, but that just made everything worse.

"Dad?"

The whispering voices grew even louder, but they remained unintelligible. They weren't speaking Primary or Cygnian. His vision narrowed to a dark, blurry tunnel, and then he felt himself racing down that tunnel toward a bright, blinding light.

CHAPTER 2

The light was so intense that it washed out every trace of detail as Darius drew near, leaving him adrift in a sheer, depthless white sea.

"Where am I?" he asked, but his voice echoed strangely in his ears as if he'd *thought* the words rather than spoken them. Details began to emerge: the thundering roar of rushing water; a dazzling streak of fiery red clouds; a twisted, beleaguered black tree bowing in the wind at the edge of a cliff.

He turned aside and looked down. A familiar person lay on a bed of crimson flower petals, her face relaxed in sleep. It was Cassandra. She lay in a metal box, her skin as pale as a freshly-fallen snow. She looked no older than her twelve years—still just a child, and now she was dead.

Horror stabbed through Darius. This had to be

a dream. He saw himself reach out to touch Cassandra's cheek, and *felt* her icy skin brush the back of his hand.

He flinched, but his hand stayed where it was, pressed to Cassandra's cheek and trembling visibly. This was too real to be a dream, but it *had to be* a dream! Just a second ago he'd been standing on the *Deliverance,* and now... here he was standing on a cliff beside a thundering waterfall, with a fiery red sky overhead, and a bright, blazing sun glaring at him over the rim of his daughter's casket.

"They killed her," a gruff voice said.

Darius followed the voice to see Tanik standing beside him. He wore a thick black cloak with the hood drawn up over his head to ward off the frigid wind gusting over the cliff. His yellow-green eyes were sharp and bright, almost glowing in the fading light.

Darius's whole body trembled with rage. His throat was so tight he couldn't speak. Hot tears slid down his cheeks. He shook his head and bit his tongue until he tasted blood.

"She tried to negotiate with them, and they killed her," Tanik went on. "This just proves that there can be no negotiating with the Cygnians. The only way we'll ever have peace is to kill them all, or subjugate them as they subjugated us."

— 33 —

"This isn't real!" Darius screamed, but again his voice echoed strangely in his ears.

He shook his head, and this time he was aware that he wasn't the one moving his body; then he heard himself speak in a hoarse whisper of a voice, and he realized that he wasn't the one speaking either. "First we're going to slaughter them. Then when there's only a few of them left, and they're on their knees begging for their lives, we'll show them mercy, but only to prolong their suffering. We'll enslave them just as they enslaved us."

"Yesss," Tanik rasped in an euphoric whisper. "That would be justice."

Darius pressed a button on the side of the casket and the lid swung shut. As it did so, he realized that this was an improvised casket, a cryo-pod, just like the one they'd used for the funeral on the *Deliverance.*

Darius saw himself extend a hand to it, and the cryo-pod floated up, hovering out over the racing rapids above the waterfall. He hesitated, blinking tears from his eyes, and then his hand fell back to his side. The pod fell, too. With a loud *splash*, it ducked briefly under the water. It bobbed back up a split second later, only to be whisked over the cliff amidst sparkling curtains of spray.

A heavy hand fell on Darius's shoulder.

"Come," Tanik said. "Night is falling. The Cygnians will be out to hunt soon."

"Let them come," Darius replied, his voice strangled with grief and barely audible over the rushing roar of the river. "The negotiations are over. It's time we showed the Phantoms what they're up against."

Darius woke up screaming.

"Dad!" Darius blinked wide eyes at his daughter. She was shaking him violently, her cheeks streaked with tears. "Dad?" She stopped shaking him and crushed him into a rib-cracking hug.

"It's okay," he whispered into her hair, but he was frowning heavily. His head pounded like it was going to explode, and he felt like he was falling, even though there was no gravity whatsoever on board the *Deliverance*. The only thing keeping them rooted to the deck was their mag boots.

"What did you see?" Tanik growled, his green eyes bright and sharp with interest.

Dyara's gaze skipped between him and Darius and she slowly shook her head. "You said this was safe."

"It is. He's alive, isn't he?" Tanik replied.

"What happened to him?" Dyara demanded.

"I..." Darius trailed off as his daughter withdrew from the hug. He saw Dyara's concern mirrored on Cassandra's face, and his mind flashed back to her lying inside a cryo-pod on a bed of crimson flower petals, pale and frozen in death. His throat closed off, and suddenly he couldn't speak.

"What is it?" Cassandra asked.

"He had a vision," Tanik explained, and Darius nodded. "What did you see?"

Darius hesitated. He had the presence of mind not to say anything in front of Cassandra, but he *needed* to know more about what he'd seen. Turning to Tanik, he nodded and said, "I saw you. Dead in a casket. The Cygnians killed you."

Tanik's eyes glittered and a slight smile curved his lips. "Did you now?"

Darius nodded shakily, trying not to let his terror show. "What did I see?"

"A vision of the future."

"A *possible* future?" Darius pressed.

Tanik's expression remained frozen as it was, but his eyes drifted out of focus. "There are two kinds of visions: one is a certainty that you cannot escape. It is self-fulfilling, and the very act of seeing the vision sets in motion a chain of events that will bring it about."

A fresh stab of horror sliced through Darius. "What? That makes no sense."

"It makes perfect sense. In order to actually see the future, a real future, one's vision of that future must be a part of its causal chain."

Darius's mind flashed back to the casket and Cassandra's corpse-white skin. His mind railed against her death being some kind of inescapable fate. "Wait, you said there are two kinds of visions."

"Yes," Tanik nodded and his eyes snapped back into focus. "The second kind is a warning showing a *possible* future. It is a kind of divine intervention that alters your choices sufficiently as to prevent the foreseen outcome."

Hope swelled inside of Darius. "So which kind of vision was mine?"

"It's almost impossible to know. Only the most powerful Revenants can discern the difference between destiny and foresight. The ones who can have the power to mold the future and change their fate. But the ones who can't tell the difference, mistake destiny for foresight and end up inadvertently causing their own fates."

"What's the point of a vision that shows you something bad and also *causes* it to happen? That implies some kind of malignant force at work, producing those visions."

Tanik nodded soberly. "And foresight implies a benevolent force. That is why it is dangerous to look into the future. There are unseen forces at work guiding those fates, some for good, and others for evil, but it is hard to tell the difference."

Darius's brow furrowed. "Can you tell?"

"Sometimes," Tanik replied.

Dyara looked dubious. "How do you know you're not just imagining things? If something you see never happens, then how do you know you really foresaw anything? I can imagine lots of possible futures and use that insight to avoid those things happening."

"Ah, but the difference is that you are guessing, whereas a vision that comes to you from the light is based on all of the available data in the entire universe, and it is not a guess."

"Right," Dyara drawled.

Darius ignored her skepticism. His eyes were locked on Tanik's, his brain burning with just one desire: to prevent what he'd seen from happening. He was tempted to believe that what he'd seen had been part of a dream and not a vision, but somehow, he knew better.

"If I train with you, will I be able to discern the difference between destiny and a foresight? Will I be able to prevent what I saw?"

Tanik smile broadened into a scar-twisted grin. "I'm touched that you care so much for me, Darius."

He blinked, confused by the comment, but then he remembered his lie about *who* he'd seen in the casket. "Yeah, well, maybe I want to prevent other outcomes, too? Besides, we kind of need you alive right now."

"Yes, you do. As to your question, I have never seen someone so recently-activated by the sprites receive a vision before. It usually takes years of training to begin to see such visions. The fact that you required no such training only confirms what *I* have foreseen: you are no ordinary Revenant."

"I thought you said we have to train to become Revenants," Dyara said.

"In some sense you become Revenants the moment you are activated, but it is more accurate to call you acolytes—Revenants in training."

Tanik snatched the empty flask out of the air, where it was floating beside Darius, and he screwed it into the top of the tank of luminous, living water. Water swirled up into the flask once more and then he unscrewed it and held it out to Dyara. "Are you ready for your activation?"

She eyed the flask dubiously. "Am I going to

have any visions if I do?"

"It is extremely unlikely. With training, eventually you will."

"Have you foreseen anything in my future?" Dyara asked, her eyes wary.

"No. Why?"

"Because I want to know if drinking that stuff will lead to my death."

Tanik grinned. "If there is any evil lurking in your future, the only hope you have of escaping it is to become a Revenant."

"So you say."

"After all these years together, you still don't trust me, Dyara?"

"Not even a little," she said, but she took the flask and pressed it to her lips. Throwing her head back, she chugged the contents of the flask for several seconds straight. When she was done, she wiped a glittering bead of luminous water from the corner of her mouth, and it went spinning away.

Darius watched it go—a tiny world with dozens of glowing sprites trapped inside. The droplet collided with the wall of Tanik's quarters and exploded in a glittering spray.

"Good. Now you're all ready to begin your training on Ouroboros."

"Ouro-what?" Cassandra asked.

Tanik turned and gestured to the viewport in his room, and Darius noticed for the first time a green-white planet the size of the tip of his thumb shining amidst the stars.

"Ouroboros?" Dyara asked. "You know this place?"

"From my time fighting the Keth, yes."

"The Keth?" Cassandra asked.

"The race of aliens that the Revenants are fighting," Darius explained. "It's the reason for the Crucible, the seals of life and death, and the designated hunting grounds in the USO. It's all part of a eugenics program designed to breed more Revenants for the war."

"So the Phantoms aren't the real enemy?" Cassandra asked.

Tanik shook his head. "They're the scapegoat the Revenants use to draft their army and control breeding in order to favor source-sensitive lineages."

"So this planet—" Darius began, jerking his chin to the green-white orb. "—it used to belong to the Keth?"

Tanik regarded him steadily. "Oh, more than that. It used to be the *homeworld* of the Keth."

CHAPTER 3

"It used to be their *homeworld?*" Darius burst out. "And you brought us here?"

"Used to be," Tanik emphasized. "It's been abandoned for centuries, which makes it perfect for our purposes."

"And what exactly are those purposes?" Darius asked. "How long are you planning to stay here?"

"As long as it takes," Tanik replied.

"How about you give us a real answer?" Darius pressed.

"A few years."

"A few *years?*" Dyara echoed.

Tanik nodded. "By then the Cygnians will either have relaxed their guard at the Crucible enough for us to slip back through the Eye, or our scouts will have located a fuel depot on this side of the Eye with enough fuel for us to make the journey home without using the wormhole."

Darius shook his head slowly. "There's no way we have enough supplies on board to last that long. We'll have to grow our own food on Ouroboros."

Tanik nodded. "We'll have to establish a colony, yes, and it will take some time for us to plant and harvest native crops, but our supplies should last until then, and there's plenty of wildlife to hunt for meat."

Darius watched as Cassandra walked up to the viewport for a better look at their new home. Darius hesitated a moment before following her there. Both Tanik and Dyara went with him to the viewport.

"Is it safe down there?" Darius asked.

"No," Tanik replied.

Darius shot him an accusing look. "Then why did you bring us—"

"Because everywhere else is either more dangerous or too far for us to reach with our remaining fuel."

"What about the Keth?" Dyara asked. "This planet used to belong to them, so how do you know there aren't any of them still living down there?"

"There aren't. I would have sensed them if they were here."

"And the Revenants?" Darius asked.

"The same. Don't worry. The only beings still alive on Ouroboros are animals."

"What are the Keth like?" Cassandra asked.

Tanik looked at her. "They're very much like us. They are what humans call a terran-type species—*humanoid*, but that is a racial slur to other species."

Darius ran a hand along his jaw. "How is it possible that so many different species can look so similar without sharing any genetic information?"

"Some say that the divine light uses a common blueprint to create life. Others think there was a master race, long dead or long gone, that seeded the galaxy with life. A common blueprint or architect would explain a common design. There are many theories."

"Yeah, so about the Keth—" Darius said. "—you once said that they make the Cygnians look tame. After meeting both Banshees and Ghouls, I don't see how any species that looks like us could make them look tame."

"It is a question of perception versus reality. The Cygnians look terrifying, but despite their numbers, their population yields a particularly low number of Revenants."

Darius snorted. "Maybe because no one is hunting *their* unproductive bloodlines to extinction."

"On the contrary, who do you think the hunters are?" Tanik replied. "Both the hunters and the hunted die on designated hunting worlds, and the Cygnians' social structure prevents interbreeding between bloodlines that haven't produced Revenants and the ones that have."

"So the Keth make the Phantoms look tame because more of them can use the source field?" Cassandra asked.

Tanik favored her with a thin smile. "Not just *more* of them. *All* of them. Every single Keth is born with an affinity for the divine light. That is why we need Revenants to fight them."

Darius blinked in shock.

"Who's winning the war?" Cassandra asked.

"We are," Tanik replied, but his smile faded to a scowl as he said that. "However, the price of victory has been too steep, and the war was unnecessary to begin with. We're fighting the Keth because of the Augur's visions."

"The who?" Darius asked.

"The leader of the Revenants," Tanik replied.

"What visions?" Cassandra put in.

"He foresaw a Keth invasion, and he started a war to prevent it. He is the one who found the Eye and established the Crucible along with the system of seals and hunting grounds, all of it in an effort to breed more Revenants. He founded the Union. Before that the Cygnians were directionless predators, scouring the galaxy for their next kill. The Augur gave them a purpose beyond killing for killing's sake."

"Is he a Cygnian?" Cassandra asked.

"No, he's a human."

That revelation struck Darius like a ton of bricks. Speechless, he shook his head and forced some moisture into his mouth. "How is that possible? The Cygnians invaded Earth a long time ago, didn't they? I thought the Union existed before they came to Earth."

Tanik shrugged. "The Augur apparently found some way to leave Earth before they invaded. For all we know, he's the *reason* they invaded."

"But that would make him... like a thousand years old!" Cassandra said.

"Older," Tanik replied.

"Why would the Cygnians let him rule them?" Darius asked.

Tanik looked at her. "The Augur is the most

powerful Revenant who has ever lived. It is likely that he compelled the Cygnian Royals to follow him, and that he compels them still."

"But what about the other Revenants?" Darius asked. "They could overthrow him. Revenants are immune to each other's abilities, right?"

Tanik slowly shook his head. "No one is immune to the Augur."

"What about you?" Dyara asked. "You're not following him."

"I learned how to hide my presence. Then I faked my death and escaped through the Eye. He doesn't know that I am still alive."

Darius considered that. "And after you escaped, you spent your time trying to destabilize the Augur's empire from within. But if he can control everyone, why bother?"

"Because not even he is powerful enough to simultaneously control *everyone* in the galaxy. He controls the leaders of the Cygnians, and the other Revenants, but everyone else is still free to do as they please."

"Free," Dyara snorted. "No one in the Union is free."

Tanik conceded that with a nod. "The Cygnians use fear and threats of force to keep citizens in line, but behind them, the Augur is the one who is really gluing everything together. Without him, the Cygnians would go back to wanton killing."

"And that's somehow better?" Darius asked.

"We have two enemies to defeat: first the Augur, then the Cygnians."

"Are there any others like the Augur?" Cassandra asked. "Revenants who can influence other Revenants?"

Tanik flashed a wan smile, and his eyes danced, as if amused by some private joke. "You haven't figured it out yet?"

Cassandra shook her head.

"Figured out what?" Darius asked.

Tanik jerked his chin to him and his smile broadened into a twisted grin. "*You*. You can influence other Revenants. That is why you are the key to everything. It is your destiny to defeat the Augur and take his place."

CHAPTER 4

Gatticus Thedroux sensed the steady thrum of power returning to his ocular units and limbs. Servomotors in his joints whirred to life in his neck as he looked around. He was floating in the back of an SB-22 Osprey.

But where was the Osprey located? And how had he gotten there?

Gatticus consulted his internal logs and found nothing but a stream of errors. Corrupted memory, files not found, sectors missing, boot failures... There was also a repair log. His nanites had repaired everything as best they could with available materials by cannibalizing non-crucial components. Gatticus frowned—a human gesture, but he was designed to look and act human, after all.

"Activate mag boots," he said, and his legs snapped straight, yanking him down to the deck with an echoing *clunk.* As soon as his feet touched the deck, he made his way down the corridor from the troop bay to the cockpit, but before he even reached the cockpit, he realized that something was wrong.

The door was open, the pilot's seat was empty, and his sensors couldn't detect any other lifeforms on board—not even the faint radiation signature of another android. He was alone.

But where was he? And how had he gotten here? He couldn't remember. He knew his own name, and most of his older memories were still intact by virtue of being stored in a backup data core. Thanks to that backup, he knew he was an executor and ambassador of the United Star Systems of Orion, the USO. He'd been on some kind of mission... but he couldn't remember what. He also knew what year it was, in addition to several different languages.

Gatticus sat down in the pilot's seat and checked the navigation panel to see where his Osprey was.

The answer wasn't encouraging. He was in deep space, far from all the nearest trade lanes and planets. Gatticus's frown deepened, and he checked the ship's log to see where it had come from.

The Osprey had launched from the *Deliverance*, a colossus-class carrier. The carrier had been stationed at another point in deep space, some fifty light years from his current location. The Osprey's autopilot had been given instructions to engage the Alckam drive and fly until the ship ran out of fuel and fell out of warp.

No fuel.

If Gatticus had possessed a heart, he was sure that it would be pounding by now. He was stranded in deep space with no fuel. There was no way back to the carrier he'd launched from, and no way to reach any nearby colonies. No one would find him drifting here in the middle of nowhere. Gatticus used the nav display to search for the nearest Union world or station.

The closest place he could call for help was a deep space re-fueling station along an elbow in a nearby trade lane. It was eleven point twelve light years away.

Even if he sent a distress call to that station, it would take too long to arrive. By then, his power cells would be utterly depleted, and even if someone reactivated him, his position and duties in the Union would have been given to some other executor. There had to be another way.

The Alckam drive was down to just fifty grams of antimatter, not enough fuel to sustain a warp bubble for a ship of this size, but it would be enough for a comm probe, if he could fashion one from the Osprey's components.

Gatticus ran the numbers in his head. Given the size of the Osprey's Alckam drive assembly, sustaining a warp bubble over twelve light years would require just over thirty grams of antimatter.

The probe would make it with fuel to spare. Now all he had to do was build it.

* * *

Darius sat in the pilot's seat of an SB-22 Osprey. "Is everyone strapped in?" he asked, glancing over his shoulder.

Cassandra nodded. "We're ready."

A couple of the other children also nodded — the black-furred Lassarian, and the chalk-white Vixxon with her staring white eyes. The Banshee child bared his long jagged gray teeth and blinked all four of his giant black eyes. He gave a low growl, and Darius suppressed a shiver. He didn't like the idea of having a Cygnian teenager in his cockpit, but Cassandra had assured him that this

Banshee was *one of the nicer kids* present. Either that said something very disturbing about the other children, or Darius was going to have to adjust his stereotypes. He hoped for the latter case.

Darius keyed the Osprey's intercom. "Is everyone secure in the troop bay?"

Tanik's voice crackled back to his ears a moment later: "Yes. Let's be on our way, Darius." There weren't enough seats in the cockpit for all of them, so Tanik and Dyara were riding in the troop bay with a squad of Marines.

Darius switched to the *Deliverance's* command channel and said, "Flight ops, this is Gray Four requesting launch clearance, over."

"Gray Four, you are second in the queue. Launch in twenty second and counting, confirm."

"Roger, Ops. Gray Four out."

Darius entered the queue and waited for the launch tube to clear out. The Vultures had already launched, but there were dozens of transports lining up to fly down to the surface with Marines and equipment. It was their job to establish a safe landing zone for the colony before they brought the rest of the crew down.

Darius's transport was the only one in the first wave that carried civilians, and only because Tanik had insisted on taking the Acolytes down with him. He'd assured Darius that they would be safe, despite the fact that Ouroboros teemed with deadly creatures.

A *clu-clunk* sounded and a jolt went through the Osprey, jarring Darius. Four dark walls rose up around them as the Osprey dropped into the vehicular airlock below. Deck sections slid shut overhead, blocking out the relatively brighter lights of the hangar.

Crimson lights flashed briefly inside the airlock and a loud *roaring* sound began as giant fans sucked all of the air out. A moment later, a pair of doors opened up in front of them, revealing the launch tube. Red lights flashed down the length of it, and a robotic voice said, "Three, two, one—"

A sudden burst of acceleration slammed them into their seats, and a few seconds later they rocketed out into space. Ouroboros loomed large and close before them, so close that it blotted out the light of the surrounding stars. Ouroboros was a mottled green and gray world, striated with blue rivers, and blanketed with white clouds. It was another arboreal planet, just like Hades, but unlike Hades, this one didn't appear to have oceans, only lakes.

Darius grimaced at the thought of what might

be lurking in the forests. He set the transport's autopilot to take them down to the designated landing zone at a safe speed, effectively freeing himself to sit back and enjoy the ride. Darius glanced at the navmap and saw a pair of Vulture fighters race up behind them, one on either side. His comms chirped with a message from one of the Vultures.

"Gray Four, this is Red Leader, be advised there's a storm building over the LZ. Unless you brought a parachute, you're gonna want to keep your speed down."

Darius recognized that voice. "Blake?"

A crackle of static burst back over the comms — a sigh. "What's up, Spaceman?"

Definitely Blake. "They let you fly again after what happened?" Darius asked. Blake had accidentally fired one too many missiles at the Crucible, killing some of the people they'd been trying to rescue.

"It was an accident," Blake replied. "And we're short on pilots. Now if you don't mind, *sir*, let's cut the chatter. I've got another fifty transports to escort down before my day is done."

"Lead the way," Darius replied, wondering for the first time what the point of a fighter escort was if Ouroboros was abandoned. What was Tanik afraid of?

After a few minutes, they hit the upper atmosphere and turbulence shivered through the transport. A growing roar sounded against their hull, and gauzy white clouds swelled below them. Before long the clouds became towering mountains, some of which were broken by the snow-covered peaks of real mountains.

As their speed dropped, the autopilot nosed down to enter the atmosphere at a sharper angle. Now they were being *pulled* against their harnesses rather than pushed into their seats.

Some of the alien children in the cockpit began murmuring and moaning with the return of gravity as their stomachs leapt into their throats. But not Cassandra. She gave a whoop of delight.

Darius smiled. She was as fearless as ever. As they fell, the clouds swept up below them, and the sky gradually lightened from black to blue. Dark specks appeared, flitting between the mountain peaks—*birds?* Darius wondered, and the clouds flashed with lightning.

"Heads-up," Blake said over the comms. "Looks like we've got some action over the LZ."

"Action?" Darius replied. "What kind of action?"

The clouds drew a thick white curtain over the

cockpit canopy, blocking their view. Darius checked the nav display and found over a hundred unidentified contacts, each of them about half the size of a Vulture. Those had to be the birds he'd seen.

A straight bolt of lightning flashed by in front of them, followed by another, and then a flickering stream of them. But lightning bolts weren't straight. These were lasers.

A split second later the clouds fell away and a scene of utter chaos appeared. Dead ahead was a sprawling green field marked with a green diamond to denote their landing zone. The hunching black shapes of several Ospreys were already landed in the field, and four Vultures were circling above them, firing flickering streams of hot-white lasers into a swarm of giant black birds.

Lasers leapt out to either side of them as Darius's escort opened fire. Birds leapt into flames and fell thrashing to the ground, raining over the LZ like meteors. Apparently the birds were more of nuisance than a threat.

But even as Darius thought that, a pair of birds latched onto one of the Vultures, and it went tumbling down. The canopy blew open as the pilot ejected. The ejection seat rode a bright blue thruster trail into the sky before deploying a parachute and drifting down slowly. The Vulture went spinning into the ground with a flash of light and a subsequent *boom* that rattled through the cockpit.

"What's going on?" Cassandra asked.

Darius took over from the autopilot and activated the Osprey's forward cannons. He targeted the nearest bird and sliced off its wings with two fat white laser beams. The severed torso of the bird fell flaming to the ground.

Just as Darius targeted the next one, he saw a pair of birds shredding the ejected Vulture pilot's parachute with their talons.

The pilot's panicked voice sounded over the comms: "Get them off me! Get them—!" His voice died in a gurgle as another bird snatched him from the air and carried him off—parachute, ejection seat, and all.

A second Vulture fighter went tumbling from the sky, and this time the pilot didn't eject.

"Fek it!" Blake roared just as that fighter dug a flaming crater in the landing zone. It was a good thing Tanik had told the deck crew to empty the antimatter from all their Alckam reactors before heading down to the surface.

Darius's Osprey hit the flock of birds, and suddenly it was hard to see for all the flapping black wings. Darius had already hauled all the way back on the throttle, but now he was forced to kill thrust entirely and hover to avoid colliding with one of the beasts.

It didn't work. No less than four birds swooped in and glommed onto the Osprey. "Blake, get them off us!" Darius snapped over the comms.

"How?" Blake demanded. "I can't shoot them without hitting you! Waggle your wings or something!"

Massive talons struck the cockpit canopy and scrabbled for purchase on the glass. Cracks fractured the canopy.

The children in the cockpit screamed, but their cries were promptly drowned out by deafening roars and a loud *whooshing* of wings. These monsters were trying to carry the Osprey away.

Thud-thud. THUD. Darius glanced up. More of them were landing on top of the transport. Claws screeched, raking on metal, and the Osprey nosed down with the added weight. The ground came racing up fast.

"We're going to crash!" Cassandra screamed.

CHAPTER 5

The cockpit door swished open and heavy boots rushed in, but Darius didn't have time to look. He fired the ventral thrusters at maximum power to avoid crashing into the landing zone, and the Osprey rocketed up. The birds clinging to them shrieked with fright and took off.

"Something spooked them!" Blake said over the comms. "They're all leaving!"

Darius regained control of the transport and banked back around to see that he was right, and it wasn't just the ones attacking his transport. They were all leaving.

"Set us down over there," a gruff voice said, and Darius turned to see Tanik standing behind him in a suit of power armor.

"What were those things?" Darius asked.

"Awks. Revenants call them Seekers because they're drawn to us. They must have sensed us coming."

"Great," Darius said.

"So why did they leave?" Cassandra asked.

"I filled their minds with terror. They won't bother us again. At least not until we've set up our defenses."

"What about the pilot they dragged off?" Darius asked.

"He's dead. Set us down over there." Tanik pointed to the far side of the grassy landing zone where a broad river raced over the edge of a cliff. A beleaguered tree clung to the cliff, and glittering curtains of spray rose above the waterfall.

Darius's mind flashed back the vision of his daughter's funeral at the edge of a river that looked just like this one.

"Darius, did you hear me?" Tanik prompted.

He said nothing, but took them down for a landing beside the river as Tanik had directed. Their landing struts touched down, and Darius spent a moment staring into a field of blue-green grass, undulating in the wind and shimmering in the sun. Clear, rippling water raced by in front of them, surging down from a soaring mountain range to one side of the landing zone.

"Let's go," Tanik said, and gave Darius's shoulder a squeeze.

Darius gave no reply. He was frozen in horror, staring at that river, the one that had carried his daughter's casket away.

"Is something wrong, Darius?"

"I saw this place in my vision," Darius said quietly. "This is where we held the funeral."

"*My* funeral?" Tanik asked. His voice was laced with irony, as if he *knew* Darius had lied about who he'd seen in his vision.

"We can't stay here," Darius said. "We have to go."

"There's nowhere else for us to go. Besides, you don't know yet what kind of vision you had. It may be easy to prevent."

Darius unfastened his harness and turned to look at Tanik. "We can stay on the *Deliverance*. Train us there."

"No, you can't. A starship is too easy to spot, and if a Keth or Revenant vessel passes through here, they'll instantly spot a ship that size with its reactor online. I'm sending the *Deliverance* away as soon as we're done offloading people and supplies."

"Away where?" Cassandra asked.

"You can't do that!" Darius said. "That carrier is our only ticket out of here!"

"Which is why we can't afford to lose it. The *Deliverance* will be safer hiding beyond the edge of the solar system, far enough away that no one should see it, but close enough to summon or fly back to when we're ready to leave."

Darius shook his head. "The Cygnians are going to come here. I saw it."

"Did you now?"

"Yes. Cassandra was—" He stopped himself, glancing briefly in her direction, then back to Tanik. "She was trying to negotiate with them. It didn't work."

"And then they killed me?" Tanik asked. His dark eyebrows hovered up behind his faceplate, furrowing his brow.

"Yes."

"Then this time we won't negotiate. Now come, we have a lot to do, and we don't want to be doing it in the dark."

Darius rose from his seat as Tanik went clomping back through the transport. Cassandra and the other children stood up too. The Banshee child bared jagged gray teeth at him. "My people are not the enemy, the Augur is." He spoke in the guttural mixture of hisses and growls of the Cygnian language.

Darius regarded the Banshee with a frown.

"Did Tanik tell you that?"

"He told everyone," Cassandra replied. "You were still unconscious at the time, so I guess that's why he told you later in his quarters."

Darius jerked his chin to the Banshee. "If your people are being controlled by the Augur, then my vision makes no sense. Why would we bother trying to negotiate if we know that the Augur is controlling your leaders?"

"Maybe what you saw wasn't a vision," Cassandra suggested. "Maybe it was just a dream."

The black-furred Lassarian Acolyte rolled his head from side to side and growled. His pointed ears twitched, and he said, "Who cares? I'm starving. Let's get out of here." With that, the Lassarian turned and left the cockpit. The Banshee child ignored him. It blinked its four giant black eyes at Darius, first the lower set, then the upper. It licked its brown lips with a long black tongue and flicked the air with its barbed tail.

"What is your name?" Darius asked.

"Gakram."

"I'm Darius."

"I know."

"Well, it's nice to meet you, Gakram."

The Banshee just went on staring at him.

Darius glanced around, looking for the other

two children. The shape-shifting Vixxon stood on the opposite side of the cockpit from Cassandra, listening quietly. Like the adult Vixxon he'd met, this one also had a ghostly-white skin, but her hair was dark and shimmering, rather than luminous blonde.

"What's your name?" Darius asked.

The Vixxon's glowing white eyes shifted to him just as the final child, a wrinkly, bony-limbed Murciago with solid black eyes came up the ramp from the gun-well below the pilot's seat.

The Vixxon said, "I am Seelka."

"And you?" Darius asked, nodding to the Murciago.

The Murciago squeaked unintelligibly at him, and Darius frowned. "I'm sorry, I don't understand. Can you speak Primary?"

The Murciago's black nose slits flared and it spread its wings. Its pinched black mouth opened to let out another series of squeaks.

Darius shrugged helplessly. "I still can't—"

"He says you can call him Flitter," Seelka interrupted. "It's a nickname that another human gave him."

Darius blinked at her. "You can understand him?"

"Of course. Murciagos come from a planet in

— 65 —

my solar system. All Vixxons have to learn Murcian."

"Darius!" Tanik's voice boomed over the intercom. "We're waiting for you in the airlock! You'll have plenty of time to get to know the other Acolytes later."

Darius used his extra-sensory implant to activate the intercom speakers in the cockpit, and then replied, "On our way."

CHAPTER 6

As soon as the airlock opened, Tanik and Dyara ran down the landing ramp, followed by the squad of Marines. Darius hung back with Cassandra and the other Acolytes until the ramp was clear, then he led the children out, stalking down the landing ramp into a rippling field of blue-green grass. Cassandra was all but skipping along beside him. The wonder of exploring an alien world had swept aside the inherent danger for the time being. Or perhaps that was just adolescence rearing its ugly head.

Darius sucked in a deep breath of the alien air. It was cold enough to make his nostrils flare and lungs burn, and it had a sharp, metallic scent to it.

Dark clouds gathered overhead, and a rumble of thunder muffled the amplified shouts and thudding feet of Marines running around in power armor. Darius grimaced, hoping it wouldn't rain. The last thing they needed at these temperatures was to get wet. The Marines would be fine in their power armor, but he and the children were only wearing jumpsuit uniforms and mag boots—and in the case of the Lassarian and the Banshee, not even that.

Cassandra ran through the field at top speed, whooping with excitement.

"Cass! Get back here right now!" Darius roared.

She stopped running and turned to him. "I'm not a kid, Dad. Besides, those birds are gone."

Darius jogged up to her, scowling. "That doesn't mean it's safe," he growled. He grabbed her arm roughly, and pointed up. Four T-shaped silhouettes riding on cold blue tongues of fire were flying in circles overheard.

"If it's so safe, what are those fighters still doing here?" Then he pointed to the still-flaming ruins of the two Vultures that had crashed. Both were on the other side of the river and pumping thick black columns of smoke into the storm clouds overhead. "Someone already died today. You want to be next?" Darius demanded.

Cassandra frowned, but said nothing to that.

Darius turned to watch the Marines work. They were all barking orders at each other and cursing as they hurried to unfold and stake down what looked like giant white tents. Making their task more difficult, a brisk wind gusted through the field, dragging the tents around like sails. As Darius watched, one of them burst free of its stakes and took flight, dragging a Marine along with it. The man cried out in alarm and began cursing viciously. His leg was tangled up in the tent ropes. Before anyone could do or say anything, the tent landed in the river and sucked the Marine in with it.

Darius released Cassandra's arm and sprinted down to the riverbank. "Hey! Somebody help him!" Darius ran along the riverbank, trying to keep up with the tent, but the current was too fast. The only sign of the Marine was the occasional glimpse of a thrashing foot or hand.

Three Marines ran by Darius in a blur with the augmented speed provided by their power armor, but one of them was far faster than the others, and he reached the edge of the waterfall first. Even he wasn't fast enough. The river swept the tent and the Marine over the cliff just a split second later.

The other two Marines reached the cliff, followed a few seconds later by Darius. He stood with his hands on his knees, gasping for air and doubled over with exhaustion. He couldn't see anything through the shimmering sheets of spray rising over the waterfall. The spray was so thick that it soaked through his jumpsuit in seconds.

All three Marines stood there in shock, staring over the cliff with water running down their black armor in glistening streams. This was their second casualty of the day, and they'd only just arrived on Ouroboros.

"What the..." One of the Marines pointed out to the horizon.

A billowing white tent appeared floating up through the swirling mist. A man in gleaming black armor dangled by his leg from ropes trailing below the tent.

The tent and its victim floated down to a safe landing in the field. Two of the Marines ran to help him, but Darius stayed right where he was, staring at the third Marine. The man's face wasn't visible through the reflections in his faceplate, but Darius knew who it had to be. "Tanik?"

"Yes?"

"How did you...?" Darius trailed off, shivering violently. He was soaked with spray from the waterfall.

"After everything you've seen me do, this

surprises you?" Tanik asked. "You'll see much greater things than this."

Darius hugged his shoulders and shook his head. He turned to look around for Cassandra, and found her striding through the field toward him.

A crack of thunder split the air, and both he and Tanik looked up at the gathering storm. The clouds were black now. Darius felt heavy raindrops land on his cheeks. "Go back inside the transport before you freeze to death. Take the children with you. I'll come get you when the habitats are ready."

Darius nodded quickly and ran across the field to reach Cassandra.

"Is that guy okay?" she called out as he drew near.

Darius nodded as he reached her side. "Tanik saved him." Another crack of thunder split the air, and the rain began falling harder. "Come on!" He grabbed Cassandra's arm again and ran back to the Osprey. By the time they reached the transport both of them were soaked. The other kids had already taken shelter inside the airlock, all except for the Banshee.

"Where's Gakram?" Darius asked.

"He said he was hungry," Seelka said, blinking her white eyes at Darius.

"Who isn't?" the Lassarian demanded.

Darius rubbed his arms in a vain attempt to get warm. Beside him, Cassandra's teeth were chattering audibly. "We'd better go back inside," he said. "Cassandra and I need to change into dry jumpsuits." Darius cycled the airlock and led the way inside. He checked the lockers in the troop bay and found a pair of spare jumpsuits.

"Come on, Cass," he said, and hurried down the corridor from the troop bay to the cockpit. Stopping just outside the open door to the cockpit, he passed one of the jumpsuits to his daughter and nodded. "You change first."

She took the jumpsuit and walked through. He waved the door shut behind her and waited, shivering in the corridor, with his back to the door. A few minutes later, Cassandra emerged in a dry jumpsuit. Her hair was still wet, and her lips were blue, but at least she wasn't shivering anymore. That was more than could be said for him.

"Your turn," she said.

He hurried into the cockpit and struggled to get changed with shaking hands. As he got undressed, he realized that he hadn't thought to look for dry underwear. Too late now. Once he was dressed, he began to feel warmer. It also helped that it was much warmer inside the Osprey than outside.

Darius left the cockpit and walked back into the troop bay with Cassandra. The black-furred Lassarian was pacing up and down.

"How much longer do we have to wait here?" he growled.

"I don't know," Darius replied. He heard a muffled peal of thunder and gestured to the ceiling of the transport. "It could be a while. At least until the storm passes."

"I am sssstarving!" the Lassarian hissed.

Darius's own stomach growled with that reminder and he went to check the lockers in the back of the Osprey for ration packs. It didn't take long to find them. He turned and held one out to the Lassarian.

The boy glared at the dull silver case with his yellow eyes narrowed to thin slits. "What is this?"

"Food," Darius said.

The boy took the ration pack and shook it beside his ear, listening to ration bars rattling around. "It does not sound like food." He sniffed the package suspiciously. "It does not smell like food either."

"Open it and try some. The red ones are meat flavored. You might like them." Darius passed out more ration packs, starting with Cassandra and ending with Flitter. The Murciago chittered something, and Darius nodded, assuming it meant *thanks*.

"Blah!" the Lassarian said. "This tastes like dirt!"

Darius barked a laugh and turned to the boy with a grin, but the Lassarian hissed loudly and bared his teeth.

"You are making fun of me! This is not food! You are trying to poison me!"

Darius wiped the grin off his face. "Sorry. It *is* food, but it's not the greatest, you're right. Look, give it here—" He held out a hand for the ration pack. The Lassarian eyed Darius's hand warily, his tail and ears flicking restlessly.

Darius crossed over to him and took one of the red ration bars inside the open pack. He took a cautious bite, chewed, and swallowed with a forced smile. "See?" he said.

"Eat more. I am not convinced."

Darius took another, bigger bite. The ration bar smelled and tasted like dog food. He'd forgotten how bad these rations tasted. This time he couldn't hide his distaste. Darius swallowed with a grimace.

The Lassarian gave a sissing laugh. "Now we are even."

Darius snorted and shook his head. "What's

your name?"

"Thessalus Arok Ubaris," the boy replied. "But you may call me Arok for short."

"Well, it's nice to meet you, Arok."

"I am sure that it is." Arok passed the ration pack to him. "You may eat the rest of the dirt. I will wait."

Darius frowned at the Lassarian's attitude, but decided not to make an issue of it. He went to sit beside Cassandra with the open ration pack.

Cassandra waggled half of a skinny brown ration bar between her fingers. "These ones aren't too bad."

Darius tried one. She was right. Instead of dog food, it tasted like biscotti. Not bad, but so dry that it caused him to cough and choke on its crumbs. Stumbling over to the lockers, he groped through them for something to drink and found a drawer full of canteens. Hurriedly raising one of them to his lips, he depressed a button and a short fat straw popped out. Darius sucked stale water from the canteen until his throat stopped itching with the need to cough. He wiped tears from his eyes and shook his head.

"Is there any more water in there?" Seelka asked, blinking her white eyes at him.

Darius nodded, and passed another canteen to

the Vixxon. Cassandra and Flitter came over, and he handed a canteen to each of them, too. Arok remained where he was, sitting on the far side of the troop bay, with his arms crossed over his chest, and yellow eyes glaring.

"Aren't you forgetting someone?" Arok asked.

Darius held out another canteen. "You want one?"

The Lassarian said nothing, but his eyes pinched into thin slits.

"Well, come get it," Darius said.

"Why don't you bring it to me."

Darius frowned. He wasn't going to pander to a spoiled brat. "Catch." he said, and tossed the canteen at the boy. Arok's eyes widened in alarm. At the last possible second, he uncrossed his arms and snatched the canteen out of the air. It had come within an inch of smacking him in the face.

"Nice reflexes," Darius said.

Arok hissed at him and jumped to his feet. "You are mocking me?" His tail lashed the deck in angry swishes.

Darius blinked. "No."

"Then you were hoping I would be slower, so that you could injure me with your cowardly assault."

"Hey, calm down, kid. I've got nothing against

you. Besides your attitude, that is."

"Attitude? What attitude?"

Flitter chirped something, and Seelka sniggered.

Arok's yellow eyes swept to them. "What did he say?" Arok demanded.

"He said you make the Banshee look friendly," Seelka said.

Cassandra laughed and nodded along with that. "It's true!"

Darius remembered her comment about the Banshee being one of the nicer children, and he wondered if it was because of Arok that she'd said that.

Arok's glare found Cassandra next and he took a quick step toward her.

Darius stepped sideways to put himself between the Lassarian and his daughter. "Hey, calm down, kid."

Arok tried to go around him, so he planted a hand on the boy's chest and gave him a gentle shove.

"I said—"

Arok hissed and lashed out with one hand, raking four sharp claws across Darius's stomach. Fire erupted in his belly and four bright red lines appeared. Darius stared dumbfounded as blood bubbled out and those four parallel gashes blurred together. Blood pitter-pattered to the deck in a steady stream at Darius's feet.

Arok grinned and held up his hand. Sharp claws protruded from the tips of all four of his fingers, dark and glistening with blood. He made an effort to peer around Darius and then tossed his head at Cassandra. "I can be funny, too. See?" he said, and roughly turned Darius by his shoulders to face Cassandra. Her eyes widened in horror at the sight of Darius's injury. She jumped to her feet with her hands balled into fists.

Darius struggled against the Lassarian, but Arok was surprisingly strong for a teenager. He elbowed the kid in the stomach, provoking a loud hiss. Rather than let go of him, Arok tightened his grip and wrapped one of his arms around Darius's throat. His claws dug in with sharp pricks, pressing dangerously close to Darius's carotid artery.

"Apologize," Arok growled.

"For what?" Darius asked quietly.

Arok tightened his grip and his claws dug into Darius's throat.

"Stop it!" Cassandra screamed.

Flitter chittered softly, but Seelka said nothing.

"Listen," Darius said. "I apologize if I did

something to offend you, okay?"

"Not good enough."

"What do you mean not—" Darius broke off in a gasp as Arok's claws dug deeper still.

"Beg for your life, *pika*."

Darius grimaced and swallowed his pride. "Please don't kill me."

"Yess, go on."

"Just leave him alone!" Cassandra screamed.

The airlock swished open in that instant, and a blast of cold air gusted in. Darius glanced sideways, being careful only to move his eyes, but he couldn't see anything. The airlock was empty.

"Who is there?" Arok demanded.

No one answered.

"Tanik?" Darius asked, wondering if he'd somehow sensed that something was amiss and had come to save his prodigy.

The airlock swished shut once more. "Nice try," Arok said. "Distracting me won't work."

"It wasn't me," Darius replied.

"Beg, pika. Beg me to spare your miserable life."

Darius was about to do exactly that when he saw a shadowy gray hand reaching down. It was exactly the same color as the inside of the transport. That hand pried Arok's claws away from

Darius's throat, and then a blast of hot, fetid breath hit Darius, and a massive, gaping maw of jagged gray teeth appeared in front of him. Four black eyes blinked open behind camouflaged lids. Banshees were practically blind in bright light. They hunted by their sense of hearing and smell instead.

Arok screamed in terror at the sight of the Banshee child. He let go, and Darius stumbled away.

Darius glanced up to see Gakram clinging to the ceiling upside down. His chameleon hide was almost perfectly blended against the metal roof of the transport.

Arok was tugging desperately to free his arm, throwing his weight against the Banshee's iron grip, but despite his best efforts his hand was inching closer to Gakram's gaping mouth.

The Banshee snapped his jaws right in front of Arok's fingers, missing them by a hair.

Arok whimpered, "Let me go!"

Gakram's eyes darted to Darius. "Say the word and I will take his hand."

Darius absently rubbed his stinging throat and his hand came away slick with blood. Tempting as it was, a hand for a few scratches wouldn't exactly be a fair trade. He shook his head. "Let him go."

"Are you certain?" Gakram asked.

"Yes."

Gakram released Arok, and the Lassarian fell on his butt with a sharp yelp. He jumped to his feet with a snarl just as Gakram dropped down in front of him on all fours. The Banshee's barbed tail skittered restlessly across the deck, and he bared his teeth.

Arok took one look at the Banshee, then spared a hateful glance at Darius, and ran for the airlock. Arok slapped the control panel until he accidentally opened it.

Once the kid was through, Darius mentally accessed and shut the doors via his extra-sensory chip (ESC). After that, they heard Arok banging on the outer doors. Darius took pity on him and cycled the airlock.

"Are you okay?" Cassandra asked. She was staring at the bloody mess Arok had made of his stomach.

Darius nodded. "I'm fine. It looks worse than it is." He wasn't bleeding anymore thanks to the nanite injections they'd received after waking from cryo. With those injections, he and Cassandra (along with all of the others from the pods) were capable of healing much faster than normal. Not to mention that they'd no longer get sick or age past their prime.

Gakram's skin gradually changed from gunmetal gray to its usual brown color, and he winked the left pair of his four eyes at Darius. "You are welcome."

CHAPTER 7

Tanik came to get them about an hour after the incident with Arok. He was still wearing his armor, but his helmet was off now, revealing his scarred face and bald head. Tanik didn't seem surprised to see the smeary puddle of blood on the deck, or Darius's shredded and blood-soaked jumpsuit.

"We're ready for you," Tanik said. The kids climbed to their feet one after another, but Darius remained seated.

"Did you see Arok?" Cassandra asked. Her hands balled into fists as she said his name.

"Who?" Tanik asked.

"The Lassarian kid."

Tanik inclined his head to her. "Ah, yes. I believe I saw him by one of the camp fires eating roasted Awk with the Marines."

"Awk?" Darius asked.

"The Seekers we shot down. I'm told that they taste just like chicken."

"You need to arrest Arok," Cassandra said.

"And why is that?" Tanik asked.

"Don't you see?" Cassandra burst out. She jabbed a finger at the puddle of blood on the deck. "He almost killed my dad!"

"That is troubling," Tanik said.

"So arrest him! Or go dump him off the cliff. I don't care," Cassandra seethed.

"Cass..." Darius chided. "I'm fine. He doesn't deserve to die."

"He tried to kill you!"

"Your girl is right," Seelka said. "He would have killed you."

"Is that true, Darius?" Tanik asked.

"Well, I don't know if he would have killed me, but he was threatening to. He told me to beg for my life."

Tanik's eyes narrowed to slits. "Did you? Did you beg?"

"I started to. My pride's not worth my life."

Tanik glowered at him. "And why didn't you fight back?"

Darius frowned. "I tried, but if I'd moved even a centimeter, he would have ripped my throat out."

Tanik scowled. "Get up."

Darius frowned. "Give me a second." He climbed gingerly to his feet, wincing as the movement tugged on the recently-scabbed over gashes in his stomach.

"Now defend yourself," Tanik said.

"What?" Darius asked.

"You heard me," Tanik said as he stalked toward Darius with his fists raised.

"Are you insane?" Cassandra shrieked. She put herself between Tanik and Darius, but he sent her tumbling with a flick of his wrist.

A hot flash of anger suffused Darius. He roared and ran at Tanik with his fists swinging. Tanik blocked his first blow, and sidestepped the next one. As Darius sailed on with his momentum, Tanik sucker-punched him in the gut.

All four of the gashes in his stomach ripped open and hot blood bubbled out once more. Darius felt a wave of dizziness wash over him, but he shook his head to clear it.

"You're soft," Tanik said. "Have you never been in a fight before?"

Darius gritted his teeth. "So what if I haven't?"

Tanik snorted. "For someone with an entire galaxy depending on him, you are remarkably complacent. Come on. Try again."

"It's not a fair fight. You're a Revenant. I haven't even been trained to use the abilities I supposedly have."

"I'm not using any abilities," Tanik replied, while advancing steadily toward him.

Darius jerked his chin to his daughter, who was just now picking herself back up. "No?" he demanded.

"Not on you," Tanik clarified.

"You're also wearing power armor."

"You don't need to injure me. First one to pin the other down wins. I've deactivated the power-assist, so my armor is a detriment, not an asset."

Cassandra ran at him, screaming incoherently.

"Don't!" Darius said.

She leapt up behind Tanik, as if to claw out his eyes. Instead, she hit an invisible wall and hung there, frozen and suspended in mid-air.

"Leave us," Tanik said, glancing at her. "Or I will put you to sleep." With that, he released Cassandra, and she fell in a heap at his feet.

Darius scowled darkly at Tanik. Enough was enough. He circled in slowly, keeping his eyes on Tanik's hands and feet.

"Good. I've got your attention," Tanik said.

Darius stopped just out of reach of Tanik, but

he continued circling, looking for an opening. He leaned in to deliver a jab to Tanik's chin, only to receive one to his own. His teeth clacked together noisily. He bit his tongue and tasted blood.

"Try again," Tanik said, smiling.

Darius tried to sweep out his legs with a kick, but Tanik caught that kick and pulled him off his feet. He landed on his backside with a jarring *thud*, and Tanik fell on top of him a second later. Cold metal armor pressed against Darius's throat as Tanik pinned him down with one arm. His other arm swept under Darius's legs, forcing them up to his chest so that he couldn't use them to deliver a kick. Not that Darius had the attention to spare. He had to use both of his hands and all of his strength just to hold Tanik's weight off his neck so that he could breathe.

Tanik shook his head, grinning. "You are pathetic, Darius! Even your daughter would put up more of a fight than this! Perhaps I should try her next. I bet she knows how to take a beating."

"Stop it!" Cassandra sobbed.

Darius's mind exploded with blinding fury, and he pushed against Tanik with all his might. Tanik's arm came away from his throat, and his other one slipped out from behind Darius's legs. Tanik began to get up, but Darius's hands found his throat and squeezed.

Tanik straightened, pulling them both up. "Much better," he croaked in a hoarse whisper. "You win. Let go."

Darius blinked in shock. He'd won? Why wasn't Tanik defending himself? He glanced away from Tanik's face and took in the scene. Both of Tanik's arms were spread from his side and wrenched behind him, as if he were straining against invisible chains. Tanik's yellow-green eyes flicked down, gesturing to the floor.

Darius followed that gesture and saw that the two of them were hovering several feet above the deck. His rage gave way to shock, and they both fell in a heap with Tanik's armor clattering loudly.

"Dad, are you okay?" Cassandra asked, hurrying over to him.

Darius sat up and nodded.

Tanik lay on the deck beside him, coughing and laughing. "Very good!" he said, while rubbing his throat. "You see? You *can* defend yourself."

"*I* did that?" he asked.

Tanik snorted. "Of course. Why would I hold myself back so that you could throttle the life out of me?"

Darius slowly shook his head. "How?"

Seelka stared warily at the two of them, while

Flitter chittered nervously.

Tanik gave a twisted grin. "Let's go find out, shall we?"

CHAPTER 8

Gatticus stood on the upper hull of his Osprey. His mag boots held him in place while he used a laser torch to weld the final pieces of his comm probe together. Stars shined all around him, dazzling in their brilliance. Gatticus took a moment to revel in the boundless beauty of the void. But only a moment.

He went back to work, firing his laser torch to join components together. The laser itself was invisible since there was no air in the vacuum to refract the light. The effects, however, were readily apparent. Hardened alloys with incredibly high melting points liquefied and flowed together like sticks of butter in a pot.

Gatticus turned off the laser, allowing the joins to cool. He ran a diagnostic on the probe's systems, checking the nav computer, Alckam drive, and comms one last time. He'd set the probe's course for Drake Depots #926, the nearest re-fueling station. It was located along a less-traveled route—the Callisto-Abbex Starlane—but hopefully it wouldn't be too long before a Union ship stopped there and received Gatticus's distress call. Failing that, perhaps the depot manager would spring for the cost of sending the message down the Starlane via comm probe. Gatticus's message promised a reasonable reward for any action which led to his safe return to Union Space. The reward would be enough to encourage civilian cooperation, but not enough to attract attention from unscrupulous freelancers who might think he was rich and try to hold him for ransom.

Regardless, as long as Gatticus's probe arrived with enough power left to transmit his distress call to the depot, his rescue was inevitable. It was a legal imperative for any Union Navy or Security vessel in receipt of a distress call to respond, and in the case of civilians, like the depot manager, they were obliged to pass along such calls at their earliest convenience.

Gatticus set the probe's maneuvering thrusters to fire on a ten second delay, and then crawled through a missing hull panel in his Osprey. The

Alckam drive was set to spin up just as soon as the probe cleared the ship. Gatticus activated his mag boots and walked through the open bulkhead into the cockpit. His transport was now a depressurized skeleton, with gaping holes everywhere. The ship was unfit for habitation by biological lifeforms, but being an android, Gatticus was just as comfortable in a frigid vacuum as he was in a warm, pressurized cabin.

Gatticus gazed out the cockpit canopy and into space, waiting. Seconds later his probe appeared, riding on small glowing blue plumes of fire.

The probe was an ugly, blocky contraption, but Gatticus felt a warm glow of pride at the sight of it. It was a testament to his skills that he'd been able to build such a vehicle at all.

A flash of blinding light tore through Gatticus's optical sensors, and the probe was gone.

It worked. Gatticus smiled. *Of course it worked.* The probe would arrive in four hours and twenty-six minutes, which meant that the soonest he could expect a rescue was about nine hours. All he had to do now was wait.

Gatticus sat down in the pilot's seat and caught a glimpse of his reflection on the inside of the canopy. His forehead was torn open, the synthetic flesh burned away and charred at the edges. The metal casing underneath was also charred, but instead of a thumb-sized hole in the center of that blast-scoring, there was a clean silver circle. His nanites had repaired his injury as best they could, but they weren't equipped to make cosmetic repairs.

Gatticus gingerly touched the charred edges of his skin, and the material crumbled into a cloud of shimmering black ashes. He scowled, wishing he could remember who had shot him and why.

Whoever it was, they deserved to be sent to the nearest Cygnian hunting ground.

* * *

Tanik led the Acolytes through the field. The storm was over, and dusk had fallen on Ouroboros. Darius looked up to see stars pricking through gaps in the clouds. The air was colder than ever, and the grassy field glistened with raindrops that quickly soaked through the legs of their jumpsuits.

The sun had sunk below the cliffs and the waterfall, but the clouds still shined with a faint orange glow. Here and there, between the soaring white domes of tents, camp fires danced with crackling flames. Marines were gathered around the fires, hunched over on stools, munching on glistening bits of roasted Awk flesh. The smell drove Darius's stomach to rumble and made his mouth water.

Another, louder rumble drew his attention to an Osprey floating down for a landing at the edge of the field. Landing lights peeled back the shadows, exposing a rippling blue pool of grass below.

A whirring sound and a flicker of movement revealed the dorsal laser turret of a nearby Osprey tracking restlessly across the night's sky. Darius wondered if that turret was set to auto-fire, or if Tanik had assigned gunners and a system of night watches. Either way, it was comforting to know that they had defenses in place in case the Awks returned.

"Dad," Cassandra whispered. "You think we could get some of that meat? I'm still starving."

Darius nodded. "Me too. Let me ask. Tanik—"

"You can eat after your lesson," Tanik said, leaving Darius with the unsettling feeling that Tanik had just read his mind.

Tanik led the Acolytes to a lonely camp fire with metal storage crates arrayed in a circle around it. "Sit," he said, and waited inside the circle until everyone found a seat. Cassandra and Darius sat together on the same crate and both leaned toward the fire, warming their hands and faces.

Arok was conspicuously missing from the group, but so was Dyara. Just as Darius wondered about them, he heard rustling footsteps and turned to see both of them approaching the fire. Firelight gleamed off Dyara's black armor and Arok's slick black fur. Arok was tearing meat off a long, glistening white bone that might have come from an Awk's leg or wing. Darius eyed the Lassarian boy warily as he approached. Cassandra suddenly stood up, as if to confront him, but Darius yanked her back down.

"Don't," he whispered.

"Please, join us," Tanik said as Dyara and Arok entered the circle of crates. They each went to sit around the fire, on opposite ends from each other, and then Tanik nodded and spread his hands to take in the group. "Welcome to Ouroboros," he said. "Your Revenant training begins tonight. We're going to start with a very simple awareness-building exercise. I want you to close your eyes and imagine yourselves floating high above this field."

Darius shook his head. "I'm not closing my eyes with Arok here. How do I know he won't sneak up on me when I'm not looking?"

Arok gave a sissing laugh. "You are wise to

fear me, human."

Tanik gave the Lassarian a cold look. To Darius, he said, "That is the point of this exercise: to be able to sense such threats, whether you can see them or not. If it makes you feel better, I will ensure that he does not interfere with your lesson."

Darius wasn't sure he trusted Tanik to keep that promise, but he gave in with a nod and closed his eyes.

"Good. Now... you're floating free of your bodies, soaring high above the field...."

Darius saw himself rising above the field. He felt the air wrap him in its icy embrace, but somehow the air felt refreshing and not cold.

He saw the shadowy field sprawling beneath him. Ospreys gleamed dimly in the flickering light of campfires, and white tents sprouted between them like mushrooms. Hunching black shadows sat around the fires—armored Marines—but they were blurry and indistinct at this distance.

Darius wondered if he was simply imagining this from what he'd already seen.

Tanik went on, "Now, reach out and *feel*. Imagine your awareness spreading, peeling back the darkness and washing over every inch of the ground below."

Darius imagined that, and the field came alive

with luminous, human-shaped specks. Some of them were hunched and huddled around the campfires, others were walking through pools of almost utter darkness between the tents. Still others were spaced out around the perimeter of the landing zone on patrol.

"What do you see?" Tanik whispered.

"I do not see anything," Arok said.

"Because you are focused on yourself. You need to look *out*, not in."

"I see the people," Cassandra said. "They're shining like giant fireflies."

"Good. Anyone else?"

Darius nodded. "Same here."

Dyara and Seelka murmured their agreement.

"I still see nothing," Arok said.

"Then sit quietly!" Tanik snapped.

Darius almost lost his focus with that interruption.

"I lost it," Dyara said.

"Try again," Tanik urged. "Relax and focus. This time broaden your awareness. You're flying higher now, seeing more of the planet. You can see the mountains rising to one side of the field, and the forest valley below the waterfall. Find the crustaceans in the riverbed, and the creatures that roost in the trees. Reach out as far as you can, and see what you can find."

Darius saw the forest and the river. They were bright and shining with millions of tiny, gleaming points of light. There were birds in the trees, crustaceans and slithering, snake-like fish in the river. The trees themselves glowed dimly with life, all the way down to their roots. He felt the slithering progress of the fish in the river, and the rush of the cold water around them. Bird feathers ruffled in the wind, and the lonely cries of two-legged carnivores echoed across the valley. The scale of his awareness was vast and giddying, as if he had just become a god.

Dyara and Cassandra both exclaimed excitedly. Seelka murmured something, and Flitter chirped.

"Now bring your focus back in, down to the clearing," Tanik said. "Find the people around you, and try to identify them by their thoughts."

Darius wasn't ready to do that yet. Instead, he tried flying higher and expanding his awareness still further. As he did so, he lost sight of the finer details. The smallest creatures disappeared, and then the larger ones did, too. He could no longer feel them, but a faint, diffuse glow remained to mark where they had been. The exception was one dazzlingly bright speck, directly below him.

Darius focused on that speck, and it resolved into eight smaller ones, arrayed in a circle. Two of them were far brighter than the rest, one which Darius instantly recognized as himself, and the other as Tanik. Darius kept pushing, higher and higher into the sky. He tried moving sideways, and the trees scrolled by below him in a bright, blurry glow. Clouds swept past, and the sun reappeared, peeking over a bed of cottony white clouds, their tips blazing with orange fire. Darius tried going higher still, heading for space. The sky darkened with his ascent, and stars appeared. From a low orbit the shining speck of the Acolytes still burned bright along the creeping black edge of the planet's terminator.

Darius imagined himself moving around the planet like a satellite, and the stars shifted around him as he raced along an orbital path. His focus remained on the planet as he flew over its day side, studying the surface. Arid bands of desert appeared near the equator, and frozen caps of snow at the poles. Everywhere else green forests and fields prevailed. Rivers and lakes abounded, and ragged gray mountain ranges rose like lumpy scars. On one of those peaks, in the middle of a semi-circular mountain range, a dazzling speck of light stood out. Darius turned his gaze to it, and everything else faded into insignificance. It was just a pinprick, but somehow it shined as bright as a sun.

Darius's view of the planet shivered and shook as he stared into the light. Indistinct whispers crowded his thoughts. Suddenly he felt watched, as if the light were looking back at him. The whispers stopped and the light vanished, leaving Darius to wonder what he had just seen. A chill came over him, and the shaking intensified.

"Darius!"

His cheek erupted with fire, and he blinked his eyes open.

He was back in the field with Tanik's snarling face mere inches from his own. Tanik's hands were on his shoulders, and Darius's body echoed with the sensation of being shaken and slapped.

"What did you see?" Tanik demanded, his eyes searching Darius's.

"I..." Darius trailed off, rubbing his stinging cheek. What had he seen? "I think I saw another Revenant."

Tanik's eyes narrowed to slits, and he withdrew with a frown. "Impossible. I would have sensed it if there were another Revenant here."

"You must have missed something," Darius said. "It looked, or *felt*, just like us, but it was only one presence, not eight. I saw it halfway around the planet from where we are now, at the top of a mountain."

Tanik said nothing to that, but the others began murmuring among themselves.

Beside him, Cassandra shook her head. "You said Revenants can communicate with each other instantly. Does that mean they know we're here?"

Darius sprang to his feet. "If they don't already know, it won't be long before they find out. We need to leave right now."

CHAPTER 9

"Sit down," Tanik said, and Darius felt an invisible hand force him back onto his storage crate. "You said you felt *one* presence."

Darius nodded. "So?"

"Assuming what you felt was real, what would one Revenant be doing all alone on an abandoned world? That suggests that he or she may be hiding here as well—or that it was not a Revenant at all. You may have sensed a surviving Keth warrior."

"That doesn't sound any better," Darius said.

"Perhaps not, but I would have felt it if someone were trying to communicate across such a vast distance."

Darius frowned. "You said that about there being other Revenants down here in the first place, and I found one."

"That's different. It is possible to hide one's presence, like turning off a lamp, but you can't shine a light from a mountaintop and still expect to hide it."

"Speak clearly," Darius said. "Are we in danger or not?"

"Not. Whoever is here with us, *if* they are here at all, they are hiding, too, and the minute they come out of hiding, I'll know. We'll have enough warning to escape. Besides, consider this, if this person wanted to be rescued, why not call for help sooner?"

Darius didn't have an answer for that.

Dyara spoke into the silence. "Let's say you're right, and whatever Darius saw isn't a threat. There's another problem."

Tanik turned to look at her. "And that is?"

"We were able to sense ourselves clearly during that awareness exercise of yours, and you said that you could tell from orbit that there weren't any other Revenants here. What if they find us in the same way? We're not hiding our presence—however you do that."

"The farther away you are, the harder it is to find someone," Tanik replied. "But I am also shielding our presence as best I can, and so is Ouroboros itself."

Darius frowned. "How can a planet hide us?"

"This is a particularly luminous world, thanks to all the animals here that evolved to use the light. Until a Revenant physically enters this system, I wouldn't worry about them finding us."

"Unless one of them is already here," Darius said. "We at least need to investigate what I saw. I'm not going to sleep until we do."

Tanik held his gaze for a long moment, but he gave in with a nod. "Very well." Turning to address the others, he said, "You're all free to get some food and sleep. Any of the Marines should be able to help you find the Acolytes' quarters." His eyes found Darius once more. "You're coming with me."

"So is Cassandra," Darius replied. After what had happened on Hades, he wasn't going to leave her behind again.

"I was going to take a Vulture...." Tanik replied. The fighters only had room for two.

"So take an Osprey instead," Darius replied. "Cassy is coming."

"Very well, but I'm flying," Tanik said.

Darius grabbed Cassandra's hand and stood up once more, pulling her to her feet beside him. "Lead the way."

* * *

Trista Leandra sat in the cockpit of her transport, the *Harlequin*, waiting for it to dock with fuel pod #16. As soon as her transport docked, a chime sounded from her comms and a prompt appeared from Drake Depot #926, asking how much antimatter she wished to purchase. Trista selected FULL and waited while the pod scanned her reactor to determine how much she needed. A moment later, a charge request popped up for a hefty four thousand seven hundred and twenty *creds*.

Trista grimaced and reluctantly approved the charge. The cargo she'd delivered to Callisto had only netted a little under ten thousand creds, instead of the anticipated fifty plus. Making matters worse, her hold was almost empty on the way back. She'd be lucky to break even for this run, which left her back where she'd started a week ago, but with an extra week of bills to pay.

Trista scowled. "At this rate, I'll have to sell my soul to pay off our debts. What do you think, Buddy? You know any dealers?"

No reply.

She glanced at her copilot, Buddy, but the furry brown Togra was curled up in his custom-sized acceleration harness, his head tucked into the folds of fat that passed for his neck. His eyes were shut, his whiskers twitching periodically. As Trista looked on, one of Buddy's legs kicked spasmodically. She frowned. Why should he be able to sleep peacefully while she was busy tearing out her hair? "Hey, mongrel. I'm talking to you." She poked him between a bulging stack of fat rolls.

Buddy opened one of his giant brown eyes and glared.

"If I'd wanted to brave the void alone, I wouldn't have bought you from that fly-infested meat market back on Polaris V."

Buddy bared his teeth at the reminder of his near brush with death.

"That's right," Trista said. "You owe me, and that means you have to listen to my gripes and cheer me up when I'm blue."

"You're black, not blue," Buddy said.

Trista frowned. "Don't be racist."

"I'm not. It's an observation. I myself am brown and white." Buddy released his harness and stood up, floating free of his seat. He stretched languorously, arching his back first one way, then the other. He thrust his arms out straight above his head and Trista heard joints popping. After that, he slumped in on himself once more and absently scratched an itch lurking somewhere under his white belly fur.

Trista looked away, out to the shining, ring-shaped fuel depot, slowly rotating around its antimatter-generating hub. The fuel pods were located a safe distance from the depot to reduce the risk of accidental or intentional incidents.

Buddy began making annoying smacking sounds with his lips. That went on for a while before Trista took the bait.

"Is something wrong?"

"I'm hungry," Buddy replied.

"You're always hungry. There's no food left."

"The depot will have something. We could flit over there in a tender and find a nice restaurant. What about seafood?"

"Money's tight," Trista replied. She couldn't afford to eat at a dive, let alone a nice restaurant. "Why don't you go on a diet?" She poked him in his fat rolls again, and this time he snapped his jaws at her.

"Watch it. I'm delicate."

Trista snorted. "You can say that again."

Another chime sounded from her comms. "Done already?" Trista wondered, but this message wasn't from the fuel depot.

"It's a distress call," Buddy said.

"Yeah, I can see that."

"There's a substantial reward."

"I wouldn't call five thousand *substantial*," Trista replied.

"But look at the coordinates," Buddy insisted. "It's close. We wouldn't have to spend much fuel to get there and back."

"Yeah..." The wheels began turning in Trista's head, and she used her ESC to run the numbers. "Four hundred and sixty-seven creds of fuel to make the trip..." She trailed off, nodding excitedly. "This could actually turn us a profit, Buddy!"

He gave a delighted chitter and rubbed his tiny hands together. Activating his mag boots, he aimed them at the deck to get down to his seat, but he was floating too high, and his boots were too small.

"Help me get back down," Buddy pleaded.

Trista reached over and roughly pushed him back into his seat with a hand on his head.

"Hey! I'm—"

"Delicate, I know." Trista disengaged from the fuel pod before her transport had finished refueling. Her comms chimed with a refund for the balance of fuel not transferred, and a trite safety reminder about not engaging her main engines until she cleared the pod.

Trista tapped her feet impatiently while she

waited for the *Harlequin's* maneuvering thrusters to push them to a hundred meters from the fuel pod.

"We really need this," Trista said, thinking about her backdated docking fees, postponed maintenance for the *Harlequin*, and the ship's next loan payment.

"Yes, we do," Buddy agreed, and gave his belly a loud slap. "Seafood here we come!"

Trista turned to glare at him. "Hey, we need that money for more important..."

Buddy's big brown eyes grew larger still, and they filled with a sudden sheen of moisture. His ears flattened against his head, and his lips began to quiver.

"Oh, fek it, I guess we can spare a few creds."

Buddy's ears popped back up and he grinned, revealing pointy white teeth. "Works every time."

"Yeah, and one of these times, I'm gonna punch you in the mouth and make you cry for real."

"Try it. I'll bite your fingers off."

"Haven't you ever heard that you shouldn't bite the hand that feeds you?"

"Haven't you ever heard that you shouldn't punch your pets in the mouth?"

Trista barked a laugh. "Fair enough."

CHAPTER 10

Darius stood behind the pilot's seat in the Osprey Tanik had chosen. He stared at a holographic rendering of Ouroboros that Tanik had generated from orbital scans of the planet. The clouds had been stripped away, and the entire rendering was illuminated, but it was still hard to pick out any distinctive features from the landscape.

"Well?" Tanik asked. "Where did you feel the presence?"

Darius used a hand to manipulate the rendering, turning it first one way, then the other as he looked for the distinctive semi-circular range of mountains that he'd seen. At this scale he couldn't see very much, so he zoomed in and tried again, but he still wasn't having any luck.

"Close your eyes," Tanik suggested. "Visualize the planet."

Darius frowned, but he shut his eyes and tried reaching out in the ZPF. The planet appeared in his mind's eye, bright and sparkling with life. He used his hands to rotate it and sure enough, he found the semi-circular range of mountains. This time there was no trace of the blinding presence he'd seen before, but he was certain that it was the spot.

Darius cracked his eyes open to see a very similar image to the one he'd held in his mind. Similar, but different. There was no sign of the mountain range. Darius frowned. "It didn't work."

"I wouldn't be too sure," Tanik replied. "Try zooming in some more."

Darius did so, and to his amazement, the range of mountains appeared. He glanced at Tanik, his eyebrows raised in question.

"When you use your awareness, things aren't always to scale. Important details can become larger than life, while the trivial ones fade away."

"I don't think we should go down there," Cassandra said.

Darius turned to his daughter. "Why not?"

"There's something... evil down there."

"Evil?" Tanik scoffed. "Don't be naive. One man's evil is another man's good. There are no absolutes."

"Really," Darius replied. "What about the Cygnians? They're evil."

"They're evil to *us*. That doesn't make them a universal evil."

Darius frowned. "Most intelligent races would agree that the Cygnians and their hunting practices are evil, even if they weren't subjected to those hunting practices themselves."

"Oh, I'm sure you're right," Tanik said, nodding agreeably. "The Cygnians hunt us and other species for sport, so that makes them evil, but consider this, if livestock could talk, what would they say about humans?"

"That's different," Darius said.

"Why?"

"Because they're not self-aware."

"How do you know?" Tanik replied.

"You know what, it doesn't matter. We're getting off topic. Cassandra felt something bad down there, and I believe her. What if this is some kind of trap?"

Tanik shrugged. "You're the one who said we should investigate. Now you want to go back?"

Darius considered that. "No. Maybe..." He nodded to the rendering of the planet. "What do *you* feel down there?"

Jasper T. Scott

"Not evil," Tanik said with an accompanying smirk. "But there is something, or an echo of something. It's worth looking into. Strap in." Tanik marked the mountain range with the green diamond of a nav waypoint, and then moved the holographic rendering to one side. The waypoint appeared superimposed on the actual planet below.

Darius went to sit beside Cassandra and strapped into his acceleration harness. As soon as he'd done so, Tanik ignited the thrusters and they were pinned to their seats.

Tanik banked toward the waypoint, and before long they re-entered the atmosphere. Clouds swept by, and then a crescent-shaped slash of gray came peeking through those clouds. They dropped below the level of the clouds and a dense green forest appeared around the mountains.

As Tanik circled down over the mountains, Darius noticed breaks in the trees, and massive skeletal structures rising out of them.

"What are those?" Darius asked, pointing to one of the structures as it soared up against the horizon, looking like a jagged black mountain.

"Ruins. The remains of the Keth cities," Tanik replied.

"They look pretty overgrown," Cassandra said.

"How long has it been since the Keth lived here?" She stared out a side window in the cockpit as they passed one of the ruins.

"About twenty years," Tanik replied. "I was with the Revenant fleet when they attacked...." Tanik trailed off, as if remembering. "It was here that I faked my death and made my escape."

"Why here?" Darius asked. "Was it because of something you saw?"

"You could say that," he replied. "Look." Tanik pointed to the mountains.

There was some kind of structure built along the side of one of the mountains. It looked like a castle—the remains of one, anyway. There were gaping holes in the walls, and the windows were broken. A series of six landing pads were arrayed around the structure, suspended over the cliff by thick metal beams. One of the pads had partly collapsed, while another held the blackened remains of a familiar-looking ship. Darius stared at it as they hovered down for a landing on the pad beside it.

"Is that..." Darius trailed off uncertainly.

"An Osprey?" Tanik asked. "Yes."

"The Revenants just left it here?" Cassandra asked.

"Does it look like they could have flown it

away?" Tanik countered.

Their Osprey touched down with a jolt and Darius unfastened his harness. He folded it away and climbed to his feet. As he did so, a chill came over him, and he shivered. He glanced out at the blackened ruin of the ship on the landing pad beside theirs. Cassandra was right. There was something *off* about this place, maybe not evil, but dark and foreboding. His gaze swept to the castle rising before them. It was like looking at a haunted house. He felt compelled to explore, but he also wanted to turn and run.

"So?" Cassandra asked. "Are we going to go take a look or not?"

Darius was just about to suggest that they stay in the Osprey when Tanik stood up from the pilot's seat and nodded to them. "Let's go."

Darius reluctantly followed him and Cassandra through the ship to the rear airlock. The foreboding grew stronger with every step, and he began to feel watched, just as he had in the field with the other Acolytes.

As they stood inside the airlock, waiting for Tanik to cycle it open, Darius shivered once more. Peripherally he saw Cassandra rubbing her arms to get warm.

"Is it cold in here?" Darius asked.

Tanik glanced at him. "No."

But he was wearing an exosuit, so how would he know? The airlock swished open, and a blast of warm, humid air swirled in. They jumped out of the airlock one after another. It was definitely warmer here than at their camp—probably closer to the equator. And yet, somehow, Darius felt colder than ever.

He looked out at the view from their vantage point. The sun was high in the sky, the forests below shining a dark and luscious green. Collapsing Keth ruins with black beams exposed soared, dotting the forest like giant skeletons.

"Come," Tanik urged.

Darius saw Cassandra staring up at the castle. Tanik strode past her and down a narrow catwalk that bridged the gap between the landing pad and the fortress. He turned to them from the other side, and called out, "Come on!"

Darius traded a glance with his daughter before walking over and grabbing her hand. "Stay close."

Cassandra nodded. "You too."

* * *

Darius walked through the gaping entrance of

the castle with his daughter, both of them treading over the thick wooden doors that had once barred the entrance. The castle was dark inside. Wind whistled in through broken windows and gaping holes in the stone walls. Old, torn and dusty furniture sat about, arrayed around a giant fireplace in the center of the room. Stairs curved up on both sides of the hearth, meeting at a balcony that overlooked the sitting area below. An old chandelier draped with cobwebs swung restlessly above the floor.

Tanik turned on a flashlight. It was a tactical light, mounted under the barrel of a laser pistol.

"Stay behind me," Tanik whispered, while sweeping his sidearm back and forth. Elongated shadows danced under the beam of the flashlight. Rubble littered the dusty floor.

"We're not alone," Tanik whispered.

Darius felt another chill come over him and quickly glanced over his shoulder to make sure no one was creeping up behind them.

"Can you sense something?" Darius whispered back. Rubble crunched under foot as he and Cassandra crept behind Tanik. Darius winced at all the noise they were making.

"No, look," Tanik said, and nodded to the floor.

There were familiar patterns in the dust.

"Footsteps," Cassandra breathed. "Maybe they're still here from when the Revenants attacked?"

Tanik just looked at her. "That was twenty years ago. With the wind gusting in as it is, those footsteps are long gone. These are fresh."

"Maybe we'd better leave," Darius said, still whispering. He glanced back through the entrance of the castle to their Osprey.

"No," Tanik said. "Let's keep looking. We need to know who's living here. Whoever it is, they're very skilled at hiding their presence from me."

"So it *is* another Revenant," Darius said.

"Perhaps," Tanik replied.

"Who else could it be?" Cassandra asked.

"One of the Keth," Tanik said as he led the way up to the fireplace.

"Let's get out of here," Darius said. "We can come back with a squad of Marines. Cassandra and I aren't wearing any armor, and you're the only one with a weapon."

Tanik crouched low in front of the fireplace and reached into it with one hand. "The coals are still warm," he said.

Darius grabbed Cassandra's hand. "We're going to wait for you in the Osprey." *And take off without you if we have to,* he thought but didn't say.

Tanik straightened and turned to them with a twisted grin. "Are you sure you want to do that?"

"Yes."

"Whatever is hiding here, it might have revealed itself to you for a reason, Darius, perhaps so that it could escape. It might try to steal our ship. You don't want to be inside it if that happens."

Darius grimaced. "Fine, we'll stay with you, but let's at least go back to the ship to get some more weapons."

"They won't do you any good against a Revenant."

"Then let's leave!" Darius thundered. His voice echoed resoundingly inside the foyer of the castle, and he cringed.

Tanik's eyes widened in alarm, and he cocked his head, listening for a reaction to the noise.

Nothing.

Darius blew out a breath, and Tanik fixed him with a scowl.

"If there's a Revenant here, then why bother whispering?" Cassandra asked. "Wouldn't they already have sensed us?"

"I'm hiding our presence," Tanik replied. "Let's go upstairs and look around. Quietly."

Just as he said that, a loud creak sounded from somewhere above the stairs, followed by the sound of a door slamming.

Darius's heart began pounding, and he tightened his grip on Cassandra's hand. He turned to run back to the Osprey just in time to see a dark, blurry shape dropping down in front of him. Tanik's flashlight swept over that shape just as it landed with a loud *crunch* on the rubble-strewn floor.

CHAPTER 11

Tanik's flashlight swept into line, revealing the face of a tall, pretty human woman with dark hair and hard gray eyes. A heavy brow shadowed long, regal features, and a strong jaw. As Darius watched, her entire body began shimmering with light, and she drew a glowing white sword from a scabbard on her back. She was using the ZPF to shield herself.

"Who are you?" Darius asked.

"Samara?" Tanik whispered.

"Tanik?" the woman replied. She dropped her sword with a noisy clatter, and it immediately stopped glowing. A split second later, so did she.

Before either Darius or Cassandra could say anything, Tanik ran by them. He holstered his pistol and crushed the woman into a fierce hug. He picked her up and spun her around in a circle, his laughter booming and echoing through the foyer like thunder.

"You two know each other?" Cassandra asked.

The woman was laughing and sobbing, and Tanik was whispering in her ear.

Darius looked on with a frown. When Tanik finally set the woman down and withdrew from their embrace, he said, "I thought you were dead."

She shook her head. "That was the plan, you *goff!* We were going to fake our deaths and escape, remember?"

"Your death was particularly convincing," Tanik replied.

"Hello!" Cassandra said. "Is one of you going to explain what's going on here?"

Tanik turned to them and gestured to the woman standing beside him. "This is Samara Gurhain. My wife."

* * *

The flat white warp disc vanished with a flash of light as the warp bubble dispersed. A double chime sounded from the *Harlequin's* sensors and Trista checked her contacts panel to find exactly one signature there, an SB-22 Osprey, designated

Gray Seven. Trista summoned a magnified rendering of the ship, and it appeared as a luminous hologram floating before her, slowly rotating.

"There she is, Buddy. Our payday. Looks like she's been in a fight..." Trista trailed off with a frown. There were hull panels missing all over the ship. How could anyone be alive in there? Even if the cockpit was still pressurized, it could only hold so much air.

"I'm not getting any life signs," Buddy said. "You think we're too late?"

"Fek it..." Trista muttered. "This is just my luck!" Now who was going to pay her that five thousand credit reward? Worse yet, she was out another four hundred and sixty-seven creds for fuel, and with nothing to show for it.

"What about salvage?" Buddy asked. "We could haul that Osprey back and sell it to an independent shipyard."

"More like a scrapyard," Trista replied. "She won't fetch much in the condition she's in, and you can double our fuel consumption on the way back with that much dead weight attached to our hull. The nearest buyer is at..." Trista pulled up a star map to check. "Abbex Prime. That's all the way at the end of the starlane!" She scowled and shook her head. "Forget it. We'll pay more in fuel to haul her than she's worth."

Buddy looked at her with big brown eyes and trembling lips. "So, no seafood?"

Trista frowned. "At this rate we'll be lucky to eat at all."

Buddy sniffed and wiped his eyes. "Why couldn't I have been rescued by a *rich* freighter captain? The universe hates me."

"You know I'm starting to see how you ended up in that meat market," Trista said.

"At least *they* were feeding me."

"Because they were fattening you up for the slaughter!" Trista sighed. "I'll get you food at the depot. All right?"

Buddy perked up. "A fillet of fish?"

"Are you crazy? No, something cheap. How about a nice loaf of bread?"

"Kill me now!" Buddy moaned.

"Don't tempt me," Trista muttered as she set a return course for Drake Depot #926.

"Wait, what's that," Buddy said.

Trista looked up from her controls to see Buddy pointing at the Osprey. At this distance it was just a tiny silver speck. But that speck was winking strangely at her.

"What the..." Trista zoomed in for a better

look, and immediately saw why it was winking. "The running lights are flicking on and off."

"Someone *is* alive in there!" Buddy crowed. "Thank the Revenants! Seafood, seafood, seafood!"

"The scans showed no life signs," Trista objected.

"Maybe it's an android?" Buddy suggested.

"An Executor? What would one of them be doing out here all alone in a derelict Osprey?"

"Must have escaped a battle. Who cares? Get in there and rescue it! Seafood, seafood, seafood!" Buddy chanted again.

"So why hasn't he tried to contact us over the comms?" Trista asked.

"Systems must be damaged," Buddy replied. "Come on! What are you waiting for?"

Trista frowned and hesitantly pushed the throttle forward. Now that she knew who she was rescuing, she wasn't sure the reward was worth it. If anyone ever found out that she'd rescued an android, she'd have a target on her back the size of a hover truck.

Androids were the Cygnians' appointed administrators. They propped up the Union by enforcing its laws—such as the law that forced parents to send their children to the Crucible as soon as they came of age. Not all of those children returned, and of the ones who did, some were marked with the seal of death and sent to designated hunting grounds for the Cygnians to prey upon. It was a barbaric system, forced upon them by an even more barbaric species. Androids, as representatives of that system, were universally hated.

Trista's mind raced, trying to come up with a way to keep anyone from finding out she'd rescued an android. Still working on the problem, she docked with the Osprey and unfastened her acceleration harness. "I'm going to suit up and board the Osprey. Stay here and watch the ship."

"Aye, Captain."

Trista rose to her feet and went up to the cockpit door, but she hesitated with her hand over the door controls. "And Buddy, if this is what we think it is, then we need to be careful, all right? You can't tell anyone that we rescued an android. Not ever. You understand?"

"Who would I tell? I'm a fortress of solitude, practically a mute."

Trista snorted. "You remember that time on Yassik Prime, when you told that hairy ape at the bar about the fire crystals we were hauling? And then he showed up at our next stop, and threatened to space us if we didn't give him our cargo."

Buddy rotated his seat to face her. His arms were crossed over his protruding belly, his brown eyes flinty. "That was one time, Tris. When are you gonna let that go?" He uncrossed his arms to hold up a tiny finger. "One little mistake."

"There was also that other time on Walros, when you—"

"Okay, okay. I get it. I won't tell anyone. I promise."

"You'd better not," Trista said. With that, she opened the cockpit door and traipsed through a small living and dining area to her cargo hold. Walked through the echoing space to a storage locker beside the cargo airlock, she reached in and removed a pressure suit and helmet. Once dressed, she left the cargo hold and strode back down the corridor between the cargo bay and living area.

Stopping halfway down the corridor, Trista bent down beside the ventral airlock. She mentally opened the airlock and climbed down the access ladder until she was standing on the outer doors. A banging sound shivered through the outer doors, right beneath her feet. Trista glanced down and peeked out the windows in the outer doors. A human man stared back at her, but his forehead was torn open revealing blackened metal. That confirmed who and what she was dealing with.

Trista scowled and held up a hand, indicating for the android to wait. She cycled the airlock and waited while fans sucked the air out. The outer doors slid open, and she grabbed one of the safety rails inside to help the android through.

As soon as the doors were shut and the atmosphere inside the airlock was restored, she nodded to the android and asked, "Who are you?"

"Gatticus Thedroux," he said, holding out his hand to her.

She accepted it with a grimace. "Trista Leandra."

"Thank you for rescuing me," Gatticus said.

"Sure. What happened to you?" She pointed to his forehead. "It looks like you got shot."

"Yes, I believe I did."

"You *believe?*"

"I don't recall what happened. My memory appears to be damaged."

"Great. Do you at least know where you're headed?"

Gatticus inclined his head to her. "Earth."

"Earth?" Trista blinked, and her nose wrinkled at the mention of her homeworld. "It's a wasteland. Why would you want to go there?"

"Because it is my posting. I am the Executor of

Earth."

CHAPTER 12

A roaring fire crackled in the hearth. Darius and Cassandra sat on stools in front of the fire, roasting chunks of Awk meat on the tips of gleaming black Revenant swords. Tanik had warned them to be careful with those weapons, because they were sharp enough to cut through mag boots and slice off their toes if they accidentally dropped them. The castle was littered with such artifacts—both Revenant and Keth weapons and armor from the battle they'd fought twenty years ago.

Tanik and his wife, Samara, sat with them, but they were too enamored with each other to bother about food.

Darius stared into the fire. Reflections of the flames flickered and danced along his glassy black blade. He withdrew the meat he was roasting to see if it was cooked yet. The outside was charred and crispy. Raising the morsel to his lips, he blew on it to cool it. Once cooled, Darius took a cautious bite. The meat was juicy, salty, tender... just like roasted chicken. A big improvement over dry rations. He made appreciative sounds as he chewed.

"Is it good?" Cassandra asked as she withdrew her sword from the fire and began blowing on her meat as he had done.

"Delicious," Darius replied.

"The good thing about Ouroboros is that Seeker meat is easy to come by," Samara said. "The bad thing is so are the Seekers." She rolled up a ragged sleeve to reveal three long parallel scars running from her elbow to her wrist.

Darius grimaced at the sight of her injury and nodded to Tanik. He had a similar set of scars running across his face. "Is that how you got yours?"

"It is," Tanik replied.

Cassandra took a break from blowing on her food. "I thought you got your scars from a Banshee?"

"I never said that," Tanik replied.

"I guess I just assumed..."

"Indeed you did."

"Are Seekers more dangerous than Cygnians?"

"To Revenants they are," Samara said. "They can hide their presence and surprise us."

"Using the ZPF?" Darius asked.

"Yes," Tanik replied.

"We're used to relying on our awareness," Samara went on. "So we're not prepared when it fails."

Cassandra nodded as she tried a bite of the roasted Awk. "You're right. This is good."

"So what now?" Darius asked.

Tanik appeared to consider that. He looked around the foyer. "What is this place?" he asked, turning to Samara.

"Seems like it was a training academy for Keth warriors," she replied. "There's a lot more to it than this. It's warm and defensible. The plumbing is solar powered, so there's water to drink and the toilets still flush. More importantly, there's a strong residual presence from when the Keth lived here."

"That must be the evil I felt when we were up in space," Cassandra said.

"Evil?" Tanik asked. "Not what I would call it, but it's quite palpable, yes."

"The Keth aren't evil?" Cassandra asked.

Tanik's dark eyebrows beetled. "Of course

not."

"Then why are you fighting them?"

Tanik snorted. "Ask the Augur. The Keth are just like us, but we were forced to slaughter them—their families, their children, even helpless babies, if you can imagine that." His eyes blazed with fury. "I still have nightmares."

Darius felt sick hearing that.

"But he made you do it, right?" Cassandra asked. "I mean, it's not your fault."

"Yes," Samara replied. "But it doesn't always feel that way. I remember enjoying the slaughter, and taking pride in the number of Keth that I killed. That's the real horror of what the Augur does. He makes you *want* to do his will."

"His days are numbered," Tanik growled.

Samara snorted. "I wish I could believe that."

"Believe it," Tanik replied. "I have found the one who can defeat him."

Samara straightened and stared at him with sudden interest. "Who?"

"He means me," Darius said.

Samara's brow furrowed. "You? You're not even trained."

"He will be," Tanik replied.

"And how do you know that he can defeat the Augur?"

"I foresaw it."

Samara frowned. "You know better than to go looking into the future, Tanik."

"I didn't. This vision came to me unbidden, and I *know* it's more than just foresight. It's his destiny to defeat the Augur. Besides that, he has the potential. Even untrained, he found you hiding here when I could not. He can affect other Revenants, just like the Augur."

A gleam of hope appeared in Samara's eyes, and Darius felt suddenly uncomfortable under the weight of her gaze. "If that's true, then we finally have a hope of ending this war."

"Let's say that's true," Darius said. "Say I defeat this Augur. Then what? There's still a bunch of blood-thirsty aliens in charge of the USO who'd like nothing better than to go back to hunting every other sentient species to extinction. Tanik said the Augur is the only thing holding the Cygnians back. If we're going to take out the Augur, we need a plan to defeat the Cygnians."

"You could do what he does," Tanik suggested. "You could *make them* follow you."

"He'll never be able to do that," Samara said, shaking her head. "The only reason the Augur gets away with controlling the Royals is because he gives them their designated hunting grounds as an outlet for their aggression. He also satisfies their need to dominate by putting them in charge. It would be impossible to completely pacify the Cygnians. Even if someone could do it with the Royals, their subjects would rise up and overthrow them the very next day. You can't change who they are as a species without changing all of them, and no one is that powerful."

"Yes, I've considered that," Tanik said. "Fortunately, there's another way."

"And that is?" Darius asked.

"The Revenants have a secret weapon."

"Oh?" Darius asked. "What is it?"

"A bomb that can tear matter apart."

Darius frowned. "You mean a nuclear bomb? That's old news. Antimatter is more powerful than that. You'd be better off venting your reactors in the direction of your target."

Tanik shook his head. "Not a nuclear bomb—a zero point energy bomb. Just one of them is enough to turn an entire planet into a cloud of dust. To do the same thing with antimatter would require all the antimatter in all the Alckam reactors of the entire Union fleet. This is far more discrete, and far more effective. It's how the Revenants are winning the war with the Keth. The technology is a closely guarded secret, but if we could steal one of those bombs and learn to develop them ourselves, we could bring the Union to its knees, one planet at a time."

Darius shuddered at the thought of destroying entire planets. He shook his head. "We can't go around killing billions of innocent citizens to defeat the Cygnians. That would make us worse than them."

"Who said anything about killing *innocent* citizens?" Tanik asked. "We would start with Cygnus Prime and work our way through their worlds from there. I assure you, even the Cygnians will surrender before they go extinct."

"So the way to stop the killing is to kill more people than ever?" Cassandra demanded.

"That's how most wars end," Tanik replied. "But let's not worry about that right now. First we need to train you and the other Acolytes." Tanik spent a moment looking around the foyer of the castle. "Perhaps this would be a good place to do that. The residual energy here will make it easier for us to hide."

"I don't think everyone will fit in here," Darius said. "And we'll still need to grow food. That means we need arable land."

"Not everyone," Tanik replied. "Just the Acolytes, and maybe a few others. The rest will stay where they are. Do you and Cassandra want to stay here while Samara and I go back for the others?"

"Hell no," Darius said. "You're not leaving us alone in here."

Tanik smiled crookedly at that. "Very well. Let's go."

* * *

The trip back to the camp was uneventful. They left the castle in the middle of the day, but arrived at camp in the middle of the night. Darius estimated it had only taken a few hours to get from one place to the other, so the two locations had to be separated by more than a few time zones.

Darius stood with Cassandra and Samara inside the open airlock of the Osprey, watching as Tanik went from tent to tent, waking up the other Acolytes. When he was done, he went to wake up some of the others as well—the Marines and Vulture pilots that they were taking back to the castle with them.

Darius shivered. He rubbed his arms, hugging his shoulders to stay warm. The air was much colder here, which did nothing to help ease the mysterious chill he'd felt at the castle. He glanced around but no one else seemed to be suffering from the cold, not even Cassandra, who was thin as a reed and wearing the same jumpsuit as him. Maybe he was coming down with something. But weren't the nanites in his blood supposed to keep him from getting sick?

After about twenty minutes, Tanik came back with the Acolytes. Darius kept an eye on Arok as the Lassarian boy hopped up beside him. Gakram, the Banshee, climbed in next, walking on all six legs, followed by Seelka and Flitter. Dyara was conspicuously absent.

Darius asked about her.

"She's flying over in the other Osprey with the Marines," Tanik said as he shut the outer airlock doors and opened the inner ones.

"I see," Darius replied. "Who did you leave in charge of the colony?"

"Ra."

Darius nodded. "Good choice." Ra had successfully led the people of Karkarus on Hades for many years. If he could keep them alive despite nightly attacks by Cygnian hunting parties, protecting a similar colony on Ouroboros should be easy for him.

Everyone followed Tanik to the cockpit and took their seats, but they were short two seats, and the troop bay wasn't designed to carry unarmored passengers.

"Where do we sit?" Darius asked. Samara was also left without a seat.

Tanik glanced at them. "Why don't you go man the gun turrets?"

Samara nodded and Darius followed her back down the corridor from the cockpit to the troop bay. Halfway to the troop bay she reached up and unfolded a ladder. "I'll take the dorsal turret," she said.

Darius nodded and waited for her to climb up to a hatch in the ceiling. She opened it and pulled herself up into a cramped space with it's own a bubble-shaped canopy. The hatch slid shut behind her, leaving Darius to figure out how to reach the lower turret on his own. He spied a matching hatch at his feet and pulled that one open. A ladder extended below the hatch to an empty seat surrounded by dark glass. Darius climbed down and dropped into the seat. Blue-green grass pressed against the glass canopy of the gun well, making it impossible to see out.

Darius reached around and folded the two halves of his acceleration harness over his chest, clicking them into place. A split second later, the Osprey blasted off, and the grass fell away in at a dizzying rate. The transport's running lights illuminated a shrinking circle of light on the rippling field. The white domes of tents appeared along with the gleaming black hulls of other Ospreys, and the still-glowing embers of dying camp fires. The glass canopy made him feel particularly exposed, inducing a brief thrill of vertigo. The dark barrels of twin laser cannons protruded slightly into his field of view, directly below his seat.

Moments later, clouds came whipping by, blotting out the view; then they fell away and rolled out in all directions as the Osprey continued on for space. The force of their acceleration was about two Gs. Enough to notice, but not enough to be uncomfortable. Clearly Tanik wasn't in a hurry to get back to the castle. The stars snapped into focus and midnight sky turned to the purest black. They leveled out, and their acceleration eased to just over one G. Darius felt his body relax. All the tension in his muscles bled away.

Fatigue swirled in, and his eyes drifted shut. It would be at least a few hours before they arrived back at the castle, and something told him that he wasn't going to sleep peacefully there, not with the whistling wind, and the cold, dark presence seeping through him.

Darius's mind wandered. He wondered what they'd find as they explored the castle. How big was it? Maybe he'd feel better about staying there if he had a chance to take a look around. He resolved to do just that as his mind succumbed to sleep.

Suddenly Darius was in the castle, standing in front of the fireplace with stairs curving up to either side. The wind howled in through the broken doors and windows, and although the air was warm, a feeling of *coldness* seeped through to his bones. Darius shivered and hugged himself for warmth.

Then he heard something: a susurrus, like the sound a field of grass made when running through it. At first he thought it was the wind, but the sound quickly rose in volume, and he distinguished *voices,* whispering furiously in his ears. They were loud enough to hear, but the words were indistinct.

"Hello?" he turned in a circle, looking for the source of the voices. He couldn't pinpoint an exact location, but he felt they were coming from behind the fireplace. Darius walked around it and discovered another staircase, this one winding down. The voices were coming from down there.

Vaguely aware that this was a dream, Darius

started down the stairs. He wound down the stairwell, past several landings with wooden doors, some of them broken, others intact. There were no windows and no lights. It should have been too dark to see the stairs, but somehow he could. He continued down and down, all the while the whispers grew louder and more insistent...

Finally, after passing nine landings, he came to a tenth at the bottom of the stairwell. A wooden door barred his way. It looked like it had been recently repaired, with fresh boards nailed over the splintered remains of older ones. The whispers were uncomfortably loud now, and impossible to ignore.

Darius reached for the door handle with a sweaty palm. His heart beat like a drum in his chest...

The door was locked, but Darius rattled it on its hinges, not willing to give up yet. The door popped open, and the whispers abruptly stopped. An old metal deadbolt fell to the floor with a ringing sound.

His palm felt slick on the cold metal handle of the door. He hesitated, terrified to open the door further, but something compelled him to go on. Darius pushed, and the door creaked loudly as it swung open.

A long hallway appeared ahead of him. The wind howled. Open windows lay along the length of the hall. Moonlight sparkled off broken wedges of glass on the dusty stone floor. Darkness pooled at the end of the hallway. Darius peered into it, and an echo of the whispers returned, urging him onward.

He crept down the hallway, broken glass crunching under foot. Beside each of the windows were small rooms with beds and wooden chests inside. The doors were either missing, or splintered open. A few of the rooms held child-sized skeletons, covered in rags and papery bits of skin. The smell of death hung in the air. Darius grimaced at the sight of the bodies. They looked like human skeletons, except for their elongated heads and three-fingered hands.

Keth children, killed in the Revenants' attack? Darius wondered if they were what he was supposed to see, but the darkness at the end of the passage still beckoned, and the whispers returned each time he looked down that way.

As Darius reached the end of the hallway, his eyes adjusted to the darkness, and he saw a vast circular chamber with no windows or doors. A pool of water gleamed in the center of the room—a well or reservoir of some kind.

More whispers.

He walked up to the edge and peered into the water. Nothing but his own reflection stared back at him in the glassy pool. About to turn away, a gust of wind slammed into his back, carrying a glowing cloud of... *Sprites.* The tiny, luminous symbionts zigged and zagged in a random pattern resembling Brownian motion, and the whispers became deafeningly loud.

The previously darkened chamber now danced with glowing white specks. The Sprites coalesced into a shimmering ball of light, and as one dipped below the surface of the pool.

Darius peered into the pool once more, and this time he saw something besides his reflection.

Dead bodies were chained to the bottom of the pool. Darius flinched in horror at the sight of the upturned faces, some of them human faces, with drifting mops of hair, others covered in fur or wrinkly hide. There had to be a few dozen people down there. The sprites dropped below one of the bodies, traveling down the chain. The chain abruptly snapped, and that body came rocketing to the surface with the Sprites on its heels. Darius rocked back on his heels and leaned away from the pool just as the body broke the surface. The Sprites burst out a second later and hovered over a woman's face.

Darius blinked in shock at the sight of her staring gray eyes. Long dark hair splayed the water around her head. She had a prominent brow, a strong jaw, and long, regal features. There was no mistaking who this was. It was Samara Guharin, Tanik's wife.

Darius stared in shock. The sprites drifted down and hovered just above her chest. There, a heart-shaped golden locket floated around Samara's neck. The whispers returned, but softly now. A split second later, the ball of sprites dispersed and went whistling by him on another gust of wind.

Darius awoke blinking rapidly and rubbing bleary eyes. They were just now making atmospheric entry over the day side of Ouroboros.

As the Osprey shivered and shook around him, Darius thought about his dream. But had it been a dream? Or was this another vision? Dreams were rarely so tangible, let alone so orderly and specific. A vision seemed more likely, but what did it mean? Clearly Samara wasn't dead. They'd met her, alive and well! But maybe this was a warning that she was going to die?

Or maybe it really was just a dream. Darius's mind flashed back to the heart-shaped gold locket around the dead Samara's neck, and he wondered if she owned such a thing. That would be the easiest way to determine if there was any truth to what he'd seen. If she owned a locket like it, then this couldn't be a dream. How else would he know about the locket?

Something else niggled in the back of his mind. Who were the others chained to the bottom of the well with Samara? He recalled that there'd been a few dozen of them. A few *dozen*.

Between the Acolytes, Marines, and Vulture pilots on their way back to the castle right now, there were a few dozen of them, too.

That hit Darius like a splash of cold water to the face. Maybe Samara wasn't the only one who needed to worry about what he'd seen.

CHAPTER 13

"We'll take you with us to the depot. You can hitch a ride with someone else from there," Trista said.

Gatticus stood behind the pilot's seat, staring into the featureless white eye of a warp disc. He marveled that although they were traveling many times the speed of light, there was no sensation of acceleration or movement—a convenient by-product of warp physics. Alcubierre-Kaminski (Alckam) drives didn't *propel* vessels through space; they compressed and expanded the space around them in a *warp bubble*. The bubble moved, while the vessel itself remained stationary within a tiny universe of distorted space-time. The flat white circle of light in front of them—the warp disc—was the only sign that the universe beyond even existed.

That was how Gatticus felt: trapped in a bubble, unable to see out, the blank sectors in his memory the only sign of what lay beyond. Fortunately only his most recent memories had been lost. His long-term memories were distributed throughout his body with several layers of redundancy.

"Hey, metal head!" Trista said. "Did you hear me?"

Buddy, her pet Togra, sniggered in the copilot's seat beside her.

"Yes, I heard you," Gatticus said. "But I wonder if I could change your mind. I'll pay you well to take me back to Earth."

"I can't risk it. If someone finds out I'm carting an Executor around, my freelancing days are over. I'll have to sign on with the USO fleet just to stay alive."

"No one needs to know. You would be taking no additional risk over what you are taking at this very moment. In fact, you could take me straight to the Union Palace on Earth. No one there would even bat an eye at seeing me step off your ship."

Trista rotated her seat to face him, and fixed him with a dry look. "Yeah, and what would my excuse be for going to the palace in the first place?"

Gatticus shrugged. "You could say you had a contract to deliver a shipment of foodstuffs."

"Let's say I do that. There's another problem. It's over two hundred light years from here to Earth."

Gatticus nodded. "How fast is your ship?"

"She'll make point four light years per hour if I push it."

Gatticus grimaced. "That's it?"

Trista's eyes flashed. "This is a civilian transport, bolts-for-brains, not a Union cruiser. Anyway, that's not the point. The point is, can you pay?"

"How much are you asking?" Gatticus replied.

"My fuel draw is just under seventy creds per light year. You'll have to at least double that if you want to make it worth my while. Say... thirty thousand."

"Done."

Trista blinked, and her copilot spun around to face him, too. His furry jaw was hanging open and his big brown eyes were bulging out of his head.

"Just like that," Trista said. There was a gleam in her eyes that Gatticus didn't like. "What's the catch?"

He decided to level with her. "I woke up on a Union vessel with a hole in my head. The ship's logs showed no sign of a fight. They indicated that I was launched from a Colossus-class carrier with the autopilot set to take me as far as possible before running out of fuel. No destination was set. Logically, that means whoever launched my ship wanted to get rid of me. If it were not for my ingenuity in fashioning a comm probe, they would have got it right."

"So?" Trista asked.

"So, I was launched from a Union ship *in* a Union ship. If the intention was to get rid of me, I am left to question who in the Union would want me gone, and how they might respond to learning that I am still around. I would like to learn the answer to that question before I hitch a ride on the nearest Union vessel."

"Aha. I get it. You want to travel incognito, and that means you've got to slum it with the civvies, but since you're an android, they all hate your guts."

"Yes. Except for you."

"No, I hate your guts just fine," Trista said. "But I like your creds, so it evens out. Price just went up. Forty thousand to take you to Earth. Plus the five promised for your rescue."

"What?" Gatticus blinked. "You already stated your price. Raising it now would be unethical."

"Said the android whose job is to sentence innocent people to death."

"We don't like our role in the Union any more than you do," Gatticus replied.

"So quit."

"We can't. Androids are not allowed to do anything else, and opposing the Union or its laws is futile. The system of tributes and designated hunting grounds is the only thing that keeps the Cygnians from committing wholesale slaughter. If we ever succeeded in overturning that system, the Cygnians would go back to hunting *everywhere*, not just on designated worlds. It is a necessary stopgap to ward off a superior foe."

"Yeah, whatever lets you sleep at night, *Executor*."

Gatticus frowned at the double-meaning behind her use of his title. "I do not sleep," he pointed out.

Trista waved her hand at him. "It's an expression. Why don't you go find a charging port or something? It's a long way to Earth, and the less we see of each other the better."

* * *

Two Ospreys and a pair of Vulture fighters

hovered down near the castle. It castle loomed large before them, cast in jagged shadows by the mountain it was built upon.

Darius climbed out of his turret just as Samara climbed down from hers. She jumped off the access ladder and landed beside him with a ringing *bang*. Darius glanced at her. No sign of a heart-shaped locket hanging from her neck. He was just about to ask her about it when Tanik came striding out of the cockpit with the rest of the Acolytes.

Samara folded the access ladder back against the ceiling and Tanik breezed by them on his way to the airlock. Darius caught Cassandra's eye, and walked with her to the airlock.

Darius noted that they hadn't brought any supplies with them, and asked about that while they were waiting for Tanik to cycle the airlock.

"The other Osprey has everything we'll need," Tanik replied as the outer doors slid open. He jumped down and started across the landing pad.

Darius and Cassandra followed him out with the others. Marines streamed from the Osprey beside theirs, while the two Vulture pilots hopped down from their fighters on landing pads beyond that.

Everyone met up on the steps of the castle. The Marines took up defensive positions at the doors and windows while everyone else walked inside.

Darius marveled that the Marines automatically knew what to do. Their training was programmed by neural mappers, not by drills and real world experience. Just a few weeks ago they'd been frozen in cryo tanks aboard the *Deliverance,* all of them terminal patients from the twenty-first century who'd been waiting for cures to their diseases. Tanik had cured them all with Cygnian nanotech, but gratitude didn't properly explain everyone's conformity with their assigned roles.

It was tempting to believe that these people were still being controlled by Tanik. Why else would they go along with his orders? *Carry a weapon, wear your armor, go to the castle, guard the castle, protect the Acolytes....*

It seemed like there should be more questions flying around and a lot less military discipline.

Tanik and Samara stopped in front of the fireplace and turned to address the group. Two pairs of Marines came in carrying metal crates and set them down to one side.

"Welcome everyone," Tanik said. "This is going to be your home for at least the next two years while you train to become Revenants."

A snort of derision echoed from the back of the group, and Darius spotted Blake Nelson standing there in his flight suit with his helmet off and tucked under one arm. Of course, *he* would be one of the Vulture pilots Tanik had chosen to join them at the castle. The other pilot standing beside him was Veekara, the Vixxon from Hades.

"Is something wrong, Blake?" Tanik asked.

"Well, yeah. I keep hearing about the *Revenants*, and the *zero point field*, and all that other kak, and I just don't buy it. Besides, what's the point? So you train them, then what? How's that going to help us get out of here? I thought the problem was we don't have enough fuel to fly around the Eye, and that we don't have enough firepower to get past the ships guarding it. Sitting around in some alien monastery for the next two years isn't going to help us. All that does is give the Cygnians more time to find us."

Murmurs of agreement rose from the Marines who'd brought the crates in from outside. Darius saw a few of them turn from their guard posts to peer in on the gathering. This was what Darius had been expecting. Despite the confrontational nature of Blake's objections, he found it reassuring to hear people thinking for themselves again. Maybe Tanik wasn't controlling them after all.

Tanik gave a twisted smile. "You mean the Revenants," he said. "The Cygnians aren't the ones looking for us on this side of the Eye."

"Whatever," Blake said. "It doesn't matter who's out there looking for us. The point is, sitting on our kakkers is a great way to let them find us."

"And what do *you* think we should be doing, Blake?"

Blake turned to address the others. "We should be sending out scouts to neighboring systems! Looking for fuel that we can steal so we can get the hell out of here. We're in the middle of a war zone. Let's go somewhere else and find some other planet to colonize. Somewhere far off the beaten track."

Heads bobbed and Veekara murmured her agreement.

"That, or we find our way back to the Union and immigrate—or whatever it is that we have to do. You said it would take three years to get to Union space if we don't go back through the Eye. How much fuel would that take?"

"More than we can possibly carry on the *Deliverance.*" Tanik replied. "Besides, you can't go back to the Union now, not after you attacked the Crucible and the Cygnians. You'd be marked for death and sent to the nearest designated hunting ground. Unless you mean that we should go back so that we can join the Coalition and the fight against the Union."

Marines and Acolytes traded worried glances with each other.

"What about us?" Arok demanded. "We didn't fight them. We could go back to the Crucible and surrender."

A few of the Marines voiced their agreement. Many of them hadn't actively fought against the Union yet.

"You Acolytes would be trained as Revenants, and then pressed into the war with the Keth. And as for the rest of you—" Tanik's gaze fell on the nearest Marine. "Assuming you won't be *grakked* by association with the rogue ship that dared to attack the Crucible, you'd be tested for your affinity to the light, just like any other tribute.

"Four out of every five people return from the Crucible with the seal of life. I see eight Marines here, so it's likely that one or two of you would be sent away to be hunted by Cygnians. I wonder who the unlucky ones would be?" Tanik asked, as his eyes roved over the group.

Silence fell, leaving nothing but the sound of feet shuffling restlessly and the whistling wind.

"We've been over this already," Tanik said.

That was news to Darius. Then again, he'd been unconscious for several days after the attack on the Crucible, so he had probably missed a lot.

"It's time we moved on to more productive conversations, don't you think?" Tanik asked.

"Two years," Blake said quietly. "Then what?"

"Then, we execute our plan to defeat the Union. Darius, why don't you tell everyone what that plan is?"

Darius swallowed nervously as all eyes turned to him. There didn't seem to be any good place to start. Taking a deep breath, he explained how he supposedly had the potential to become the next Augur, and how Tanik had foreseen him sitting on the throne of a new Union with the Cygnians as their slaves. That explanation met with skeptical looks from everyone, including and especially the other Acolytes.

"You're basing all of this on a vision?" Blake scoffed. "How is *one* man going to somehow defeat an interstellar empire of blood-thirsty aliens?"

Tanik spoke next. "By defeating the Augur. I already told you that the Augur is the one controlling the Cygnian Royals. When the Augur dies, they'll snap out of it, and the Union will erupt in civil war. That is when we will make our move."

"What move?" Blake demanded.

"We're going to turn Cygnus Prime into a cloud of dust."

A low growl sounded from Gakram, the Banshee Acolyte in the group, but everyone ignored him.

"You mean figuratively?" Blake asked.

"No, literally." Tanik went on to explain about zero point energy bombs and his plan to steal them and use them against the Cygnians.

Silence reigned in the castle once more, but for Gakram's growls.

"So the Cygnians are just going to surrender after that?" Blake asked.

"My people will never surrender," Gakram replied, baring his long gray teeth at them and hissing. "For every one of us you kill, we will kill thousands of you."

"We'll keep destroying your worlds until you do surrender," Tanik replied.

Gakram let out a thunderous shriek, and lunged. Tanik held out a hand and the Banshee stopped, hovering in mid-air, growling and thrashing against unseen forces.

Exclamations of shock and confusion rose from the group. For many of them, this was the first time they'd witnessed proof of Tanik's abilities.

"We may be able to negotiate a peaceful resolution," Tanik said.

That set off warning bells in Darius's head. In

his vision Cassandra had been killed for trying to negotiate with the Cygnians.

"Your people could use an ambassador, someone who's seen what they're going to face and who can warn them to back down before it's too late. But it's your choice, Gakram. You can also throw your life away by fighting me, if that makes more sense to you."

Gakram snarled, and Tanik smiled. "I'm going to release you now." With that, Tanik dropped his hand, and Gakram fell, landing on all six of his limbs. He hissed loudly, and the quills on his back rose like hackles, but he made no move to advance on Tanik. The air sang with tension as the two of them stared at each other.

"A simple threat combined with a demonstration on an unpopulated world in the Cygnus System may be enough," Tanik said, giving in with a shrug. "It will be your job to convince your people to back down after that."

Gakram hissed once more, but he seemed less agitated now. "I will try."

Blake cleared his throat. "Well, that sounds like a nice plan—assuming those weapons exist, *and* that you can get your hands on them."

"They do and we will," Tanik replied.

"Sure, sure. Here's a sidebar for you: let's say

that *I* don't want to be a part of it. What then?" Blake asked.

Tanik spread his hands, palms up, to take in the whole group. "The choice is yours. You're not prisoners."

"So we can go back to the camp?" Blake asked.

"I'd prefer it if you stayed for a while," Tanik said. There was a hint of menace in his voice, and Darius wondered if it was a threat.

Blake said nothing, but he crossed his arms over his chest and glared.

Tanik nodded. "Good. Now that that's settled, why don't you open those crates and start distributing our supplies?" Not waiting for his reply, Tanik's gaze skipped to one of the Marines. "Sergeant Davies, you and your squad can get started setting up the generator and the lights."

"All right," the Marine replied. His face was hidden by his helmet, but Darius committed the voice to memory.

"And let's get started boarding up those entrances!" Tanik said, now shouting to be heard over the sound of booted feet *thunking* on stone. "We don't want Seekers surprising us in the night."

Darius took a moment while everyone was busy to have a word with Samara. Cassandra followed him. "Hey, Samara," Darius whispered.

She just looked at him.

"Yes?" Tanik asked.

Darius felt a chill come over him under the weight of their combined stares, and he could have sworn he heard urgent whispers echoing at the edge of his hearing. He forced a smile and nodded to Samara. "I wanted to ask you something."

"Then ask," Samara replied.

Darius thought about mentioning his vision of her, but something told him not to say too much. "Did you ever own a gold locket?"

Samara's eyebrows inched upward. "Why do you ask?"

"I found one when we were here earlier. I thought maybe it was yours."

"Show it to me," Samara replied.

Darius flashed an apologetic smile. "That's the thing. I lost it."

Samara's eyes narrowed swiftly. "Then why are you telling me about it?"

Darius shrugged. "Because if it was yours, I thought you might want it back. I wondered if I should try to find it again." He glanced at Tanik as he spoke, but there was no sign of recognition on his face, either. Maybe his vision had just been a dream after all.

Samara shook her head. "Don't waste your time. It probably belonged to one of the Revenants who died here twenty years ago."

Darius nodded slowly. A warm breeze gusted through the castle and Darius rubbed his arms to keep warm, wondering as he did so, why a *warm* breeze left him feeling chilled.

Darius frowned. "We should get another fire going."

"And waste firewood?" Tanik asked.

Samara stared at him. "Are you feeling all right, Darius?"

"Yeah, it's just drafty in here," he said, and jerked his chin to the open windows. "I'm sure I'll feel warmer once the Marines board them all up."

"Yes," Samara replied. "I'm sure you will."

"Sorry to waste your time," Darius replied. He grabbed Cassandra's hand and led her back to the others.

"What was that all that about?" Cassandra whispered.

Darius shook his head. "Nothing. Don't worry."

Cassandra regarded him with her eyebrows skeptically raised, but she left it at that.

"Make a line!" Blake said as he dug through a supply crate with Dyara.

Darius shuffled into line with Cassandra and the others, wondering about his vision while he waited. Samara's comment about the locket belonging to one of the dead Revenants had sparked a new line of thinking: maybe he hadn't seen a vision of the future, but of the *past*. And if that were the case...

Did that mean the real Samara Gurhain was dead, and that this one was an impostor? He had to admit, Tanik meeting her here after twenty years seemed like a big coincidence.

Darius glanced at Samara. She caught his eye and smiled. He forced himself to return the smile before looking away. No, Tanik had recognized her, so she must be his wife.

Unless she'd deceived him somehow. Darius had witnessed Tanik use his abilities to make a Cygnian King think he was Captain Okara of the *Deliverance*. With that plot, they'd snuck past the Cygnian fleet guarding the Eye. But Tanik was a Revenant and Revenants were immune to each other's abilities.

Darius frowned, unable to make sense of his suspicions. Something wasn't adding up. He and Cassandra reached the front of the line, and Dyara handed him a bundle of supplies while Blake passed a second bundle to Cassandra.

"There's a flashlight, a sidearm, three fresh jumpsuits, two ration packs, and two canteens for water," Dyara explained. "Any questions?"

Darius shook his head and said, "Thank you."

Dyara nodded, and he went to stand at the foot of the stairs with the others who'd already received their supplies. Darius glanced at Cassandra's bundle and was happy to note that she hadn't been given a weapon.

"What now?" Cassandra asked.

"Now, you get your weapons," Tanik said, striding over to them with two of the glassy black swords they'd used a few hours ago to roast Awk over the fireplace.

Samara joined him, carrying two more of the swords, in addition to the one she carried in the scabbard on her back.

Darius watched in horror as they passed the swords to the kids, starting with Arok and Cassandra, then Seelka and Flitter. Gakram was the only kid who didn't get one.

"You can't be serious," Darius said.

"Is something wrong?" Tanik asked.

"You said those swords are sharp enough to slice off our own feet if we're not careful, and you're passing them out to children like they're toys."

"Don't worry," Samara said. "There are scabbards in the armory with the other weapons. We're going there now. Keeping the weapons sheathed when not in use should prevent any accidental dismemberment."

"Yeah, and what about the intentional version?" Darius asked.

Arok grinned and flourished his blade in the Banshee's direction. Gakram jumped back, hissing and flicking his barbed tail back and forth. He stood on five feet, clutching his supplies to his chest with one arm.

"I hate to say it, but I agree with Darius," Blake said, walking up to them with his own bundle. "This is a bad idea." His free hand rested on the butt of a sidearm holstered at his hip as he eyed the sword-wielding teenagers.

Cassandra held her bundle of supplies under one arm while she held her sword aloft with the other.

"Revenants are warriors," Tanik said. "And warriors need weapons. Would you prefer it if your daughter were helpless to defend herself when the Awks attack?"

Darius glared at Tanik, but he decided not to press the issue any further.

"Samara, would you please take us to the

armory?" Tanik asked.

"Of course, follow me." She led the way behind the stairs and the fireplace to a shadowy stairwell, curving down.

Darius froze, blinking in shock. It was the exact same stairwell he'd seen in his dream.

CHAPTER 14

Tanik used the tactical light under the barrel of his sidearm to light the way, but Samara went on ahead, content to walk in the dark.

One by one everyone followed her and Tanik down the stairs, but Darius held Cassandra back, letting the other kids with their swords go first. He didn't want her accidentally running into one of those blades in the dark.

Dyara and Blake hung back with them. When it was just the four of them, Blake gestured to the stairs and said, "After you, Spaceman."

"That nickname doesn't even make sense anymore," Darius replied.

"How about Chosen One? Or maybe Your Highness? Does that work better for you?"

Darius ignored him. He took the flashlight

from his supplies and flicked it on to illuminate the stairwell. "Stay close," he said to Cassandra, and then followed the sound of footsteps and muffled voices down.

They passed several landings with wooden doors, just like Darius had seen in his dream. Darius wondered if he'd find a locked door at the bottom, and behind that, maybe a long hallway with a well at the end...

He didn't have a chance to find out. Everyone was waiting for them on the other side of a splintered door on the next landing. Darius walked through with the others, and Samara gestured to the walls of the room.

"Welcome to the armory," she said.

Cracked and broken windows lined the left wall, letting in slanting beams of sunlight that danced with gleaming specks of dust. All kinds of weapons hung on the walls between those windows—swords, spears, daggers, rifles, and pistols, as well as a few others that Darius couldn't identify.

The floor was wide open and padded with a spongy black material. Thick, curving wooden beams supported a high ceiling overhead.

"This is where the Keth trained," Samara explained.

"It should work for us as well," Tanik said.

He went over to the wall and removed three gleaming black swords, while Samara went to collect the scabbards she'd mentioned. Tanik joined Darius and Dyara at the entrance of the armory and stared pointedly at the supplies in their hands. "Everyone, put your belongings down for now. We're going to be here a while."

Darius left his things on the floor beside the entrance with Cassandra's and Dyara's bundles.

Blake stood in the doorway looking on with a frown. "Maybe I should go help the Marines while you guys do... whatever it is you're going to do."

"By all means," Tanik replied.

Blake left the entryway without further comment, his footsteps echoing as he climbed the stairs.

Tanik hefted the swords in his hands. "Darius, Dyara? Take your weapons."

They each went to take one. After that, Samara passed out the scabbards. They were looped through thick black belts, creased and cracked with age.

"Strap these on and sheath your swords," Samara directed.

They all took a moment to do so while Tanik and Samara went to stand in the center of the room.

"Gather round and watch," Tanik said.

They formed a loose circle. A moment later Tanik's black armor turned bright and shimmering with light, as did his face. He drew his sword to reveal that it was glowing brightly, too.

Seelka gasped, her white eyes blinking in shock, while Flitter spread his wings and chirped excitedly.

"Revenants can focus the divine light in a shield to protect themselves," Tanik explained. "They can extend that shield around other things that they touch—weapons, armor, or other people.

"There are different kinds of shields. Some are for defense, while others can turn an ordinary blade into a superheated beam of plasma."

As they watched, Tanik's sword grew brighter. He walked over to the nearest wall, and swiped the weapon through the stones.

The rocks exploded with a thunderous *boom.*

Darius wrapped himself around Cassandra to shield her as shards of rock zipped by them in a stinging hail. "Hey!" he said. "Are you crazy?"

Tanik turned to regard them with a thin smile. "With training, you can learn to focus different shields at the same time, both to protect your person and to empower your blade."

"Why not just use guns?" Cassandra asked.

Darius recalled asking that same question when he'd seen Tanik using a sword during the attack on the Crucible.

"Because lasers and projectiles would reflect off the inside of our shields and kill us. There's no way to shoot and protect ourselves at the same time. Now, I want you all to try shielding yourselves as I did. Imagine yourselves wrapped in a blanket of light."

Darius tried it, and in that same instant he saw dazzling light pouring out from him in all directions. He stared at his hands in shock, blinking against the glare as he turned them over first one way, and then the other.

"Snaz!" Cassandra blurted out as she began glowing, too.

One by one, the other Acolytes all lit up the room, some more brightly than others.

"The brighter your shield, the stronger it is," Tanik replied. "You'll learn to strengthen them over time, but right now they are an indication of your innate potential."

Darius looked around, comparing himself to the others. It was hard to be sure, but it looked like he and Cassandra were glowing the brightest, while Arok's shield glowed the least.

"As you can see," Tanik began, "Darius's shield is almost as strong as my own."

All eyes turned to Darius, making him feel very uncomfortable. Samara's gaze was the worst of all. There was a wary gleam in her blue eyes that was either jealousy or malice. He couldn't tell which.

"Cassandra's not far off," Dyara pointed out.

"Yes, she appears to be very strong as well," Tanik agreed. "Perhaps she has a talent for shield projection."

"A talent?" Cassandra asked.

Tanik nodded. "Every Revenant has one ability that is stronger than the others. A talent."

"What's mine?" Darius asked. His shield faded as he lost his concentration, and one by one the others did, too.

"Your talent is the same as the Augur's," Tanik replied. "It is the ability to affect other Revenants with your mind."

"And what about me?" Seelka asked, her white eyes pinched into speculative slits.

"You'll each discover your talents during the course of your training," Tanik replied.

"What's yours?" Darius asked. "And Samara's?"

Tanik smiled. "We are both skilled in many

different abilities."

"That wasn't an answer."

"No," Tanik agreed. "In time I'm sure you'll be able to guess what our talents are. Consider it a training exercise. Right now, we need to choose your sparring partners."

Darius didn't like the sound of that. He laid a hand on Cassandra's shoulder. "I choose Cass." Better that she train with him than someone else, like Arok or Samara.

"I'll choose your partners," Tanik said. "Darius you're with me. Cassandra, you'll face Samara."

Panic stabbed through Darius at the thought of his daughter facing that woman. He hadn't had time to figure out what his vision meant, but there was something about her that gave him the creeps. "Hang on—" he said. "Wouldn't it make more sense to put Cassandra and I together? You and Samara are both already trained Revenants."

"And therefore less likely to accidentally slice you in half," Tanik said. "Consider yourselves lucky. As for the rest of you—Arok, you'll face Flitter. Seelka and Dyara, you'll both face Gakram."

"Two against one?" Gakram growled in Cygnian.

"You have six limbs. That leaves four arms free

to wield swords, and four eyes to track them. Cygnian Revenants are rare, but they are terrifying in battle." Tanik held up his robotic arm and flexed it with an audible clicking sound. "I should know."

Darius remembered how Tanik had fought a Revenant Ghoul at the Crucible, only to return later with his sword arm missing at the shoulder.

"Spread out with your partners," Tanik said. "And don't forget to use your shields. Your swords will be deadly, but fragile without them, and we can't afford to lose any of them or you."

Samara walked over and nodded to Cassandra. "Come with me, girl."

Darius grabbed Cassandra's hand and shook his head. "I don't think so."

"Don't worry. I will make sure no harm comes to her," Samara said. "You can trust me, Darius."

But that was the problem. He didn't trust her at all.

CHAPTER 15

Darius leapt over Tanik's sword, narrowly missing a swipe to his legs. The glowing blade swept back in a zigzag before he even touched ground, forcing him to parry in mid-air. The two blades struck with a sizzle of energy, and a metallic *clank.*

Thump. Darius's boots hit the padded floor, and he backpedaled quickly to get some space. But not too much space. Behind him Dyara and the Vixxon girl, Seelka, were sparring against Gakram and his four swords.

"Good!" Tanik said, and flung away a bead of sweat from his shining brow. "Now let's try something new."

Darius glanced around, panting with exertion as he looked for his daughter. Cassandra was on the attack, grinning wildly as she pushed Samara back with a fast series of strikes. Darius watched them with growing concern. What if one of those blades slipped? All of them were shielding themselves, but were those shields enough to keep them from getting hurt?

As he wondered about that, a blinding splash of light dazzled his eyes, connecting with his shoulder. He felt the impact, but it wasn't the sharp bite of a sword; it was the heavy blow of a bludgeon.

Tanik stepped back, flourishing his blade. "Your concern for your daughter is your weakness," he said. "You will never become a Revenant if you are always focused on her. It could get you killed, Darius."

He nodded slowly, all the while thinking that Tanik wasn't going to kill his own prodigy. He glanced at Cassandra once more, just in time to see her desperately fending off Samara's series of counter attacks. One blow slipped through Cassandra's guard, and she cried out, followed by another, and then two more. Cassandra tried to parry the final blow, but Samara knocked the blade out of her hand. Cassandra retreated frantically, but she tripped over her own feet and fell backward. Her shield flickered and failed and she held up her hands in surrender as Samara loomed over her.

That woman took another step, her sword swinging down for a decapitating blow...

He ran, faster than he'd ever run in his life, and batted her sword away with his own.

"What are you doing?" he demanded, as he used his sword to shove Samara back a few steps. "She surrendered."

Samara arched an eyebrow and smiled thinly at him. Her free hand came up, and Darius went flying across the room. He hit the nearest wall and the back of his head slammed into the stones with a ringing *thud* that should have cracked his skull open. His shield must have saved him.

"I was going to sheath my blade so that I could help her up," Samara explained, somehow standing in front of him already.

Darius frowned, replaying the scene in his mind. Was it possible that she'd been putting her sword away rather than swinging it for a killing blow?

"That's enough sparring for today!" Tanik shouted to be heard above the sounds of swords clanking and booted feet thumping on the floor. "Put your weapons away and gather your things. It's time to assign sleeping quarters."

Darius sheathed his own sword, which he surprisingly hadn't dropped while being thrown like a doll. He watched as Samara went to help Cassandra up.

Once on her feet, Cassandra limped across the floor to collect her blade. A fresh stab of anger shot through Darius at the sight of that, and he hurried to her side.

"Are you okay? Let me help you," he said.

"I'm fine," Cassandra snapped as she retrieved her sword and slipped it into the scabbard at her waist.

"Hey, watch your tone, young lady."

Cassandra rounded on him, her blue eyes flashing. "I'm not a young anything anymore, Dad. I'm not a kid."

Darius's brow tensed into a knot. "You're only twelve years old."

Cassandra fixed him with a dark look. "You treat me like I'm made of glass, like I'm always about to break."

Darius nodded to her leg. "You're limping, and I swear it looked like she was going to kill you."

Cassandra gave an exasperated sigh and shook her head.

Samara walked over to them with Tanik. "Why would I want to do that, Darius?" Samara asked.

He met her gray eyes and glared at her for a handful of seconds. "I don't know," he admitted. "But I don't like this. Any of it."

"Any of what?" Tanik asked.

"Giving weapons to kids, teaching them how to kill." Darius shook his head. "You said I'm the key to everything, right?"

Tanik's eyes narrowed to thoughtful slits. "Yes..."

"So if you want my help to hunt down and kill the Augur, then you have to leave my daughter out of it. No more swords, or guns. She can go off and be a regular twelve-year-old with other kids her age."

"No," Cassandra said.

Darius rounded on her. "I'm still your father, Cass. So what I say goes."

"Or what?"

Darius blinked. "Excuse me?"

"What are you going to do? Kick me out? Ground me and send me to my room?" Cassandra shook her head. "This isn't your house."

Darius's whole head felt hot. Veins in his temples were pulsing like they were about to explode. "When did you become such a brat?" he asked quietly.

Cassandra's lips quirked into a bitter smile.

She turned and walked away, heading for the exit.

"Hey! You come back here, right now! We don't know if it's safe out there!"

But Cassandra only walked faster.

Darius took a few hasty steps to follow, but Dyara stepped in front of him, shaking her head. "I'll go after her. You can come find us later. Let her cool off first."

Darius accepted that with a stiff nod and watched as Dyara ran after Cassandra.

"She's right," Tanik said quietly.

Darius rounded on Tanik with a scowl. "Who's right about what?"

"Your daughter. She has a right to make her own decision about training."

"She's twelve!"

"In your time I assume that means she's too young to go to war, but in this time, children of her age with her potential have no choice."

"You send twelve-year-olds into combat?"

"No," Tanik shook his head. "We send fourteen and fifteen-year-olds. It takes two years to train them."

Darius snorted. "I'm not going to change my mind. If she trains, I won't, so it's up to you."

"Is this because of your vision?" Tanik asked.

"What vision?" Darius's eyes narrowed

swiftly, and he became peripherally aware of the other Acolytes gathering around.

"The one where you claim to have foreseen my death. Except that it wasn't me you saw in that casket. It was Cassandra."

Darius fixed Tanik with a wary look. "How would you know what I saw? Are you reading my mind?"

Tanik shook his head. "I cannot. Revenants are immune to each other, remember?"

"So how did I get thrown across the room a few minutes ago?"

"That's different. We're only immune to each other's *minds*."

"Then how would you know who I saw?"

"It was clear from the way you acted. You wouldn't be so concerned if you had foreseen *my* death." Tanik gave him a twisted smile. "I doubt you would have even mentioned it if you had. It's okay. We don't have to be friends."

"We aren't. What does my vision have to do with Cassandra's training?"

"You said that she died trying to negotiate with the Cygnians. Does that sound like something that could be a consequence of training her to fight? It may very well be that she dies in the future you saw because you denied her the training that would have saved her life."

Darius considered that with a heavy frown.

"Does owning a gun make you a soldier?" Tanik pressed.

"No."

"Then neither will a sword. There is no inherent danger in her training. It's what she decides to do with it that you should concern yourself with."

Darius wasn't sure he agreed with that analysis, but Tanik had raised a good point about his vision. When and if the Augur was defeated, the galaxy was going to erupt in a bloody civil war, and Cassandra would be better off if she knew how to defend herself when that time came.

"I'm going to go find her," he said.

"Of course," Tanik replied.

"We'll be on the upper levels," Samara added. "That's where the sleeping quarters are."

Darius nodded and took off at a run. He had the presence of mind to grab his flashlight on his way out. After ten minutes of searching the levels on different landings of the stairwell, he gave up and went back up to the entrance hall of the castle.

But she wasn't there either. On a whim he went outside and spotted Cassandra with Dyara, the two of them sitting on the edge of the only empty landing pad. Seeing Cassandra's feet dangling over the edge of a thousand-foot drop with the wind gusting as it was made him wince. An image of Cassandra falling, her limbs flailing all the way down flashed through his mind.

Darius shook his head to rid himself of the unsettling thought. He stopped a few feet behind Dyara and Cassandra and softly cleared his throat, afraid to scare them.

Cassandra turned to see him standing there, and quickly looked away. Dyara glanced over her shoulder next. She smiled and waved him over.

Darius sat down beside Cassandra, doing his best to ignore the dizzy thrill that coursed through him at the sight of the distant tree tops.

Darius looked away from the view and nodded to Cassandra. She did her best to avoid his gaze. "Listen, Cass," Darius began. "We fought your cancer together, so you should know why I treat you like you're made of glass. For the past few years all I could think about was keeping you alive."

"But I'm cured now," Cassandra said.

"It's only been a week since you were cured. My brain is still trying to catch up, and now there are other threats to deal with, and in some ways they're a lot worse. I thought I'd lost you on Hades,

Cass."

"I know," Cassandra said, staring at her feet. "I'm sorry."

"For?"

"I shouldn't have spoken to you the way I did."

Darius smiled. "Thank you. I appreciate that, and I'm sorry too. I'll try to be less protective, but I also need you to be careful and not put yourself in harm's way."

"Just because I'm training to fight doesn't mean that I have to fight," Cassandra pointed out.

"That's what Tanik said," Darius replied, nodding. "He thinks it would be safer for you if you knew how to defend yourself. And he's right, so I'm going to let you train. But not with Samara."

Cassandra looked up. "Why not?"

"I'll get to that in a minute. First, you remember that vision I had when Tanik gave me the water with the sprites in it?"

Cassandra nodded. "You said you saw Tanik, dead in a casket."

Darius shook his head. "I saw *you* in that casket, Cass. Tanik and I were at your funeral. I lied because I didn't want to scare you."

Cassandra's brow wrinkled.

"It was probably just a dream," Dyara said.

"I thought so, too, but then we landed on Ouroboros and I saw the exact same setting. In my vision, we had the funeral by a river. At the end I shut the casket and it went over a waterfall. It was the same setting as where we landed—the river, the field... the waterfall."

"So... I'm going to die?" Cassandra asked, her blue eyes huge and blinking.

"No, listen, in that vision Tanik and I were talking about how you tried to negotiate with the Cygnians and they killed you. I think Tanik is right. The simplest way for you to avoid what I saw is to not negotiate with them. Do you understand? If someone needs to go talk to them, now or later, it *can't* be you."

Cassandra nodded. "Okay, but what does that have to do with me training with Samara?"

"I had another vision, recently, on our way back to the castle. I haven't told anyone yet, but it was about Samara."

Dyara's gaze pinched with concern. "What did you see?"

Darius told them about the stairwell that he couldn't possibly have known about. He described the locked door he'd seen at the bottom, and the well with bodies inside, one of which looked like Samara. Then he mentioned the gold, heart-shaped locket around her neck.

"What do you think it means?" Cassandra asked.

"At first I thought maybe those bodies were ours and the vision was a warning that we're all going to die here. So I asked Samara about the locket."

"So that's what you were going on about," Cassandra said.

Darius nodded.

"What did she say?" Dyara asked.

"She said she's never owned anything like that, and Tanik didn't seem to know anything about it either."

"So maybe she's going to find the locket later?" Dyara suggested. "What you saw might still be a vision of the future. Maybe the two visions are connected and it means that the Cygnians are going to find us here."

"Maybe," Darius admitted. "But there's another possibility. What do we know about Samara? It's a hell of a coincidence that she and Tanik were reunited here after twenty years, and without either one of them actively searching for the other."

"What are you suggesting?" Dyara asked.

"Maybe she isn't Samara. Maybe the real

Samara did die here, and her body is at the bottom of that well. This Samara could be using the zero point field to make Tanik think she's his wife. I saw him do that, convincing a Ghoul king that he was the real captain of the *Deliverance* on our way through the Eye to reach the Crucible."

"She'd have to fool all of us, too," Dyara said, shaking her head.

"No she wouldn't. We don't know what Samara looked like, so she would only have to fool Tanik."

Cassandra looked skeptical. "Except Tanik said Revenants are immune to each other's abilities, so how could Samara trick him like that?"

Darius nodded. "He also said there are exceptions to that rule, like the Augur, and supposedly me. What if this Samara, whoever she is, is another exception?"

Cassandra's eyes went huge again. "Kak..." she whispered. "What if she *is* the Augur? I mean, I know he's a man, but what if he's making us all see a woman instead?"

Darius smiled wryly. "Something tells me Tanik would figure that out pretty quick."

Cassandra's brow furrowed. Then she appeared to get it, and her nose wrinkled. "Eww, Dad!"

"Well, they've been separated for twenty years, right? And anyway, according to Tanik, people like the Augur are immune to each other. There's no way Samara is the Augur, but Tanik never said that the Augur and I are the only ones who can influence other Revenants. She could be like me, sent here by the Augur to infiltrate our group."

"How would he know we're coming?" Dyara asked.

"Maybe he's had a vision of his own death, and that vision told him where to look for the one who's going to kill him."

"You mean you," Dyara said.

Darius shrugged. "Or Tanik. He's the one plotting to kill the Augur."

Dyara pressed her lips into a determined line. "We need to go find that well. If there are dead bodies chained to the bottom, and one of them has a gold locket around its neck, then I'd say your vision is pretty clear. If not, then it was a vision of the future, and we should leave this place before we all end up in that well."

Darius nodded. "I agree."

"So what are we waiting for?" Cassandra asked. "Let's go!"

"Not yet," Darius said. "We should wait until everyone's asleep. Until we know what we're dealing with, we can't risk that Samara or anyone else finds out what we're doing."

Dyara nodded slowly. "If she can fool Tanik into thinking she's his wife, she can probably read our minds."

"Maybe," Darius said. "Although I don't think she can read my mind."

"That's why she didn't figure out why you were asking her about the locket," Cassandra said.

Dyara appeared to consider that. "Or it's because she really is Tanik's wife, and she can't read our minds any more than he can."

"I really hope that's true," Darius replied. "Because if it isn't, there's probably a Revenant fleet on its way here right now."

CHAPTER 16

"You promised," Buddy said. His lips began to quiver, and his eyes grew round.

Trista didn't like the idea of stopping at the depot for food when they had an android on board, especially not with Buddy's loose lips, but it was a long way to Earth. They would have to stop somewhere sooner or later anyway.

"All right, fine, we'll go get something, but you'd better shut the hell up about our metal friend."

"Who?" Buddy asked with squinty eyes.

"Gatticus."

Buddy shook his head as if he didn't recognize the name. Then Trista got it. "Very funny. Save the routine for strangers on the station."

Buddy grinned. "Yes, Captain."

Half an hour later Trista docked their tender ship with the outer ring of Drake Depot #926. They climbed the ladder through both airlocks and hauled themselves up inside a boxy security checkpoint. Their tender had already been scanned and physically searched by security drones on the way over from the *Harlequin*, but now it was time for a final check.

Trista waited with Buddy while a hovering drone scanned them with a flickering blue fan of light. Space stations were all the same—paranoid about terrorists. Something about owning a multi-billion-credit piece of interstellar real estate made people jumpy.

The drone flitted sideways and a robotic voice said, "You may proceed."

Trista started toward the exit of the checkpoint, both loathing and loving the sensation of artificial gravity. It had been a week since they'd left Callisto—a week in space with nothing but mag boots to pin them down.

The door swished open and Trista followed the signs to the station's food court.

"Hey, wait up," Buddy panted. "My legs are shorter than yours!"

Trista snorted. "You sure that's the problem?"

"What are you trying to say?"

Trista smiled. "You know what you find when you look up *Togra* on the datnet? Sleek little furballs running through fields, and leaping from tree to tree."

"It's not my fault I have a slow metabolism. Besides, gravity's lighter on Togora, and we don't have any fields or trees, so how do you know I can't run or leap like those show offs you saw?"

Trista snorted, but she stopped and waited for him where their corridor ended in a T. She glanced back to see Buddy's belly dragging on the deck as he ran on all fours to catch up.

"Can I pick the restaurant?" he asked as he stopped beside her and rose up on two legs once more.

"Don't start," Trista warned.

"But—" Buddy cut himself off as a trio of armored Ghouls stalked by in front of them, all of them walking on two legs, with their heads brushing the ceiling. Weapons dangled from holsters strapped to their broad torsos, one for each of their four hands—not that they needed weapons with their claws and teeth.

"Great," Trista muttered as soon as they were gone. "There must be a Cygnian cruiser re-fueling here. Stay close," she said, and glanced down at Buddy. But he was gone. "Buddy?"

A heavy weight landed on her shoulder, and she winced as sharp claws bit through her jumpsuit.

"Right here, Captain," Buddy whispered.

Under other circumstances Trista would have complained about carrying a twenty-pound ball of fat on her back, but it would be safer for both of them this way.

She joined the corridor, still following signs to the food court, but making sure to keep a good distance from the Ghouls up ahead. A large communal dining area opened up to their right, and the Ghouls peeled out of the corridor, heading for a restaurant with whole animal carcasses dangling above the counter. Trista scowled. Just her luck. The Cygnians were hungry, too. She picked the restaurant farthest from them, a burger place that looked like it would be fast and cheap.

Buddy groaned as she walked up to the counter. "If you're not going to get me fish, you could at least get something that doesn't taste like it was kakked out of a *Slog*."

The proprietor of the burger place, a *Slog* himself, overheard that comment and chased them off, shaking his fist and cursing.

"Nice work," Trista said. "Keep it up, and I'll ask those Cygnians if they wouldn't prefer fresh meat."

"You wouldn't dare," Buddy said.

"Try me."

Trista went to another restaurant and ordered a pizza for them to share. She asked for anchovies on Buddy's half to make him happy. It turned out to be a bad idea. He went from a sulking ingrate to a bubbly maniac. By the time he reached his third slice, he was standing on the table and singing an ode to the pizza.

"Shut up and sit down," Trista snapped, noticing looks they were drawing from people dining at adjacent tables. Fortunately the Ghouls didn't seem to care. They were hunched over a table in the far corner of the dining hall, tearing bloody chunks off an entire *ciervak* carcass.

Trista looked on in disgust. As she watched, she spotted a flicker of movement in the shadows behind their table. The Ghouls were too focused on their meal to notice.

It was a human woman, sneaking up behind them with what looked like a pair of butcher's knives. Trista's whole body tensed in anticipation. *She's going to attack them.* Her mind raced, wondering how to save the woman from herself, but there was no time and she was too far away.

The woman lunged out of the shadows and

stuck both knives deep into the neck of the nearest Ghoul. She yanked them out, screaming and stabbed again. Black blood spurted in her face. The Ghoul rounded on her with an outraged roar. He caught her next attack on two of his four arms, while his other two swiped at her head with razor-sharp claws. Her throat and face disappeared in a crimson tide, and she slumped to the deck.

The wounded Ghoul tore the knives out of his arms, threw back his head, and let out a deafening roar; then all three of them fell upon the dead woman, claws and teeth flashing.

Trista looked away with a sickened grimace. She caught a glimpse of the red sauce on her pizza, and nearly retched the contents of her stomach all over Buddy.

He was still standing on the table, his jaw slack and brown eyes huge as he watched the Ghouls feed. "Why would she do that?" he asked. "She didn't even kill him."

"There's no shortage of reasons to hate the Cygnians," Trista whispered, and glanced back at the scene. There was a man wearing a bloody butcher's apron standing off to one side, looking on in horror. He took a step toward the Ghouls, and then another, as if unable to help himself.

"Kak," Trista muttered. "That *goff* is going to

get himself killed! Stay here." She jumped to her feet and ran.

"What are you doing?" Buddy shrilled.

Trista reached the butcher just as he called for the Ghouls' attention. "Get away from her, you *vagons!*" he yelled in a cracking voice.

All three of the aliens looked up, their faces and jagged gray teeth smeared with blood. One of them rose to his full height and turned, his armored tail skittering as it swished across the deck. "Is that a challenge?" The Ghoul growled in Cygnian.

Trista flashed an apologetic smile and tried to pull the butcher back, but he resisted. "Are you crazy?" she hissed in his ear.

He turned to her with tears in his eyes. "That was my wife."

"She was your mate?" the Ghoul thundered, all four of his black eyes pinching with sudden interest.

"No," Trista said and bowed her head in a gesture of submission. "He said that was a waste of a *life.*" She pulled the man back a few more steps, and this time she managed to turn him away and point him in the direction of his restaurant.

The Ghoul snarled and went back to feeding.

"Don't look," Trista whispered as she led the

butcher behind his counter and from there through a metal door into one of the back rooms. It turned out to be a freezer with more carcasses hanging inside. She shut the door behind them, and the man sank to the floor, sobbing. Trista looked on with a frown, wondering if she should stay or leave.

The butcher's sobs grew quiet, leaving him spent and staring at the wall in a catatonic daze.

"Why did your wife do that?" Trista asked.

"Now I have no one," he said, as if he hadn't heard the question.

"Well, at least you're alive. You won't be if you go and do something stupid like she did."

"You don't understand," he said, shaking his head. "They took her from us."

"Took who?" Trista shivered and rubbed her arms. The cold air in the freezer was starting to get to her.

"Our daughter, Cora. She came back from the Crucible with the seal of death. We didn't even get to say goodbye before they shipped her off to Deggros as designated prey."

"Fek. I'm sorry," Trista said. She felt a flash of hatred for the Cygnians and their arbitrary system of choosing prey, but she clamped down on the feeling with a scowl. She wasn't going to change anything by raging against the system.

It's their own grakking fault, she thought. *They knew the score and they decided to have a kid anyway.* Maybe they thought they'd be the lucky ones, or maybe that was why they'd only had one. This was why Trista had never settled down.

"Are you going to be okay?" she asked, shivering and rubbing her hands together to stay warm.

The butcher gave no reply. He had to be just as cold as she was, but his grief took precedence over mundane physical concerns.

"Take care of yourself, okay? And don't do anything stupid." Trista left the freezer at a brisk pace and rounded the counter, doing her best not to look at the Ghouls. They were still gorging themselves on the butcher's wife.

When Trista reached her table, she found Buddy lying on an empty pizza pan with his belly in the air and a few crumbs scattered around him.

"Let's get out of here."

Buddy glanced at her with half-lidded eyes. "You'll have to carry me."

Trista glared back. "Did you even wait to see if I was okay before you ate my half?"

"That sounds like a trick question."

Trista snorted and shook her head. "I should

leave you here." But even as she said it, she picked him up and carried him off, cradling him in her arms like a baby.

"You'd miss me too much," he said, gazing up at her with big brown eyes and a faint smile.

CHAPTER 17

Darius sat on a twenty-year-old mattress in his and Cassandra's assigned quarters, watching through the jagged remains of a broken window as the sinking sun splashed fire on the clouds. Cassandra and Dyara sat beside him, eating a few of their rations.

"I wonder why all of the windows are broken?" Cassandra asked.

Darius shrugged. "Storms?"

"Or birds pecking at them, trying to get in for shelter," Dyara suggested.

"Seekers?" Cassandra asked.

"I don't think so," Darius said. "Not these windows, anyway. They're too small for Seekers to climb through."

They sat in silence, watching the night fall. The

room turned hazy with darkness, and the air grew cold. Darius shivered.

"How much longer do we need to wait?" Cassandra whispered.

"A while yet," Darius said, shaking his head. In theory everyone had already gone to bed, but he doubted that included Tanik or Samara, and especially not the Marines who were probably still boarding up entrances and stringing lights through the common areas.

Cassandra covered a yawn and shook her head.

"Why don't you get some sleep?" he suggested, and nodded to the dusty mattress. An ancient-looking brown blanket and a pillow sat on the foot of the bed. He passed the pillow to Cassandra and waited for her to lie down before spreading the blanket over her. She rolled over to face the wall, and he looked on with a smile. "Good night, sweetheart. I love you."

"Night, Dad. Love you, too."

He glanced at the door; it was barred and locked. The castle had plenty of rooms with missing or broken doors, but there were enough that still had them for the Acolytes to have a measure of privacy and security. Dyara's room was across the hall from Darius and Cassandra's, but since they were planning to go sneaking around the castle together it didn't make sense for her to wait there by herself. That, and she didn't want to be alone.

Darius sat in silence with Dyara. Stars came out, winking at them—the cold eyes of the night.

"What's it like?" Dyara whispered.

Darius arched an eyebrow at her. "What's what like?"

She jerked her chin to Cassandra. "Having kids."

"Oh, it's amazing. And terrifying. And exhausting. Frustrating..."

"All that?"

"I could go on," Darius said. "It's a bit of everything, but mostly it's great. I would have had more kids if I'd found the right person, and if it hadn't been for Cassandra's cancer."

Dyara nodded slowly. "I wish I could have kids."

"You can't?" he asked.

"No, I can. I just don't want to."

"But you said..."

"I wish there were some way to have them and keep them safe. My parents sacrificed everything to get me this." She turned over her wrist, revealing the seal of life, a glowing triangle with an eye inside of it. "They sold their home, cashed in their savings, and moved to a remote planet, all so they could get me this forgery and keep me from going to the Crucible." She shook her head. "And look at where it got me. I ended up getting sent to a designated hunting ground with Tanik. Then I went to the Crucible anyway, and now I'm training to become a Revenant, the same as my brother and sister did. My parents did everything to keep me safe and it still wasn't enough.... I wonder if they're even still alive."

"Your parents?"

"No, my brother and sister."

"Maybe. How long ago did they go to the Crucible?"

"I was ten when Jade left. Jace left the following year. I'm twenty-nine now."

"So they left... nineteen and eighteen years ago," Darius said. "Have you ever asked Tanik about them? He said he fought the Keth for thirty years before he made his escape."

Dyara nodded. "And after he escaped he led the Coalition fleet for twelve years, and he spent the last eight on Hades with me and the other exiles. If you do the math, that means he just missed them."

Darius frowned. "Well, there must be some

other way to find them. Maybe when we go hunting for the Augur we'll have a chance to look for them."

"I'm not sure there's going to be a *we*. Tanik seems to think you're the only one who can defeat the Augur."

Darius snorted. "Yeah, and after two years of training, I'm supposed to go up against a Revenant who's so old that he was actually born before me. Except he didn't spend all that time in cryo like I did. What do you suppose two years of training will do against more than a thousand years of practice and experience?"

"I'm sure Tanik has a plan. Maybe there will be some way that we can help you."

"Maybe." Darius covered a yawn and nodded to the empty bed on the other side of the room. "You can get some sleep if you like. I'll wake you when it's time to go."

Dyara grabbed his hand, and Darius felt a thrill go through him as her cold fingers laced through his. "You should sleep, too. We can set an alarm with our ESCs."

"Right," Darius replied. "I forgot about that. But there's only one bed."

"We can share," Dyara said. She stood up and pulled him over to the other bed, not giving him a chance to object. Darius looked on with a frown as she laid out the blanket and fluffed the pillow. She climbed in with her mag boots and flight suit still on and then held the blanket open for him to climb in beside her. Darius thought about removing his boots, but decided against it. They needed to be ready to run or fight at a moment's notice. With the thought that Samara could be a Revenant impostor stuck in his head, Ouroboros didn't feel safe anymore—not that it ever had to begin with.

He glanced at the weapons rack at the foot of the bed, making sure he knew where to find his sword and pistol if he needed them.

"Well?" Dyara prompted.

Darius climbed into bed beside her. She curled up against him and laid her head on his chest. He supposed that meant she'd forgiven him for siding with Tanik during their brief coup on the *Deliverance*, but still, an apology probably wouldn't hurt.

"Hey," he said. "I'm sorry for what happened. I should have found some way to make Tanik release you, or at least visited you while you were in the brig. And I'm sorry for siding with him. He made me a deal I couldn't refuse."

"It's okay. I get it. Tanik promised to save your daughter, and he did, so..." she shrugged. "I get it."

"Thanks." Darius wrapped his arm around her shoulder. Somehow it didn't feel like she was a stranger, even though he'd barely known her a week. She'd made her intentions known early on, and he'd made it clear that he just wanted to be friends, but now, lying beside her with the smell of her hair and the feel of her body tucked against his, it was hard to remember why he hadn't reciprocated her interest.

Whatever the case, now definitely wasn't a good time to start anything, and taking it slow seemed like the only way forward when he had an adolescent daughter to think about. But, if nothing else, he had to admit it was nice not sleeping alone for a change.

"What time should we set our alarms for?" Darius asked as he mentally checked the time via his extra-sensory chip. It was only 1823, but his ESC was still set to interstellar standard time. He suspected it was quite a lot later in the local time zone.

"How about twenty-one hundred hours IST?" Dyara suggested. "By then only the night watch should still be awake."

"Hopefully," Darius replied. He set his alarm for 2100 and checked the door one last time, making sure that it was locked and barred. It was, but that would likely do nothing to keep a Revenant out. He frowned, wondering what he could do about that. An idea occurred to him and he got out of bed.

"What's wrong?" Dyara asked.

He removed his sword from its rack and sheath and walked over to lean the blade against the door handle. Satisfied, Darius went back to bed.

"What's that for?" Dyara inquired.

"If someone manages to open the door while we're asleep, we'll hear my sword fall on the floor."

"Smart," Dyara said as she snuggled against him once more.

Darius let out his anxiety with a sigh and allowed his eyes to drift shut. It wasn't long before exhaustion overcame him and he fell asleep.

In the next instant he was standing next to Tanik on the bank of the river running through camp, and gazing into Cassandra's casket. Her expression was serene, with no sign of whatever had killed her. Darius felt cold all over.

"They killed her. She tried to negotiate with them, and they killed her," Tanik said.

No, Darius shook his head. *This is a dream.* He knew it was a dream, but somehow that didn't make it any less real.

Cassandra's eyes sprang open and she smiled. "Don't worry, Dad. I'm just sleeping."

"Cass?" he asked, his voice echoing strangely in his head. He tried reaching for her, but just as he did so, her smile vanished and her eyes slammed shut. "Cass!"

He awoke with a shout.

Dyara flinched and sat up quickly. Her eyes were wide and blinking as they searched the room. But there was nothing in the room with them. She turned to him with a puzzled frown. "What's wrong?"

"I had a nightmare," he whispered. "Sorry I woke you. You can go back to sleep."

"Another vision?" Dyara asked.

Darius glanced at Cassandra. She was too still. His heart pounding, he left the warmth of the covers to stumble over to her bed. He placed a hand on her back and waited to feel the subtle rise and fall of her breathing.

Once she did, Darius let out a shaky sigh. It was an old routine. Having fought cancer with Cassandra for so many years, he was no stranger to nightmares of her dying that chased him into the waking world. Maybe these weren't visions, after all. Maybe these were just fears messing with his head.

But he knew better than to believe that. He couldn't have known there was a river like the one in his dream on Ouroboros before they'd landed there.

Darius shook his head, confused. He'd already warned Cassandra about his vision. Why would she try to negotiate with the Cygnians if she knew that it could lead to her death?

Darius caught a flicker of movement in the corner of his eye and felt a warm hand slide into his. He turned to see Dyara standing beside him.

"It was about Cassandra again?"

Darius nodded. "The same vision as last time. I have to get her out of here, Dya. It's the only way to keep her safe."

"Depending what we find in that well, we all might have to leave. We should wake her. It's time to go."

"It's twenty-one hundred already?" Darius asked.

"Almost." Dyara went to her bundle of supplies and grabbed a flashlight. She turned it on and shined the beam on the weapon rack to find her sword and sidearm. "There's no point trying to go back to sleep now," she said as she strapped on her weapons.

Darius shook Cassandra by her shoulder. "Cass. Wake up, honey," he whispered. "It's time to go."

"Already?" she groaned, rubbing her eyes and crawling out of bed. She stumbled over to the weapons rack to collect her sword.

Darius followed to get his gun. Strapping it on, he crossed the room to get his flashlight and promptly flicked it on. As he shined the beam on the door, the light bounced off his glassy black blade, and he went to retrieve it.

Once they had their weapons and flashlights, he and Dyara lifted the wooden beam that barred the door, and set it aside. Dyara unlocked the deadbolt, but hesitated with her hand on the door handle. "Flashlights off," she said, glancing over her shoulder at them. "We don't want anyone to see us leaving."

All three flicked off their flashlights at once, and Dyara opened the door with a loud groan of rusty hinges. Darius cringed at the noise, and they all froze.

Dim white light spilled into their room from a string of lights the Marines had hung from the top of the opposite wall.

Darius waited for a handful of seconds, staring into the hall, and listening for the sound of another door opening, but all he heard was the steady thumping of his heart. *So far so good,* he thought.

"Let's go," Dyara whispered.

CHAPTER 18

Hushed voices drifted to Darius's ears as they neared the balcony above the foyer at the end of the hall. He identified two different voices, both male, and neither of them familiar. *Marines on the night watch.* Just as they started down one of the curving stairways, he picked out a third voice. It was Blake's.

Great, Darius thought. The last thing they needed right now was to have to explain themselves to him.

As they crept down the stairs, Darius saw the two Marines, as well as Blake, all with their backs turned and guarding a pair of improvised wooden doors. Both doors were wide open, revealing a black sky full of stars, and the Marines' rifles were on the ground, leaning against the doors.

So much for a night watch, Darius thought. He glanced around the foyer as they reached the bottom of the stairs. The windows were boarded up, but only with a few planks each. Not much of a deterrent for the Seekers, but better than nothing.

Dyara quietly led them around behind the fireplace to the spiral stairs leading down. A string of lights illuminated the stairwell, too, making their flashlights unnecessary. Dyara waited at the top of the stairs, and this time Darius took the lead. He led them down past the armory and the landings below it, until they reached the bottom. The string of lights ended on the landing above, giving barely enough light to see by. At the bottom of the stairs a patched wooden door barred the way, just like in Darius's vision.

"Is this it?" Dyara whispered.

"Yes." Darius nodded and reached for the door handle. It turned easily in his hand. He frowned. In his vision the door had been locked. As he opened the door, he listened for the sound of the deadbolt falling out and hitting the stone floor, but he heard nothing.

Behind the door they found a long corridor lined with broken windows on one side and doors on the other, just like he'd seen in his vision.

Darius walked through, and something

metallic skittered under his feet. He stopped, and scanned the floor. A metallic gleam revealed the deadbolt. He'd kicked it as he walked in. The lock had already fallen out.

"Someone's already been down here," Darius said.

"How do you know?" Cassandra breathed.

"Because in my vision the door was locked, and the deadbolt fell out when I forced it open. Now the door's unlocked, and the deadbolt is already on the floor.

"That's a pretty specific vision you had," Dyara commented.

Darius nodded slowly. He stepped aside to let the others through, and then clicked on his flashlight and shined the beam down the corridor. Familiar patterns appeared on the dusty floor.

"Look," he said, pointing the beam of light at the floor.

"Footsteps," Dyara said. "You're right. Someone was down here already."

"Maybe it was one of the Marines?" Cassandra suggested.

"If it was the Marines, why aren't there lights strung up down here, too?"

"Maybe they ran out of lights," Dyara said.

"Or they never came down here, and those are

Samara's footsteps," Darius replied. "Maybe she came to erase the evidence."

"If she can't read your mind, how would she know to do that?" Dyara asked. "I didn't tell anyone about your vision."

"Me either," Cassandra said.

"We met her again after we spoke on the landing pad, when she and Tanik were passing out blankets and assigning rooms. Maybe she sensed your suspicion and read something in your minds?" Darius belatedly recognized how strange that sounded. He was shocked by how fast this was all becoming normal to him—visions, mind-reading, and other supernatural phenomena. It all seemed impossible even after seeing and experiencing it for himself.

Cassandra's and Dyara's flashlights clicked on and their beams joined his.

"Let's not get paranoid yet," Dyara said, brushing by him in the doorway. "Let's go see what we can find." She led the way down the corridor.

Darius drew his sidearm, waiting for Cassandra to go next. He brought up the rear to make sure no one snuck up behind them. Broken glass crunched underfoot as they went. Darius peered inside each of the open doors to his right, looking for the child-sized humanoid skeletons he'd seen in his vision, but found no sign of them—just dusty old mattresses, stripped bare, and a few wooden chests.

At the end of the corridor, Darius noticed their flashlights bouncing off something smooth and reflective. *The water in the well?* he wondered.

They reached the end of the corridor, and he saw that was exactly what it was. A round pool of water, smooth as a mirror, gleamed in the center of a cavernous room.

"There's the well," Dyara said, walking up to the edge of it. Darius and Cassandra followed, and all three of them shined their flashlights into the well. The glassy pool reflected some of the light, while the rest illuminated a few feet of murky, sediment-filled water.

"Great," Darius muttered. "We're going to have to dive in to find out what's at the bottom."

Cassandra's nose wrinkled. "Dive *in*...? With dead bodies in there? No thanks."

"Not you, and not without the right equipment." He turned to Dyara and looked her up and down.

She held up her hands. "Don't look at me."

"You're already wearing a flight suit. All you need is your gloves, an oxygen tank, and a helmet, and you'll have a complete set of diving gear."

"I left all of that back in the Osprey outside the castle. I'd have to explain why I'm going to get it to those Marines—and to Blake."

"I'm sure you could come up with a good excuse," Darius said.

"Like what?"

"Like..."

"We could tell them the truth," Cassandra suggested.

"And risk Samara finding out what we were up to?" Darius asked.

"Actually, that might not matter," Dyara said. "If we don't find bodies in the well, then your vision was some kind of warning about the future, and we'll have to tell Samara, anyway. And if we *do* find bodies down there, then we'll have to tell Tanik what you saw so that we can confront her and find out who she really is. Either way, we won't be skulking around again after tonight."

Darius frowned. "And what if she's already been down here to erase the evidence?"

Dyara waved her flashlight around, searching the room; then she began walking around the well, checking the floor.

"What are you looking for?"

"Muddy footprints. Puddles."

"Puddles?" Cassandra asked.

"If Samara beat us down here and went into the well herself, then there'd be water around it," Dyara explained.

"Why would she do that?" Cassandra asked.

"To remove the bodies. Or the locket. Or both."

Dyara finished walking around the well and slowly shook her head. "There's nothing, not even a drop of water. I bet if we ask the Marines upstairs they'll tell us that they came down here earlier as part of a security sweep, but no one's been in the well yet. You two wait here. I'll be back," Dyara said.

"Are you sure you don't want us to come with you?" Darius asked. "Safety in numbers."

Dyara flashed a smile. "I'll be fine. See you soon." She took off at a run with her sword slapping her hip and her flashlight bobbing as she went.

Once she reached the stairwell and disappeared, Cassandra said, "I like her too."

Darius blinked. "What? I don't..."

Cassandra snorted. "Yes, you do. It's okay. You don't have to ask for permission or anything. And it's about time you went on a date."

Darius frowned. "A date? Here? What would I do? Hunt and kill an Awk and then invite her to the barbecue?"

Cassandra shrugged. "Sounds like a plan. I bet that's how the cavemen did it, and obviously it worked for them, or we wouldn't be here to discuss it."

"Ha ha," Darius said.

"The point is, you don't have to be alone."

"I'm not. I've got you."

Cassandra arched an eyebrow at him. "What's wrong, scared she'll turn you down?"

Darius frowned and gestured to their surroundings. "Look at where we are, what we're doing—our primary concern right now is survival." He shook his head.

Cassandra smiled. "Doesn't that just add to the romance? You know, live for the moment because you might not have tomorrow?"

Darius narrowed his eyes at her. "And what would you know about that, young lady?"

She gave him a dry look. "Nothing. I'm *twelve*, Dad."

He nodded slowly. "Then stop acting like such an adult."

"Just think about it, okay? She likes you. I can tell. I mean, she invited you to sleep in her bed last night. That's got to count for something."

"You were awake?"

Cassandra grinned.

Darius snorted and looked away, shining his flashlight back down the corridor. He kept his aim on the open door at the end, just in case Dyara wasn't the one who came down those stairs.

And she wasn't.

Darius's finger tightened on the trigger.

"Hey there, Chosen One!" Blake called, and waggled the beam of his flashlight in greeting. Dyara came down the stairs behind him, wearing her helmet and gloves. Darius slowly lowered his weapon and waited while they approached.

Blake stopped in front of him, grinning from ear to ear. "What's this I hear about you becoming a grave robber?"

Darius frowned. "If you're not going to take this seriously, then why did you come?"

"Who says I'm not taking it seriously? I'm the one who's been telling you from the start that there's something off about that Tanik guy. It won't be any surprise to me if his wife turns out to be a zombie."

Darius turned to Dyara with a furrowed brow. "A zombie? What did you tell him?"

Dyara threw up her hands and shook her head. "He hears what he wants to hear," she said, her voice muffled by her helmet.

"What else do you call a dead chick who's somehow walking around again?" Blake asked, still smiling.

Darius offered a smile of his own. "You think we're crazy."

"I don't think it. I know it." Blake jerked his chin to the well. "Prove me wrong. Go find me a skeleton for Halloween."

"Hallo-what?" Dyara asked.

Darius waved his hand to dismiss that reference and nodded to her. "Are you ready?"

Dyara nodded back and reached around to grab the air hose dangling from the oxygen tank on her back. She inserted it into her helmet, and gave a thumbs-up. That done, she passed him her flashlight and removed her sword belt and gun belt. She slid a coil of zero-G tether off the gun belt, and clipped one end of it to a metal loop on her flight suit. She gave the other end to him.

"Don't let go."

"I won't," Darius replied, and clipped the other end of the tether to his own gun belt.

They walked to the edge of the well together and peered in once more. Darius shined his flashlight into the murky depths and passed Dyara's back to her. She shook her head and turned on her helmet lamps instead. "These are waterproof," she explained.

He nodded and set both flashlights down on the edge of the well so that he could manage the coil of zero-G tether.

Dyara swung her feet over the edge of the well.

"Tug twice on the line when you're ready to come back up," Darius said.

Dyara nodded.

"Don't spring a leak!" Blake added.

Everyone glared at him.

"You're a real kakker, you know that?" Cassandra said.

Blake snorted, but his smile faded with the rebuke.

"I'm going in," Dyara said, and pushed off the edge of the well with a splash.

Darius fed the tether to her as she sank into the murky depths of the well. Her headlamps illuminated the water from within, revealing a lot more than they'd seen earlier with their flashlights. Thick black clouds of sediment appeared all around her, like dead flies in a jar.

The murky water soon swallowed Dyara whole, leaving nothing but a vanishing green glow. Darius kept feeding the tether into the water, faster and faster as she fell. He was running out of line to give her.

"It's not going to be long enough!" Darius said.

Blake slapped him on the back. "I guess you'll just have to jump in with her."

Darius scowled at Blake, and the other man held up his hands in surrender.

"It's that, or you cut her loose. I'm just telling it like it is."

A moment later, the line pulled taut and yanked Darius against the edge of the well. He cried out as his gun belt pulled painfully against the small of his back, and he hauled up on the tether to try to take some of the weight off, but it was too thin and slippery to get a good grip. Darius panted with exertion and pain. Dyara was no lightweight wearing all of her gear.

"Help him!" Cassandra cried, and her hands joined his on the tether.

Blake appeared on the other side of him and grabbed the tether, too. With the three of them pulling, they managed to get some slack on the line. Darius gasped in relief.

Then the line went suddenly slack and they all staggered back a step. "What the... she unclipped it," Darius said, blinking in shock. "How's she going to get back up?"

"Well, I guess she could always swim," Blake said.

Darius gave him a dark look. "If she could do that, then what was the point of the tether?"

He shrugged. "Extra safety?"

"Should we pull it out?" Cassandra asked.

Darius shook his head. "No. Maybe she was close to the bottom when she unclipped, and she can still reach it."

Time dragged by as they waited. Darius counted the seconds, watching the water for any sign of movement below.

Nothing. The seconds turned to minutes, and Darius began to worry. Dyara could last for a while down there with her oxygen tank—at least an hour if it was full—but if she was trapped at the bottom of the well, then sooner or later they were going to have to find some way to get her out. Darius glanced at Blake. "You're wearing a flight suit."

"And?"

"If you give it to me and go get me a helmet and an oxygen tank I can go down and get her."

Blake looked dubious. "If she doesn't come back up, what makes you think you will?"

Just then Darius felt a tug on the tether, followed by another one. Then he felt a heavy weight yank him against the side of the well once more. "She's back! Help me pull her up."

The three of them hauled on the line together

until it was coiled in giant loops around their feet. The ghostly green glow of Dyara's headlamps reappeared, rising fast, and then a few seconds later she broke the surface. They grabbed her hands to pull her out.

"What did you find?" Darius asked as she sat on the edge of the well.

Dyara pulled out her air hose and unfastened the seals on her helmet. Darius noticed that her gloves were dripping with black muck, so he helped her get the helmet off.

"There's nothing down there," Dyara said, shaking her head.

"Surprise surprise," Blake muttered.

"No bodies?" Darius asked. "Are you sure?"

Dyara nodded. "Positive. I searched the bottom, but there's no bones. There's just a thick layer of mud." She held up her hands, letting it drip from her gloves with noisy *splats*. "Either your vision was just a dream, or it was a vision of the future."

"I'll take door number one," Blake said. "Dreams are the kak of the mind, my friend," he said, and slapped Darius on the back again.

Darius gave him a look of strained patience. "So how do you explain that I knew this well was here before we ever came down here?"

Blake shrugged. "Maybe you heard about it from the Marines. They were down here earlier."

"Well, that explains the footprints," Cassandra said.

Darius shook his head. "But it doesn't explain my vision. I had it while we were still in orbit, on our way here."

"But you were at the castle before that," Blake pointed out.

"He didn't come down here," Cassandra said. "He was with me the whole time."

Blake snorted. "And I suppose I should just take your word for that."

"Why would we lie?"

"I don't know, maybe to make us think your Dad is as special as everyone says he is?"

"Shut up, Blake," Dyara said.

"No problem. I was just leaving," Blake said, and stalked away.

Dyara turned back to Darius. "In your vision, were the bodies decomposed, like they'd been there for twenty years? Or did it look like they'd died recently?"

Darius shook his head. "They were recent."

Dyara nodded. "Then all signs point to a vision of the future, not the past. We need to go tell Tanik before it's too late."

"What about Samara? And that locket?" Cassandra asked.

"I guess she really is his wife. As for the locket, she's probably going to find that later on," Dyara said. She nodded to Darius. "Regardless, between this vision and your other one, it's pretty clear that Ouroboros isn't safe for us. We need to leave this planet."

Darius nodded slowly and absently peered into the depths of the well once more. "Let's hope Tanik sees it that way."

CHAPTER 19

Darius raised his fist to knock on the door to Tanik's room, but the door swung open before his knuckles even touched the wood.

Samara stood there in the dim light spilling from the hall, wearing a jumpsuit from the *Deliverance*. "Hello," she said.

"Can we come in?" Dyara asked. "It's kind of a long story."

Samara turned to defer the question to her husband. "Tanik?"

"Let them in," he growled.

Darius walked in, followed by Cassandra and Dyara. Samara closed the door behind them, shutting out the light from the hall, and they flicked on their flashlights to peel back the shadows once more.

Tanik's room was larger than the one Darius and Cassandra shared. There was a large bed in the center, flanked by two broken windows. A pair of wooden nightstands sat beneath those windows, and the ragged remains of ancient curtains fluttered restlessly along the top. Darius noticed a wooden chest at the foot of the bed, and two wooden wardrobes along the walls.

"Well?" Tanik prompted. He was sitting on the edge of the bed, glaring at them. His chest and arms were bare, revealing rippling cords of muscle. He didn't have an ounce of fat on him. Samara walked over and sat beside her husband.

Darius explained about his vision and their trip to the well. Samara and Tanik listened without interrupting. Darius omitted their suspicions that Samara might be an impostor, since that no longer seemed like a serious possibility.

"We didn't find anything," Dyara added. "No bodies, and no locket. So we have to assume that what Darius saw hasn't happened yet."

"As opposed to something that had already happened?" Samara asked with a faint smile. "Don't tell me you were expecting to find *me* at the bottom of that well?"

"Well..." Darius trailed off. "I thought maybe the real Samara was already dead, and that you might be some kind of impostor."

Tanik snorted and shook his head. "And she somehow fooled me into thinking that she's my wife? How would she do that? And why would the woman in your vision have the same features as Samara? Unless you're suggesting this is my wife's clone."

"Is that a possibility?" Darius asked.

"No. It would take more than twenty years to mature a clone to the same apparent age as my wife, and we've only been separated for twenty years. Besides, this Samara has all of the same memories, and the same personality as the one I remember."

Darius nodded. "I guess I was just being paranoid."

"Indeed," Tanik replied.

"Is that why you were asking me about a necklace?" Samara asked.

"Yes," Darius replied.

Samara stood up and walked over to the nightstand. She retrieved something from the top drawer, turned, and held it dangling from her fingertips. "Did it look like this?"

Darius gaped at the sight of it, and crossed over to her for a better look. The necklace was black with age, and the heart-shaped pendant wasn't any cleaner, but there were still glimmers of the golden color it had once had. It certainly *looked* like a twenty-year-old necklace, but for some reason it had looked new in his vision.

"Where did you find it?" Darius asked.

"In one of the rooms on the lower levels," Samara said. "I was going to clean it up and wear it myself."

Darius considered that with a frown. "Well, I guess you're not going to die because of the necklace."

"Unless it's cursed," Cassandra suggested.

Darius arched an eyebrow at her. "You've been watching too many horror movies."

"No, Darius is right," Tanik said. "The necklace is unimportant. Wear it or not, it won't change anything."

"Then I'll wear it," Samara said.

"Is there something else you'd like to tell us?" Tanik asked.

"Both of my visions involved people dying here," Darius said. "Maybe that necklace has nothing to do with it, but clearly this planet does. We need to leave before the things I saw start to happen."

Tanik held his gaze for a long moment. "We don't know how far into the future these visions are. They could be things that are going to happen a hundred years from now. What did Cassandra look like in your vision? Older, or the same?"

Darius consider that. "I don't know..."

"Think."

"Maybe a year older. Or two. No more than that."

Tanik nodded. "Then let's not overreact. As for your vision of Samara, she doesn't age, so there's no way to be sure that what you saw is imminent. If you have another vision, let us know. Perhaps that will reveal more. Until then, we're staying right here."

"Another planet would be safer," Darius insisted.

"Would it?" Tanik replied. "This planet is abandoned and not frequented by Revenants. Furthermore, our presence is masked by the planet and this place," he said, gesturing to the castle walls. "We won't find another planet like it within range of our remaining fuel supply, and we're going to need that fuel to leave here when the time comes."

"And when will that be?" Darius asked.

"Once your training is complete and you are ready to fulfill your destiny to take the Augur's place. Now, if there's nothing else..."

Darius frowned. He wanted to insist further, but he'd run out of arguments for them to leave. If it came to it, he supposed there was nothing stopping him from leaving by himself and taking Cassandra with him. Maybe Dyara, too, if she wanted to go.

"No, there's nothing else," Darius said. "Sorry to wake you."

"No need to apologize," Samara replied as she stood up and walked with them to the door. "You did the right thing by coming to tell us what you saw, but I suggest that the three of you go get some sleep now. You'll need your energy for tomorrow's training."

"Sure. See you tomorrow," Darius said as he stepped out into the hallway with the others. The three of them walked back to their room in silence. Once they were inside, they locked and barred the door. Dyara stripped out of her muddy boots and gloves, and then her flight suit. A rotten smell began to saturate the air.

"Yuck," Cassandra said, waving her hand in front of her nose. "Maybe we should leave that out in the hall."

"Or leave it on," Darius suggested.

"Leave it on?" Dyara echoed, shaking her head. "It's wet. I can't go to bed in that."

"I'm not sure that we should go to bed. We need to get out of here."

"Do *you* know a safer planet than this one?" Dyara challenged.

"Well, no but..."

"It makes no sense to avoid one threat by running headlong into another," Dyara insisted.

"I think she's right, Dad," Cassandra said.

Darius glanced at her. Two against one. He let out a breath and walked up to the window to get some fresh air. The night's sky was bright and dazzling with stars. A warm breeze caressed his face, bringing with it alien smells. He shut his eyes for a moment, and focused on his breathing, trying to still his racing heart. He felt a hand slide into his, and turned to see Dyara standing beside him.

"Come to bed," she said. "We can worry again in the morning."

Darius allowed her to lead him back to bed. Cassandra was already curled up under the covers on the other bed with her eyes shut.

Once he was lying in bed with Dyara's head on his chest once more, he realized how wide awake he was. Something was bothering him, something he couldn't put his finger on.

Dyara's leg twitched, and Darius glanced at her to find her face relaxed in sleep. He looked to

Cassandra, she seemed to be sleeping, too. How could they both fall asleep so easily while he was still wide awake? And how was it that they'd been in agreement to leave Ouroboros right up until they'd talked to Tanik and Samara? Now both Cassandra and Dyara were singing the same tune as Tanik and Samara.

Were they convinced by Tanik's arguments? Or something more sinister? *If Samara is an impostor, and capable of influencing or controlling other people's minds, then maybe she's doing that with Cassandra and Dyara.*

But she can't affect my *mind,* Darius thought. *Maybe that's why I'm wide awake and worrying while everyone else is sleeping soundly.*

Darius frowned up at the hazy stone ceiling. He didn't know enough about visions or the zero point field. Could Samara have somehow removed the bodies from the well without leaving any water or mud on the floor? Maybe she'd thrown the bodies out a window. No one would find them in the forest a thousand feet below the castle, unless they went down there purposefully to look.

Darius took a deep breath and let it out slowly. Maybe he was just being paranoid. The fact that Samara had found that locket *could* be evidence that what he'd seen was a vision of the future. Or it could be that Samara had dredged that locket from the well in order to make him think that.

Darius rubbed his eyes and kneaded his temples, trying to massage away his headache. There was only one way that he was going to settle his doubts. He needed to find some excuse to go looking at the base of the cliffs below the castle. If he didn't find anything down there, then maybe he could finally put his suspicions to rest.

CHAPTER 20

Darius only managed to sleep for an hour before waking up to the sound of a fist thumping on his door, followed by Tanik's voice. "It's time to get up. Meet me in the armory in ten minutes."

Cassandra groaned and sat up. "What's going on?"

"Time to train," Darius said, as he stumbled out of bed.

"It's four in the morning!" Dyara said. "The sun isn't even up yet."

Darius walked to the window and peered down at the horizon. He saw a faint blue glow of dawn building there, but no hint of a sunrise yet. Cold air caressed his face and made him shiver. "I guess a cup of caf would be too much to ask for," he said as he turned from the window.

They ate a quick breakfast of dry rations and washed it down with stale water from their canteens before hurrying down to the armory.

The morning's training involved more sparring with swords, and then practicing a new ability— *concealment,* which they could use to hide their presences from each other. Tanik had them practice by playing hide and seek in the castle.

Darius wasn't comfortable with being separated from Cassandra and not knowing where she was, especially not with his lingering suspicions about Samara. Whenever possible he'd hide with or near Cassandra. In the latter case, he used his awareness to keep track of her, despite her best efforts to keep her presence concealed.

She wasn't the only one who couldn't hide from him. When it was his turn to *seek*, none of the Acolytes could hide from his awareness. He could see all of them, bright and shining, even with his eyes open—and even through the castle walls. Only Tanik and Samara might have been able to hide from him, but they weren't playing.

In the final game, Darius found a particularly good hiding spot. He climbed out one of the windows in the armory and stood on a ledge around the corner from it, with his fingers wedged into gaps between the stones in the wall. He used concealment to hide his presence, and waited for Arok to find him.

After waiting for what felt like at least half an hour, his fingers were numb and his arms and shoulders were stiff. Still, he clung there, using his own awareness to track people through the wall of the castle.

The other Acolytes had gathered inside the armory, on the other side of the wall from him, while Arok searched the upper levels of the castle. Tanik and Samara stood to one side of the group, recognizable from their height and the tone of their presences. He didn't dare to reach for their minds and thoughts, lest he reveal himself, but he did manage to extend his awareness into the armory to hear what was going on.

The Acolytes were grumbling about lunch. After a few minutes of their whining, Darius wondered if he should reveal himself, but he resisted the temptation, hoping that Tanik, or better yet, Samara, would grow tired of waiting for Arok and try to find him for themselves. If it turned out that he could hide from them, too, then that might give him a chance to sneak out and go snooping for evidence at the base of the castle later on.

"Arok's never going to find him," Dyara said.

"Why don't you go find Darius and tell him that he won?"

"I would, but I cannot sense him anywhere," Tanik replied.

"Nor can I," Samara said. "You were right about him. He must have exceptional potential to be able to hide from us with so little training. We will have to look for him with our eyes. Everyone spread out and look."

Despite his aching muscles and growling stomach, Darius smiled. When everyone had left the Armory, he snuck back in through the window and crept up behind Cassandra.

"Boo," he said.

She jumped with fright and rounded on him. "Not funny!"

He grinned. "I think it was."

"Where were you! We've been looking everywhere for you."

He shook his head, still smiling. "That's my secret. Come on, let's go find the others."

Darius stopped hiding his presence, and it wasn't long before Tanik and Samara found them.

"Very impressive," Tanik said as they stood on the steps outside the castle.

"Yes," Samara added, her eyes thoughtfully narrowed as she studied Darius. He didn't like the way she was looking at him, but after a moment, she tore her gaze away to look at Tanik. "Why don't you get us some lunch while I round up the others?"

Tanik nodded, and she disappeared inside the castle.

Darius expected more dry, gummy rations, but instead, Tanik told them to wait on the steps while he walked down to the end of one of the landing pads. Once there, he raised his arms to the sky, and Seekers came flocking to him from the forests below. He called out a warning to the Marines on guard duty, and they shot at the Seekers while they were still circling above Tanik's head. Three of the beasts fell with mighty *thumps* at Tanik's feet; then he dropped his hands and the remaining birds fled, squawking and shrieking with fright.

Twenty minutes later, the Acolytes gathered outside, watching while Marines tied the birds to spears from the armory and piled scrap wood in a circle of rubble that they'd arranged at the bottom of the steps. Darius watched with the others, thinking about the food chain on Ouroboros. Maybe these giant birds were a threat to Revenants because they could hide their presence and sneak up on them, but Darius was beginning to see the other side of the equation: Revenants were far more of a threat to the Seekers than the other way around.

Cassandra sighed. "I'm starving! When do you think the food will be ready?"

Darius shook his head. "Not for a few hours, at least."

Cassandra groaned, and Darius favored her with a smile. He reached over and mussed her sweaty hair.

"Hey!"

"You need a shower, young lady."

Her nose wrinkled. "You too."

"You first," he replied.

"They're communal showers," Cassandra complained.

He looked around. "Everyone's out here. I bet you'll have some privacy right now, and I can watch the door for you to make sure no one else goes in."

"Yeah, well, what about my jumpsuit? I've only got one left that's clean. Maybe it would be better to let the stink accumulate for a few days. We don't have laundry chutes and maintenance bots like we did on the *Deliverance*."

"We'll have to find a way to wash our own clothes," Darius said. "What we need is soap...."

"We can make some after we eat," Samara

said, striding by them.

"How are we going to do that?" Darius called back to her. She was by the bonfire helping the Marines secure one of the Seeker carcasses.

"With fat and ash," Samara replied. "I'll teach everyone later."

Darius watched her and three Marines stand up and carry a dead bird tied with zero-G tethers to a frame of two parallel spears. They hoisted the frame up and balanced the ends of the spears on a pair of supply crates that they'd turned on their ends beside the fire. It was a clever setup.

"Darius," a gruff voice said. He turned and saw Tanik hurrying down the steps of the castle.

"Need something?" he asked.

Tanik stopped in front of him and Cassandra and pointed to the small pile of scrap wood beside the fire. "Yes, more firewood," he said. "You and I are going to go get some."

"How?" Darius asked.

Tanik nodded to one of the Ospreys. "We'll fly down and land in a clearing. Our swords will work just fine to fell dead trees and chop them up. We should be back long before the food is ready."

Darius's stomach growled, and he frowned. "Yeah, and that sounds like hungry work to do on an empty stomach."

"There's more rations in the Osprey. Come on. We're going to need that wood if we want to eat anything else."

"What about Cassandra?"

"She can stay here."

"I'd rather she came with," Darius said.

"And I'd rather that she stay." Tanik held his gaze.

Darius frowned, and Tanik clapped a hand on his shoulder. "Collecting firewood is a man's work, am I right?"

"That's sexist," Cassandra complained. "I can cut wood just as well as you."

Tanik arched an eyebrow at her. "Perhaps you can cut it, but can you carry it? You can't weigh more than a hundred pounds."

"So?"

"So, you can help us once you've packed on some more muscle. Besides, I'm sure your father doesn't want you to get crushed by a falling tree."

Cassandra glared at Tanik, but Darius relented with that argument. "All right, let's go."

"Seriously?" Cassandra said. "You're going to leave me all alone? Remember what happened the last time?"

Darius gave her a tight smile. "You'll be fine up here," he said, and pointed to the Marines standing guard with their laser rifles. "Besides, after today's training you must be feeling more confident about protecting yourself, right?"

"I guess..."

Darius looked around for Dyara. He spotted her standing to one side of the bonfire. "Stick with Dya," he said. "I'll be back soon."

"Fine," Cassandra relented. "You be careful."

"I've got Tanik with me," Darius said with a shrug. "I'm sure we'll be fine."

Tanik smiled thinly at that. "Yes. Let's go."

Darius dropped a kiss on top of Cassandra's head while Tanik turned and strode for one of the two Ospreys. "Be safe," Darius whispered before hurrying after Tanik.

"You, too!" Cassandra called after him.

CHAPTER 21

Darius watched Tanik quietly as he flew them to the forest below the mountain. There was a clearing on the slope not far from the castle, just a few kilometers from where Darius had hoped to look for the bodies from the well.

He felt an uneasy flutter in his stomach as he wondered about that. After spending all day trying to think of a way he could get down to the forests, now Tanik was taking him down there, along with the perfect excuse—to gather more firewood. Was Samara was onto him? Darius's heart began to pound. Or, maybe Tanik was onto Samara, and he wanted to get Darius alone so that they could talk.

Darius cleared his throat. "You must be happy to have your wife back after all these years, especially after you thought she was dead."

"Yes," Tanik agreed, bringing the Osprey down between the tops of bright green trees with spiky, cone-shaped leaves that gleamed like jewels in the sun.

"Sorry for waking you both last night," Darius went on. "I guess visions can be misleading sometimes."

"Most times," Tanik amended.

Darius frowned. This conversation wasn't going anywhere. The forward landing struts touched down with a *crunch* of gravel, followed by the rear ones as the Osprey landed on the slope. Tanik rose from the pilot's seat with a twisted smile.

"You're not very subtle, Darius."

His whole body turned to ice, and he fumbled with the release lever for his acceleration harness. "I'm sorry?" Darius asked with a furrowed brow.

"Subtle. You're still suspicious of my wife." Tanik said, walking down the sloping deck to loom over Darius. He stood with his hand on the hilt of his sword.

Darius hesitated to reply.

"You really think I wouldn't be able to recognize my own wife?" Tanik asked.

"Well..." Darius trailed off with a nervous laugh. "I guess that is pretty stupid."

"Indeed," Tanik agreed as he went to open the cockpit door. "You don't want to go losing your head down here, Darius."

Apprehension shivered down Darius's spine. *Was that a threat?* He finally managed to release his harness to join Tanik in standing, but he almost fell back into his seat thanks to the steeply-slanting deck.

"Lose my head?" he asked.

"Yes." The cockpit door slid open, and Tanik regarded him with a cold smile that never reached his eyes. "It's an expression from your time, is it not?"

"Yeah..." Darius nodded, wondering how Tanik would know that. He smiled back, trying not to let his unease show, and followed Tanik down the sloping corridor.

Tanik waved the airlock open as they crossed the troop bay. Darius walked in behind him. The inner doors slammed shut, and then the outer ones slid open.

Tanik hopped down, seeming almost to float to the ground. He took a few steps, pebbles crunching loudly underfoot, and then turned to Darius. "Well?"

Darius landed on the slope with a sharp spike of pain in the arches of his feet, and fell on his hands and knees—a stark contrast to the graceful, floating landing that Tanik had executed. Picking himself up, he saw Tanik already walking down the slope, heading for the trees.

As Tanik reached the trees, he began to glow brightly with the gathered energies of the zero-point field. He drew his sword, also glowing brightly, and swept it through the trunk of a dead tree. The tree leaned over and slowly fell, snapping the branches of its neighbors before hitting the ground with a loud *crash*.

Darius stopped and stood off at a safe distance, watching as Tanik's blade swept through a second snag, felling it with another crash. Tanik moved onto a third, but this time it was a live tree.

Darius felt a prickling thrill of warning. Before he could figure out why, a shadow fell over him and he saw a massive tree swinging down toward his head. Darius ducked and rolled to one side.

Sharp branches carved fiery lines in his back, and spiky leaves pricked his skin like cacti, but the trunk missed him. The crashing thunder of the falling tree died away, replaced by the booming peals of Tanik's laughter.

"Good! I was hoping you'd make this a challenge."

Darius spun to face Tanik, drawing on the ZPF

to activate his own shield even as he drew his sword. "What are you doing?" he screamed, partly from the pain of his injuries.

Tanik walked around the fallen tree, flourishing his own blade. "Tanik was right about you. You are a threat to the Augur."

It only took Darius a second to figure out why he was speaking in third person. "Samara?"

"My real name is Nova."

"You've been pretending to be Tanik's wife this whole time," Darius said.

"That's a banal observation at this point, don't you think?"

"You don't have to kill me," Darius said, backing away in the direction of the Osprey. "I don't want any part in killing the Augur. That was all Tanik's idea."

Nova's lips stretched into a smile, and the yellow-green eyes of the body she'd somehow possessed danced brightly in the light of a ZPF shield. Nova stopped advancing for a moment, but Darius kept backpedaling.

"I believe you," Nova said. "But there's just one problem. I've also seen Tanik's vision—the one with you sitting on a throne, ruling the Union, and I'm afraid that there's only one way to prevent that from happening."

"I'm not a threat," Darius said.

"That little stunt you pulled in the fortress earlier is just a taste of what's to come. If you can already hide yourself from me, imagine what you'll be able to do when you're fully trained?"

"I'm not a threat," Darius repeated.

"No? You're idealistic, and when you realize that you actually have the power to change things, you'll try. You'll try to be the hero and save the galaxy from itself. You *are* a threat, Darius, whether you know it now or not, and there's only one thing to do with such threats."

"Let's say you're right. Why don't you be the hero and save me the trouble? Or does the Augur control you so tightly that you can't think for yourself?"

Tanik's body began advancing again, a helpless avatar for Nova. "And what heroic agenda would you have me pursue? Defeat the Cygnians? Destroy the Crucible? Free the hunted?" Nova smirked. "You're not the first misguided fool to think that we should be fighting the Cygnians instead of the Keth.

"There are two problems with that—you're assuming that the Cygnians are the greater threat, and you're assuming that a fair and democratic Union would be peaceful. Do you have any idea how many different wars the Cygnians prevented by unifying and subjugating all the different species in Orion? Right now everyone has a common enemy. They're like ants, raging against the boot that crushes them. Take that away, and they'll turn on each other—assuming they survive your war with the Cygnians."

Darius was still backing away, but Nova outpaced him easily. He fought the urge to turn and run. He couldn't risk turning his back on this fight.

"I have a daughter," Darius said, shaking his head. "Don't do this."

"Begging is a disgraceful way to die," Nova chided.

"The others will find out that you killed me. You won't be able to make it look like an accident. Not anymore."

"Perhaps not, but I doubt it will matter." Nova flashed another smile. "They're not thinking very clearly right now." Nova's free hand rose, and hundreds of large rocks floated up all around Darius's head.

"Goodbye, Darius."

Nova flicked Tanik's wrist, and the rocks flew toward Darius's head at high speed. He thrust up his hands in an attempt to shield his face, and his eyes winced shut in anticipation.

But nothing happened. He cracked his eyes open to see the rocks hovering in mid-air, some of them bare inches from his nose.

Nova looked puzzled. "How are you doing that?" She looked at Tanik's hand. "Tanik must be weaker than I thought. What a pity."

Nova dropped Tanik's hand, and the rocks fell with a noisy clatter. The larger ones came rumbling down the slope. Darius glanced over his shoulder to see the boulders knocking other ones free, jumping and skipping down the mountain in a thundering rock slide. Darius leaped over one of them, and dodged two more. Just before the rock slide had finished rumbling past him, a third boulder glanced off his hip and knocked him over. He dropped his sword and fell on his hands and knees once more.

Panting from the sudden exertion, Darius looked up and glared at his adversary. The rocks parted like a wave around Tanik, missing him entirely. Darius grabbed his sword and climbed to his feet.

Nova laughed. "I guess we'll have to do this the hard way." She leapt through the air and landed with a crunch of gravel right in front of Darius.

Nova swung her sword swung down, and Darius just managed to bring his up in time to block. The blades crashed with a sizzling metallic clatter. Nova slid her blade down along Darius's, then slipped it out from under, and thrust.

Darius turned his body to avoid that attack, but it still grazed his stomach with a crackling hiss and a searing flash of heat. Darius jumped back, recoiling from the blade. He glanced down to find his jumpsuit char-blackened where the sword had grazed him.

Darius backpedaled in earnest now, heedless that he might trip. "Snap out of it, Tanik!" he screamed.

"It won't work," Nova said. "He can't hear you."

Darius turned and ran down the hill, willing himself to run faster than he ever had in his life. Gravel skittered under his boots as he dashed down the mountain, weaving around boulders and leaping over others. He heard hurried footfalls behind him, and glanced over his shoulder to see Nova keeping pace with him.

"You can't run from me, Darius!"

But Darius ran even faster and reached the trees. Branches and tree trunks blurred around him. Jutting roots forced him to jump while fallen logs and low-hanging branches made him duck. His lungs burned and his legs ached, but still he ran.

"Watch your step!" Nova called out, sounding farther away now.

Darius didn't understand until the trees abruptly parted in front of him and clear blue sky appeared. Going too fast to stop, he sailed right over the cliff and into open air with his legs still churning. He cried out in alarm, and his head swam as he looked down. A carpet of green and blue trees sprawled out far below his feet. It was a sheer drop, at least a hundred stories. He picked up speed quickly, with the wind ripping at his jumpsuit and hair, forcing his eyes to shut.

He managed to squint them open just as he hit the forest canopy. Branches slapped, snapped, and scratched as he fell, some of them breaking through his shield. Then he hit the ground with a sickening *thud.*

He lay there on his back, unable to breathe. The treetops spun around his head. His whole body felt warm and numb, like it was vibrating, or falling still. Shredded bits of green and blue vegetation fluttered down like rain. A broken branch crashed down beside him with a *thump.* Darius's mind swam. He thought he might be sick, but he couldn't find the strength to move. His eyelids slammed shut like they were made of lead. He forced them open, only to have them slam shut again. Even with his eyes shut, it felt like the world was spinning.

I must have a concussion... can't sleep now... he thought, even as his thoughts slipped away like water through a sieve. Would Nova come down to look for him?

His mind flashed back to the game of hide and seek at the castle, and he used what little strength he had left to hide his presence as he had then. He only hoped that it would work while he was asleep—unless this smothering carpet of darkness was the shadow of death, in which case it wouldn't matter anyway. Darius sucked in an aching breath and let it out in a shuddering sigh.

CHAPTER 22

Dim light slipped in through a blurry veil of eyelashes. Darius's eyes opened wider. Sensation and memory came back in broken fragments, like staring at his reflection in a shattered mirror. He remembered falling, slamming into the ground and lying there numb and fading.

He no longer felt numb. His entire body ached, his skin itching and tingling. That had to be a good sign. He tried sitting up, but a sharp pain stopped him, and he saw the jagged, bloody point of a branch protruding from his side.

Kak... he thought, his heart pounding and head swimming. He couldn't pull that branch out. It was likely the only thing stopping a deadly hemorrhage.

Darius blinked at the slivered fragments of a

dark blue sky. Night was falling. He must have been unconscious for several hours already. That meant his injuries were holding—at least for now—and that Nova had given him up for dead.

Darius focused on keeping his presence small and concealed while he thought about what to do next. He was alone in a forest teeming with Seekers and who-knew-what other kinds of predators, badly injured, and with no supplies to treat those injuries.

The nanites in his blood might be enough to keep him alive if he pulled out that branch. Darius tried sitting up again, using his arms to prop himself up. Searing pain lit his stomach on fire. He bit his lip to keep from crying out and forced himself upright.

As soon as he did so, he realized he had another problem, besides the branch. Both of his legs were broken, folded up under him at impossible angles. One of them was broken so badly that he could see a bloody white bone poking out.

Darius gasped, and his breath hitched in his lungs. His stomach heaved at the sight of the injuries, drawing a fresh stab of pain from the puncture wound in his side.

No wonder Nova had given up on him. There

was no way he'd be able to survive without urgent medical attention. Feeling like he might faint, Darius lowered himself onto his back. That movement activated his injured abdominal wall and he gasped from the pain. With his mind and heart racing, he laid his head on a bed of broad blue leaves, and prickly cone-shaped green ones. The world was spinning again. He thought about Cassandra, of leaving her an orphan in a hostile galaxy, forced to fight and die in the Revenants' war, with her mind and will no longer her own.

He couldn't leave her to that fate. He had to find some way to get through this. To survive. First he needed to remove the branch. Then he'd have to set and bandage his broken legs and fashion splints.

Darius glanced around, noting the broken branches around him. He could fashion splints with some of them and secure them with strips of fabric from his jumpsuit. But it could take days or weeks for his nanites to heal his legs. He'd have to find water and food long before then.

One problem at a time.

Darius lifted his arms. At least they weren't broken, but they were badly scratched. Blood had crusted in long crisscrossing lines, running all the way down both of his arms. He grabbed the end of the stick protruding from his side, about to tear it out but thought better of it. It would be easier and safer to pull it out the same way it had gone in. He forced himself back into a sitting position and felt around behind him for the other end of the branch. It was slick with blood, and there wasn't much to grab onto.

He had to push it through from the front until he had something to grab at the back. Grimacing, Darius wrapped both hands around the stick... and pushed.

Stars exploded in his head. White-hot pain tore through him, and there was no stopping the scream that burst from his lips. Tears streamed down his cheeks and hot blood bubbled over his hands. Darius stopped, gasping and shaking, weak with shock. He blinked spots from his eyes and shook his head. He couldn't pass out now. He'd die for sure.

With blood still pouring from his side, he reached around and found the other end of the stick. It was slippery with his blood, but he found a knot in the wood to grab onto. Knowing that time was precious, he gritted his teeth and ripped the branch all the way out. Darius felt things pulling and shifting inside of him, and almost fainted from the pain and loss of blood. He tossed the branch aside and clapped a hand to the front and back of the puncture to slow the bleeding. Gasping from the pain, he held pressure on the wounds with shaking hands.

There wasn't much else he could do. He couldn't spare his hands to rip off pieces of his jumpsuit for a bandage, so he just sat there, in a world of pain, with his life slipping through his fingers.

After a while, the flow of blood slowed, and a spreading numbness eased his pain. It was utterly dark now. The only sight an occasional glint of eyes watching from between the trees. His eyelids grew heavy once more. He fought it, but exhaustion overcame him, and his head hit a pillow of dried leaves.

Darius thought he heard branches snapping; then a sudden ruckus of startled animal cries, one of them cutting off in mid-scream.

He tried opening his eyes, but was too far gone, bobbing away on a black sea of oblivion. Dark shadows seemed to move around him, and the trees scrolled by. At some point he felt sharp, grinding stabs of pain that made him want to cry out in agony, but his lips refused to move. Trapped, a prisoner in his own body while shapeless horrors hulked about, torturing him. *Am*

I in hell? The sensations didn't last, but neither did his awareness.

Some time later, he awoke fully and lay staring at the treetops. Branches clung like cobwebs to the glaring blue sky. Darius's brow furrowed. He must have slept through the night.

Flexing his arms, Darius propped himself up on his elbows. His pain was gone. Clean skin had replaced the bloody puncture hole in his side, and his legs were laid out straight, with no sign of the jutting white bone he'd seen earlier.

Did I dream those injuries? he wondered

Darius checked the date and time via his extra-sensory chip. The time was 1340 IST, and it was the 321st day of the year 1520 AU. He hadn't thought to check the date before, so he had no way of knowing how much time had passed.

He'd have to rely on other means of time-keeping. He smacked his lips and worked some moisture into his mouth. His throat hurt from dehydration, and his stomach was dissolving in its own acid, but he would be in much worse shape if more than a day had passed. Not to mention he'd be lying in a pool of his own filth.

Comforted by his reasoning, Darius got up and tried walking. It didn't hurt, and his legs worked just fine. Whether he'd imagined his injuries or not, those nanites must be miracle-workers. *No one takes a hundred-story plunge and then gets up and walks around the next day like it was nothing.*

Darius cast about, trying to figure out which way he should go. Before he did anything, he needed to find water. And where was his sword? He felt sure he'd had it in his hand when he fell.

Broken branches with their cone-shaped green leaves and broad, papery blue ones littered the forest floor. Those leaves were already dry and losing their color. Darius wondered about that, but then he saw his sword lying gleaming in a freckled pool of sunlight, and his mind turned to more important matters.

Darius went to retrieve the weapon. Twigs snapped and leaves crunched as he went. He sheathed the sword in the scabbard at his side.

Now what? Water. And then food. He felt around for his sidearm. By some miracle, it was still in the holster at his side. Darius breathed a sigh and nodded to himself. He could hunt and kill something with that weapon. He could also use it to start a fire and cook the meat.

After that, he needed to find some way to get back up to the castle to rescue Cassandra—Dyara, too, if he could. He'd probably have to stun them both and drag them away if Nova had them under her spell. But then he'd still have to find some way to steal a ship.

Darius frowned. How was he going to do all of that with Blake and the Marines guarding the castle and the transports?

It might be easier just to sneak up to Nova's room in the middle of the night and kill her. He couldn't hope to best her in combat, but he'd already proven that he could hide his presence from her and Tanik. He just had to find some way to get into their room while they were asleep.

Darius gave a grim smile. *I'm coming for you Nova.*

CHAPTER 23

Trista sat at an illuminated onyx bar tracing the fissures with her eyes as she sipped an icy wheat beer with a slice of orange in it. It was hard to say if the beer or the slice of orange had come from Earth, but it was a nice reminder of her ancestral home all the same. Hats off to the owner of Drake Depot #920. She and Buddy had come to the bar for a much-needed break from the confines of her ship. They'd been traveling for more than a week already, but they still had twenty days to go before they reached Earth.

Beside her, Buddy gulped down his third beer and let out a thunderous belch. Heads turned their way, and Trista offered an apologetic smile on his behalf.

Buddy patted his bulging stomach. "I'd better

go to the restroom before I spring a leak," he said, and climbed down from his bar stool. "See you soon."

"You do that," Trista said.

"Trista Leandra? Is that really you?"

Trista froze. She knew that voice. Of all the people to run into... *Don't be Jaxon, don't be Jaxon...*

A familiar man hopped up on the stool that Buddy had just vacated. "By the Revenants, it really is you!"

Trista reluctantly turned to face him. "Oh, hey Jaxon. Imagine meeting you out here. I thought you got married to what's-her-name and settled down on Praxis?"

Jaxon grinned, his cheeks dimpling. He ran a hand through his dark wavy hair, and Trista experienced a flashback to eight years ago—meeting Jaxon at a bar not unlike this one. She'd made the mistake of letting him take her back to his ship, of getting sucked into his web of lies and empty promises.

"Yeah," he said. "I did."

The bartender slunk over to them, a white-furred Lassarian female with piercing blue eyes. "Drink?" she asked.

Jaxon nodded. "Beer. Whatever's the cheapest."

The Lassarian grabbed a mug and filled it from a nearby tap. A cloudy brown ale poured out. She slid the mug over to Jaxon and left.

He took a swig, grimaced, and reluctantly swallowed. "Oh, that's vile!"

"What happened to the high life?" Trista asked, nodding to his drink.

"Sedasa left me, and her Daddy's lawyer made sure I got nothing. They made it look like I cheated."

Trista arched an eyebrow at him. "Did you?"

"I'm not that stupid. I know a good thing when I've got one. Besides, even if I did cheat, I wouldn't have got caught. Sedasa got bored with me, that's all, and then she had her father take care of it. I can't prove it, but I'm pretty sure he bribed the judge."

Trista frowned. "An android? You can't bribe Executors. That's one of the reasons Cygnians use them."

"No, not an android. Nowadays only criminal cases go before the Executors. They're stretched thin with all their other duties, so the civil cases go to biological judges that they appoint."

Trista blinked. "I had no idea. I'm sorry?"

Jaxon waved a hand to dismiss that sentiment. Not that she actually felt bad for him. He took another swig of his ale. "I'll find another ride. Speaking of which, where are you headed?"

Trista shrugged. "Places."

Jaxon looked at her. "Places? What places?"

"Why do you want to know?" Trista asked over the rim of her beer mug.

"Why don't you want to tell?" Jaxon countered. He lowered his voice to a conspiratorial whisper. "What kind of contraband are you hauling?"

"I'm not."

"So why can't I know where you're going?"

"Maybe because I don't want you following me. You lost the right to know my business when you cheated on me with that horny *vix*. Now that she's dumped your useless kakker, don't think I'm going to give you a second chance."

Jaxon's brow furrowed. "I apologized for that."

"Sure, and I forgave you."

"Because I gave you my ship."

"You transferred your loan to me," Trista corrected. "And that was *before* we broke up. Besides, as I recall, you only did that so you could declare bankruptcy and not lose your ride in the process."

"We can argue about the details all day, but the fact is, you came out ahead. I had ten percent down on the *Rogue.* That's a bundle of creds. Two hundred and fifty thousand. At the very least, you owe me that."

"I don't owe you kak. The *Harlequin* is mine," Trista said. "Legally you've got no claim to her."

"You changed the name? What was wrong with *Rogue?*"

Trista shrugged. "The *Rogue* turned out to be a cheating *vagon.*"

"All right, let's do something. You give me a ride to wherever I need to go, and we'll forget all about you owing me."

Trista regarded him steadily, staring into those slanting blue eyes and wondering how she hadn't seen how full of kak he was from the start. He was right, she had made out pretty well thanks to his stupidity in transferring his ship into her name, but she didn't feel like she owed him anything, much less a free ride to wherever he wanted to go. Besides, knowing Jaxon, that wouldn't be the end of it. He was just trying to get his foot in the door. He had something else in mind.

"I'm sorry," she said, getting up from the bar. "I don't have room for extra baggage. Now if you'll excuse me, I need to use the lady's room."

Jaxon regarded her stonily. "Sure."

Trista left in a hurry. She passed Buddy along

the way, staggering and hiccupping on his way back to the bar. "Hey, go back to the docking bay," she said, bending down to catch his arm. "I'll meet you there as soon as I get the supplies we need."

"We're leaving?"

"The *Harlequin's* old owner showed up. He seems to think I owe him something, and I don't want you getting mixed up with him."

Buddy nodded slowly, his big black eyes pinching into thoughtful slits. "I could bite him for you if you want."

Trista shook her head. "Better not. You might catch something. I'll meet you back at the tender."

Buddy nodded. "See you soon."

It took Trista half an hour at the depot's market to find the supplies she needed—mostly food and cosmetics. After that, she headed to the docking bay, pushing a full cargo crate's worth of supplies on a rented dolly.

She cleared the security scans at the berth where she'd docked her tender. There was no sign of Buddy, but that wasn't a surprise. He was probably waiting for her in the cockpit, sleeping off all those beers. For a creature his size, three beers had to be like twenty.

Trista pushed the dolly into the center of the docking elevator and gestured for it to take her down. The platform sank and the outer doors of her airlock rose into view. The platform jerked to a stop at the bottom of the docking tube, and she keyed in her security code. Both sets of doors swished open at the same time. No point wasting time to cycle the airlock when both sides were fully pressurized.

Trista walked through a small cargo space behind the tender's cockpit. It was only big enough for two crates. Station drones typically handled the loading and unloading of transports, but the handling fees were exorbitant, and there was no point in paying those fees for just one crate of supplies that she could easily push around by herself.

Trista slid the cargo crate onto one of the magnetic cargo racks and pulled the dolly out from under it. After returning the rented dolly to the cargo elevator, she went back inside to shut the airlock.

As soon as it slid shut, Trista turned and waved the cockpit door open. "Hey, Buddy, wake up!" she said as she approached.

He gave no reply. *Probably drunk out of his mind.* Trista scowled. "You need to start earning your keep around here, furball," she said, glaring at the copilot's seat as she stepped into the cockpit.

The pilot's chair rotated to face her. "Hey there, Tris."

Her hand went straight to her hip, but her gun wasn't there. Weapons weren't allowed on the station, so she'd left hers aboard the tender, and now Jaxon had it, and he was pointing it at her.

"How did you get past the security checkpoint?"

"Buddy here authorized me." Jaxon kicked the seat beside him, rotating it to face her. Buddy was tied up with zero-G tether and a sock had been stuffed in his mouth. His cheeks were bulging and his eyes were wide and darting, his chest rising and falling in quick, rapid breaths.

Trista blinked in shock. "Why would he authorize you?"

Jaxon held out his palm and a black insect buzzed out of it.

"What is that?"

"A stringer drone. One bite and you'll be dead within an hour." Jaxon nodded sideways to indicate Buddy. "Ten minutes for a little furball like him. The antidote is very specific. Nanites can't produce it. No station has it."

Trista's eyes flicked to Buddy. No wonder he looked so scared. "You poisoned him?"

Jaxon's lips twisted in a sly smile. "Well..." He

glanced at Buddy and shook his head. "It's actually harder than you'd think to get a weaponized drone past a security sweep these days. Luckily for me, your friend here is quite gullible."

Buddy's hyperventilating stopped, and his eyes narrowed swiftly. He murmured a curse against the sock, and Jaxon laughed.

"You didn't meet me here by accident," Trista realized. "You've been following me."

Jaxon clapped his free hand against the butt of her sidearm, leaving his drone to hover beside him. "Very good."

"How did you know where to find me?"

"You forget, the Callisto-Abbex run was *my* route. I taught it to you."

Trista scowled. "What do you want?"

"What do I want?" Jaxon asked, tapping his chin with the tip of her gun, as if he didn't know the answer.

She thought about jumping him now that he wasn't aiming the gun at her, but she knew better than that.

"Well?" she prompted.

"I want what's mine, woman. Give me my ship back."

"Over my dead body," Trista spat. "She's mine now. Who do you think's been making payments while you were gone? It's been a long time, Jax, and I've got easily as much invested as you did. Probably more."

Jaxon shrugged. "So buy out my share."

"How about we compromise. You wanted a ride, right? I'll take you wherever you're headed. No charge."

"No, I'm afraid that offer has expired. You can pay out my share, or you give me my ship back. Take your pick."

"And if I refuse?" Trista demanded. "What are you going to do? Kill me? Steal the *Harlequin*?" She shook her head. "Either way you'll get caught and sent to the nearest hunting ground. You wouldn't dare."

Jaxon's smile faded, and his blue eyes turned to ice. "Maybe I'll just tie you up and haul you around the galaxy with me while I make back the creds that you owe. No one bothers to search transports these days, not if you don't dock them, and that's what this tender is for, isn't it?" he said, grinning and patting the armrest of the pilot's seat. "I wonder how long it will be before anyone realizes that you've been taken hostage aboard your own ship? A year? Ten years? A hundred? It's a pity your parents decided to go and get themselves killed in the Coalition."

Trista gaped at him. Her thoughts went to Gatticus. If the android was half smart, he'd figure out what had happened and lie low until he could get the jump on Jaxon.

"What are you thinking about?" Jaxon asked with narrowed eyes. "Did you booby-trap my ship?"

Grak it. He'd always been good at reading her. "I've got a boyfriend," Trista lied, to distract him from other possibilities. "He's waiting for me on Abbex. He'll come looking for me if I don't show up."

Jaxon barked a laugh. "A frigid vix like you has a man?" He shook his head. "I don't think so. I'd bet a million creds that this little mascot of yours is the only person you have in the whole galaxy—if you can call him a person, that is." Jaxon gave her a wicked leer. "But don't worry. You have me now, so you don't have to be lonely anymore."

"Touch me and I'll cut it off."

Jaxon laughed. "The only thing you'll be cutting off is the circulation to your wrists. He reached around behind him and pulled out a coil of zero-G tether. He tossed it at her. "Be a darling and tie yourself up for me, would you?"

"Go fek yourself."

"I'd rather wait for you to do it." Jaxon pulled

the trigger, and the electric-blue muzzle flash of her own gun was the last thing Trista saw.

CHAPTER 24

Darius used his awareness to get a bird's eye view of the surrounding forest and found a nearby river. He ran to it and drank greedily. Distracted by his thirst, he didn't notice, or sense, the Seeker creeping up beside him. It cried out and lunged, stabbing at him with its beak. Darius fell in his hurry to get away, and it leapt into the air, swooping down for the kill, talons reaching for his stomach.

Darius pulled his sidearm and fired twice into the monster's belly just as it landed on top of him. It went limp, pinning him to the ground under what must have been at least two hundred pounds of dead weight.

Darius grunted and heaved, crawling out from beneath the dead bird. He heard another Seeker screeching in the distance, and looked up to see three black specks. They'd be here soon. Darius holstered his sidearm and drew his sword. He took a second to examine the Seeker carcass before picking up a leg and slicing it off. It came away in his hand, charred-blackened and sizzling. *Good enough.* He sheathed his sword and dashed back into the forest, putting some distance between him and the river. He hadn't seen Seekers hunting on the forest floor, and he suspected they wouldn't, since they couldn't easily fly down there.

Once he was a safe distance from the river, Darius chopped down a dead tree. It fell with a crash, and he set to work slicing it into blocks of firewood with his sword. He piled them up and set his pistol to *beam* rather than *burst* to start a fire. The pile of wood burst into flames and Darius held the Seeker leg over the fire to roast it. When the whole thing was as black as coal, he peeled away the burned bits to check inside. The meat was white. He blew on it, and tried a bite. It could have used some salt, but otherwise it was delicious.

Once he finished eating, Darius used his awareness to cast his mind up, high above the forest, to search for the castle. He found it in seconds, burning bright with the luminous silhouettes of its occupants.

As Darius returned to the forest floor, he found two particular trees on a line pointing toward the castle to use as landmarks. He walked by those trees and kept on going in that direction. It wasn't long before he found himself back at the base of the cliff he'd fallen off. It was too high and too steep to safely climb, so he walked along it, looking for a way up. After about twenty minutes, he spotted something: a long diagonal fissure in the side of the cliff, running all the way from the base to the top. As he drew near, he saw steps inside the fissure, carved out of the rock. He couldn't believe his luck.

Darius tracked the steps all the way up. There had to be thousands of them. Maybe this was how the Keth had gotten to their fortress. Where else would those steps lead? A thrill of excitement coursed through him at the thought, but seeing again how *many* stairs there were gave him pause. He was going to be very thirsty by the time he reached the top. It was a pity he hadn't thought to bring a canteen along when Tanik had asked him to help gather firewood.

Darius wondered if there was a way he could fashion a canteen, maybe from the skin of the Seeker carcass at the river. But that sounded time-consuming, and fraught with difficulty. Without any survival training to draw on, how long would it take him to figure that out? He'd have to clean the skin and maybe dry it in the sun, and then tie it up with something. Sinew? Grass?

Fashioning such a thing would probably take him the better part of a day. The longer he waited to deal with Nova, the longer she would have to call reinforcements. When those reinforcements arrived, he somehow doubted everyone would stay here. Nova would probably evacuate the Acolytes to a proper Revenant training facility in another star system. If that happened, he'd end up stranded on Ouroboros with all the time in the world to figure out how to make a canteen from Seeker hide.

Darius grimaced and shook his head. He couldn't afford delays right now. He'd already lost a day lying unconscious on the forest floor.

Letting his reservations go with a sigh, he started up the steps. His legs were burning and trembling before he'd even made it halfway up, and he'd been right about needing water: sweat was dripping from his brow, and his mouth was so dry that his tongue stuck to the roof of his mouth. Dizzy with exhaustion and gasping for air, Darius sank to his hands and knees on the steps. His head spun at the sight of the distant treetops, reduced to toothpicks once more. It was a long way down.

Once his breathing had slowed and his legs had stopped burning, Darius pushed himself back up and forced himself to climb the rest of the way to the top. Once there, he found himself looking up a grassy, pebbly slope. The stairs continued up that slope, all the way to a sheer black cliff where the castle loomed, shrouded in thick white clouds.

Darius thought about the running water in the castle. If he could sneak in, he'd be able to get something to drink. He swallowed past his dry, burning throat, and forced himself to go on. *Onwards and upwards...*

He hoped no one was looking down from the castle to see him climbing the slope. Then again, he'd probably look like an ant at this distance, so it wouldn't matter even if they did see him.

By the time Darius reached the foot of the cliffs below the fortress, he was delirious with thirst and exhaustion. His legs were trembling violently and he felt nauseous. The steps continued ahead of him, chiseled from the side of the cliff and rising another thousand feet. Whoever the Keth were, they had to be born athletes.

Darius walked off the path and collapsed in the shade of a few trees. He lay there gasping with his heart hammering. The heat of the day pressed down on him like a physical thing. He was drenched in sweat, the tattered remains of his jumpsuit sticking to him. His mind was foggy, his muscles burning and aching at the same time, and his feet felt like they were made of blisters. He needed to rest and shut his eyes for a minute.

A warm breeze blew, caressing his face, and a rotten smell filled Darius's nostrils, making him gag. His eyes popped open and he frowned. That smell was familiar. It smelled like... like the mud that had been dripping from Dyara's boots and gloves after she'd gone diving in the well. Darius sat up quickly and looked around. He couldn't see anything in his immediate vicinity, so he stood up and walked around, looking for the source of the smell. He found it about twenty feet away, behind a pair of thick tree trunks. The smell was from a pile of bones, coated in dried black mud. They were crawling with insects. Darius recognized some of the bones—a piece of a human skull, a femur... a shattered hip.

This was the proof he'd been hoping to find. Nova *had* found the bodies in the well and thrown them out the window. His vision had been of the past.

That seemed like a pointless victory now, but it did serve to reinvigorate him with outrage. Nova had lied to them from the start.

Darius stalked back to the steps and began the arduous climb to the top. All along the way, he concentrated on staying hidden, on keeping his presence small. Near the top of the cliff, he reached a landing that led to a sturdy wooden door. Darius walked up to the door and tried the handle. It was locked. He tried forcing the door open, but it wouldn't budge.

With a sigh, he continued up the stairs until he saw the landing platforms arcing out overhead and heard voices. Darius crept off the path and crouched in the shadow of the nearest landing pad. He calmed his breathing, and cocked his head to listen. One of the voices belonged to Blake.

"It's been a week since the Revenants got here, and they're *still* sending supplies down! You'd think when they can lift things with the twitch of a finger that they'd offer to help unload the cargoes, but no. They'd rather watch us grunts do all the work!"

"Shut up and carry. You want them to hear us?" another man said in a hushed voice. Booted feet went clomping down the walkway.

Darius blinked in confusion and shock. *It's been a week since the Revenants arrived?* How was that possible? He couldn't have been unconscious for a whole *week*. Not without water, food... shelter. He slowly shook his head, casting back to the time after he fell. He remembered waking to find a hole in his side, both of his legs broken, and long, bloody scratches running down both of his arms. Then he'd passed out and dreamed of dark shadows moving around him.

Darius's heart thudded in his ears. The conclusion was inescapable. Someone had treated his injuries, but who, and where were they now?

CHAPTER 25

Trista awoke tied into an acceleration harness in the passenger's cabin of her own ship. She looked around. The other five seats in the cabin were empty.

"Buddy?"

No answer.

He needed a custom-fit acceleration harness, and the only such harness was bolted to the copilot's seat in the cockpit. Hopefully that's where he was, and not tied down like luggage in the cargo bay. Trista strained against the zero-G tether tying her hands together, struggling to reach the release lever of her acceleration harness. She twisted in that direction, using the odd half an inch of wiggle room that the harness gave her.

But it was no use. The release lever remained

half a foot out of reach, and her harness held her in place more effectively than the loop of metal tether wrapped around her wrists.

Trista bit back a scream. She wasn't going to give Jaxon the satisfaction. Then again... where was Gatticus? Did he even know what was going on? If not, screaming might actually be good for something.

So she screamed, and screamed again, until her lungs were empty and her throat hurt.

Heavy footsteps came clomping down the corridor outside the cabin. Trista tried to determine if they were coming from the cockpit or from one of the ship's sleeping quarters, where Gatticus might have found a charging port. She couldn't be sure since both the cockpit and the sleeping quarters lay in the same direction.

The door swished open. "Hey there, Tris." Jaxon grinned and leaned against the jamb. "You shouldn't waste your breath. Haven't you heard? In space, no one can hear you scream."

Trista glared at him. "Where's Buddy?"

Jaxon waved a dismissive hand at her. "He's fine. Don't worry, he's too valuable to throw out an airlock."

Trista's eyes narrowed at that. *"Valuable?"*

"Of course. Don't tell me you never thought of

selling him. Togras are highly-prized companions."

"Selling him?" Trista shrieked. "You sell him and I'll drop you at the nearest hunting ground."

Jaxon barked a laugh and clucked his tongue at her. "You're hardly in a position to be making threats, Tris. But thank you for the idea of what to do with you if you become too much of a burden."

Trista gaped at him.

And he gaped back.

Her eyebrows scrunched together in a frown; then she saw the subtle jittering of Jaxon's limbs, followed by electric arcs of blue fire leaping off his clothes. His eyes rolled up and a familiar face appeared over his shoulder.

"Gatticus! Where the hell have you been?" she demanded.

"A simple thank you would suffice," Gatticus replied. "Who is this?" He jerked his chin to Jaxon, who was unconscious, but still standing thanks to the zero-G environment.

"Long story. Would you mind helping me out of my harness?"

Gatticus retrieved Trista's sidearm from the holster on Jaxon's hip and then squeezed around him to help her out of her acceleration harness. He pulled the release lever and folded her harness out of the way. Trista stood up on cramping legs.

"How did you stun him?" she asked, noting that the gun in his hands had been in Jaxon's possession until just a moment ago.

Gatticus held out his free hand, palm up, and she saw blue arcs of electricity leaping out of it.

Trista snorted. "Nice to be an android."

"Indeed it is," Gatticus replied.

"Well, let's stun him properly, just in case." Even as she said that, she realized that something was wrong. She leaned to one side for a better look. "Kak! He's already gone!"

Gatticus glanced over his shoulder. "He appears to have revived himself. He's an unusually resilient individual."

"We need to hurry," Trista muttered. "Help me free my hands."

Gatticus took a moment to examine the zero-G tether wrapped around her wrists, then he aimed her sidearm at it. "Do not move," he said, and flicked the setting on the side to *beam*.

"Wait!" Trista said.

He pulled the trigger and a solid white beam of energy hit the tether. In a matter of seconds it began glowing red-hot. The cord branded her skin and she cried out in pain. Then it snapped and she was free.

"Fek it!" Trista snatched her gun away from

Gatticus. "What the hell were you thinking?"

"I was thinking that we need to hurry, just like you said."

"Come on," Trista growled, and ran from the passenger cabin with her wrists red and stinging. She turned, heading for the cockpit, but a hand landed on her shoulder and pulled her back.

"Wait," Gatticus whispered. "He's in the tender."

Trista glanced back at him. "How can you tell? Never mind. Tell me later," she added quickly. "He must be trying to make a run for it. If he gets away in that ship, I'm grakked!" She ran down the corridor toward the tender's airlock. By the time Trista reached it, she could already hear the tender's engines rumbling on the other side.

She slapped the airlock door controls and the inner doors parted. Her finger tightened on the trigger in anticipation of the kill, but the airlock was empty. Stalking through to the outer doors, she slapped that control panel, too, but this time it spat out a depressurization warning.

"What?" Trista blinked in shock at the control panel. And a split second later the rumbling roar of the tender's engines disappeared. She was too late. He was already gone. Trista turned and darted out the airlock, almost knocking Gatticus over on her way out.

"Where are you going?" he asked.

She gave no reply, saving her energy to run. She pounded down the corridor, cursing under her breath all the way to her cockpit. When she arrived, she fell into the pilot's seat and activated the *Harlequin's* defensive turret. Out of the corner of her eye, she noticed Buddy sitting beside her, tied and harnessed into the copilot's seat with that sock still stuffed in his mouth. His cheeks puffed out with a muffled demand for her to cut him loose, but there was no time, so she pretended not to notice.

Finding the tender on her contacts panel, she targeted the engines—then thought better of it. Engines were expensive to repair. She targeted the tender's cockpit canopy instead. Using an infrared overlay she located Jaxon and aimed at his chest. Just as she was about to pull the trigger, a hand reached around and pulled her arm away from the joystick. A second hand canceled her targeting solution before she could pull the trigger mentally.

"What the fek! Let me go!" Trista roared.

"I cannot allow you to kill him," Gatticus said. "Murder is a crime. I'd have to send you to the nearest hunting ground if you kill him."

"But he's stealing my ship!" Trista said. She

— 290 —

made a grab for the joystick with her other hand, but Gatticus grabbed that arm, too. "Fek you! Am I supposed to just let him get away?"

Even as she said that, the tender turned and directed its thrusters at her, making an inexpensive kill shot impossible. Those thrusters flared bright blue as Jaxon hit the throttle.

Trista's comms chimed with an incoming message, but she ignored it. She used her ESC to mentally access the turret controls. Just as she was about to get a lock on the tender, Gatticus released her wrist to cancel the targeting solution once more. Her hand was only free for a fraction of a second before Gatticus's iron grip closed around her wrist once more.

"Grak it! Let me go!" Trista screamed, half from pain and half from outrage as she strained against Gatticus's hands, further injuring the burns that he'd inflicted earlier. "At least let me disable its engines!"

"There's a one in three chance that you'll hit the Alckam reactor and destroy the tender if you do. That would also earn you a murder charge. Is it worth the risk? I don't believe you want to find out."

"It's a tender! It doesn't have an Alckam drive!" Trista said. That was a lie, but how would

Gatticus know that? The only reason her tender was warp-capable was because Jaxon had owned it before her. He'd spent a fair portion of his career smuggling illegal goods past Union patrols, so he'd needed a getaway ship.

Gatticus pointed to her targeting display. The tender was bursting with gamma rays, a telltale sign of matter-antimatter reactions. "He's about to jump."

A split second later, the tender vanished with a dazzling flash of light.

The fight left Trista, and she slumped in her seat, blinking spots from her eyes. Gatticus released her wrists. Seeing the blinking red light on her comms panel, she remembered the message she'd received just before Jaxon had jumped. She keyed it for playback.

Jaxon's voice came slithering out of the speakers: "That was a nice trick, Tris. I never would have had you pegged for a friend of the metal heads, but I guess you never really know a person, huh? See you around. Oh, and I'd lay low for a while if I were you. Yuri isn't going to be happy to hear about your new friend."

Trista gaped at the comms.

"Is something wrong?" Gatticus asked.

"I'm done!"

"You're alive. You're free. You're welcome, by the way."

Trista glared at him. "Do you have any idea what you've done? My career is over!"

Gatticus cocked his head. "And why is that?"

"Do you know who Yuri is?"

"I'm afraid I do not."

"Yuri *Mathos?* You don't know who Yuri Mathos is?"

Gatticus's eyes widened in recognition. "The terrorist?"

"He'd prefer to be called a freedom fighter, but yeah. Jaxon goes way back with Yuri. Thanks to you, every pirate and terrorist this side of the Union is going to find out that I'm carting a *metal head* around with me, and now they're going to be looking for me. When they find me, they'll seize my ship, and either force me to join them, or kill me. Either way, I'm grakked."

CHAPTER 26

Darius lay in the shadows below the walkway with his head spinning. A *week* had passed. How could he have survived that long? Something wasn't adding up, but he didn't have time to figure it out. He needed to find water before he passed out. His head felt hot, while the rest of his body felt chilled, signs of heat stroke.

Darius cocked his head, listening for more footsteps. All was quiet. He crept out from under the landing pad and back to the stairway. There was a landing nearby, leading to a door just below the castle's entrance hall. Darius walked to that door and found it locked, just like the one on the first landing he'd encountered.

The last few dozen steps led straight to the front steps of the castle, within clear view of the front entrance. He couldn't go up there without being seen. Glancing back to the door in front of him, he wondered if there was a way he could break in. His sword. His hand found the hilt of his sword. If it could chop down trees, it would definitely slice open a wooden door. But would he reveal himself to Nova by drawing on the ZPF to shield himself and his blade? Darius grimaced. He'd have to risk it.

He activated his shield, and a pale white glow peeled back the shadows around the door. He drew his sword and pushed the tip as gently as he could through the edge of the door. The wood splintered and smoked, glowing bright orange around the blade. A curling tongue of flame appeared. Darius pulled the sword out. He waved the smoke away, cringing at the acrid smell. He couldn't afford to start a fire so close to the entrance of the castle. One of the Marines might smell it or see it and come down to investigate.

Darius studied the door once more. This time he pushed his sword into the seam on the right-hand side of the door, and swiped it down in a quick, smooth motion. A wooden beam clattered on the stone floor behind the door, making him wince. Hopefully, no one had heard it.

He projected his awareness beyond the door,

Darius found that the way was clear. Encouraged, he carefully opened the door. The remains of the beam dragged and bumped along the floor as the door swept them out of the way. He winced again at the noise.

A dark and windowless corridor lay before him. A good sign. The Marines hadn't bothered to illuminate this part of the castle, which meant that no one was using it—not yet anyway.

Darius sheathed his sword and bent to pick up the severed pieces of the wooden beam. He carried them outside and carefully laid them behind the stone landing. He went back inside and eased the door shut behind him, hoping the wind wouldn't blow it open.

The corridor was so dark that it was hard to see. Darius blinked his eyes a few times, giving them a moment to adjust to the light. There was a faint glow coming from the end of the corridor. He crept toward it, using his awareness to make sure no one down here with him. But the nearest people were on the level above, probably gathered around the fireplace in the entrance hall.

As he traveled down the corridor, Darius glanced through the open doors. They were storage rooms, filled with dusty wooden chests and empty shelves. He vaguely remembered this part of the castle from the game of hide and seek he'd played with the other Acolytes. At the end of the corridor, Darius saw another door. It was cracked open and letting in a bright wedge of light from a circular stairwell. He heard voices and footsteps approaching, and hid behind the door.

"I thought I felt something..." Cassandra said.

"Like what?" Dyara asked.

"I don't know. Something."

Darius held his breath, and plastered himself to the wall behind the door.

"I think it was through here..." Cassandra said.

The footsteps stopped, and the door groaned as someone pushed it open. It swung toward Darius's face and he winced, willing the door to stop before it hit him and bounced off...

It stopped within an inch of his nose.

"There's nothing through there, just empty storage rooms," Dyara said.

"Maybe a Seeker found its way in? We should take a look to be sure," Cassandra replied.

Darius eased his sidearm out of his holster and flicked it to *stun*. A few more footsteps sounded, and then—

"Dyara, Cassandra! A word, if you please. It's urgent."

Tanik's voice.

"Coming," Dyara said. "Let's go," she added in a hushed voice.

"But—oh, fine," Cassandra relented.

Darius heard their footsteps retreating up the stairs and let out a shuddering breath. He checked the luminous silhouettes around him to make sure no one else was nearby before darting around the corner to hide in one of the storage rooms. Somehow Cassandra had sensed him down here.

The question was, had Nova also felt something? Or was it just Cassandra?

Regardless, Darius realized that there was some good news. For whatever reason, Nova hadn't evacuated everyone from Ouroboros. She was bringing down supplies instead. Whatever her reason, it meant he had some time on his side. The bad news was that the Revenants were here, so even if he killed Nova to get rid of her influence, it wouldn't be good enough anymore. The other Revenants in the castle were almost certainly under the Augur's influence, and they would remain that way until the Augur died. Still, if Tanik, the Marines, and the other Acolytes were freed to think for themselves, maybe they could escape Ouroboros.

Darius swayed on his feet and almost fell over from dehydration. He had to get to the kitchen, or at least to the nearest restroom so he could find water.

Making sure to keep his presence hidden, Darius opened his mind further to locate and track everyone inside the castle. Bright and shining silhouettes appeared through the walls, floor, and ceiling. There had to be at least fifty people— *Revenant reinforcements.* Nova definitely had everyone under her influence if she'd managed to bring in reinforcements without a fight. Darius cringed at the thought of trying to keep track of so many people, but he was going to pass out if he didn't get something to drink soon.

Keeping an eye on the larger and closer silhouettes, Darius made sure that none of them were going up or down the stairs.

They weren't. The way was clear—at least for now. Darius crept out of the storage room, around the corner, and out the door. Remembering that he was on the level below the entrance hall, he went down, heading for the armory. A string of lights lit the way.

Thanks to the game of hide and seek he'd played with the other Acolytes, Darius knew that there was a restroom with communal showers a few floors down, just above the armory.

Darius hurried down the steps as quickly as he

dared. He passed two landings before walking through the door on the third. His eyes fell on a tray sink and the dripping faucets above it. He ran to the nearest one and opened the valve with a shaking hand. Leaning over, he let the water run into his open mouth. It was the sweetest thing he'd tasted in his entire life. He drank until almost blacking out for lack of oxygen, then straightened and stood leaning on the sink, gasping for air. In that moment booted feet came *clomping* down the stairs. Darius shut off the faucet and ducked into the nearest shower stall.

Using his awareness, Darius counted seven luminous silhouettes walking down the stairs. He held his breath as they passed his level and entered the armory below. Their presences shined brightly through the floor. Darius let out a shaky breath. *That was close.*

They'd probably gone down to the armory for more training. That meant soon they'd be coming up here to refill their canteens.

Darius wiped drops of water from his mouth and leaned against the side of the shower stall. He had to find somewhere to hide. He thought about the storage rooms where he'd come in, but Cassandra had expressed an interest in searching them. The lowermost level with the well might work, but he had no way of knowing if it was still abandoned, and he'd have to sneak by the open door of the Armory to get there.

No, the safest thing would be to find a hiding place somewhere outside. Darius crept out of the bathroom and back up the stairs to the corridor where he'd come in. He hurried down to the end and slipped out through the door.

He headed down, planning to hide somewhere along the steps. *But what if someone finds the door I sliced open?* If they did, it might lead them outside to search the stairs he'd climbed.

Darius slowed to a stop just as he reached the cliff ledge that ran below the landing pads. He remembered hiding there to listen in on Blake's conversation with one of the Marines. It wouldn't work as a long-term hiding spot, but the ledge ran all the way around the front of the castle to the other side. He couldn't sense anyone guarding that side of the castle. Maybe he could find a place to hide there. It was on the opposite side from the door where he'd broken in, which was an added bonus.

Darius checked the landing pads and the walkways leading to them.

No one up there. Good.

The nearest people were higher up, guarding

the front of the castle. Darius crawled on all fours along the ledge. He knocked the occasional loose rock or pebble free, sending it plummeting a thousand feet to the trees below. The noise of his knees and scabbard dragging against the rocks was like thunder to his ears, but he doubted anyone could hear him from the front steps of the castle.

He reached the last landing pad and saw the side of the castle soaring up three stories from his ledge. There was a row of windows on the third level that Darius suspected to be the sleeping quarters above the entrance hall.

Checking to make sure no one had a line of sight on him, Darius crawled around the side of the castle for a better look. He spied scraps of curtain fluttering in the last two windows, and his mind flashed back to the tattered curtains in Tanik's and Nova's room.

Darius's pulse began to race. He couldn't believe his luck! He'd found their room from the outside. If he could just find some way to climb up there, he'd be in a perfect position to ambush Nova after she went to bed. Darius studied the wall of the castle, looking for a way to climb it, but there were no ledges or handholds that he could see, only the sills below the windows, and they were at least twenty feet up.

Despair gripped him. If he couldn't climb through Nova's window, he'd have to wait until everyone was asleep and then somehow sneak past the night watch. That might be doable, but then he'd still have to find a way through the locked door to Nova's room. There was no way he'd be able to break through that door without waking her or Tanik up. He *had to* find a way to climb up to those windows.

Darius looked around once more. The side of the mountain behind the castle rose up within six feet of one of the windows. The slope looked climbable, but he'd have to jump to reach the window sill. There was a ledge just above the level of the windows. Maybe he could jump from there.

Darius hurried over to the base of the cliff and studied it for handholds. Finding the first one, he started up the cliff. It was actually relatively easy going. There were a few points along the way where he had to dangle by his hands to reach the next handhold, but he eventually made it to the ledge he'd spotted.

Pulling himself up, Darius perched there with his knees drawn up to his chest. From up here he saw that the gap between the cliff and the window was more than six feet; it was at least nine. Darius's heart sank. There was no way he'd be able to jump that far. Not without a running start, and there was barely enough space on the ledge to stand or sit, let alone run.

Darius considered his dilemma, wishing there were some way to float or fly across the gap. That thought triggered a memory. He recalled watching Tanik appear to float down from the airlock of the Osprey as if he weighed no more than a feather. He'd also seen Tanik move things telekinetically....

But Tanik wasn't the only one who'd done that. Darius had done something similar himself, without even realizing it. Right after they'd arrived on Ouroboros.

Darius concentrated on taking deep, calming breaths, and shut his eyes to focus better. Awareness, Concealment, and Shielding all worked through some form of mental visualization. Perhaps the same would be true for this? Darius tried visualizing himself floating above the ledge.

At first nothing happened, but then he felt something shift. The hard pressure of the ground beneath his feet and rear disappeared with a subtle tug of upward motion. Darius cracked his eyes open to find himself hovering several inches above the cliff. He grinned, elated by his discovery—

And then fell back down with a jarring *thud.*

He pitched forward, losing his balance on the cliff and fell headfirst toward the ground below.

Darius stifled a scream and shut his eyes, imagining himself caught up in a powerful updraft that held him floating above the ground on a cushion of air.

He hit the ground with a stinging *crunch* of gravel, spat out a mouthful of pebbles, and blinked his eyes open. That fall should have broken his neck. Something he'd done had worked. Maybe it explained how he'd survived a 100-story fall. He had a whole new set of reflexes.

Darius pushed off the ground and stood staring up at the windows. Floating in midair didn't seem like an easy thing to accomplish, but if he could slow a fall, he could probably augment a jump.

Darius bent his legs and leapt for the window sill, imagining and visualizing his success in reaching it even as he did so.

To his amazement, he flew straight up to the window. His hands found the ledge and he clung there. It took a moment for the full weight of gravity to return, and once it did, he almost lost his grip.

Darius hung there, panting and straining to hold on. His arms and hands were still weak from climbing the cliff. Before he climbed through, he opened his mind, checking to make sure no one was in the room or coming up to investigate. If someone had sensed something from his use of the ZPF, they might be on their way....

But they were all elsewhere. No one was nearby. Reassured, Darius pulled himself through the window and climbed over the nightstand into Tanik and Nova's room. He cast about, looking for a hiding place. A large bed sat between the windows, two wardrobes lay along the far wall, and a wooden chest was at the foot of the bed.

Darius went to the wardrobes and checked both. The first one had fresh jumpsuits hanging inside, along with towels, soap, and other supplies piled on the bottom. The second wardrobe was empty, and more than big enough for Darius to hide in. He sat inside the wardrobe and pulled the doors shut, sealing out the light. He heard his breath reverberating inside the small, dark space and worked to slow his breathing. Darius hoped Nova or Tanik wouldn't forget which wardrobe they were using and accidentally look inside the wrong one.

As his breathing slowed, he turned his mind to keeping his presence hidden. He'd been using concealment ever since he'd fallen from the cliff.

During training, Tanik had explained that as long as the intention to stay hidden was fixed in the back of his mind, he would be hard to detect, but now Darius put a conscious effort into the ability. He imagined himself as a tiny speck, dark and invisible. While doing that, he used awareness to gaze through the wardrobe doors and the walls of the castle. Dozens of people milled about on the lower levels. Darius kept expecting one of them to turn and head up toward him, but that never happened. Somehow he hadn't alerted anyone to his presence.

Some of the tension left his body. He'd done it. Now all he had to do was wait. What weapon would he use when the time came? He groped in the darkness for the butt of his sidearm, and then for the hilt of his sword, reassuring himself that they were both still there. Either weapon should work if he had the element of surprise.

Darius's legs began cramping and he stretched them as best he could in the confined space. How much longer would he have to wait here? He checked the time via his ESC. It was 1615 IST. He recalled that the last time he'd planned to go sneaking around the castle in the middle of the night, he and Dyara had set their alarms for 2100 IST. That left about five hours—five hours of waiting inside this closet with his muscles cramping. Just then his stomach rumbled. The Seeker meat was long gone after climbing two thousand feet of steps.

Darius grimaced. This was not going to be easy. He laid his head back against the side of the wardrobe, willing himself to sleep to pass the time. Exhaustion from the climb washed over him like a wave. Darkness swirled inside the wardrobe, the only light a thin bar on the back of the wardrobe spilling through the gap between the doors. Darius shut his eyes and waited for sleep to come. It wasn't long before he fell into a deep, dreamless sleep. Despite not having dreams, he did experience something: a feeling of utter despair, of being trapped, and confined, unable to move or speak, of being forced to do unspeakable things that left him feeling empty and alone, as if he had become the very darkness that enveloped him. Death lurked in that darkness.

Darius awoke with a start, his heart pounding, and panic buzzing in his veins. He was still in his dream, trapped in the dark, unable to move. Despair curled in his gut. He felt an urgent need to run, to escape, to throw himself out the window, and plummet to his death just to make it all stop. He almost burst out of the wardrobe in that moment, but calm rational thought trickled back before he could. Just as well. His ears picked up the sound of muffled voices in the room beyond. The gap between the doors was dark. He checked the time via his extra sensory chip. Somehow he'd slept until 2100. 2105, to be exact. The muffled voices sounded like they belonged to Tanik and Nova. He couldn't make out what they were saying, but they sounded sleepy.

Darius waited in the dark, biding his time. Minutes passed and their voices grew quiet, but still he waited. His legs and feet were cramping, his bladder bursting, and his back spasming, but he ignored it all. If he revealed himself too soon, Nova would kill him, and this time she'd make sure he was dead.

Darius kept an eye on the time, waiting for fully half an hour to pass. Time dragged at an agonizing pace—literally. Finally, the clock hit 2150. *Good enough,* he decided.

Darius pushed the wardrobe doors open and climbed out into the room. Starlight streamed in through the windows. After enduring the utter darkness inside the wooden box, it was more than enough to see by. Darius identified two people lying on the bed under the covers, each of them curling away from the other with a large gap in between. *Not the spooning type, I guess.* That made sense, considering that Nova wasn't actually Tanik's wife, Samara.

Darius identified Nova by the pool of long dark hair splayed around her pillow. *This was it.* He crept over to her side of the bed and wrapped his hand around the butt of his pistol. Drawing the weapon, he flicked it from *stun* to *burst* and aimed it at her head...

And hesitated with his finger on the trigger. Plotting to kill Nova was one thing. Doing it, like this, in cold blood, was another.

The lapse in his resolve only lasted for a second. Nova had left him for dead and all but possessed his daughter. She had to die. His finger tightened on the trigger—

But Nova's eyes flashed open and he flew backward through the air. He hit the nearest wall and smacked his skull against the stones before sliding to the floor. Nova appeared to float out of bed, bright and shining in the light of the ZPF. She stalked toward him, wearing nothing but her underwear, and Tanik belatedly rose from the bed, asking, "What's going on?"

"Your prodigy, Darius, is alive, darling," Nova said.

"He is?" Tanik asked, sounding confused.

"Yes, he thought he could kill me in my sleep, but don't worry, he won't be alive for much longer." Nova held out a hand to the second wardrobe and it flew open. There came a screech of sharpened steel, and the dark flash of a blade. Nova's sword slapped into her hand and immediately began glowing as her shield enveloped it.

Darius jumped to his feet, drew his sword, and summoned his own shield just as Nova's blade came flashing toward his neck.

Their swords met with a *clank* and a sizzling roar of energy. Nova pushed him back against the wall and laughed in his face. Darius saw a flicker of movement and his eyes darted aside to see Tanik rising from the bed, his gaze found them, but his eyes were blank and staring.

"Tanik!" Darius gritted out. "Snap out of it! I can't face her alone."

"He can't help you, Darius," Nova said through a sneer. "No one can."

CHAPTER 27

Darius shoved as hard as he could against Nova's blade, imagining in his mind's eye as he did so that he could send her flying as she'd done to him.

She staggered back a few steps, blinking in shock. "You've learned some new tricks since the last time we fought."

Darius took his chance to get away from the wall, and circled around, looking for an opening to attack. "Who are you?" he demanded.

Nova smiled. "I thought we covered that already?"

"No." He shook his head. "You gave me your name. That doesn't tell me anything. How did you know to find us here? This world was supposed to be abandoned."

"It was," Nova agreed. "And I already told you how I found you here. I foresaw you, just as Tanik did. My visions led me here."

Darius continued circling Nova, using the conversation to distract her. "So you came on your own initiative—not because the Augur sent you."

Nova smiled cryptically. "Yes and no."

Darius fetched up against the side of the bed, within arm's reach of Tanik. The man's yellow-green eyes were glazed, and he was staring blankly at the wall, as if in a trance.

Darius glanced at the door, a plan forming in his mind. He jumped onto the bed, and bounded down the other side in an attempt to escape through the door. But Nova ran by him in a blur and cut him off.

"Yes and no?" Darius echoed, as he tried to think of a new way out. He glanced at the open window beside him. He could dive through it and down to the ground below. He'd have to use the ZPF to cushion his fall, but he'd already done that once. He could do it again.

"Yes, I came on my own initiative, and no, the Augur *did* send me."

Darius regarded her with a furrowed brow, his plans for escape momentarily forgotten. "How is that possible?"

Nova flourished her blade. "Because I *am* the Augur, Darius."

He slowly shook his head. "How... the Augur's a *he*."

"He was a he. The *Augur* is a title, Darius. It is given to the most powerful Revenant. The original Augur died, lured to his death by a Keth warrior, and I replaced him. I was his right-hand. The most powerful of the Luminaries."

"Then..." Darius trailed off, shaking his head. "Why are you trying to kill me? I could join you. We don't have to fight each other."

"Join me? You want to join the war against the Keth?"

Darius hesitated.

"I didn't think so." Nova advanced a step.

Darius held up a hand to stop her. "Wait."

She stumbled back once more, suddenly frowning. "How did you... *this* is why you have to die," she said. "You're untrained and barely aware of what you are doing, and you're forcing *me* back." She tried advancing on him again, but this time she bounced off an invisible barrier. She let out a frustrated scream and thrust out her free hand.

Darius saw the air ripple and felt a gust of wind slam into him. This time he was the one who stumbled backward. She raised her sword and strode toward him. "Clearly I've been going too easy on you."

Darius waited until she was close, then thrust out his hand and imagined her flying away from him on a gust of air, but this time she was ready for it, and nothing happened. Her blade swung down toward his outstretched arm and he barely managed to pull it back and block before she could slice off his hand.

This time she didn't lock blades with him, but broke away and struck again, aiming low for his legs. He parried, then countered when he saw an opening, but it was a trick. She batted his sword away with such force that it flew out of his hand.

She hit him with another gust of air; he went flying over the bed and into the wall. This time he blacked out when his head cracked against the wall. When he came to, he sat slumped on the floor, and Nova was rounding the bed to reach him.

"That's more like it," Nova said. "Any last requests?"

"My daughter," he breathed. "Don't make her fight."

"Oh, I'm afraid I can't grant you that, Darius. She's no Luminary, like you or I, but she has great potential nonetheless, and we're short of soldiers, especially with all of the other Luminaries fighting me for control of the Crucible."

A loud knock sounded on the door. "Is everything all right in there?" a woman asked.

Darius didn't recognize the voice. Before Nova could reply, the wooden beam barring the door exploded, and a pair of women in silvery armor stormed in. They immediately began glowing in the light of their shields, and they drew their swords.

"Madam Augur, do you need assistance?" one of them asked.

"Stand down, Adept! I'm fine. This will be over in just a moment." Nova bent down in front of Darius and lifted his chin with one finger. She placed her glowing blade right under his chin, and flashed a wicked smile. "I'll say goodbye to Cassandra for you."

Darius felt cold fury burning inside of him. His ears began ringing, and he saw red. He couldn't see or think straight, but he managed to focus his thoughts enough to imagine ripping the swords out of the hands of the Revenant soldiers standing behind Nova to send them plowing through her chest from behind.

One of the soldiers shouted something, but the

sound was muffled, reaching Darius's ears as if from a great distance. He heard whispers, loud and furious in his ears, just like he had in his visions.

Nova's eyes widened in outrage and shock, her lips moving, but no sound coming out. She half-turned away from him, her sword leaving his throat to block an unseen attack. She was just in time to bat two glassy black swords out of the air. They shattered and exploded into gleaming shards at the touch of her blade.

Darius seized the moment and reached into the ZPF once more. He imagined his fallen sword flying into his hand as if drawn by a magnet. Darius saw a dark flash as the weapon sailed through the air, and he jumped to his feet just as the hilt of his sword slapped against his palm. Nova rounded on him, but her arms were pinned rigidly to her sides, and her blade dangled uselessly from her fingers, as if it suddenly weighed too much for her too lift.

"How..." she trailed off, veins in her arms and neck bulging as she strained against the invisible forces holding her.

Darius let loose an unintelligible roar and charged. Nova's eyes widened in horror just before he ran her through. His glowing blade disappeared in her chest, halfway to the hilt, sparkling and crackling against her shield.

Nova's mouth formed an "O" as shock registered on her face. Her sword fell from nerveless fingers, and her shield vanished. Darius's sword remained buried in her chest, smoking and sizzling with the sickening smell of roasted flesh.

Her skin curled away in glowing orange sheets, like bark from a burning branch, and then she burst into flames.

Nova recoiled from his sword, stumbling away as he pulled it out, and fell thrashing to the floor. A moment later, she lay still, but the flames roared over the charred black mound of her corpse.

In the background Tanik started, as if waking from a dream, and his head turned to regard Darius with a faint smile. "I told you it was your destiny to kill the Augur."

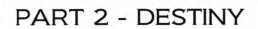

PART 2 - DESTINY

CHAPTER 28

"How did you know she's the Augur?" Darius asked Tanik, all the while watching the two Revenant soldiers who had burst in. They both still stood by the door, seemingly frozen in shock at the sight of Nova's charred corpse.

Tanik glanced at them, then back to Darius. "Don't worry. They're coming to their senses now. I'm sure they're nothing but grateful that you killed her. As am I. Thank you."

"You didn't answer my question," Darius said slowly. "How did you know she's the Augur?"

"I heard everything she said to you. Controlling another person's mind doesn't disengage their faculties, only their will."

"So it's true? The original Augur is dead?"

Tanik glanced over his shoulder once more.

"Perhaps these Adepts can answer that."

One of the two women in the doorway nodded. Without knowing their names, Darius differentiated them by their hair. One was blonde, the other a redhead.

"Yes, he's dead," the blonde said. "He died here, on Ouroborus, twenty years ago. That was when Nova took over."

"That might explain how I was able to escape his influence...." Tanik mused.

The woman looked at him. "Who are you again?"

"We've already been introduced, have we not? I am Tanik Gurhain, a former Sentinel in the Augur's army."

"Tanik Gur..." the woman trailed off, shaking her head. "I don't recognize you."

"I've been gone for twenty years, hiding in the Union. I'm Samara Gurhain's husband," Tanik supplied.

"Samara." The blonde looked to the redhead. "She was the one with the locket, wasn't she?"

"Yes," the redhead nodded. "I remember her," she went on. "She never took it off, not even to shower. She was really in love with you."

Darius's brow wrinkled at the mention of that necklace. He strode over to Tanik, giving Nova's corpse a wide berth.

"You didn't seem to know what I was talking about when I mentioned that locket in front of you," Darius said.

"It's been twenty years, and I was under Nova's influence when you asked," Tanik explained.

Darius arched an eyebrow at that. "I thought you said being controlled by another Revenant doesn't affect your faculties?"

"Perhaps I should have said it doesn't affect your *memory*. Nova suppressed my recognition of the locket to avoid drawing suspicion to herself," Tanik replied.

"I don't remember you from the battle of Ouroboros," the redhead interjected.

Tanik offered her a thin smile. "It's been twenty years. Besides, I wasn't in the first wave with my wife. I was in the second. By the time I arrived, the battle was almost over."

"I was also in the second wave..." the redhead said.

"Then you must have missed me. It was chaos down here."

"I didn't catch your names," Darius interjected.

"I'm Adept Lora Addison," the redhead said. She pointed to the blonde. "This is Adept Asha

Wilks. Who are you?"

"Darius Drake."

"Nova said that you're a Luminary. Is that true?"

"It is," Tanik confirmed.

"What does that mean?" Darius asked.

"It means you have the ability to influence other Revenants, like the first Augur, and Nova."

"Oh," Darius said, glancing behind him at Nova's smoldering corpse. "So it's another title—like the Augur."

"Yes," Tanik confirmed.

"Dad?"

Darius's head spun around at the sound of the voice. Cassandra stood in the open door behind Lora and Asha. Dyara was with her. He grinned. "Cass!"

"Dad!" Cassandra came running. She slammed into him and wrapped him in a fierce hug. "They told me you were dead, but I couldn't... it's like I was someone else." She sniffled against his chest. "I couldn't even cry!"

She was crying now, her tears soaking into his tattered jumpsuit. Darius kissed the top of her head. "I know, sweetheart. It's okay. Samara was controlling everyone, even Tanik. Her real name was Nova."

Cassandra looked up, her blue eyes bright and shining with tears as they searched his. She withdrew to an arm's length and looked to Tanik. "How is that possible?"

"She was the Augur."

Cassandra gasped. "I was right! But I thought the Augur was a he?"

Tanik explained how Nova had taken over twenty years ago.

Dyara came in and stood awkwardly to one side. "Hey," she said, smiling wanly at Darius. "It's good to see you again."

Something stirred inside of Darius at the sight of her, and he withdrew from Cassandra's embrace. Crossing quickly to Dyara, he took her face in both of his hands and kissed her, long and hard. For a moment she was too shocked to react, but then he felt her kissing him back.

A few seconds later, she leaned away to regard him with a puzzled look. "I thought—"

"Life's too short," he said, cutting her off with a shake of his head. "And I've already wasted enough of mine."

Tanik cleared his throat. "You two can profess your lust for each other later. We have important matters to attend to."

Darius turned to Tanik with a frown. "Can't it

wait a minute?"

"No." Tanik jerked his head to Lora and Asha. "Gather the other Revenants. We have much to discuss."

"Who put you in charge?" Lora asked.

"I was a Sentinel. You're an Adept." Tanik jerked a thumb at Darius. "And he's a Luminary."

"Untrained," Asha pointed out. "And you just admitted that you've been AWOL for twenty years."

"Untrained or not Darius is all that's standing between you and blind servitude to the next would-be Augur, so I'd suggest you treat him well."

"How do we know he's going to be any better?" Lora asked, while tucking a loose strand of red hair behind her ear.

"We should get out of here while we still can," Asha said in a low voice, her eyes darting between Darius and Tanik.

"And go where?" Tanik demanded.

Asha grimaced and chewed her lower lip, but Lora wasn't so easily intimidated. She drew herself up, and said, "We still have control of the Crucible, and the Eye. We could brand ourselves with the seal of Life, take our ships, and go to the Union. It will take a while before one of the other

Luminaries realizes that Nova is dead and comes to fill the power vacuum."

"And then what? Go into hiding?" Tanik asked.

"You did," Lora pointed out, nodding to Tanik's wrist, the one bearing the glowing triangle with an eye inside of it—the seal of life.

Tanik snorted and turned over his other wrist, revealing the glowing, sickle-shaped seal of death. "And look where it got me."

"We'll be careful," Lora insisted. "You must have done something to earn that."

"I did. I led the Coalition fleet against the Union for twelve years," Tanik said.

"Then you're a bigger fool than I thought. And anyway, you're not a Luminary, so you can't make us stay here. Even if you could, why bother? The Keth are gone. The war is over. It's time to go home."

Darius cleared his throat. "Excuse me."

"What?" Lora crossed her arms over her chest.

"If you have control of the Crucible and the Eye, don't you think you should use the opportunity to change how the system works?"

"Change it how?" Lora asked.

"You could send *everyone* home with the Seal of Life. Keep identifying the ones with the potential to become Revenants, but let them choose if they want to be trained or not. Send the ones that do to a training facility *in* the Union, somewhere that their parents could visit them."

Lora smirked at that, but Darius noticed Asha nodding along. Tanik was quiet but smiling from ear to ear.

"Don't you think that would be better for everyone?" Darius pressed.

"Sure it would," Lora said. "Right up until the Cygnians wonder why they're not getting any fresh meat for their hunting grounds, and they start picking people at random to prey upon."

"The hunting grounds need to be disbanded, anyway," Darius said.

"Good luck with that," Lora scoffed. "You'll trade one war for another! The Keth are hiding, defeated. Done. But the Cygnians are more powerful than ever. Do you have any idea how many people would die in a war with them? And without them holding the Union together, it won't be so unified anymore. You'll splinter it in a hundred pieces, and none of those pieces will be strong enough to fight the Cygnians."

"So we unite the Revenants and fight them ourselves," Darius said.

"You'd have to kill all the Luminaries first.

They're convinced that the Augur was right about the Keth and that the Crucible is a necessary evil. And who knows? Maybe they're right. Or at least they *were*. We'd never have conquered Ouroboros without the Crucible feeding us fresh soldiers."

Darius frowned. "How many Luminaries are there?"

"Besides Nova? Another six, each with their own fleet and their own star system. You'll never be able to defeat them all. Nova was arrogant enough to fight you herself, but the others won't be that careless once they realize what they're up against. You'll either have to destroy their fleets, or infiltrate their palaces and fight through swarms of soldiers to get to them. Even if you force us all to fight for you as Nova did, we can't beat them all. The only way to win would be to use the Crucible to swell your numbers until your fleet is stronger than all of the others combined, and that would take years."

Darius sighed, stymied by Lora's objections.

Tanik placed a hand on his shoulder and nodded to the Adepts. "Gather the other Revenants. Give me a chance to tell you about *my* plan. Darius knows the end goal, but he hasn't given enough thought to all of the steps along the way. Once you've heard what I have to say, you can decide if you still want to leave, and if so, no one's going to stop you."

"Fine," Lora said. "But your plan had better be brilliant, or you're going to lose your army before you ever have a chance to use it."

Tanik nodded agreeably. "I'm aware of that, Adept."

Darius watched as both Lora and Asha left the room. "What plan?" he asked after they'd left. "I thought your plan was to kill the Augur and threaten the Cygnians with weapons of mass destruction? Well, we killed the Augur, but now we've learned that there's six more just like her. We could probably still threaten the Cygnians, but what good would it do if the other Revenants are fighting us from behind?"

Tanik answered that with a cryptic smile. "Patience, Darius. You'll have your answers soon. In the meantime, why don't you go down and wait for me in the entrance hall? I need to get dressed."

Darius's gaze lingered, but Dyara's hand slid into his, and he felt her tugging him toward the door. "Let's go," she said. He nodded, and Cassandra went ahead of them, leading the way.

Whatever plan Tanik had in mind, Darius hoped it was good enough to convince the other Revenants. They needed help if they were going to defeat the Cygnians.

CHAPTER 29

It was standing room only in the entrance hall of the castle, but Darius had found his seat before all of the others had arrived. He was sharing an empty storage crate with Cassandra and Dyara, each of them sitting to either side of him. Besides the seven Acolytes, there were eight Marines, and thirty Revenant soldiers in their shiny silver armor.

Tanik stood at the center of the gathering, in front of the fireplace, dark with soot and coals. Like the other Revenants, Tanik was also wearing armor, but his was black power armor from the *Deliverance,* the same as the Marines wore.

"Now that everyone's here, I can explain why you shouldn't all go run and hide in Union space," Tanik began. "The first and most obvious reason, is because whoever the next Augur is, they won't let you go. They'll come looking for you. You'll be hunted and dragged back to the Crucible, having gained nothing for your trouble. And the second reason, is because we have a chance to take over the Union for ourselves."

"What about the Cygnians?" one man asked.

"How many ZPF bombs do you have in your fleet? A hundred? A thousand?"

"More than a thousand," a woman said. Darius recognized the voice. It was Lora Addison.

"And how many do the Cygnians have?" Tanik pressed.

"None," someone else replied.

Tanik nodded sagely. "So we press our advantage. Threaten their worlds. Give them a demonstration, and warn them what will happen if they don't respect the Union's independence."

"They won't," Lora said. "So you're suggesting we commit xenocide."

"If it comes to that, yes," Tanik replied. "In a society divided into predators and prey, the rule is kill or be killed."

"And then what?"

"Then, we install our Luminary as the new regent of the Union."

Hushed murmurs spread from one Revenant to the next. Darius recalled that only Lora, Asha, and the other Acolytes knew about his potential.

"Darius, would you stand up please?" Tanik asked.

He stood, and offered a tight smile to all of the Revenants who suddenly turned to stare at him with a mixture of suspicion and hostility.

"We should kill him while we still can!" someone said. Heads bobbed, and someone started pushing through the crowd with his hand on the hilt of his sword.

A sharp jolt of adrenaline lanced through Darius and he raised his hands. "Wait. I'm not like the others. I have no interest in controlling anyone. I never even met the original Augur. Nova tried to kill me twice before I eventually killed her, because—"

"Because you wanted to take over as the next Augur!" someone accused.

"No! Because she'd foreseen me, sitting on a throne, ruling over a new Union with the Cygnians defeated."

"That's a lie," Lora scoffed.

A low growl built into a roar from somewhere in the back of the room. Darius suspected that was Gakram, the Banshee Acolyte voicing his discontent.

"It's not a lie," Tanik insisted. "I've seen the

same vision, and if you take the time to look into the future for yourselves, you will, too."

"What's the point? The future is too elusive to predict," another Revenant said.

"It *is* elusive," Tanik agreed. "But some things can be seen with certainty, and this is one of them."

"Let's say your plan works," Lora said. "Why Darius? Just because he's a Luminary?"

"Yes. He's the only one whose visions can be wholly trusted, and therefore, the only one who can be trusted to guide the new Union safely through turbulent times."

"We'll never win," Lora insisted. "Even if we defeat the Cygnians. The other Revenants will come through the Eye behind us and fight us for control of the Union."

Murmurs of agreement followed that objection, and Darius had to admit she had a point. This was the argument that had given him pause and made him doubt Tanik's plan in the first place.

Tanik raised a hand for silence. "There is one way we can stop them. We collapse the Eye behind us, trapping them on this side of the galaxy."

"That's impossible," one man said.

But Tanik shook his head. "Wormholes are held open by exotic matter. The zero-point field is capable of interacting with that matter, and it's possible to use the field to both open and close wormholes. One ZPF bomb, detonated in the right place, should be enough to collapse the Eye."

"I've never heard of such a thing. Wormholes are an enigma. No one knows how they're formed or how they can be destroyed," Lora said.

"You're wrong. I know how."

"Prove it," Lora said.

"As you wish." With that, he raised both of his hands, and a bright orb appeared, hovering above their heads. It expanded rapidly to fill the hall. Everyone gasped and leaned away from it, but Darius peered into it, watching as it went from an opaque ball of shimmering light to a translucent sphere.

Stars appeared, and in that instant a roaring wind whipped by them, blasting them from all sides and sucking them toward the light.

Darius wrapped his arms around Cassandra and Dyara and grabbed the handles of the storage crate they were sitting on, pinning them all to it. He felt his legs, suddenly weightless, drifting up toward the shimmering portal.

"Grab onto me!" he yelled as he felt Cassandra slipping toward the light.

But the wind died just as suddenly as it had begun, and Darius's legs hit the floor with a *thunk* of mag boots on stone. Darius turned to look just as the room burst into heated discussion. Tanik gazed into the crowd with a smug smile, twisted into a sneer by the scars running across his face.

"How did you do that?" Lora shouted to be heard above the furor.

"I'm afraid that knowledge is too dangerous to share," Tanik replied. "Suffice it to say, I know how wormholes are made, and I also know how they are unmade."

"You said you need a ZPF bomb to shut the wormhole," Darius said.

Tanik nodded. "I'm not strong enough to collapse a wormhole the size of the Eye by myself."

"If you can open and close wormholes at will, how do we know that one of the Luminaries won't be able to do the same thing?" someone asked.

Tanik waved that concern away. "If they knew how to open wormholes, don't you think they would have done so to ambush you and take over the Crucible by now? Besides, opening a small portal for a brief period is one thing. Opening one large enough for starships to cross, and holding it open while they do so is much more difficult."

Awe at what they'd witnessed set in, and a hush fell over the entrance hall.

"Why did we get sucked toward it?"

Cassandra whispered.

"Because he opened the wormhole into space," Dyara replied. "He depressurized an entire planet."

Lora said, "This plan of yours might actually work. Regardless, I'm not the one you need to convince. We're all Adepts here. The Advocates and Sentinels are the ones you need to speak to, starting with Admiral Ventaris."

Tanik nodded. "I'm ready when you are, Adept."

CHAPTER 30

—THREE DAYS LATER—

The nonessential crew cabins on the *Deliverance* were all large rooms with tiered rows of seating, arrayed inside a dome of holo panels. Each seat had its own acceleration harness and configurable holo display, while the holo panels around the cabin showed the ship's surroundings. Right now those panels showed the distorted region of space inside of the Eye of Thanatos as they crossed it on their way to Union space.

Three days ago Tanik had gone with Adepts Lora and Asha to give a demonstration of wormhole creation/destruction aboard the Revenant fleet's flagship, the *Harbinger*. Admiral Ventaris must have been impressed, because immediately thereafter he'd given the order to evacuate Ouroboros. Now the crew of the

Deliverance was back on board, along with a handful of Revenant soldiers. The *Deliverance* had joined the Revenant fleet at the Crucible, refueled, and then flown through the Eye behind all of the other ships.

Darius didn't enjoy the return to a zero-G environment, but leaving Ouroboros behind more than made up for it. His vision of Cassandra's funeral had shown a setting from the surface of the planet. The farther they could get from it, the better. As soon as Tanik shut the Eye behind them, there'd be no way to return to Ouroboros, and therefore, no way for his vision to come to pass.

Darius let out a shaky sigh and glanced around the crew cabin. Cassandra and Dyara sat to either side of him along the front row of seats, while the other Acolytes sat further down the same row. Everyone in the cabin stared fixedly at their holo displays, or at the holo panels on the walls. Anticipation and boredom mingled with hushed voices and fidgeting limbs. It reminded Darius of flying on a commercial airliner back in the 21st century.

"It looks like we're almost through the Eye," Cassandra said, studying a star map on her holo display. "Do you think they dropped the bomb already?"

Darius shrugged. "Maybe."

"Hopefully it works," Dyara added.

Darius nodded along with the sentiment, and reached for Dyara's hand. She laced her fingers through his and smiled.

He smiled back. In the past three days he and Dyara hadn't had much of a chance to figure out where their relationship was going, or what their expectations were, but they'd spent last night alone in her quarters, and this time they'd done more than just sleep. It had been an unusual experience in zero-G, but surprisingly not awkward. And since then, Darius hadn't noticed any awkwardness or diminished interest between them, which he took as a good sign.

"Here we go..." Cassandra said.

Darius looked to the holo panels and watched as the star field seemed to invert and peel away from a backdrop of stars, undistorted by the warped space inside the wormhole.

He pulled up a star map on his holo display. Green blips appeared in a long line ahead of their position, while a cluster of yellow ones—the Cygnian Fleet, sat to one side, unmoving.

That was a good sign. It meant that so far Admiral Ventaris and the other Revenants were managing to do their part, exerting themselves to control the Cygnian leaders aboard their fleet. Darius wasn't sure how much they knew about the Revenants and their war with the Keth, or for that matter, the real reason for the Crucible and their ritual of sending children to it. Now that the Augur was dead, the Cygnians were supposed to be in the slow process of coming to their senses—whatever that meant. From everything he'd been told, Darius suspected it meant that a bloody civil war was coming.

Darius watched on his map as they followed the Revenant fleet to a safe distance from the Cygnian fleet. The *Deliverance* was the last ship through the Eye, since it was Tanik's ship, and he had to close the wormhole behind them.

As Darius watched their progress, he felt the *Deliverance's* engines periodically engage, pressing him into his seat, or against the sides of his acceleration harness. Silence reigned in the cabin. Everyone watched their displays in breathless anticipation, waiting to see the Eye suddenly disappear.

"How do we know if it worked?" Cassandra asked.

"I don't know..." Darius said. "Maybe I should try to contact the bridge for an update."

Dyara's hand tightened around his. "Wait,"

she breathed. "Look."

Darius glanced at her display. She'd zoomed in on the Eye. It looked the same as ever, a gleaming soap bubble bathed in stars. He shook his head. "I don't see..." And then he did. The bubble was rapidly shrinking. "It worked!" Darius crowed.

Speakers crackled to life inside the cabin amidst a rising clamor of excited exclamations. "This is Captain Gurhain. The Eye is now collapsing behind us, and we are en route to the star system that will serve as our staging ground for the next six months. If you see the Cygnian fleet moving to attack us, don't be alarmed. We won't be in-system much longer."

Attack us? Darius stared at his holo display. The group of yellow blips was moving, changing shape as the Cygnian fleet began inching toward them. The deck in the crew cabin began glowing faintly with the light of the ZPF, and in the next instant, bright green lasers flickered out of the void, lashing the Revenant fleet.

"Why are they attacking us?" Darius wondered aloud. "I thought the Revenants were controlling them."

"They're obviously not very good at it," Dyara said. "Maybe Cygnians are harder to control than humans?"

"Or it takes a Luminary to control them," Cassandra suggested. She glanced at Darius as she said that. "Maybe you should try?"

He shook his head. "I wouldn't know where to begin. Anyway, the Revenants are shielding us at the moment, and Tanik said we won't be here much longer."

Even as he said that, he saw the lead ship of the Revenant fleet jump to FTL with a corresponding flash of light. Consecutive flashes raced down the line of ships like a chain reaction, and in a matter of seconds the *Deliverance* was the only ship left.

"Why aren't we jumping?" Cassandra asked.

But before Darius could venture a guess, the holo panels blazed a blinding white, and faded to black around the flat white circle of a warp disc.

The intercom crackled to life once more. "This is Lieutenant Fields from the helm—we have established warp and ceased maneuvering. You may now disengage your harnesses. ETA to our destination is twenty-one standard days. For updates please consult the nearest holo display. Fields out."

Darius frowned, staring into the unblinking eye of the warp disc. *Twenty-one days! It must be a long way to the staging ground.* No wonder they'd refueled the *Deliverance* at the Crucible.

The sound of releasing harnesses and mag-booted feet shuffling filled the cabin, but Darius lingered in his seat, troubled by his thoughts.

Cassandra folded away her harness, stood up, and stretched. Dyara did likewise. "Are you planning to stay there?" she asked.

Darius belatedly released his harness and stood up, frowning at Dyara as he did so.

"What's wrong?" she asked.

"The Cygnians attacked us before we jumped. They attacked us despite the Revenants' best efforts to control them."

Dyara shook her head, not getting it. "So?"

"So, we're going to spend the next twenty-one days flying to our staging ground, and after that, six *months*, doing who knows what while we prepare to face them."

"I'm pretty sure Tanik plans to continue training us," Dyara said.

"And while we're off play-fighting with swords, what do you think the Cygnians are going to be doing in the rest of the galaxy? Now that Nova is dead, no one is keeping them in line anymore. If what we saw was a sample of their aggression in spite of the other Revenants' best attempts to control it, then how many people are going to die while we sit around doing nothing?"

Cassandra frowned and shook her head. "Maybe nothing will change. They're not all bad. Gakram is—"

"Just a kid," Dyara interrupted. "And as far as I can tell, he's unusually passive for a Cygnian. Darius is right. The Cygnians are probably slaughtering people as we speak. We should talk to Tanik," Dyara said.

"Talk to me about what?"

Darius turned to see Tanik striding from the entrance of the cabin, walking against a steady outflow of crew. The other Acolytes were already on their way out, probably heading for their quarters or the nearest mess hall. Darius spotted Gakram, the Banshee Acolyte, skittering along the ceiling on six legs to avoid the crowds.

As soon as Tanik reached them, Dyara asked why they were waiting so long to address the Cygnian threat and launch their coup.

Tanik gave a thin smile. "Six months is how long it will take for us to get our ships into position and simultaneously threaten all of the Cygnians' worlds. Rest assured, we're not delaying any more than we have to."

"But you said we'll be spending the next six months at the staging ground," Darius pointed out.

"*We* will, yes. That's because our target, Cygnus Prime, is closer to the Eye, and to the staging ground, than all of the other Cygnian worlds. We will remain there with the *Deliverance* and the *Harbinger* until all of the other ships reach their targets. While we wait, we will conclude your training."

"I thought it takes two years to train Acolytes?" Cassandra asked.

Tanik inclined his head to her. "Ideally, yes, but we don't have that much time anymore. And speaking of training, your next lesson starts in one hour. Tell the others. I'll meet all of you in the aft cargo bay."

Cassandra nodded.

"I have one more question before you go," Darius said.

Tanik's left eye twitched. "And that is?"

"Why couldn't you and the other Revenants keep the Cygnians under control?"

"Only the Augur and the Luminaries are powerful enough to completely control another person's mind."

Cassandra nodded.

Tanik went on, "Our control over the Cygnians at the Eye was fleeting at best, enough to dampen their suspicions when we came through, but not enough to keep them in line after the Eye collapsed."

"Why should they care about that?" Cassandra asked. "They should be relieved. Now they don't have to send their kids to the Crucible."

Tanik looked at her, his expression a mixture of amusement and strained patience. "The Eye is the symbol of their religion, the Church of the Divine Light. It's their connection to the after-life, to their dead ancestors and to their children who never came home from the Crucible. They call those lost ones *Gah'hussi*, translated to mean Revenants. We know that those people never really died at all, but the Cygnians don't know that, nor does the rest of the galaxy.

"So when the Eye collapsed, it took their entire belief system with it, annihilating their hope for a life after death. They blamed our arrival for that event. They think we're devils come to kill them all." Tanik smirked. "Ironically, that's not far from the truth."

"If the collapse of the Eye was the catalyst," Darius began, "then maybe the civil war won't start until we confront the Cygnians."

Tanik shook his head. "I doubt it. Word of our arrival and the collapse of the Eye will spread, and now that the Augur's influence is gone, the

Cygnian Royals won't take long to change their minds about who can and can't be preyed upon. Once that happens, no one will be safe anymore."

"Then we should jump straight to Cygnus Prime and threaten them *now*, not in six months' time," Darius said.

"If we have our ships in position to threaten all of their worlds at once, it will be much more effective than simply threatening their home world and waiting for them to relay that threat to the rest of their people. A simultaneous threat will prompt a simultaneous reaction from all of the royal houses, otherwise we risk getting a partial or fake surrender."

"They could still offer a fake surrender," Darius replied. "Pretend to back down, wait for us to leave, and then attack when our guard is down."

"Indeed," Tanik replied. "That is a valid concern, which is why we won't back down until we're sure that it is safe to do so. Rest assured, Darius, Admiral Ventaris and I have discussed this strategy extensively, and we will do everything we can to limit the loss of innocent life. Now, I trust that answers all of your questions?"

Darius gave in with a hesitant nod. "It does."

"Good. Then I'll see you three in the aft cargo bay for training." Tanik turned and walked back up the aisle to the exit.

"I don't trust him," Cassandra said. "There's something he's not telling us."

Darius snorted. "There's a lot he's not telling us."

"Whatever he's hiding, one thing's for sure: he's right about the Cygnians. They're going to go *goffity* when they hear that the Eye is gone."

CHAPTER 31

—SEVENTEEN DAYS LATER—

Trista sat watching the jump timer counting down the last ten minutes to their arrival in the Sol System. They'd spent the past seven days in FTL, partly because they already had all the supplies they needed, but mostly because Trista wanted to avoid any unfortunate run-ins with Yuri's gang.

Gatticus had offered her a job as palace courier to keep her safe. The offer came with a Union-issued clipper, so she could sell the *Harlequin* before her reputation as a *friend of the metal heads* caught up with her. It would also mean a steady salary and plenty of benefits that she'd missed out on as a freelancer.

The down side? Less excitement, less freedom, and giving up on her life-long dream of owning her own ship and being her own boss. Trista had told Gatticus that she'd think about it, but the truth was, thanks to Jaxon, she didn't have much of a choice.

Trista glanced at Buddy. "You're unusually quiet."

"Are you going to take the job?" he asked, not looking at her. Apparently he was thinking about the same thing as her.

"Well... yeah, I think I am."

"Then I guess this is goodbye."

Trista did a double take. "What? Why?"

"They're not going to let me be your copilot. Togras aren't citizens. People think all we're good for is being cute and cuddly, and keeping *real* people company. We're just pets to them."

"Not to me. You're intelligent—more intelligent than a lot of so-called *real* people that I've met. In my book that makes you just as much a citizen as anyone else. I'll tell them we're a package deal. They'll have to hire us both, or I won't take the job."

Buddy looked at her, his big brown eyes sad, and his chubby cheeks drooping. "They won't go for it."

"Maybe not, but you don't have to leave just because they won't let you ride in the cockpit. We'll save some creds and wait for Yuri to get bored of looking for us. Give it a year. After that, we can resign and buy a new ship so that we can go back to doing what we do best."

Buddy regarded her with wide eyes and his furry brow hopefully furrowed. "Promise?"

Trista nodded. "You bet."

The jump timer hit one minute, and the cockpit door swished open. Trista glanced over her shoulder to see Gatticus stepping in. "Ready to empty your bank account into mine?" she asked.

"Your fee will hardly empty my account. Executors are highly paid, and we have fewer reasons to spend money than biological lifeforms," Gatticus replied as he folded out an extra seat and acceleration harness beside the door.

"Must be nice," Trista said.

The timer hit zero and a flash of light suffused the cockpit. The contacts panel chirped for her attention, followed by the comms, with a blinking red light to indicate a waiting message. Earth appeared dead ahead, a shining blue and white jewel. Trista checked the contacts panel as a matter of routine, and icy dread trickled into her gut.

"What the hell?" She checked her nav panel for confirmation and saw the same thing there.

The *click* of an acceleration harness releasing reached her ears, and Gatticus appeared, looming over her shoulder.

"That's a Cygnian Fleet," he said, pointing to the contacts panel.

"No kak," Trista replied. "But what's that?" She traced a clump of unidentified gray blips on the nav panel. It was a rhetorical question. She already knew what she was looking at, but she didn't want to believe it.

"Debris," Gatticus replied in a quiet voice. "See if you can get a visual on them."

"One second..." Buddy said.

A magnification box appeared, overlaid directly on the cockpit canopy. Debris filled the box, jagged black shapes tumbling against the cloud-streaked blue backdrop of Earth's oceans. Trista caught a glimpse of something familiar in the debris field. "What's that?" she wondered aloud as she magnified a particular piece of debris. A hull fragment with charred white lettering appeared. Trista read it aloud, "*U.S.O.S*—they attacked a Union Fleet! The Cygnians are the rulers of the Union. Why would they destroy their own ships?"

"That's a good question," Gatticus replied. He pointed to the blinking red light on the comms panel. "Maybe that message will help us answer it?"

Trista checked the sender's ID tag.

ADMR COVATHUS 12th USON FLEET

Then she checked the message characteristics.

NO ENCYRPT, AUTO REPEAT, OPEN CHANNEL

She keyed it for playback and a human voice issued from the cockpit speakers: "This is Admiral Covathus of the 12th Fleet to all incoming vessels: the Cygnians have attacked us without provocation or warning, and they are not responding to comms. They are invading Earth. Run and spread the word. The Cygnians can no longer be trusted to uphold the laws that they themselves established. As of this moment, the Union is at war with itself."

"Grak it!" Trista said. "Turn us around, Buddy!" She checked her Alckam drive and grimaced. They were down to 10% fuel. Where could they go with so little fuel? More to the point, where could they go that might be safe?

"Hang on," Gatticus said. "I'm the Executor of Earth. They won't attack us if they know that I'm on board."

Trista snorted. "Yeah, I'll bet that's what that Admiral thought right up until they sneak-attacked him."

"We have to at least try to open a dialogue.

Maybe I can figure out what started this conflict and negotiate more favorable terms for Earth's surrender."

Trista eyed him dubiously. "You heard the admiral—he said the attack was unprovoked and they weren't answering hails. If they'd wanted to talk, they would have done so before blasting the entire 12th fleet to scrap."

"We have to try," Gatticus insisted. "There are billions of people down there. Are you willing to sacrifice all of their lives just because you were too afraid to stick around and see if you could help?"

"Grak it, bolts-for-brains! Fine, get on the comms! The Alckam drive still has to cool down, anyway, but I'm not waiting any longer than I have to."

Gatticus nodded. "I need your authorization for remote access to the comms."

Trista spotted the access prompt on her main holo display and granted his request. "Done. Start flapping that silver tongue of yours—and sit down. I need to engage the engines to get us headed away from Earth."

"Of course," Gatticus replied. A moment later, Trista heard his harness *click* into place, and then she engaged the thrusters at one and a half Gs. The engines roared and her stomach lurched as the acceleration pressed her against her seat. As the initial sensation passed, the steady pressure became a welcome reprieve from weightlessness.

"Buddy, keep an eye on those Cygnian kakkers, and let me know if any of them start heading our way."

"Aye-aye, Captain," Buddy replied.

Trista used the nav panel to find all of the star systems they could jump to with their remaining fuel. There were only two options—the Centauri System at just over four light years, or Barnard's System at just under six. She picked Centauri, hoping that whatever had sparked the conflict on Earth it hadn't spread to Earth's colonies yet.

Gatticus's voice interrupted her thoughts as he recorded a message. "This is Executor Gatticus Thedroux of Earth to the 9th Cygnian Fleet. I am returning to Earth aboard the independent transport, *Harlequin.* See the attached ID code and credentials for confirmation of identity. Please confirm friendly status. Over."

Trista didn't hold out much hope for his negotiations. About ten minutes later, the comms chirped with a reply. Considering they were only a few light seconds from Earth, the Cygnians had obviously taken their time to reply. Trista was just about to play the message, when Gatticus beat her to it.

A series of hisses and growls rumbled through the speakers. "This is Queen Rissara of the 9th Fleet. We confirm friendly status for the *Harlequin,* but do not bother returning to Earth. We have seized the planet and re-designated it as an active hunting ground. Do not interfere with our hunters."

Trista scowled. "You want to ask them *why* they seized the planet?"

Gatticus recorded his reply, "My Queen, if I may know the answer, why did you seize Earth? Perhaps there is some way we can resolve this dispute without subjecting the entire population to your hunters?"

This time the reply was much quicker, and it was not the queen who replied, but a computer-generated approximation of a human voice: "Executor Thedroux, please dock your vessel with the *Rissara's Wrath* and report for reprogramming and reassignment."

"So much for friendly status," Trista said.

"What are we going to do?" Buddy asked.

Trista kept an eye on the Cygnian fleet as she considered that very question herself. "We've still got two minutes left before our Alckam drive finishes cooling," she said.

"And then it has to warm up," Gatticus pointed out. "We'll never make it."

"So what do you suggest? We give up?"

"No. Turn around. Make it look like I'm complying with my orders."

But before Trista could do anything, a proximity alert sounded and a yellow blip appeared right behind them, well within effective weapons range. It was a Cygnian transport. The comms chirped with another message, this time from that transport. Trista's hands began to shake. She clamped them around the armrests of her chair and used her ESC to play the waiting message.

More growls and hisses. "Power down your engines, and prepare for boarding."

"Fek that," Trista muttered.

"You can't hope to win a fight with them," Gatticus warned. "You have to do what they say. Perhaps they will show you mercy."

"Sure," Trista snorted. She hauled back on the throttle with one hand to make it look like she was complying with their orders, but with her other hand she activated the *Harlequin's* defensive turret and used the targeting camera to aim for the Cygnian transport's cockpit.

"They're powering weapons!" Buddy said.

Trista pulled the trigger and held it down. Her

target camera flashed with golden lances of fire that stabbed repeatedly through the enemy transport's cockpit. A moment later, it blew open in a glittering rain of shattered glass. The pilot appeared to be dead, but the co-pilot began thrashing in the suddenly airless cockpit. Folding metal shutters rolled out, re-sealing the cockpit. She tried aiming for those, hoping to breach the cockpit once more. Two more lasers snapped out from her turret, drawing condensing white streams of escaping air. Trista grinned, but her elation was short-lived as those gusts of air sputtered out. *They must have plugged the holes.*

Her surprise attack was spent. There was only one thing left to do. "Buddy, spin up the Alckam drive!"

"Where to?"

"No destination! Emergency jump," Trista said as she shoved the throttle up to six *G*s, and activated an automated evasive routine.

"Ayyyye-ayyye!" Buddy howled as the sudden burst of acceleration drew out his syllables.

Trista gritted her teeth against the rib-cracking force of the engines, and switched to hands-free control of the *Harlequin*.

The Cygnian transport returned fire, sky-blue lasers flashing by on all sides. A moment later the

Harlequin's combat computer produced a hissing *crunch* to signal an impact. A damage alert squawked, and Trista glanced at it.

"We're losing cabin pressure!" Gatticus announced, reading the report before she could. He didn't sound at all fazed by the high Gs they were pulling.

Must be nice to be an android, Trista thought. The Alckam drive began spinning up, and a jump timer appeared at the top of Trista's main display. *Eleven minutes.* She grimaced. That was fast for a transport, but not nearly fast enough under the circumstances. She wished now that she'd found some way to upgrade the drive system. She also wished that she'd had the sense to wear a pressure suit. As it was, wearing just a jumpsuit, all it would take was one lucky hit to the cockpit, and she'd be in big trouble.

Trista used her ESC to keep up a steady stream of return fire with the *Harlequin's* defensive turret. Golden laser beams snapped out to punch holes in the enemy transport's outer hull, but there were no telltale bursts of escaping air. *It must have thick armor,* Trista thought.

The jump timer hit nine minutes, but it may as well have been counting down from infinity. Trista desperately targeted another part of the Cygnian transport, hoping to score a lucky hit on its antimatter containment tanks.

Another *crunch* sounded from her combat computer, followed by another damage alert.

"Cabin pressure is down to sixty percent!" Gatticus announced. "I can't deploy repair drones until you stop accelerating."

We stop accelerating and we die, Trista thought. *We don't need air in the cabin right now.* Buddy's eyes darted to hers, wide and bulging with terror. She tried to offer a reassuring smile, but the Gs they were pulling turned her expression into a grimace.

She directed her attention to the *Harlequin's* targeting systems, and aimed for another part of the Cygnian transport. Golden laser beams stabbed its hull once more, again to no effect. Being a military transport, the Cygnian ship probably had two hulls.

"They're not firing missiles at us," Gatticus said. "They must be trying to take us alive."

Probably so they can send us down to Earth to be hunted with everyone else, Trista thought. *Too bad, kakkers, you're gonna have to kill me.*

Another *crunch* sounded from the *Harlequin's* combat computer, but this time the noise was drowned out by a much louder *roaring* sound. Trista's ears popped and her guts clenched. A violent wind whipped by her, tugging at her hair and making her eyelids flutter.

"The cockpit's been breached!" Gatticus yelled to be heard over the sound of escaping air. "You have to kill the engines!"

Trista fought to stay conscious in the increasingly-thin air. She mentally activated an airflow sensor to identify the location of the leak, and watched on her main holo display as a holographic representation of her ship appeared. The hull panel directly above her head began flashing. Straining to look up, she spotted a thumb-sized hole glaring back at her. It wouldn't take much to plug it, but all the loose articles in the cockpit were securely stowed under her and Buddy's seats, and the hull patch kit was in a compartment under the floor, out of reach. Trista began to hyperventilate in the thin air.

"Trista!" Gatticus screamed. He sounded very far away. "Kill the engines!"

I guess we're dead anyway, she thought, with heavy lids sinking over blurry, dimming eyes. She killed the engines with a final lucid thought, and then blacked out.

CHAPTER 32

When Trista came to, she heard the slapping sound of a butcher's mallet tenderizing meat. The meat turned out to be her cheek, and the mallet was Gatticus's hand.

"Wake up!" he said.

"Ouch," she mumbled and rubbed her stinging cheek. It had certainly been tenderized. Dead ahead, the white eye of a warp disc glared at her. "What the..." Trista trailed off.

A *thunking* noise sounded from the cockpit door.

"We've got company," Gatticus explained.

Adrenaline stabbed through Trista's veins, and her eyes flew wide. "Cygnians?"

Gatticus shook his head. "No, your ex."

The thunking noise returned, followed by the

muffled sound of a familiar voice. "Open the door, Tris!"

Trista's eyelids fluttered in shock. "What? *How?*"

"Jaxon followed you to Earth on one of Yuri Mathos's ships, the *Death's Head*. He must have checked the course you plotted before we forced him off the *Harlequin*."

Trista gaped at Gatticus. "What about the Cygnians and the breach in the cockpit?"

"Repair drones sealed the breach, and the *Death's Head* took care of the Cygnians. They docked and jumped away with us before the Cygnians could send reinforcements. Under the circumstances, we are very fortunate to have been followed."

"I don't believe it," Trista muttered. "How long was I out?" She caught a flicker of movement in the corner of her eye and turned to see Buddy shaking himself awake.

"I'm alive!" he crowed.

"A few hours," Gatticus replied. "I had to stun you both to slow your metabolisms and keep you alive until the cockpit was re-pressurized."

"How does that work?" Trista asked.

Gatticus handed Trista her sidearm, and hefted a portable oxygen tank with a mask dangling from it. "Stunning you slowed your breathing. The air in the cockpit was too thin to breathe, and I could only find one emergency oxygen tank for the two of you. It was mostly empty. You must have forgotten to refill it."

"Are you going to open this door, or do I have to cut it open?" Jaxon demanded.

Trista pulled the release lever for her harness and held her sidearm in a tight grip as she rounded the pilot's seat to face the door. Aiming her gun at the door, she waved it open.

Jaxon stood there in an armored pressure suit, his face clearly visible through the transparent visor of his helmet. He was aiming a laser rifle at her chest.

"Get off my ship," Trista demanded.

"*Your* ship?" Jaxon scoffed and shook his head. "You're welcome, by the way."

"For what?"

"For saving your life!"

"Is that what you were doing? I suppose re-possessing the *Harlequin* had nothing to do with your heroism."

Jaxon gave a sly smile. "Does it matter? You're alive, aren't you?"

"Enough. Move," a new voice growled. Jaxon stepped aside, and another individual in an armored pressure suit walked in.

Trista's whole body went cold as she recognized the man. His face was covered in pitch-black fur. He had a square jaw, a short snout, and piercing blue eyes. Most humans had a hard time telling aliens apart, but Trista could have picked this one out of a crowd of black-furred, blue-eyed Lassarians.

"Yuri," Trista said, smiling crookedly to hide her terror. "I'm flattered that you came for me personally."

He stepped into the cockpit, heedless of the fact that Trista was pointing a gun at him. His own weapon remained in a low-slung holster on his thigh.

"Hello, Trista," he said, and lifted his chin so that he was peering down his nose at her. "It's been a long time."

"Not long enough. You must be scraping the bottom of the barrel to come after a small fish like me."

Yuri flashed a mouth full of sharp, pointed white teeth and nodded over her shoulder to Gatticus. "This must be the Executor you were transporting."

"I am," Gatticus confirmed. "The Executor of Earth, to be exact."

"Former Executor of Earth," Yuri corrected. "Based on the... unfortunate situation we found you in, it would seem you had a difference of opinion with your Cygnian masters about the invasion of Earth."

"You could say that," Gatticus replied.

Yuri nodded, and his bright blue eyes found Trista's once more. "I would like to extend an invitation for you to join my organization."

Trista snorted. "And become a terrorist like you? I don't think so."

Yuri rolled his head from side to side. "The Cygnians attacked and seized your home world with no provocation. There is no longer any distinction between terrorists and freedom fighters. Now, there are only two sides: those who stand with us, and those who do not."

Trista shook her head. "That sounds like a familiar tune. Just because some people aren't actively fighting the Cygnians, doesn't mean you can steal their cargoes and commandeer their ships."

Yuri conceded that with a nod. "I admit we have been forced to do some disreputable things to survive, but now that is coming to an end. Word of Earth's fate will spread, and as it does, entire star systems will flock to join the Coalition."

"The Coalition?" Trista echoed with a knitted brow. "*You're* part of the Coalition? I thought the Union wiped them out years ago."

Yuri smiled. "The Coalition Fleet was wiped out, not the Coalition itself. So, what do you say? Are you ready to fight back?"

"I am," Gatticus said.

Trista glanced over her shoulder to find him nodding.

Yuri flashed his pointy white teeth in a grin. "Having an Executor on our side will add great legitimacy to our cause."

"I'm not a citizen," Buddy said. "Can I still join?" He was perched on the back of his seat, his claws digging into the material to keep from floating away.

"Of course," Yuri replied. "All are welcome to join the Coalition, not just those the Cygnians deem worthy of inclusion in their Union."

"Then I'll join if you do, Tris," Buddy said.

Trista turned back to Yuri with a frown. "What if I say no?"

"Then we'll drop you at the nearest Union station or planet."

"Without my ship," Trista guessed.

"I'm afraid there's some confusion as to its rightful owner." Jaxon chuckled at that, and Yuri grinned once more. "Regardless, we need every ship we can get, so I'm afraid we cannot allow you to keep it—especially not after risking all of our lives to acquire it. Look at it this way, if we hadn't come after you, your life *and* your vessel would have been forfeit. Now you are only losing the latter."

Fekking thieves, Trista thought. But Yuri was right, he *had* just saved her life—even if that hadn't been his primary concern. Besides, she couldn't keep or sell her ship now—not after using it to attack a Cygnian transport. Come to think of it, since that vessel was registered to *her,* and not Jaxon, there was no question as to who had fired on that transport. She was an outlaw already, whether she liked it or not. Yuri's invitation to join his gang was just a formality.

"All right," Trista said in a resigned voice. "Count me in."

Yuri grinned and held out one four-fingered hand. She hesitated before shaking it.

"Welcome to the Coalition," he said.

CHAPTER 33

—FOUR DAYS LATER—

The Osprey shivered and shook with the turbulence and friction of atmospheric entry. The clouds parted, and Darius saw the surface of Cratus appear—a vast planet-wide ocean speckled with dense clusters of crescent-shaped green islands. The islands formed familiar patterns— partial circles of varying sizes. Tanik explained that the islands were actually the partially-submerged rims of impact craters. Asteroid impacts were an on-going threat, which was why the planet remained uninhabited and had never evolved intelligent life.

Cratus's proximity to Cygnus Prime, at just three light years away, made it worth the risk to establish a forward base there.

As Tanik flew them down to one of the larger

islands, Darius noted that it was surrounded by pristine white beaches and sparkling blue-green water. It looked like one of the Caribbean islands from Earth.

"Wow!" Cassandra said from the seat behind his. "Now *this* is my kind of planet! You think the ocean is safe to swim in?"

"Perfectly safe," Tanik replied. "Shallow, too."

"Mega snaz! I'm going to the beach as soon as we land!"

"After your training," Tanik corrected.

Dyara flashed a smile at Darius. She was sitting across the aisle from him on the other side of the cockpit.

"I do not know how to swim," Gakram growled. Darius couldn't see him, since he was sitting at the back of the cockpit beside Cassandra, but he could imagine the Banshee's four black eyes squinting speculatively, and his lips curling away from six-inch gray teeth in his version of a frown.

"It's easy. I'll teach you," Cassandra said.

Darius didn't like the idea of them spending any more time together than they already did, but there wasn't much he could do about it. Gakram and Cassandra had forged an unlikely friendship over the past several weeks. Darius wasn't sure what to think of it. He tried not to judge Gakram by his species, but it wasn't easy. Cassandra was training to join a war with Gakram's people, and somehow Darius was supposed to believe that Gakram didn't mind? Then again, Gakram was also training for that war, and he wasn't the only Cygnian being placed in that position.

There were more than fifty Cygnian Revenants aboard the *Harbinger* alone, and over a thousand of them scattered throughout the Revenant fleet. What did they think of Admiral Ventaris's battle plans?

In theory, they would only attack if their threats and ultimatums failed, but from everything Darius knew about the Cygnians, he doubted threats would be enough. Where would the Cygnian Revenants' loyalties lie if it came to a fight?

A pair of Ospreys roared by trailing bright blue tongues of fire from their engines. They reached the landing zone, stopped, and hovered down into a green field with scattered black-trunked, red-leafed trees. Tanik brought their Osprey down beside one of the trees. The wind produced by their landing jets sent leaves raining down all over the cockpit canopy. They looked like rose petals.

"Beautiful," Dyara whispered, peering up as

rose petals fluttered down from a clear blue sky.

The Osprey touched down with a jolt and a muffled *thud-unk,* and the roar of the transport's engines faded to a ringing silence.

Tanik released his harness with a loud *click* and turned to face them as he stood. "Welcome to Cratus."

* * *

Four hours later, Ospreys and shuttles were still roaring down from orbit. The grassy green field that was their landing zone had disappeared under white rolls of habitat canvas. Large white domes sprouted like mushrooms.

This time it wasn't just the crew of the *Deliverance* who were setting up camp, but a full complement of 4,560 Revenants from the *Harbinger* as well.

Darius and the other Acolytes had spent the last four hours helping to set up camp, but now, after a short break for rations and water, Tanik pulled them aside for training. He took them down a gentle slope toward the water, getting some distance from the noisy bustle of the camp.

Before long, beads of sweat were streaming down Darius's back and face and soaking through his jumpsuit. Cratus was a hot world. *At least we're not wearing suits of armor like the other Revenants.* Trainees weren't given armor because Tanik said they might be tempted to rely on it instead of their ZPF shields, which would be a deadly mistake. Darius had never really bought that excuse. He would have liked the added buffer against the threat of dismemberment and death, but now, he was glad not to be wearing any extra layers. *Unless those suits are air conditioned...* They probably were. All the Revenants he'd seen on the surface so far had been wearing their helmets. There had to be a reason for that. *Keep the cold air in,* Darius thought, with an accompanying flash of jealousy.

Tanik stopped walking and turned to face them. They were at least a kilometer from the ocean, but here the grass thinned out to scraggly clumps, and sand was mixed liberally with the dirt.

"Break into your usual sparring teams, and spread out," Tanik instructed. "Now that we have some real space to work with, I want you to practice what I taught you aboard the *Deliverance* — jumping, running, and kinetic attacks."

People broke off into their usual pairs: Dyara went with Seelka, the white-eyed Vixxon. Arok, the black-furred Lassarian, went with Flitter, the flying, bat-like Murciago, and Cassandra went with Gakram. That left Darius to face Tanik—as usual.

Tanik gave him a snarling grin. "Perhaps this time you will be able to offer more of a challenge."

Darius drew his sword and summoned a shield to envelop both himself and his blade. Tanik did likewise, and they began circling each other at a distance. Darius reached out into the scrubby field, using the ZPF to look for any loose rocks he could throw at Tanik, but all he found were pebbles. He was just about to give up when he felt something much bigger than a rock. It was a rotting log, lying far away on the beach. Darius picked it up with his mind and sent it sailing toward Tanik. Because of the distance, it took a few seconds to reach Tanik. By the time it did, it was moving so fast that it was nothing but a blur.

Right before the log could slam into Tanik, he leapt over it, flying at least twenty feet into the air. The log plowed into the field behind him with a thunderous roar, pushing up an impressive bow wave of sand and dirt.

Tanik landed lightly, laughing. "Nice try."

So much for that, Darius thought. He circled closer, realizing he'd have to rely on swordplay to win this fight—not that winning seemed possible.

Tanik's free hand twitched, and Darius

stopped advancing, wary of a trap. Thick clouds of sand and pebbles floated up all around them, shimmering in the sun until they blotted it out and blocked Tanik from view.

Groping in the sudden twilight and choking on sand, Darius used his awareness to look for Tanik—

Just in time to see him come soaring down directly overhead. Darius blocked a heavy swipe of Tanik's luminous sword, but his knees buckled with the sheer force of the attack, and he was forced to use the imparted momentum to roll out of the way. As he did so, clouds of pebbles and sand battered him on all sides, driven by howling, hurricane force winds. Soon pebbles began breaking through his shield with bruising force. The pain was enough to break his focus and collapse his shield entirely. At that point things went from bad to worse. The pebbles beat him senseless and sand dug into his skin in fiery waves.

The attack ended and Darius lay there stunned and bleeding, gasping against the pain, and wincing up into a blinding yellow sun. Tanik's shadow fell over him a moment later. His glowing sword swept down for the kill. Darius focused on shielding himself once more and brought his own blade up just in time to avoid being cut in half. He lay there, furious from the pain, and pushing feebly back with both arms as Tanik pressed down with all of his weight. Darius tried to knock him away with a kinetic blast, but Tanik was ready for it, having rooted his feet to the ground.

"You disappoint me, Darius. Perhaps I should just kill you now and rid myself of the burden of your training."

Darius gritted his teeth and shook his head. "You're bluffing."

"Am I?" Tanik smiled wickedly and pressed harder, pushing Darius's own blade down to his chest. The luminous white edge touched the very same shield that enveloped it, and created some kind of a feedback loop that roared with deafening force. Moments later, Darius felt the sharp bite of his own sword slicing through his skin and cried out in pain.

The weight on his sword abruptly lifted as Tanik whirled away to block some unseen attack. Darius pushed himself up on one elbow to see Cassandra locked in a frantic battle with Tanik, her sword flashing against his in a frenzy of strikes. She was actually pushing him back.

Darius scrambled to his feet to help her, but as he did so, a cloud of sand and pebbles rose shimmering into the air. Darius imagined

Cassandra being pummeled with sand and rocks until she was a bloody mess like him, and a flash of fury burst within him.

He dropped his shield and sword to better focus his energy into a kinetic assault. Darius found Tanik inside the hovering cloud of sand and pebbles, picked him up, and threw him as hard as he could. Sand and pebbles fell in a clattering rain, and the air cleared as Tanik lost his focus.

Cassandra stood with her sword frozen in mid-parry and confusion written all over her face. Tanik had disappeared.

Darius whirled around, expecting a surprise attack from above or behind, but none came. Reaching out in the ZPF, he found Tanik—a luminous white speck sailing down into the ocean with a visible splash.

For that plume of water to be visible at this distance, Tanik had to have hit the water *hard*.

"Did *you* do that?" Cassandra asked.

"I..." Darius trailed off, shaking his head. He could feel Tanik's mind, but only dimly. The man was sinking below the waves. "Grak it, I think I knocked him out!"

Darius ran to the beach, drawing on the ZPF to go faster. He heard footsteps pounding after him as the other Acolytes followed.

As Darius reached the water, he used his awareness once more, and found Tanik drifting in darkness, some five hundred meters out. Darius grabbed the man with his mind and carried him swiftly over the waves to the hard-packed sand at the water's edge.

Darius reached Tanik's side and fell on his knees to check for a pulse. The others arrived and clustered around.

"Is he dead?" Dyara asked.

"He's not breathing," Darius replied.

"He's just pretending!" Cassandra scoffed.

Seelka shook her head. "I cannot sense him."

"Quiet!" Darius snapped, struggling to remember his CPR training. He turned Tanik's head to the side and yanked his mouth open. A stream of water poured out. As soon as it slowed to a dribble, Darius turned Tanik's head back to the center, pinched his nose shut, and blew into his lungs several times in a row. He leaned back to check for a pulse, but didn't get one, so he went back to blowing air down the man's throat.

About halfway through his third breath, a gout of warm water leapt into his mouth, and Darius recoiled, spluttering.

Tanik was awake, coughing and gasping for air, his whole body spasming with the effort to clear his lungs. Gakram and Arok helped turn him on his side, but he slapped their hands away, and vomited all over the beach.

Tanik stumbled to his feet and opened his mouth. A stream of water gushed out and splattered on the sand, pushed from his lungs by unseen forces. Wiping his mouth on his sleeve, Tanik's green eyes narrowed in a scowl and flicked to Darius.

Expecting an attack, Darius began to draw on the ZPF to shield himself, but before he could, Tanik smiled and said, "Very challenging indeed."

CHAPTER 34

After Tanik's brush with death, he declared the training session over and led them back to camp. He and Darius both recovered their swords along the way.

The Acolytes followed Tanik up the long, gentle slope to the grassy field of the landing zone. As they crested that rise, a gleaming city of white domes sprawled out before them, arranged in a large circle with streets radiating from the center like the spokes of a wheel. The Ospreys had all been moved to a dedicated landing field to one side of the camp, along with a few squadrons of Vulture and Shrike fighters.

It looked like all of the habitats were set up at this point, and Darius couldn't see or hear any more transports coming down from orbit. Tanik led them down the other side of the hill to the edge of camp. They passed a pair of perimeter guards and started down a street of trampled grass. A pair of six-wheeled rovers rumbled down the street ahead of them, kicking up grass and dirt. Revenant soldiers in silvery armor worked along the sides of the street planting metal poles in the ground and stringing lights between them with the ZPF.

Side streets branched off between the habitats periodically, but Tanik showed no sign of changing course. He was heading straight for the center of camp, where a particularly large habitat rose like a mountain above the others.

"Where are we going?" Cassandra whispered, finally breaking the silence.

"To the command center to get our hab assignments," Tanik replied.

They walked on for at least two kilometers, passing hundreds of habitats along the way. As they drew near to the large habitat module in the center of camp—what had to be the command center—Darius noticed two six-wheeled rovers parked out front, and a pair of armored guards stood outside the doors. To one side of the command center, another half a dozen rovers were parked in a cordoned field, facing four two-legged mechs with nine-foot versions of the Revenants' swords.

Darius wondered about those mechs. *The Revenant version of a tank?* He slowly tore his eyes away, just in time to see Tanik come to a sudden stop. He held up a hand, indicating for the Acolytes to do the same.

Darius sent Dyara a questioning look. She shrugged and shook her head. A moment later he had his answer. He spotted a group of six giant Cygnians in black armor advancing on the front doors of the command center. From their massive size and the fact that they were walking on two legs, rather than six, Darius assumed they must be Ghouls rather than Banshees.

The two Revenant soldiers standing guard outside the command center adopted a wary stance and turned toward the incoming Ghouls.

Just then, Admiral Ventaris burst outside. The doors of the command center flapped restlessly in the wind of his passing before resealing themselves along a magnetic seam. The admiral was a giant of a man, at least six and a half feet tall, with broad shoulders and a thick chest, but the Cygnians were a head and shoulders even taller than him, and far more impressively built. They stopped a few feet away and glared down on the admiral with the four glowing red eyes of their helmets.

Each of them wore four short swords that dangled from their chests and hips, and they stood with their hands either resting on the hilts or with long, curving claws twitching restlessly beside them.

Darius cringed at the sight of the standoff, but Admiral Ventaris didn't seem intimidated.

"Can I help you, Sentinel?" he asked.

The front most of the Cygnians tossed his head and growled in an amplified voice. "You gave orders for my people to be reassigned to the *Nomad*, and to make camp on a separate island."

"That's right," Admiral Ventaris replied. "Is there a problem with that?"

"The *Nomad* is the smallest and weakest vessel in the fleet."

Admiral Ventaris spread his hands in a shrug. "Your numbers are few. It makes no sense to give you a larger ship."

The Cygnian hissed loudly. "*Why* did you reassign my people?"

"To prevent unnecessary incidents. We are preparing to threaten and possibly attack your worlds. Some of the other Revenants are starting to see you as the enemy, so the less they see of you the better, wouldn't you say?"

The Cygnian raised two fists and shook them

in the admiral's face. "Do *you* see us as the enemy?"

"Of course not," Admiral Ventaris said, smiling blandly in the face of the accusation.

"I don't believe you. I think you are trying to consolidate us in one place so that you can kill us more easily. I also do not believe that you are planning to *threaten* my people. You are planning a preemptive strike to attack all of our worlds at the same time. You are planning xenocide."

Admiral Ventaris appeared taken aback. "If that is what you think, I am surprised you haven't already tried to rip out my throat!"

"Perhaps I should," the Cygnian growled, looming toward him.

"You are welcome to try." The Admiral grabbed the hilt of his sword, as did the guards standing behind him, but no one drew their weapons—yet.

Darius could feel the zero-point field crackling with tension. Like the calm before a storm, the air felt heavy with dark and violent rumblings.

"We'd better back him up," Tanik said, and took off at a run. Darius and the other Acolytes hesitated before running after him.

The Cygnians turned to look as they approached, momentarily distracted by their arrival. The glowing red eyes of their helmets glared.

Tanik reached the admiral's side first and fixed the Cygnians with a dark look. "Is something wrong?" he asked.

As Darius and the others arrived, the Cygnians wordlessly turned and stalked away.

"Thank you, Tanik," Admiral Ventaris said, watching the Cygnians go. He ran a hand through his short, crew-cut black hair and shook his head. "That was about to get ugly."

"Is it true?" Cassandra asked. "You separated them from us?"

A low, unintelligible growl sounded beside her, and Gakram bared his teeth in a fearsome snarl.

The admiral smiled thinly at them. "I'm afraid I had no choice. Several deadly fights already broke out while we were in-transit to Cratus."

"Twenty-one days is a long jump," Dyara said. "Some degree of tension is to be expected. You're going to make things worse if you start separating the Revenants into groups of *them* and *us*."

The admiral snorted. "I don't see how things can get much worse. A Vixxon Adept on my ship had his arm ripped off by a Banshee. He nearly died. The Banshee responsible was thrown out an airlock. On another ship, a group of three Lassarian Advocates ambushed a pair of Ghouls in their sleep. Only one of the Lassarians escaped, but he later died of his injuries in the med bay. There have been several other, lesser incidents as well, that merely resulted in disfiguring scars. Under the circumstances, segregating the Cygnians is the safest thing for everyone."

Gakram growled once more, but this time his words were perfectly clear. "What about me? Do I have to go to the other island?"

Admiral Ventaris nodded. "I'm sorry, but yes. It's as much for your sake as for anyone else's. We don't want anyone trying to sneak up on *you* in your sleep."

Gakram hissed. "Let them try."

The admiral favored him with a dry look. "Yes, while I'm sure that you can take care of yourself, I'd rather not lose any more people." Ventartis's hazel eyes slid away from Gakram to regard Tanik once more. "Was there something you needed?"

Tanik nodded. "Hab assignments for my Acolytes."

"Of course. Go inside and ask for Staff Sergeant Asaris. She's the Advocate in charge of those assignments. When you're done, come back and find me. I need to speak with you—" His eyes flicked briefly over the Acolytes standing behind Tanik. " —privately."

"Of course," Tanik replied.

At that, Darius heard a clamor of whispering voices, all demanding his attention at the same time. It was the same sound that he'd heard in his visions, and while waking on a few occasions. Each time he'd heard the sound, it seemed to be a warning, maybe from the Sprites themselves, but what were they trying to warn him about this time?

Darius wondered about that as they walked through the doors of the command center. A degree of secrecy was normal in the upper echelons of any army, but Darius had a bad feeling that this was something else—something much more sinister.

CHAPTER 35

After receiving her hab assignment, Cassandra asked for permission to go find Gakram and say goodbye. Darius made a face like he wanted to say no, or like he was about to invite himself along, but Dyara whispered something in his ear to stop him from being such a *Dad*.

Cassandra smiled. She'd been abandoned by her real mother, so she didn't have anything to compare to, but so far Dyara seemed pretty *snaz* for an adult.

Cassandra found Gakram standing around one of the Ospreys with the Ghouls they'd seen back at the command center. They were in the middle of what looked to be a heated discussion, but they abruptly stopped talking as she'd approached. The Ghouls turned to glare at her with their black helmets and glowing red eyes. Cassandra wasn't sure what was more terrifying—a Cygnian helmet, or their regular faces.

"Hey, Gakram!" Cassandra called out, and waved to him from what she judged to be a safe distance.

He bounded over on six legs and growled at her in a low voice. "What do you need?"

"I..." Cassandra glanced at the Ghouls. All six of them were staring at her. She suppressed a shiver and looked away. "I thought maybe we could go down to the beach together."

Gakram hesitated. "I have to go soon."

"Right now?"

"Let me ask when they are leaving." Gakram hurried back over to the Osprey. He spoke for a moment with one of the Ghouls, and then darted back to Cassandra. He flashed a fearsome grin. "I have two hours."

Cassandra smiled. "Good enough! Let's go!"

They hurried through the camp at a brisk pace, passing countless soldiers along the way. When they reached the edge of camp, Cassandra said, "Race you to the water!" and took off at a run. She drew on the ZPF until her legs turned to a blur. The grass rustling past her legs became a steady roar. Gakram ran by her a split second later.

"Hey no fair!" Cassandra said. "You've got six legs!"

He reached the beach a minute before she did. She found him seated on his haunches at the edge of the beach with all four of his arms crossed over his chest. His mouth hung open in a gaping grin. "You are slow," he growled.

"No... you're fast!" Cassandra panted. She collapsed and lay on the warm sand, squinting at the sun, dizzy with exhaustion. "It's too hot!" she breathed, rolling her head from side to side. "I have to get in the water."

Gakram padded up beside her like a giant dog. "Let me help you."

Cassandra's brow furrowed as she tried to figure out what he meant by that. In the next instant she felt his arms reaching under her and scooping her off the beach.

"What are you—heeeyyy!" She broke off in a scream as Gakram leapt into the air with her cradled in the lower two of his four arms. The beach fell away in a dizzying swirl, and clear blue water took its place, rushing up fast. Wind ripped at Cassandra's hair as they fell. She had just enough time to suck in a breath and hold it before they hit the water.

As they plunged below the surface, Gakram let

go, and she kicked her way to the surface. It wasn't easy with her boots on, but she managed to compensate by drawing on the ZPF to *push* herself up. She broke the surface, spluttering salty water. A soggy curtain of hair hung in front of her face. She swept it away with one hand, while treading water to stay afloat. "That wasn't funny, Gakram! I thought you couldn't swim!" She looked around for him. "Gakram? Kak!" She sucked in a breath and dived back down. Forcing her eyes open despite the sting of salt water, she searched the sandy bottom. She spotted a dark, blurry shape up ahead, at least ten feet down, and striding along the bottom on six legs like a crab.

Cassandra kicked back up and swam for the shore. When she was still a dozen feet from the beach, Gakram's head broke the surface in front of her. She swam up beside him and they walked out together. Cassandra collapsed in the wet sand at the water's edge, and he sat down beside her.

"You didn't tell me... you could breathe underwater!" Cassandra accused, gasping for air again.

"I can't," Gakram growled. "I held my breath."

"That long?"

"Yes."

"Well, how did you walk along the bottom like

that?"

"Cygnians don't float. We sink. That is why I don't know how to swim."

Cassandra snorted and shook her head. She pushed herself up onto her elbows and looked out over the shimmering water as she caught her breath and calmed her racing heart. Waves swished up the beach, tickling her hands and carving hollows in the sand around her fingers. A somber silence grew between them as they sat there drip-drying in the afternoon sun. Cassandra wasn't ready to say goodbye. Would she even be allowed to visit Gakram on his island? It wasn't fair.

"I have something I want to tell you," Gakram said slowly.

She turned to him and waited for him to go on.

"It's a secret," he added, not looking at her. "You cannot tell anyone. Not even your father."

"I won't. I promise."

The muscles around two of Gakram's eyes twitched, and then his giant head turned to meet her gaze, his black eyes blinking and squinting. The slits in his neck flared as he sucked in a deep breath. "We are leaving Cratus."

"We are?" Cassandra asked.

"Not you. We. My people."

"What?" Cassandra couldn't contain her outrage. "Ventaris is making you leave? He can't do that! You're Revenants, too!"

"He is not *making us* leave. We are leaving because we know that we must. Because we know what is coming. Perhaps the admiral does, too, and that is why he gave us our own ship—to make it easier for us to go."

"You know what's coming...?" Cassandra trailed off. "What do you mean?"

"The war, Cassssandra," he replied, drawing out her name in a hiss. "The admiral is planning to slaughter my people. He isn't going to give us any warning, or any chance to surrender. He's just going to jump in, drop his bombs, and leave. My people are not prepared to fight Revenants, or weapons that can destroy entire planets. They have no idea what is coming. So we are leaving. We have to warn them."

"But..." Cassandra shook her head. "Then they'll be ready for us when we come."

"Yes. That is the point."

"A lot of Revenants could die, Gakram! *I* could die!"

Gakram said nothing to that. "That is why I am telling you. So that you know to stay away."

"What about my dad? And Dyara? What about

Seelka and Flitter!? You said I can't tell anyone, so how do I warn them?"

"You cannot. Not if they will tell the admiral."

Cassandra shook her head. "There has to be a better way, Gakram. Maybe we can negotiate..." She trailed off, remembering her father's recurring vision. He'd seen her dead, killed for trying to negotiate with the Cygnians, and he was still having that vision. He never said anything to her anymore, but she'd overheard him talking to Dyara about it a few times on their way to Cratus.

"Yes, we could try to negotiate," Gakram growled. "And that is the other reason I am telling you that we are leaving. There is an ancient Cygnian prophecy about an alien child who comes to warn my people of the return of the Destroyers."

"The Destroyers?" Cassandra echoed. "Wait— an *alien child?* You mean like *me?*"

"You could fit the description, yes," Gakram said.

"Why are you only telling me this now?"

Gakram's barbed tail slapped the sand behind him. "It did not seem relevant before. Now it is. If you come with us, we might be able to convince the Old Ones to grant the Union its independence without a fight."

Cassandra shook her head. "No. My dad

warned me about this. I can't go. They'll kill me if I try."

Gakram gave a hissing reply, "Tanik told us that visions are not always certain. And even if you *are* killed, does that mean that the negotiations failed? Perhaps your sacrifice could save us all."

"If your people *kill* me, I think it's safe to say that the negotiations fail. I'm sorry, Gakram. Prophecy or no prophecy, I can't go."

"I understand. It takes great courage to see one's own death coming and not flinch as it approaches."

Cassandra grimaced, chagrined by her own cowardice—if that's what this was. She wasn't ready to call it that. "Maybe if you'd told me about this prophecy thing sooner..." she trailed off, shaking her head.

"It is okay, Cass. I cannot ask you to risk your life for my people. That is my burden, not yours." With that, he stood up and shook himself dry like a dog, spraying Cassandra with water.

"Hey!"

Gakram's mouth hung open in a rueful grin. "Goodbye, Cass. I will miss you."

Cassandra jumped to her feet. "Hang on. I'll walk you to your ship."

They walked back to the camp under a heavy

blanket of silence. Halfway there they ran into Tanik. He just stood there on the slope, staring off into the distance, as if in a daze. Cassandra watched him with a frown. As they approached, he snapped out of it, and his green eyes found them with a wan smile. "Did you have a nice swim?"

"Yesss," Gakram hissed.

"What are you doing out here?" Cassandra asked.

Tanik nodded to her. "Your father is looking for you."

"So *you* came looking for us? Why isn't *he* here? And why were you just standing there like a statue."

"He is helping to prepare dinner. And I was just standing there because I sensed your approach. I decided to stop and admire the view while I waited for you come to me."

Cassandra glanced over her shoulder at the view: a clumpy field rolling out to a bar of white sand and a thin blue line of water along the horizon. It wasn't much to look at.

"Come. We should not keep your father waiting." With that, Tanik about-faced and led them the rest of the way back to camp.

CHAPTER 36

That night they ate grilled fish under the stars. Apparently some of the Revenants had gone down to the water and caught those fish earlier.

Gakram's absence around the camp fire made Cassandra feel hollow inside. Her dad kept trying to cheer her up with stupid jokes, and Dyara wanted her to talk about it, but she just wanted to be alone. When she finished eating half a fish, Cassandra excused herself to take a shower in the outdoor facilities, which had running water thanks to pumps with snaking pipes that ran from a nearby stream.

When she was done, Cassandra strolled aimlessly down the grassy streets, looking for the Acolytes' habitat. Silver light bloomed from the strings of lights on the street poles overhead. It was just barely enough to illuminate the gleaming white letters beside the doors of the habitats as she went by—*C-26, C-27, C-28...* The Acolytes' complex was *D-42*. She was on the wrong street.

Cassandra cut through the next side street to reach "D." The side streets were unlit, so it took Cassandra's eyes a moment to adjust to the sudden plunge into darkness. Once they did, she saw a pair of glinting eyes watching her.

Her hand fell to her sword. "Hello?"

"Cassandra," a guttural male voice whispered. The man stepped forward, closer to the light pooling from the street behind her, and she caught a glimpse of shiny scars running across his face. "We need to talk."

It was Tanik. Cassandra frowned. A warm breeze blew down the side street behind her, and she shivered. She felt oddly chilled. Maybe it was because her hair was still wet. "About what?" she asked.

Tanik took another step into the light, and glanced around furtively. "About the Cygnians," he explained. Someone went thumping down the street behind her, and Tanik quickly stepped back into the shadows.

Cassandra glanced behind her and saw a willowy Dol Walin walk by on long, skinny legs.

"Follow me. We can't talk out here," Tanik said, and then started down the alley ahead of her.

Cassandra hesitated. Tanik was not the kind of person she really wanted to follow down a dark alley. And what was he being so secretive about, anyway? Unfortunately, there was only one way to find out. Cassandra crept after him. They reached "D" street, and Tanik led her to the doors of the habitat on the corner—*D-30*. He keyed the magnetic door flaps open from an adjacent control panel and then stepped inside. Cassandra hesitated again, watching the door flaps flutter in the wind of his passing. The chill inside of her had turned to ice. She rubbed her arms and looked around once, quickly, before following Tanik inside.

The habitat was cool and dry inside, just like all the others. The temperature was regulated by the canvas itself, which became cold on the inside, and hot on the outside when connected to an electric current. Moisture condensed naturally on the inside and ran in rivulets down the inside of the domes to collect in drains along the floor, and that water served to flush the habitat's toilets, albeit sparingly.

Cassandra had thought it was a brilliant system when she'd first learned about it, but right now it was doing nothing to help with how cold she felt. She rubbed her arms and shivered. Maybe she was getting sick.

"Come sit down," Tanik said. He was already seated in a high-backed inflatable armchair. Cassandra headed for an inflatable couch and sat in the corner farthest from Tanik. Her sword made sitting awkward, but she maneuvered it so that it dangled to the floor while she perched on the edge of the couch.

"So? What did you want to tell me about the Cygnians?" Cassandra prompted.

"They've all been reassigned to the *Nomad*."

"I know, I was there."

"Yes, but what you don't know is *why*."

Cassandra shook her head. "The Admiral said—"

"He lied. I just came from a meeting with him and a few other high-ranking Sentinels. Before they gave the *Nomad* to the Cygnians, they sabotaged the antimatter containment system. They also re-calibrated the sensors to make sure the problem wouldn't be found until it's too late."

"What? Why would they do that?"

"As insurance. The sabotage won't do anything—unless the Cygnians try to jump away, say for example... to warn their people that we're coming." Tanik's green eyes sharpened, and a faint smile curved his lips.

"I'm sure they wouldn't do that..." Cassandra lied, remembering that Gakram had told her not to tell anyone about his people's plans. She glanced at the door to Tanik's habitat. She had to send Gakram a message to warn him about the sabotage!

"Let's not waste time with lies, Cassandra. Gakram confided his people's plans to you on the beach."

Cassandra's head snapped back around. "How do you know...?"

"Because I was using the ZPF to eavesdrop."

Cassandra blinked in shock. "*That's* what you were doing out there in the field?"

"Yes."

Cassandra shook her head. "Why are you telling me all of this?"

"For two reasons. One, because I don't believe we should start this war by killing our own people. And two, because I'm not sure we need to fight."

Cassandra arched an eyebrow at him. "You think we can get the Cygnians to back down?"

"Gakram told you about the prophecy."

Cassandra's eyes widened. "You know about the prophecy, too?"

"Of course. Anyone who knows anything

about the Church of the Divine Light knows about their prophecies of the end of days."

"Then you think I should do it. You think I should get myself killed by trying to negotiate with them."

Tanik shook his head. "Let's start with the most immediate problem. The *Nomad* is going to jump away, and when it does, it will explode and kill everyone on board. Boom." He mimed an explosion with his hands. "No more Cygnian Revenants. But if someone were to warn them, they could fix the sabotage and jump out safely."

"So get on the comms!" Cassandra snapped. "Why are you wasting time telling me?"

Tanik favored her with a condescending look. "Any message we send would be intercepted and eventually decrypted by Admiral Ventaris. We would be executed for treason. There is, however, a more subtle way to deal with the issue.

"When Gakram told you about the prophecy, let's say that you agreed to go with the Cygnians. A little while later, I learned that you had left. Knowing what I do about the admiral's sabotage, I naturally decide chase after you and bring you back. But when I arrive on the *Nomad* to pick you up, you refuse to leave, so the only way I can save you is by revealing the faulty containment field.

Unfortunately, after that revelation, the Cygnians take me prisoner, and you continue on as planned to fulfill your destiny as the harbinger who was prophesied."

"What?" Cassandra blinked furiously as she tried to understand the point of Tanik's convoluted story. "Wait—we're actually going to go with them to warn their people? Why?"

"To fulfill the prophecy."

"And die! No way." Cassandra shook her head vigorously. "You can go if you want to, but I'm staying on Cratus."

"I'm not the one who was prophesied. The Old Ones won't listen to me. But you won't die. I promise. I won't allow it."

"How can you possibly make that promise? You know about my dad's visions."

"And I also know that visions are rarely cast in stone. The reason the ZPF shows us what it does is so that we can do things differently to avoid the negative outcomes we see. The Sprites are not evil—showing us unavoidable horrors just to torment us. They show us things in order to help us reach our destinies, and your destiny, whether you like it or not, is to negotiate with the Cygnians before they are all wiped out.

"Why do you think *you*, of all people, were the

only one to befriend the Banshee child, Gakram. And why do you think *he* befriended you? It is your destiny to save them, and it is my destiny to save you—should the need arise."

"I don't..." Cassandra frowned, but then a smile quirked her lips into a mischievous grin. "Your destiny is to save a teenage girl? I guess it's all downhill from there, huh?"

Tanik's eyes twinkled with amusement. "This is why you are my favorite student. You have a fine sense of humor."

Cassandra did a double take. "I thought my dad was your favorite student."

"No, your father is a pain in the kakker."

Cassandra burst out laughing. It took a while before she regained her composure, and by the time she did, there were tears streaming from her eyes. She swiped them away and forced herself to be serious. "You promise I won't get killed?"

"I swear it to every god and Sprite in the universe. May they all strike me dead if I fail."

Cassandra let out a slow breath. "Okay, but maybe we should tell my dad."

"No. He won't let you go. You know how he is. He'd grak the whole galaxy just to save your life."

Cassandra snorted. "True. Fine. Let's do it. Do I have time to go back to my hab first?"

"What for?"

"Well, to take a few changes of clothes, at least. The Cygnians don't wear jumpsuits, and even if they did, I have a feeling they wouldn't fit me."

"You have ten minutes to pack a bag. If you run into your father or anyone else, tell them the bag has dirty laundry in it and you're going to wash it in the machines by the river."

"Good thinking."

"When you're ready, meet me at the end of street A. I'll be waiting there, beside a pair of Vultures."

"*Two* fighters? What for? We could both ride in one, and we probably should, since I've never flown anything before."

"Yet you have the training," Tanik pointed out.

She and the other Acolytes had all downloaded flight training modules during the time they'd spent flying to Cratus. But since they'd been in warp the whole time, there'd been no way for any of them to practice that training. "I don't know... I don't even have a flight suit."

"It's a short flight, and you can use the autopilot the whole way. As for the flight suit, I'll make sure there's one waiting for you in the cockpit."

"What if I crash and die? How are you going to

protect me from that?"

"Now you're sounding like your father. You will know what to do once you're in the cockpit. Make sure you engage the fighter's stealth mode to avoid detection. I'll follow you an hour later in the second fighter."

Cassandra's brow tensed. "Do we have enough time for you to wait a whole *hour* to follow me?"

"The Cygnians won't leave until they've evacuated all of their people from the other island. I can still sense some of them there, but they're getting ready to leave, so I suggest you hurry."

"Fine." Cassandra stood on shaking legs. Were they shaking from excitement or fear? Maybe a bit of both. "See you soon," she said, and then turned and ran out the door.

CHAPTER 37

"Here," Tanik whispered, and handed Cassandra an oxygen mask.

She fitted the mask over her mouth and nose; then Tanik handed her a helmet. As she slipped it over her head, the helmet came to life with a series of tones and chimes. Glowing HUD icons appeared. One of them was a blinking O_2 indicator.

"Ready?" Tanik asked.

Cassandra glanced around. Her breath reverberated noisily inside the mask and helmet. She and Tanik were hiding in the shadows between two Vulture fighters at the edge of camp. So far they'd managed to avoid awkward run-ins with Revenant patrols, but Cassandra wasn't sure how much longer that would last.

She'd also been lucky to have avoided a run-in

with her father back at the Acolytes' habitat. When she had arrived at the habitat, Seelka had told her that her dad and Dyara were together in their shared sleeping module. She had taken advantage of their inattention to pack a bag and sneak out. When Seelka had asked where she was going, she'd told the Vixxon exactly what Tanik had told her to say: *"I'm going to do some laundry."*

Seelka had looked confused, probably because Cassandra had never been in a hurry to do chores, so Cass had added *"I don't want to start smelling like Arok."*

Seelka had wrinkled her nose and smiled. *"Good idea."*

Tanik interrupted her thoughts, bringing her back to the present. "Remember to engage stealth mode before you take off," he said.

Cassandra nodded and mentally activated her helmet's external speakers. "Will that be enough?" she whispered. "Won't someone hear me take off?"

Tanik shook his head. "No, because you're not going to light your engines. Not yet, anyway."

"How am I going to take off without engines?"

"I'm going to use the ZPF to launch you."

Cassandra sucked in a quick breath. "You can do that? Is that safe? What happens when you let go?"

"*Then* you light your engines. At that point you'll be far enough away that no one will hear a thing. I've already plotted a course for you in the nav. You can let the autopilot take you the whole way, but do not stray from that course. When the *Nomad* contacts you asking about your approach, tell them that Gakram invited you."

Cassandra's stomach was doing nervous flips, but she nodded. Snatching her pack of supplies off the ground, she turned toward her fighter. The rim of the open cockpit lay just out of reach, and there was no ladder to climb.

"Let me help you," Tanik said.

Invisible hands picked her up, and she hovered into the pilot's seat. She stowed her pack in the webbing under it. *Now what?* she wondered, as she studied the dark squares of three separate holo displays. Her eyes roved over the flight stick and the sliding throttle control, to the numerous banks of switches, buttons, and levers that adorned every available surface. It was overwhelming. Cassandra's heart pounded in her chest and her palms began to sweat inside her gloves. She felt a vague sense of familiarity with the cockpit and its control systems, but she was in the grip of a panic, and couldn't think straight.

"Connect your air hose. It's under your seat,"

Tanik said.

Cassandra fished around under the seat. She found the snake-like hose after just a moment and slotted it into the opening in the chin of her helmet.

"Now secure your acceleration harness."

Cassandra folded out the two halves of the harness. It was more flexible than the ones she was used to. An additional clip fastened a springy cage around her helmet for added support. Cassandra wondered about that as she clipped the harness together.

"Close your canopy," Tanik said. "And find the ignition switch. Don't hit it until I release you. Understood?"

In lieu of a reply Cassandra flashed a thumbs up over the side of her cockpit. She found and depressed the *open/close canopy* button, and the beak-shaped canopy swung down over Cassandra's head with a pneumatic groan. A split second later, her fighter leapt soundlessly into the air, squashing her into her seat. The camp fell away below her, a dizzying sea of white domes with grassy, illuminated streets radiating like spokes from the command center.

It wasn't long before she lost sight of the camp entirely, and the jagged black mountains at the center of the island scrolled into view. Moments later they fell away, too, and the star-dappled sky took their place. Cratus's moon shined down on her, a skinny silver crescent, the same shape as the island below.

How high is Tanik taking me? But even as she thought about that, the upward motion ceased, and Cassandra felt herself being pressed back into her seat as the fighter turned. Soon the island was rolling by beneath her. From this altitude the Revenants' camp looked like an alien growth on the darkened landscape.

A minute later, the island was behind her, and the moonlit canvas of the ocean scrolled out before her like a roll of tinfoil. Then the pressure of acceleration ceased, and the nose of her fighter pitched down. The weightlessness of free fall set in, and Cassandra gripped the armrests of her seat in white-knuckled fists. Air whistled around the fighter as it picked up speed.

Cassandra panicked. *Where's the ignition?* She'd forgotten to identify it earlier. Her eyes skipped around the cockpit, checking switches at random and trying to read their labels. It was too dark to read anything. *Which one is it!?* She needed a flashlight. With a thought, Cassandra activated the headlamps on her helmet, and the inside of the cockpit snapped into focus. She began reading the miniature fonts that identified the various buttons and switches. Air roared around her fighter as it bucked and shivered with turbulence.

Cassandra glanced up. Her fighter couldn't be more than a thousand feet above the water now, and it was descending rapidly. She was out of time. Supposedly she already knew what to do because of the flight training module she'd downloaded. Cassandra stopped worrying for a minute and let her thoughts flow.

To one side of her main holo display she spied a bank of four red switches, linked together. She flicked the switches, even as her eyes registered the words *Engine Start* written above them.

There came a throaty roar, and the cockpit erupted with glowing lights and displays. A bright green heads-up-display flickered into view, projected on the faceplate of her helmet.

Trusting herself, Cassandra grabbed the flight stick, pulled up hard, and slid the throttle forward. Acceleration slammed her into her seat and threatened to rip her hand from the stick, but she tightened her grip and held on until the Vulture leveled out. She let out a ragged sigh and spotted her altitude on the HUD—*three hundred and ten feet*. Another second or two and she'd have been dead.

Cassandra's pulse hammered in her ears. She

carefully rolled some of the tension out of her shoulders and took a moment to orient herself. A blinking green arrow pointed to the right side of her HUD, indicating a nav waypoint. Wondering how to reach it, Cassandra tested the rudder pedals with her feet. The left pedal sent the fighter's nose drifting to the left, and the right pedal sent it drifting to the right. Cassandra tried pushing harder on the right pedal, using rudder alone to bring that nav point into view. It didn't work. Her fighter began trembling with a noisy roar of turbulence. The nose dipped down, and the left wing kicked up. She quickly released the rudder pedal and used a combination of stick and left rudder to bring the Vulture back to straight and level flight.

Again, she had to force herself to rely on instinct. *Don't think. Just do.* This time, Cassandra tilted the stick to the right, applied rudder from the *left* pedal, and pulled up gently on the stick.

To her amazement, the Vulture's nose drew a straight line above the horizon, and a moment later the green diamond of the waypoint swept into view. It was two hundred and four klicks away, and forty thousand feet up.

Cassandra began pulling up to reach that altitude. That was when she remembered Tanik's instructions to engage the fighter's stealth mode. Letting instinct guide her, she found the toggle switch on her dash and flicked it. The noisy roar of her fighter's engines quieted and the Vulture slowed its ascent.

Cassandra let out another sigh and flicked off her helmet lamps to gaze up at the stars while she climbed. As the range to her waypoint scrolled down, she noticed the *Autopilot* button at the bottom of her nav display. She recalled what Tanik had said about using the autopilot, and she touched the button. A series of options appeared, but the course was already laid in, just as Tanik had said it would be. Cassandra engaged the autopilot and the flight stick went limp in her hand. She released it to rest her hands in her lap, settling in for the journey ahead.

Tanik had said he'd follow her after an hour. But how long would it take to reach the *Nomad*? Cassandra mentally queried the autopilot and the answer flashed at the bottom of her HUD.

ETA 1:21:34

Almost, Cassandra nodded to herself. Tanik would be taking off in his fighter just before she reached the Cygnians' ship.

Cassandra's thoughts turned to what lay ahead after that—negotiating with the Cygnians.

Cassandra couldn't believe she'd let herself be talked into it, especially after all of her father's visions. But Gakram would be there to protect her, and so would Tanik. Besides, why would the Cygnians want to kill her anyway? What could they possibly stand to gain by shooting the messenger?

Cassandra laid her head back and allowed her eyes to drift shut. With the autopilot doing all of the flying, she could afford to rest for a little while.

* * *

The autopilot took Cassandra into orbit and halfway around Cratus to reach the *Nomad*. When she was just a hundred klicks out, the Cygnians sent her a curt message, demanding that she identify herself. At that point, Cassandra told them what Tanik had said she should—that Gakram had invited her. They left her waiting for about two minutes, no doubt while they checked with Gakram to confirm her story, and then she'd been granted clearance to land on pad 4B.

It took her most of the way to the *Nomad* to figure out how to feed a specific landing pad into the autopilot.

As the *Nomad* swelled before her, she struggled

to spot the hangar bay. Where was the autopilot taking her?

Her fighter slowed to a crawl and swooped down along the Nomad's hull. *I'm going to crash!* Then she spotted lights flashing down the length of a flat, skinny line in the side of the ship's hull. A pair of magnetic docking clamps came racing down the strip, and a *clu-clunk* sounded as they captured her fighter.

The clamps braked her remaining momentum, and she slammed into her acceleration harness with bruising force. The Vulture shivered to a stop in the center of an illuminated green landing pad, marked *4B* in holographic letters floating on her HUD. In the next instant, the landing pad flipped 90 degrees and carried her sideways into the ship. A pair of metal doors slid shut to her left, sealing the outer hull, and a loud roaring began as air pumped into the space around her fighter. As soon as the sound died away, another pair of doors opened to her right, and the landing pad carried her fighter down a set of rails and into a darkened hangar. Gleaming fighters and Ospreys occupied dozens of matching landing pads and rails.

Cassandra slowly shook her head, peering into the hangar and searching for any signs of life. Why was it so dark? Then she remembered that

Cygnians had very sensitive eyes. They were practically blind in brightly-lit areas. They compensated with their sense of smell and hearing, which was apparently acute enough to create full mental images of their surroundings even with their eyes closed.

She pulled the release lever beside her seat to disengage the harness. Next she removed her air hose and pulled off her helmet. She took a moment to revel in the cool air caressing her hair and face. Stowing the helmet at her feet, she shut down the Vulture's engines and punched the open/close canopy button. Cassandra grabbed a handrail inside the cockpit as it opened, and stood up carefully in the zero-G environment. "Hello?" she called out.

But there was no answer. The hangar was deserted. That was definitely strange. Why was there no one here to greet her? Cassandra reached out in the ZPF and found a Banshee loping toward her on six legs.

"Welcome to the *Nomad*, Cassss," the Banshee said.

"Gakram!" Cassandra recognized that voice. She groped in the dark to find the railings of the staircase that should have folded out beside her cockpit. Finding the railings just below the rim of the cockpit, she climbed down to the deck. Her mag boots drew tinny *clangs* from the steps as she went.

"I am glad you changed your mind," Gakram said.

Cassandra turned to face him. "So am I."

"Why did you?" Gakram asked. She saw his giant head tilt to one side, then the other, like a dog. Cassandra smiled at the memory. She missed dogs.

"Tanik spoke with me. He convinced me to come."

"Why would he want you to join us?" Gakram asked. "He is no friend of my people. It was his plan to threaten us and demand independence for the Union. And it was his idea to use the ZPF bombs to do it."

Cassandra shrugged. "Maybe he is more of a friend than you think. He told me something, but... I think he wanted to be the one to tell you. He'll tell you when he lands."

"Lands?" Gakram echoed with a growl. "*Tanik* is coming? We did not invite *him* to join us. *Why* is he coming?"

"It's a long story."

Gakram bared his teeth. "He cannot come."

"He has to! Admiral Ventaris did something to

— 419 —

your ship."

"What did he do?"

Cassandra chewed her bottom lip. "Well, I guess there's no harm in me telling you now..."

Cassandra went on to explain about the sabotage, and Tanik's plan to accompany her to Cygnus Prime as a bodyguard, in case the negotiations didn't go well.

Gakram held his tongue until she was done speaking, but as soon as she stopped, he let out a terrifying shriek that sent her reeling back a step and left her ears ringing. "This treachery will not go unpunished!" Gakram spun around and darted away, bounding across the hangar.

"Wait! Where are you going?" Cassandra called after him.

"To stop Elder Arathos from using the jump drive before we all die!" Gakram replied.

CHAPTER 38

Darius woke up sweating and shuddering with horror. His chest was tight, his breathing shallow. He sat up and the covers fell away, making him shiver. He stifled a sob, and worked to control his breathing.

A dark shape sat up beside him, and a warm hand rubbed his back. Dyara's chin came to rest on his shoulder. "It's okay. It's not real," she breathed beside his ear.

"Not yet," Darius replied. "This is the fifth time I've seen myself at her funeral in as many nights. It's getting more frequent."

Dyara's chin left his shoulder. "What do you think that means?"

"I think... I don't know. Maybe the Sprites are trying to tell me that what I'm seeing could happen

— 421 —

soon. I have to talk to Cassandra." Darius stood up from the inflatable bed, and walked over to a modular closet to put on a jumpsuit.

"You've already warned her. Why wake her up just so you can repeat those warnings? It can wait until morning."

"No," he shook his head. "It can't."

"It doesn't even make any sense," Dyara insisted. "Why would she try to negotiate with them after you've warned her not to? And we can't get back to Ouroboros anymore, so how could we possibly have a funeral for Cassandra there?"

"I don't know. Maybe the setting isn't important. Or maybe the setting could change. All I know is there has to be a reason I keep seeing the same thing, over and over again."

"I don't know what to say," Dyara said. "Maybe it was just a dream, and you've turned it into a recurring nightmare by fixating on it so much."

"I hope that's true," Darius replied. He finished putting on his jumpsuit and padded barefoot down the hall from their sleeping quarters.

Breezing through the magnetic door flaps at the end of the hall, he stepped into the common area of the habitat. The overhead lights were still on, but turned down low. It was enough to see by. On his way through the room, Darius's bladder gave an insistent twinge. He hesitated, and his gaze strayed to the door of the Acolytes' shared bathroom. Then he shook his head. He could hold it.

Sweeping through the door flaps barring Cassandra's room, Darius walked down a darkened hallway to her bed. He sat on the side of it, and the inflatable mattress sank under his weight. He felt around for her under the covers. "Cass?" The bed was still made.

A jolt of adrenaline shot through Darius's heart, and his pulse began thundering in his ears. Suddenly he was out of breath, as if he'd run a marathon. *She probably stayed out late,* he decided. But what would she be doing in the middle of the night?

Darius took a deep breath, shut his eyes, and reached out into the ZPF. He expanded his awareness rapidly, picturing himself floating through the top of the habitat and soaring high over the camp, looking down. Luminous beings were everywhere, mostly inside the habitats, sleeping in their beds. Darius tried to find the familiar tone and texture of his daughter's mind, but he couldn't sense her anywhere in the camp.

He broke out in a cold sweat; a flash of panic coursed through him, but he clamped down on it and cast himself higher still, until his awareness covered the entire island. He saw bugs creeping in the dirt, birds roosting in the trees, fish darting through the water—even a giant sea monster roaming in the deep...

But there was no sign of Cassandra. Darius gave into the panic. He cast his mental presence higher and higher until the island fell away and the dark crescents of adjacent islands appeared. From that altitude he sent himself racing over the surface of Cratus, circumnavigating the entire globe in a matter of seconds. He couldn't find his daughter anywhere.

There was no sign of the Cygnians either. Their island had been abandoned, leaving only swirling echoes of their presence. Darius directed his attention to the stars and cast himself out into space.

He found her—aboard a lone destroyer, on the other side of the planet far away from the rest of the fleet. All of the beings around Cassandra felt intensely alien, their thoughts dark and violent. *Cygnians.*

Darius's eyes flew open and his heart kicked against his sternum. He flew out of Cassandra's room, yelling, "Dyara! We have to go!"

She and several of the other Acolytes burst out of their rooms as he reached the common area.

"Go where?" Dyara asked.

Darius hurried through the room. He needed to put on his mag boots and sword. "The Cygnians have her," he yelled, as he reached the doors to their room.

Dyara stood blocking the way. She blinked at him. "You mean like a hostage?"

Darius shook his head. "I don't know! Maybe! She's on their ship!" He grabbed Dyara's shoulders in iron grips and forcibly moved her out of the way.

"She probably just went to visit or something."

"No. They evacuated Cratus. I can't sense any of them down here with us."

"They did? How do you know?"

He breezed down the corridor to their room, and Dyara followed close on his heels. "Talk to me, Darius!"

"It's happening, Dya!" he said. He reached their room and started pulling on his boots. "They're leaving to warn their people that we're coming, and Cassandra's on board. She's going to try to negotiate with them, and they're going to kill her."

Darius went to the wardrobe and fetched his sword. Dyara clapped a hand to her mouth and slowly shook her head. "Why would she do that!"

"I don't know, but we can't let them take her. We have to stop that ship from jumping away."

* * *

Darius burst through the doors of the habitat and onto the grassy street. Dyara came out right behind him.

"We should find Tanik," she said.

Darius shook his head. "I already tried. He's not in the camp."

"Then where is he?"

"I don't know, but it doesn't matter." Darius nodded to the command center. "The admiral will know what to do. Come on." He sprinted down the street, drawing on the ZPF to enhance his speed. He ran so fast that his boots kicked up clods of dirt and grass behind him. Dyara kept pace beside him. Habs blurred into white streaks as they ran by. Revenant patrols stopped and stared. Some of them called out to ask why they were in such a hurry, but Darius didn't stop to explain.

They reached the command center in just under a minute. Darius slowed as he reached the building, but he didn't stop. The soldiers guarding the doors moved to block his way. One of them held out a hand, and he slammed into an invisible wall and bounced back a few steps. "Halt," the man said. "Go back to your habitat, Acolyte."

Darius glared at the man. "I need to speak with the admiral. It's urgent."

The soldier traded a dubious look with his fellow guardsman. "About what?"

"About the fact that my daughter is aboard the Cygnians' ship."

"So?"

"So, they've evacuated their island!" Darius thundered.

"Maybe they don't like the heat."

The other guard snickered at that.

Darius scowled. He didn't have time for this. He reached into the ZPF and shoved the guards aside as hard as he could. They went flying in opposite directions and bounced off the nearest habitats.

"Darius!" Dyara protested. "You could hurt them!"

Darius ignored her, and directed his attention to the doors of the command center. He tried pushing through them, but they were locked, so he drew his sword and sliced them open. The canvas doors slumped to one side, and Darius swept into the command center. Dyara struggled to keep up as he stormed through the entrance, past the mess hall and the Command Information Center (CIC) to the admiral's quarters. There was another guard standing there. He straightened at the sight of their approach.

"What are you doing here?" the man demanded.

This time Darius didn't bother trying to argue; he picked the man up and physically moved him out of the way, holding him in a mental vice with his feet dangling three feet above the floor. The guard struggled against Darius's hold, but to no effect. Darius sliced the Admiral's door open. "Hey!" the guard said in a strangled voice. "I need backup!" Darius squeezed him harder to make him shut up.

The lights were on in Admiral Ventaris's room. He was up and busy strapping on his sword. "You didn't have to tear the place apart," he said. "I sensed you coming."

"They have my daughter," Darius explained.

"I know. I heard your conversation with the guards as you approached."

Just then, the very same guards came rushing up behind Darius and Dyara. They drew their swords with a *screech*.

"Darius! Look out!" Dyara cried as she drew her own sword.

"Enough!" Ventaris boomed. "We're all on the same side here. Darius, please release Adept Thebasian before you kill him."

Darius glanced at the guard he held frozen in the air to one side of the door. The man's face had turned blood red, and his lips were blue.

"Sorry," Darius said, and released the Adept. The man fell three feet to the ground and collapsed in a heap, gasping for air.

"Now perhaps you can explain yourself a bit better," Ventaris intoned. "You said they have your daughter. How do you know?"

"She's not in her room. I used the ZPF to find her. She's in space. On the Cygnians' ship."

Ventaris closed his eyes and took a deep breath. His eyes snapped open a split second later. "You are right, but she's not the only one. Tanik Gurhain is with her."

Darius blinked in shock. "Tanik is there? Why would he join the Cygnians?"

"That's a very good question, but I have a bad feeling that I know the answer. We need to get to the CIC before it's too late."

CHAPTER 39

By the time Tanik came aboard the *Nomad*, the sabotage had been found, and the Cygnians were busy fixing it. As a result, he wasn't the one they credited with saving their hides—Cassandra was. That won her a measure of trust and a tentative standing on board the ship, one which enabled her to roam the corridors freely. As for Tanik, he'd been allowed to stay aboard the *Nomad*, but only as a prisoner. He'd made a half-hearted attempt to convince Cassandra to leave with him and go back to camp. She refused, just as they had planned, and Tanik had refused to leave, too, so the Cygnians confiscated his sword and arrested him, taking him down to the brig.

Cassandra and Gakram stood outside a heavily-reinforced cell designed to hold a

Revenant—though Cassandra wondered if it would hold a *Cygnian* Revenant. She stepped up to a holo panel on the wall of Tanik's cell and waved it to life. They weren't allowed to enter his cell to communicate with him directly.

Tanik appeared on the screen, floating above the deck with his legs crossed and eyes closed.

"Tanik?" Cassandra asked.

His eyes snapped open and flicked to the screen on his side of the cell. "You came to visit me. How nice." His voice oozed with sarcasm.

"How are you going to protect me now?" Cassandra demanded. "You're locked up! This wasn't part of the plan."

"No, it wasn't," Tanik agreed. He uncrossed his legs and his mag boots yanked him to the floor with a metallic *clunk.* He went to the holo panel in his cell and glowered at her. "Who told you to tell the Cygnians about the sabotage?"

"I... you didn't tell me not to!" Cassandra objected.

"I did. Indirectly, at least. I gave you our story. You were supposed to have joined the *Nomad* in order to accept Gakram's invitation and fulfill the prophecy, nothing more. I was supposed to come and tell them about the sabotage, but only *after* I was forced to tell them in order to save your life."

"Well, what's the difference?"

"The difference is, now the Cygnians aren't grateful to *me* for saving them, so they've locked me up, and if the Admiral ever figures out that you told them about the sabotage before I arrived, then we'll both be liable for treason—me for telling you classified information, and you for relating it to the Cygnians."

Cassandra gaped at him. "Well... we can still stick to your story when we get back. How will anyone ever know any different?"

Tanik scowled. "Indeed, just be sure that you *do* stick to that story."

"You didn't answer my question," Cassandra prompted. "How are you going to protect me now?"

"I'll figure something out. In the meantime, it would be best if you didn't talk to anyone, about *anything*, except for Gakram."

"Well, what do I do when we arrive at Cygnus Prime? What about the prophecy?"

The Ghoul guard who had accompanied them to Tanik's cell glanced their way as she said that, the four red eyes of his helmet glaring.

Tanik's eyes darted to that Ghoul, then back, and he smiled thinly at her. "I'll figure something out," he repeated, and fixed her with a meaningful look.

She took the hint and nodded hastily. "Okay."

The guard stalked over to them on two legs, his massive head brushing the ceiling. He growled at Gakram. "We have to strap in."

"We're jumping out already?" Cassandra asked.

The Ghoul glared at her once more, then looked back to Gakram. "We have detected six squadrons of fighters incoming. Elder Arathos is going to try to outrun them."

Gakram hissed and tossed his head. "Lead the way, master."

* * *

Darius stood with Dyara in the CIC, watching his worst nightmare unfold. He was bursting with the urgent need to *do* something, but there was nothing he could do. Even if he took off in a Vulture right now, he'd never be able to reach the *Nomad* before they jumped away, or for that matter, before the fighter squadrons Admiral Ventaris had launched.

Revenant Sentinels with the rank insignia of Lieutenants and Lieutenant Commanders manned the various control stations in the room. The admiral walked from station to station, checking in with each of them.

"Flight Ops, how long before our fighters reach weapons range with the *Nomad?*" Ventaris asked.

"Fifteen minutes, sir."

"And how long before the *Nomad* can jump?"

"They haven't started spinning up their Alckam drive yet, but once they do, they'll need at least twenty minutes to complete the warm-up cycle, sir."

"Grak it," Admiral Ventaris muttered. "Authorize your pilots to use whatever force necessary to stop the *Nomad*. We can't let it get away."

"Understood, sir."

That hit Darius like a bucket of ice water. "Hold on a minute," he said.

Admiral Ventaris glanced at him. "Yes?"

"You're going to shoot them?"

"How else do you expect me to stop them from leaving?"

"My daughter is on board," Darius said.

"I am aware of that, Acolyte."

"I don't think you are!" Darius thundered. "And I don't think you care if she becomes collateral damage."

"Be careful how you speak to me. You are not

the Augur yet. And I assure you, we will do everything we can to capture the *Nomad* in one piece."

Darius scowled at him. "And what if you destroy the ship? Then what? You'll give me your deepest condolences?"

"Calm down and shut the hell up before I throw you out of the CIC."

Darius clamped his mouth shut, but he could feel his eyes popping with fury. Blood vessels pulsed at his temples. Admiral Ventaris turned away and continued walking down the line of control stations.

"Comms, report! Any reply to our hails?"

"None yet, sir."

"Warn them again. If they don't power down their engines and submit to boarding, we *will* fire on them."

"Yes, sir. It might help if we had a better excuse. Why are we boarding them if they haven't even begun spinning up their Alckam drive?"

"It's enough that we suspect they're going to warn their people. If we waited for them to actually jump, it would be too late."

"Yes, sir," the comms operator replied.

Dyara came to stand beside Darius. She slid her hand into his and gave it reassuring squeeze.

"She's going to be okay. They'll stop the *Nomad* before it jumps."

Darius shook his head slowly, unconvinced. "I just don't understand why she left. She knew about my visions. What could have convinced her to go? And why didn't she say something to me!"

"She must have had a good reason."

Darius arched an eyebrow at her. "And what about Tanik? What's he doing there with her?"

"Maybe..." Dyara trailed off. "I'm sure they'll have a good explanation when we speak with them."

"Yeah," Darius frowned. "They'd better."

"The *Nomad* is spinning up its jump drive! ETA twenty minutes," someone announced.

"Ops!" Admiral Ventaris bellowed. "How long to firing range?"

"Ten minutes!" the lieutenant at the flight ops station replied.

"That gives us ten minutes to stop them," the admiral mused. "Arm the ZPFs."

"The ZPFs, sir?"

"You heard me, Lieutenant!"

ZPFs? What are those? Darius had a guess, but he didn't like it, and he needed to be sure. Reaching out with his awareness, Darius cast his mind toward Admiral Ventaris to get a feel for his intentions. He didn't like the deadly resolve he found in the Admiral's aura, so he pushed deeper until he was inside the Admiral's head, surrounded by whispering voices and fragments of thought. Darius couldn't *see* the admiral's thoughts as much as he could *hear* and *sense* them. It was as if he had possessed the admiral's body, and his thoughts were now Darius's thoughts, too.

If our fighters have them pinned down with lasers, they won't be able to drop their shields to fire back, so our missiles should get through... unless the Cygnians on board use the ZPF to deflect them. But if we're using ZPF warheads, just one missile will be enough to take them out. No shield is strong enough to repel that.

Darius reeled in shock. *You can't destroy that ship!*

What are you doing inside my head? Admiral Ventaris demanded.

Before Darius could formulate a reply, he received a violent shove that broke his concentration, and suddenly he was back in his own body.

The admiral rounded on him and pointed a finger at his chest. "Do that again, and I'll have you executed."

"You don't care if you destroy them!" Darius accused.

"And you don't care if everyone in the entire fleet dies, just so long as your daughter lives," Admiral Ventaris countered.

"You don't have to destroy them," Darius replied. "You can board them instead."

"Assuming we can physically catch up with them before they jump away, which does not look like a serious possibility. Our missiles will be lucky to catch them, let alone our fighters."

"Then follow them to Cygnus Prime! That's where they're headed, isn't it?"

"Our entire battle plan is predicated on the element of surprise! One swift strike to cripple the Cygnians' infrastructure and win the war. If we go to Cygnus Prime now, they'll withdraw their fleets from Union space to defend their other worlds."

"You never intended to threaten them," Darius said. "You've been planning to wipe them out this whole time."

"Of course I have! I'm not stupid. Why risk all-out war when we can cripple the other side and end the war before it starts? You need to stop thinking about yourself, and start thinking about the greater good. If your daughter has to die to save billions of lives, does that not justify her sacrifice? Besides—*I'm* not the one who sent her aboard the *Nomad*. I isolated the Cygnians aboard that ship for a reason. She's the one who chose to join them. She's chosen her side in this war."

"You don't know that. She could be a hostage."

"Then why hasn't the *Nomad* contacted us to make demands? What is the point of taking hostages otherwise? Face it, Darius, she went willingly."

"Tanik, too?" Darius challenged. "Wasn't he the brains of this entire operation? Why would he join the Cygnians?"

A muscle in Admiral Ventaris's cheek twitched. "Hopefully, to bring your daughter back. If not, he may have betrayed us all even more deeply than she did. Now, stop wasting my time. If you can't keep quiet, you'll have to leave. There's nothing you can do to help your daughter." The admiral turned back to the officer at the flight ops station. "ETA to firing range?"

"Three minutes, sir, but the *Nomad* is now shielding itself, and they're still trying to make a run for it."

"Fire the ZPF missiles. There's only so much they can shield."

"Yes, sir."

A jolt of adrenaline stabbed through Darius's heart, and his legs began to shake. He had to do something! But what? His hand fell to the hilt of his sword and his gaze darted around the CIC to get a feel for his opposition. Even if he sneak-attacked the admiral and somehow managed to kill him, his officers wouldn't call off the attack. Besides, he only had a few minutes to work with. The guards standing by the doors noticed his hostile stance, and started toward him.

"We should go..." Dyara whispered, and grabbed Darius's arm in a warning grip. "You don't have to stay here for this."

"No," Darius shook his head. "I do."

He released the hilt of his sword and shut his eyes. He pushed his mind into the thoughts of the approaching guards, and told them to go back to their posts. There was a brief flash of confusion as they resisted, but Darius pressed harder, not taking no for an answer. He cracked his eyes open and saw the men walking back to the doors, their eyes glazed and staring, as if he'd put them in a trance. Darius couldn't believe it had worked. He struggled to quell their suspicions and smooth away their doubts. Now he reached in a new direction—back to the admiral, and forced his way into the man's thoughts. Ventaris immediately began shoving him out, but this time Darius pushed back as hard as he could. It worked. All at once the admiral's resistance faded to a subtle pressure, and suddenly *he* was in control.

"Call off the attack," Darius said, but it was the Admiral's voice that he heard.

"Sir?" The lieutenant at flight ops turned to him with a bemused frown.

"You heard me, Lieutenant! Now! Before they open fire."

"Yes, sir... fighters are standing down."

"Recall them," Darius said.

"They're already on their way back, sir. Is there some reason for your change of heart?"

Darius thought quickly, coming up with an explanation on the fly. "I've just received new information via my ESC. It's Tanik. He and Cassandra infiltrated the *Nomad* by pretending to be on the Cygnians' side. He says it's too late to stop them. They've already sent messengers ahead to Cygnus Prime, so there's no point in destroying the *Nomad*."

"But sir, we've been monitoring the entire system day and night. We have probes everywhere. We would have detected the jump emissions if any ships had left the system."

Darius's mind raced, trying to come up with an explanation for that. He took a gamble. "Not if they flew far enough away first and then executed their jump in the shadow of a large planetary body."

"*Maybe*, but gamma rays are hard to miss, sir."

"Stop questioning me, Lieutenant. I trust Tanik. If he says they sent out messengers, then they sent out messengers. We can figure out how they pulled that off later."

"Yes, sir."

"Comms, ready the fleet," Darius went on, still using Ventaris. "Tell them to plot a course for Cygnus Prime and start spinning up their Alckam drives—and sound the evacuation. We're all leaving for orbit immediately."

"Yes, sir," the comms officer said.

A klaxon started screaming from loudspeakers outside, and through smaller ones dangling from the ceiling of the CIC. The comm officer's voice bubbled out a moment later. "General quarters, general quarters! All personnel to your transports. We are evacuating Cratus. This is not a drill. I repeat, all personnel to your transports. This is not a drill."

Darius struggled to maintain his hold on the admiral's mind, despite the constant pressure of his resistance. He released the guards by the door in order to focus more squarely on the admiral, and then he risked splitting his focus in order to take back control of his own body.

Dyara was shaking him by his shoulders.

"Darius! What's wrong? Answer me!"

He blinked, slowly coming back to his senses—literally. "I'm fine." He glanced at the Admiral. Ventaris stood there, frozen, obviously still under his control. Darius instructed him to leave the CIC and head for his transport.

"I'll see you all in orbit," Ventaris said as he left.

Darius hadn't even needed to put those words in the admiral's mouth this time. *Interesting,* he thought. This was a looser form of control, but a lot easier to manage. The mental pressure from Ventaris's mind remained, like the beginnings of a headache, but it was tolerable.

Darius followed Ventaris out of the CIC and Dyara kept pace beside him. "Wow," Dyara breathed as soon as they cleared the doors. "That was really lucky."

Darius looked at her. He couldn't risk telling her what he'd done. Someone in the command center might overhear. He tried planting his reply directly in her thoughts instead.

It wasn't luck. I'm controlling him. I made him back down. He jerked his chin to the admiral. Ventaris was striding purposefully down the hall to the front doors of the command center.

Dyara's mouth dropped open and her eyes

widened. *Darius?* She thought back at him.

Yes?

"*You're* the one who made them stand down?" she whispered in a sharp voice.

"Quiet!" Darius snapped, and glanced behind them to make sure no one had overheard.

"Darius... this isn't right. You can't just take control of someone like that!"

I had no choice, he thought at her. *I couldn't stand by and let him kill her! Besides, the admiral was planning xenocide. You heard him. He admitted it! Now that we're in control, we can look for a diplomatic solution.*

Dyara shot him a skeptical look as they breezed out the front doors of the command center. It was chaos outside. The klaxons were louder out here, and the comm officer's message played on repeat. Revenant soldiers ran about in squads, snapping orders at each other.

Admiral Ventaris cut right, heading for an open stretch of field beside the command center where a pair of Ospreys hunched in the grass.

"A diplomatic solution..." Dyara trailed off as they followed Ventaris to the field. "You mean like *negotiating* with the Cygnians? Isn't that what got Cass killed in your visions?"

Darius grimaced at that reminder. "Maybe if I

negotiate for her, she won't be tempted to try herself," he said.

"Maybe..." Dyara replied.

But Darius wasn't convinced that negotiating would work. Admiral Ventaris was probably right to think that the Cygnians wouldn't back down unless they were already defeated. Darius shook his head to clear it. He shouldn't be in charge. Taking over gave him a chance to save Cassandra. As soon as they arrived at Cygnus Prime, he'd find a way to rescue her and get the hell away from the fighting before they ended up dead. *This isn't our war, and we're not soldiers.*

CHAPTER 40

—FOUR HOURS LATER—

Cassandra watched the *Nomad* drop out of warp on the holo panel in her quarters. Gakram kept her company. They'd spent most of the past four hours sleeping after their lucky escape from those squadrons of Revenant fighters. Gakram had scoffed at the Revenants' sudden retreat, saying that no Cygnian would back their prey into a corner only to step aside at the last minute and let them go. He'd suggested that perhaps the Admiral was afraid to actually start a war with his people.

Cassandra said nothing to that, but she'd been secretly disturbed by Gakram's reaction. She was seeing a new side to him, and it didn't give her much hope for negotiating a peaceful resolution. *Maybe I shouldn't even try*, she thought. *My dad's visions can't come true, if I don't negotiate.* And with

Tanik locked up, he couldn't defend her if she did. It wasn't worth the risk.

"This is it," Gakram growled. He turned his massive head to her. "Are you ready to fulfill your destiny?"

Cassandra swallowed thickly. "Right now?"

"Why not?" Gakram asked.

"Well, don't you need to wait to take me down to Cygnus Prime or something? I mean, how am I supposed to talk to your Old Ones from here?"

"We will hail them over the commsss," Gakram hissed. "We cannot delay. The admiral may follow us."

"Ah..." Cassandra faltered for another excuse.

"Come," Gakram intoned. "There's no time to waste." He got up and loped toward the door, and Cassandra slowly followed. She reached out with her awareness to find Tanik, hoping by some miracle to find him nearby.

He was two floors down, hovering in his cell with his legs crossed and his eyes shut, just as he had been the last time she'd seen him. Cassandra's heart sank.

Gakram waved the door to her quarters open, and Cassandra followed him into the corridor. He ran ahead, but she dragged her feet. *Maybe he'll lose track of me.*

Gakram stopped and glanced back at her. "Hurry!"

She flashed a wan smile and picked up the pace, her mind racing to come up with a way out. Maybe she could just tell Gakram that she'd changed her mind. They'd have to find some other harbinger of doom.

They reached a bank of elevators, and Gakram hit the call button with one claw. Cassandra willed the elevators to take their time, but one of them opened almost immediately and Gakram stepped inside. He snarled and glared at her. "Are you coming, or not?" His tone was brimming with aggression.

Cassandra stepped through the elevator doors and they swept shut. She eyed her friend as the elevator carried them up. "What's wrong with you? You're not acting like yourself."

Gakram gave a chilling hiss and bared his teeth at her. His black eyes were intense in the dim light of the *Nomad's* glow panels.

"Stop it!" Cassandra said. "You're scaring me."

Gakram gave a *sissing* laugh. The elevator stopped on the command deck and Gakram brushed by her on his way out. His barbed tail flicked within inches of her face as he left.

Cassandra recoiled from it and said, "Hey! You

almost hit me!"

"Sorry," Gakram said as he slunk down the corridor to the bridge.

Cassandra started after him, but then thought better of it. "I'm not going."

Gakram glanced back at her. The predatory look in his eyes had faded somewhat, and he looked more himself again.

"I am sorry," he said. "You must understand, when we are anticipating a hunt, our bodies produce many chemicals and hormones that make us more aggressive than usual. I apologize if that is scaring you. It issss hard to resist one's instincts in moments like these."

Cassandra shivered and crossed her arms over her chest. The chill that she'd felt on Cratus was back, and this time her hair wasn't wet from a shower. "I don't think this is a good idea," she said. "I think it was a mistake for me to come."

"You cannot run from your destiny, Casssss," Gakram hissed.

Just then, an elevator opened and Tanik stepped out. Cassandra gaped at him, and Gakram hissed. "How did you get up here?"

"There's no time to explain," Tanik said. Nodding to Cassandra, he added, "Are you ready?"

She shook her head, blinking in shock. "Ready for what?"

"To speak to the Cygnians. We'll go together. They won't be able to harm you with me there to protect you." Tanik patted the hilts of two Cygnian short swords, one on each hip.

"Where did you get those?" Cassandra whispered.

"From the guard outside my cell."

"Is he..."

"Don't worry. He's alive."

Gakram hissed again.

Cassandra thrust out her chin and nodded to him. "I'll speak to your people, but *only* if Tanik joins me on the bridge."

"As you wish," Gakram growled. "Now let us go before it is too late."

They followed him to the bridge and waited while Gakram announced them to the pair of Banshee guards outside the doors.

A moment later, the doors swished open, and an armored Ghoul appeared. His helmet was off, revealing a fearsome snarl. He pointed a long, gleaming gray claw at Tanik. "What is *he* doing here?"

"He found a way to escape, Elder Arathos."

"And you did not kill him?"

Gakram bowed his head. "Forgive me, master. He surprised me on my way here. The girl would not deliver her message without him."

"What message?"

"This girl is the one who was prophesied to herald the return of the Destroyers. Tanik is her guardian."

The Ghoul hissed and tossed his head. "The girl does not fit the description. The one who was prophesied must have lived even longer than the Old Ones."

"And yet still be a child," Gakram added. "Cassandra *is* that one. She was born fourteen hundred years ago."

"Impossible."

"She was frozen on her world, master, and only awoke recently. She *is* the herald."

Cassandra saw the Ghoul's eyes glazed and staring off into the distance, as if deep in thought.

"If what you say is true," Arathos began slowly, "then she must speak to the Old Ones for us."

Gakram growled and tossed his head. "That is why I invited her to join us aboard the *Nomad*, master."

"And you were right to do so." The Elder's gaze fell on Cassandra next, and he bared his teeth at her. "I will open a channel for you."

CHAPTER 41

"How long before we arrive in the Cygnus System?" Admiral Ventaris asked.

"ETA thirty minutes, sir," the officer at the helm replied.

"Good. Keep me posted, Lieutenant."

"Yes, sir."

Darius's eyes were closing of their own accord. Holding his grip on Admiral Ventaris's mind for so many hours had taken its toll. The closer he was to the admiral physically, the easier it seemed to be, but even here on the bridge, it was still exhausting. Darius wasn't sure how much longer he could keep it up.

Fortunately, he didn't need to control Ventaris for much longer.

Darius nodded to Dyara where she sat in a

spare acceleration harness beside the doors to the *Harbinger's* bridge. "I have to go," he said.

Dyara looked at him, her eyes full of concern and accusation at the same time. "Where?"

I'm going to take a fighter and board the *Nomad,* he thought at her.

By yourself? she thought back.

He shrugged. *Who else is going to come?*

Dyara's mouth twisted into a bitter smirk. He could guess what she was thinking. Why go alone when he could make the admiral give the order for a whole team of Revenants to join him?

But the truth was, he wouldn't be able to trust the Revenants once he released his hold on Admiral Ventaris. Besides, he felt guilty for dragging everyone along on his personal crusade. It had seemed to make sense at the time, but he hadn't been thinking very clearly. Now, having had the past four hours to reflect on his actions, Darius questioned his decision to send the entire fleet after the *Nomad.* They could be flying into a trap.

Darius shook his head. It was too late to worry about that now. Hopefully Admiral Ventaris would be able to lead them to victory, or at least to a successful retreat. Darius pulled the release lever beside his seat and folded his acceleration harness aside. He stood up and turned to leave the bridge, only to find Dyara already on her feet and waiting for him by the doors.

I can't ask you to come with me.

You didn't ask. I'm offering.

Why?

More for Cass's sake than yours.

He nodded. *That's fair. But we could die out there. We're going to be up against a whole destroyer full of Cygnians. Trained Revenant Cygnians.*

We could also die in here, Dyara thought back at him.

"Thank you," he whispered.

"Sure." Dyara waved the doors open and they ran down the corridor together. Darius struggled to keep up with her. His mental fatigue had begun to affect him physically, making it hard just to put one foot in front of the other. He hoped he wouldn't pass out in his cockpit....

* * *

Cassandra stood before the holo panels on the *Nomad's* bridge, staring into a darkened chamber somewhere on the surface of Cygnus Prime. Four sets of *four* black eyes glinted in the gloom. Jagged, gaping rows of teeth gleamed below the eyes, but that was all Cassandra could make out clearly. On her side of the transmission, Elder Arathos stood in front of her and slightly to the left, while Tanik stood behind her, and slightly to the right.

"Who am I speaking with?" one of the Cygnians in the transmission demanded, glaring at them with pinching eyes. "You are one of us, yet you come to us on a human vessel. Explain."

Elder Arathos bowed his head. "My lord, I am Elder Arathos, a Revenant returned from the Eye."

Silence answered that declaration. "Then the Augur is dead."

Cassandra frowned at that. The Old Ones *knew* about the Augur? Tanik had said that the Augur had been controlling the Cygnians like a puppeteer, but if their leaders *knew* about him, it implied a more willful association.

"Yes..." Elder Arathos confirmed, his voice trailing off uncertainly. "This human girl behind me is the herald foretold by the prophecy of the Destroyers. She comes to you with a dire warning."

A loud murmur of hissing and growling thundered through speakers on the bridge as the Old Ones reacted to that news. Cassandra couldn't make out individual words, but she thought the general tone of their voices was confusion rather than shock or concern.

As the noise died away, one of them spoke: "*What* prophecy?"

Cassandra's blood turned to ice and she shot Tanik a questioning look. He looked equally confused.

Elder Arathos went on slowly. "The prophecy about the return of the Destroyers, My Lords..."

"Have you lost your mind, Elder? Or are you trying to insult our intelligence? There is no such prophecy. And who are these *Destroyers* you speak of?"

"I... I am sorry, My Lord, I must be confused..."

"Yes. Are you certain that the Augur is dead? I sense a powerful hold over you. Who is giving you your words, Elder?"

Cassandra's brow furrowed, and she glanced at Tanik once more. *You?* She mouthed.

Tanik shook his head and mouthed, *No.*

"No one holds sway over me, My Lord. My words are my own. I must have encountered a false prophet during my time fighting the Keth. I apologize for wasting your time, but the dire warning remains: the Revenants are no longer under the Augur's influence. A fleet of them is coming. They bring weapons with them, weapons that can destroy entire planets in an instant. They were planning a cowardly surprise attack to destroy all of our worlds at once. We came to warn you."

The Old Ones murmured amongst themselves once more. "What is the nature of these weapons?"

"Explosive devices that use the power of the Divine Light. They are more powerful than an entire ship full of antimatter, and yet still small enough to be launched from a fighter."

"Are you certain these weapons are as powerful as you claim? Have you seen them used?"

"They are, My Lord, and I have. It is what the Augur used to defeat the Keth."

"Curious that he never mentioned that in his reports... Did this fleet follow you here?"

"I cannot say, My Lord. Perhaps."

"Then we will take the necessary precautions. Now, we would like you to prove that you are not under any influence but your own."

"How should I prove that, My Lord?"

"Kill the human emissaries."

"As you wish."

Cassandra rocked back on her heels, and Tanik yanked her behind him just as Elder Arathos rounded on them and drew all four of his swords with an echoing screech.

"Shield yourself!" Tanik screamed, just as the

bridge of the *Nomad* erupted in a deafening chorus of alien shrieks. Elder Arathos began glowing brightly in the light of his own ZPF shield, and all four of his black swords shined like frozen laser beams.

Cassandra activated her shield and drew her sword at the same time as Tanik drew the two he'd stolen from the Ghoul guarding his cell.

Arathos hissed at them and hunched down to their level. He held all four of his glowing blades out straight, preparing to skewer both her and Tanik at the same time.

Just then, Cassandra caught a flicker of movement in the corner of her eye. Gakram was creeping up behind the elder, his chameleon skin blended perfectly against the dull gray of the *Nomad's* deck.

"They have us surrounded! Watch my back!" Tanik said.

Cassandra turned her back to his, and saw three more Cygnians approaching from behind, glowing bright with shields and brandishing four swords each.

CHAPTER 42

The cockpit shuddered as the Vulture's engines roared to life. Glowing holo displays and lights appeared on every available surface. The comms beeped with a message and a red light blinked. Darius checked the panel to see that it was from *SF76-G1*, Dyara's fighter. He played the message and set all future messages from her to auto-play.

"Darius. What's the situation with your hand puppet? Can we expect friendly fire after we launch?"

"I'll hold onto the admiral's mind as long as I can, but the farther away we get, the harder it's going to be."

"That wasn't much of an answer," Dyara grumbled.

"I'll warn you before I lose control of him."

"Thanks."

Lights flashed down the length of the launch tube as doors parted in front of Darius's fighter. An automated voice sounded inside his helmet: "Three, two, one—"

Darius slammed into the back of his seat as the fighter roared down the launch tube and into space. Stars exploded into view on all sides. Cygnus Prime lay to one side. It appeared to be the size of a golf ball—red and brown with specks of blue that might have been lakes.

The sensors chimed insistently, and the comms crackled with Dyara's voice. "Kak... are you seeing this, Darius?"

He shook his head. "No?"

"Check your contacts panel."

Darius glanced at it and immediately saw what she meant. The Cygnian home defense fleet, comprised of several *hundred* capital-class vessels, was belching out Blade Fighters at a furious rate. By contrast, the Revenant fleet only had twenty capital ships.

"We're outnumbered," Darius said as he found and targeted the *Nomad.* He banked toward it and pushed the throttle to three Gs.

"*Badly* outnumbered," Dyara gritted out as she

matched thrust with him and followed him through the maneuver. Her fighter swept into view, all four of its thrusters burning with bright blue tongues of fire.

"We can draw on the ZPF to shield ourselves. They can't," Darius said.

"Yeah, but we can't shoot through our shields. It won't be long before the whole fleet is pinned down under fire. All we'll be able to do is weather the assault. We need a different strategy. What was the Admiral planning to do?"

Darius shook his head. "I don't know."

"Well, what are *you* planning to do?"

Darius couldn't concentrate with Admiral Ventaris's mind pushing constantly against his, trying to take back control. He heard the admiral's bridge officers clamoring for attention, but distantly. It was all he could do to hold Ventaris back, respond to Dyara, and pilot his fighter. If controlling just one person was this hard, how had Tanik managed to control a crew of a thousand people after waking them from cryo?

"Why aren't we launching fighters?" Dyara demanded.

"I..."

"You didn't give the order?"

"Hang on!" Darius shut his eyes and cast his

mind back to the *Harbinger*. Suddenly he was sitting on the bridge in the command chair.

"Sir! We need to launch our fighters now, while we still can," the lieutenant at the Flight Ops station said. He sounded distressed.

"Sir!" The comms officer turned to him. "Our captains are still waiting for your orders. They're getting impatient!"

The pressure of Admiral Ventaris's mind had become a loud, constant buzzing in Darius's ears. He couldn't think. He couldn't...

Suddenly all was silent but for the roar of the Vulture's engines. Darius's eyes snapped open. It felt like a crushing weight had been lifted. "I lost him," he said. "The admiral is back in control."

"No offense, but thank the gods for that!" Dyara replied.

The hairs on Darius's neck stood straight up; then came the urgent squawk of an enemy target lock.

"Dya, jink hard! Shields up!" Darius screamed. His fighter glowed dimly in the light of a ZPF shield. He stepped on the rudder pedals in a seesaw motion while hauling back on the stick. The rudder pedals activated the Vulture's maneuvering jets to mimic the motion of an atmospheric rudder. The result was a climbing slalom.

A split second after Darius began the evasive maneuver, bright crimson lasers snapped out all around his cockpit. Crimson was the color of heavy Union lasers. He wasn't going to be able to shield too many of them. "The *Harbinger* is firing on us with everything they've got!" Darius warned.

"No kak! I hadn't noticed that!"

"Keep juking!" Darius said through gritted teeth as a laser scraped his left wing with a hissing roar of dissipating energy. "The *Nomad* hasn't launched fighters yet, so now is the time to board them." The *Nomad* probably *couldn't* launch fighters, come to think of it. It was a Union ship, and there wouldn't be any Cygnian-sized fighters on board.

"Who's in charge here, you or me?" Dyara quipped. They'd agreed that she would take the lead in this rescue mission, at least while they were in their cockpits, but Darius wasn't used to a chain of command.

"You are," he said, just as an enemy missile lock began beeping urgently in his ears.

"In that case, activate your ECM and turn off your point defense turret before it gets you killed. That thing's on auto. It doesn't know we're using ZPF shields. You don't want all that energy back-firing into your own ship."

"Oh, kak!" Darius deactivated the turret and activated electronic countermeasures instead. The screaming alerts of missile lock warnings overlapped each other in a steady roar.

"Good. Now juke like your tail's on fire, because we've got sixty Hornet Missiles incoming, and I doubt our shields will hold against more than two or three."

"*Sixty?*" Darius echoed, and stared wide-eyed at his nav panel. Missiles streamed toward them in snaking lines from the *Harbinger* and the two cutter-class destroyers flanking it.

"The admiral must really want you dead," Dyara said. "You'd better start thinking about where we're going after this—assuming we survive, that is. Something tells me we're not going to be welcome on the *Harbinger*."

Darius thought about it as he continued executing a randomly weaving evasive pattern. She was right, but they had more immediate concerns. The missiles were closing fast, and there was no way the ECM would be able to scramble them all....

CHAPTER 43

Elder Arathos engaged Tanik just as two of the other three Ghouls attacked Cassandra. Eight swords windmilled before her eyes, threatening to chop her into bite-sized pieces. There was no way to block them all, so she didn't even try. She leapt straight over their heads, and used the ZPF to pull herself down behind them in the zero-G environment. Their barbed tails flicked reflexively toward her, the tips gleaming with deadly drops of venom.

Cassandra limboed deftly away from one tail as it swept by just inches from her nose. She blocked the other with her sword, slicing the tip off and sending it tumbling away. The Ghoul screamed and rounded on her, its jaws gaping in pain. It dropped all of its swords, leaving them drifting in the air, and lunged at her with claws and teeth flashing. Cringing, Cassandra thrust out her free hand to deliver a focused kinetic attack.

The Ghoul tumbled away, and Cassandra blinked in shock. She couldn't believe it had worked. As her opponent sailed past Tanik, he diverted one of his swords and slashed open the Ghoul's neck. Black blood spurted out in a drifting wave, splashing Tanik's face and jumpsuit. The creature howled in pain, thrashing and bucking as it drifted through the air. The second Ghoul rounded on Tanik with a loud hiss, and joined Elder Arathos in attacking him. Now Tanik was the one fending off eight blades at once.

Cassandra sensed the third Cygnian, unaccounted for until now, creeping up behind her. She twisted around just in time to block slashes from two of its four swords. The sheer momentum of that attack sent her sprawling. Cassandra scrambled to her feet, backing away from her new attacker. As she did so, she caught a glimpse of the Old Ones watching on the forward holo panels.

This is entertainment for them! Cassandra realized, just as she fetched up against one of the holo panels running around the bridge. She was out of room to run.

Thrusting her free hand toward the advancing Ghoul, she delivered another kinetic attack, this time with a steady pressure. The Ghoul stumbled back a step, then sheathed one of its swords and held out a hand of its own to counter her attack. It was a standoff, but she had managed to stop the Ghoul from advancing. *Now what?*

Her opponent snarled, pushing harder, and suddenly she couldn't breathe. The Ghoul began inching toward her. *Where is Gakram?* she wondered, pushing back as hard as she could. It wasn't enough. The Ghoul flourished its three swords, and its jaws yawned wide open, as if to swallow her whole.

"Gakram!" Cassandra called out in a breathless gasp.

A dark, blurry shape pushed off the ceiling and floated down, abruptly swelling with the light of the ZPF. There came a flash of glowing claws, and suddenly the pressure on Cassandra's chest lifted. The Ghoul who'd been advancing on her was gushing black blood from where its trachea used to be.

Cassandra blew out a shaky breath, and nodded to Gakram. "Thank you."

"Look out!" Tanik called.

They turned just as four swords flashed

toward Gakram. He threw up two arms to block them.

"Gakram!" Cassandra screamed

All four blades connected with Gakram's arms and his shield gave way with a *pop!*

Gakram's arms were vaporized up to the shoulders in a fiery burst of embers and ash. He screamed in agony and thrashed as the stumps smoldered with a sickening stench. He lost his grip on the deck and floated free. Cassandra ran in to block a second attack, aimed for Gakram's head. She caught two swords with her own and used the ZPF to telekinetically hold back the other two.

She felt a sharp stab from behind and stood blinking at her attacker in shock. *His tail.* The Ghoul's mouth popped open in a grin of interlocking nine-inch gray teeth.

"Goodbye," he growled. Cassandra recognized the depth and tone of his voice: it was Elder Arathos. He let loose a *sissing* peal of laughter and withdrew to join the fight against Tanik. The message was clear. She was a goner.

On his way to Tanik, Arathos leapt after Gakram and sliced off his head. It was vaporized instantly, and his body burst into flames.

No! Cassandra wanted to scream, but somehow she couldn't. Her sword drifted from nerveless fingers, and she stumbled away, her head suddenly light. Her eyes blurred with tears at Gakram's passing. Cassandra's back pulsed with waves of fire where she'd been stabbed, but the pain quickly faded to numbness. She tried to recover her sword as it floated past her head, but she couldn't move. The Ghoul's venom had paralyzed her! Her feet were pinned to the deck by her mag boots, leaving her to stand and watch the fight through blurry, tear-filled eyes.

Tanik sliced one Ghoul in half with a burst of fiery embers, and assailed Elder Arathos from all sides with sailing black swords. Those blades were dark and unshielded, so they shattered to gleaming bits on Arathos's shield, but that momentary distraction was enough. Tanik slipped one of his swords past Arathos's guard and ran it straight through the Ghoul's chest. Arathos shrieked and his shield failed with a loud *pop*. Tanik withdrew the blade and deftly sliced off the Elder's legs at the knees. The severed limbs disappeared with a puff of glowing ashes, and Arathos spun away, shrieking. His arms and swords slashed at empty air in a vain attempt to strike back, but he could no longer reach Tanik. He used his tail instead, whipping it toward Tanik's head, but Tanik saw it coming and sliced off the barbed tip with a flick of his wrist. Unlike the Ghoul's legs, mysteriously the tail wasn't vaporized by Tanik's sword.

Cassandra noticed the forward holo panels return to an uninterrupted vista of stars and space. The Old Ones had ended their transmission. Tanik grabbed the severed tip of Arathos's tail as it floated by his head. Brandishing it like a club, he rushed to Cassandra's side, leaving Arathos to die slowly from his wounds.

"Where are you hurt?" Tanik demanded.

Cassandra tried to speak once more, but again, her lips wouldn't move.

"He got you with this, didn't he?" Tanik asked, and shook the severed tail in front of her by way of indication.

Cassandra wanted to nod, or blink, but she couldn't do either. Fresh tears leaked from her eyes with the frustration of the attempt.

"We have to hurry," Tanik said. As he turned to leave, Cassandra saw herself float free of the deck and drift along behind him. The doors of the bridge swished open, and Banshees and Ghouls came crowding in brandishing their claws and swords.

They parted before Tanik like a wave hitting the bow of a ship. The Cygnians snarled and shrieked at them, their arms straining against invisible bonds as Tanik walked by. Cassandra floated along on his heels, watching the Cygnians. Her mind was fading fast, and confusion swirled through her thoughts. *If he can hold them back like that, why didn't he do that with the ones on the bridge?*

As Tanik strode down the corridors of the ship, the Cygnians they encountered were struck by the same invisible forces and roughly shoved aside. Tanik was an unstoppable force storming blithely through their ship in plain sight.

Cassandra began lapsing in and out of consciousness, catching only faint glimpses of their surroundings. She had a bad feeling that it meant she was running out of time. *I'm sorry, Dad...* she thought, while reaching out for him in the ZPF. She was surprised to find him nearby, racing toward the *Nomad* in a fighter. *I should have listened,* she went on.

Cass, is that you? Her dad's voice echoed inside her head. *Why did you leave!*

They said I was the only one the Old Ones would listen to, but they didn't listen! The prophecy... she trailed off, her thoughts flickering.

Hang on! I'm coming!

So are we... she thought as she and Tanik entered the hangar where they'd landed. He ran for one of the Ospreys, and she zipped along behind him, drawn by an invisible tether.

CHAPTER 44

—TEN MINUTES EARLIER—

Darius and Dyara managed to escape the incoming missiles by using the ZPF to push them off course and smash them together. Dyara had a close call with three of them, but Darius had managed to help her push them off course.

Soon after clearing the Revenant Fleet, they passed into weapons range with the *Nomad.* Curiously, the destroyer didn't fire on them. It wasn't shielded, so that wasn't the reason.

"Don't they see us coming?" Darius asked.

"Stay sharp..." Dyara warned. "They might be waiting for us to drop our guard."

Keeping up an evasive flight pattern as they approached, Darius reached out to the *Nomad* to determine the intentions of the ship's commander. What he found instead was Tanik and Cassandra, locked in a deadly struggle with the Cygnians on the bridge.

"We have to hurry!" Darius called out over the comms.

"What's wrong?" Dyara asked.

He explained what he'd sensed on the bridge.

"Don't worry. We'll be there soon," Dyara replied in a tight voice.

The next few minutes passed with agonizing slowness. Darius reached out periodically to check on Cassandra, each time finding her alive and fighting. He struggled to take heart from that even as despair and foreboding swirled inside of him. He was so close! Just a few more minutes!

Darius checked his range to the *Nomad.* It was still more than a hundred klicks away—ETA ten more minutes. He resisted the urge to push the throttle higher. It wouldn't help. If he went any faster, he'd be unable to slow down in time to dock with the *Nomad.*

Darius started to check on Cassandra once more, when her voice came echoing through his thoughts—

I'm sorry, Dad...

He reached back. *Cass, is that you?* Stupid question. *Why did you leave!?* A better one. But it was too late for recriminations now.

They said I was the only one the Old Ones would listen to, but they didn't listen! The prophecy...

Hang on! I'm coming! Darius thought back at her.

So are we...

Darius shut his eyes, heedless of the risk, and cast his mind into the *Nomad* in an attempt to see what she was seeing. He caught a glimpse of a shadowy hangar, and of Tanik running toward an Osprey.

His eyes snapped open. "They're coming out!"

"What? How do you know?"

"They're going to launch in an Osprey. They'll need us to escort them to safety."

"Safety?" Dyara echoed. "With the Revenant fleet behind us and the Cygnians in front there's no such thing as safety. We need to plot a jump and get the hell out of here."

"So plot a jump!" Darius snapped.

"Where?"

"Back to Cratus," he decided. "It's close. We can re-group and figure out where to go from there."

"Good enough for me," Dyara replied.

Darius plotted a jump of his own, keeping an eye on the nav panel as he did so to look for signs of an Osprey launching from the *Nomad*.

A few more minutes passed with his Alckam drive spinning up, and a jump timer ticking down.

"We'll have to hold the jump until we can sync with them," Darius said.

"Are you sure they're coming?" Dyara asked. "I don't see..."

Darius's contacts panel chimed and an Osprey shot out the front of the *Nomad*. It went evasive immediately, but the destroyer didn't fire on them. Not yet anyway.

Darius sent a message immediately. "Tanik! Is Cassandra with you?"

The reply came back a split second later. "Yes. But she's hurt. One of them stuck her with its tail."

"Did you get the tail?" Dyara asked quickly.

"No," Tanik replied. "I couldn't. We were cut off at the time, so I didn't see which one stabbed her. It was all I could do to escape with her before they killed us both."

Darius's heart pounded erratically in his chest. "She's alive?"

"Yes, but unconscious from the venom. I had to freeze her in a cryo-pod to keep her alive."

Darius let out an uneasy breath. She was alive. That was the important part. "We'll figure out how to deal with the venom later," he said.

"You need the tail of the Cygnian who

poisoned her!" Dyara said. "Without that, there's no way to synthesize an antivenin. It's like trying to solve a puzzle with half of the pieces."

Darius scowled. "So we'll find another Cygnian and use their tail!"

"The venom and antivenin is unique to each Cygnian, Darius! We'll have to board the *Nomad* and find the one who stabbed her. It's the only way."

"She's right," Tanik said. "But it's too dangerous. There are too many of them...."

Darius couldn't believe what he was hearing. "I'll find him," he said, already throwing his Vulture into a high-G turn. "Just get Cass to safety!"

"I'll set a course for the *Harbinger*," Tanik replied.

"No, not the *Harbinger*," Darius said. "We're not welcome anymore. Go back to Cratus."

"Why aren't we welcome?" Tanik asked.

"Long story," Darius replied. "We can trade explanations later. I'm expecting a good one from you."

"Of course," Tanik replied. "I'll see you at Cratus."

Darius nodded to himself. "Dyara? Are you with me?"

"We're going to have to take the whole ship, and somehow capture all of them alive..." She trailed off uncertainly.

"So?"

"So, how are we going to do that, Darius?! They're all fully trained Revenants—*Cygnians* no less—and we'll be outnumbered. We won't stand a chance."

"Then tell me there's another way to save Cass."

"I can't, but... maybe we can find some way to track down the Cygnian who stabbed her later. She's in cryo. She's stabilized. We won't help her by throwing our lives away."

Darius gritted his teeth, warring with himself. He couldn't just leave! But Dyara was right. "Fine. Sync our jumps, Dya, and let's get out of here."

"Way ahead of you," she replied, her voice relayed by the extra-sensory chips (ESCs) in their brains. She must have been pulling too many Gs to physically move her lips.

A request to sync jumps began blinking at the bottom of Darius's nav. He accepted it and lined up his fighter with the blue arrow of the jump vector. As soon as he did, his throttle shot up of its own accord, and his thrusters began roaring at nine Gs.

Darius fought to stay conscious and breathe against the immense pressure squashing him into his seat. His oxygen mask and flight suit helped, but not enough.

He glanced at his nav to figure out why they were making such a fast getaway. It didn't take long to see why. More than a dozen squadrons of fighters raced toward them from the Revenant fleet, and several *hundred* Cygnian squadrons approached from behind the *Nomad*. Dyara was trying to get them out of the area before they got caught in the middle of a massive battle.

As the squadrons drew near to each other, Revenant fighters opened fire on the *Nomad* with streaking swarms of missiles and flickering yellow lasers.

"No!" Darius roared. He mentally toggled a target camera to watch the *Nomad* weather the assault. The destroyer was shielded, but that meant it couldn't fire on the incoming missiles, and it had no fighters to protect it. The Cygnian squadrons would arrive too late to save them.

The *Nomad* slowly turned, its thrusters flaring bright blue in a belated attempt to run. Golden lasers lashed the destroyer's shield, provoking fading flashes of light as they dissipated harmlessly. Then the missiles arrived—a glinting hail of metal bullets riding on tiny blue thrusters trails.

The impacts came one after another, explosions blossoming in roiling clouds of fire. The *Nomad's* shields burned bright, repelling the onslaught. Darius held his breath. They just needed to last a little longer...

But then the shields failed and the *Nomad's* hull darkened. Explosions ripped holes through the side of the ship. Debris and bodies gushed out.

"No!" Darius screamed again, staring helplessly as a massive explosion tore the *Nomad* apart from the inside. The antimatter storage had been breached.

Darius gaped at the empty space where the destroyer had been. Whoever had stabbed and poisoned his daughter, had just been vaporized.

Blinking hot tears from his eyes, Darius battled to breathe against the combined weight of acceleration and loss. Rage boiled inside of him, urging him to turn back and kill as many Cygnians as he could.

"I'm sorry," Dyara said, her voice echoing through his thoughts over their ESCs, and giving him pause.

Then the jump timer hit zero, sweeping away Darius's plans for revenge in a blinding flash of light.

As the intense pressure of acceleration vanished, Darius slumped against his harness, sobbing and gasping for air.

CHAPTER 45

Clouds swept by Darius's cockpit and the surface of Cratus peeked through—lush green islands and tropical waters as far as the eye could see. Darius's eyes weren't seeing much. He'd set the autopilot to follow Tanik's Osprey, because he was in no shape to fly. After spending the last four hours alone with his thoughts, he'd cried himself into a stupor.

There had to be some other way to save Cassandra. He refused to accept that his visions had somehow inexplicably come true.

Whispers from the ZPF—or the Sprites, whichever—echoed at the edges of Darius's hearing, but they were as unintelligible as ever. None of this made sense. *Why* had Cassandra gone with the *Nomad?* What could she possibly have been thinking? In their brief telepathic dialogue, Cass had mentioned something: she'd said the Cygnians convinced her to speak to their Old Ones, because of a prophecy, whatever that meant.

But if the whole thing had been their idea, then why did they attack her? Why *kill* her for trying to help them? It boiled Darius's blood and blurred his eyes with a fresh sheen of tears.

Tanik had a lot of explaining to do. That was part of the reason they were landing on Cratus now. The other part was to *see* his daughter, if only through the frosted glass of a cryo-pod. They also had to gather supplies from their abandoned camp and figure out what to do next.

Darius knew what *he* wanted to do. He was going to find some way—*any* way—to make the Cygnians pay. If they could kill a twelve-year-old girl after she'd tried to save their lives, then they deserved to die too.

Tanik landed his Osprey on a flat grassy plateau above the camp. Dyara's fighter set down to one side, and Darius's to the other. The subtle jolt of landing skids touching down jarred Darius out of his thoughts and brought him back to the moment. He wasn't wearing his helmet or oxygen mask anymore—he'd turned them into a snotty mess and had to remove them—so he simply pulled the release lever for his harness, opened the canopy, and jumped down. His legs collapsed under him, but he picked himself up and ran to Tanik's Osprey.

The airlock opened just as he arrived, and a cryo-pod floated out ahead of Tanik. Darius peered into that pod as it settled in the grass at his feet—

And saw Cassandra's face.

It was true. He placed both palms against the icy glass. The steady *hum* of the pod's cooling systems shivered through his bones.

"I did everything I could to save her," Tanik whispered.

Darius rounded on him and grabbed him by the collar of his flight suit. "What were you doing on the *Nomad* in the first place!? Did *you* take her there?"

Tanik shook his head. "No. She went on her own. I followed her. When I found out that she'd gone to join Gakram on the *Nomad*, I went after her to bring her back."

"Why didn't you tell *me?*"

"There was no time, and because I knew that the admiral had sabotaged the *Nomad's* Alckam drive and rigged it to blow when they jumped. Telling you that would have been an act of treason."

"The admiral did *what?*"

"When Cassandra refused to come back with me, I was forced to reveal the sabotage, and the Cygnians arrested me. I later broke out, but by the time I got to Cassandra it was already too late."

"I sensed you both fighting together on the bridge..." Darius said. "You said you were separated when she got poisoned."

Tanik nodded. "We were. It happened before I arrived. It took a few minutes for Cassandra to succumb to the venom, and by the time I realized what had happened, we were already on our way to the hangar."

Darius glared at the man, not ready to give up, but he was out of accusations. Pushing Tanik away, he turned back to Cassandra's cryo-pod.

Dyara approached them, long grass rustling against her legs. Darius noticed the grass, as if for the first time—*green* grass, bowing in the wind; then a sound reached his ears—running water. He looked up and saw that Tanik had landed them beside a rushing stream. To one side, jagged black cliffs, to the other, a thundering waterfall with a scraggly black tree beside it.

Darius gaped at the scene. It was almost identical to the landing zone on Ouroboros, and it definitely matched his visions. Darius barked out a broken laugh.

He saw Dyara shoot him a bemused look as she came to stand beside him. She was probably wondering what he had to laugh about. Maybe she'd never suffered enough to know that madness and laughter were a refuge from sorrow.

"This is it," he whispered, smiling like a maniac. "It's all come true!" He slowly shook his head and laughed again. "I guess we may as well have the funeral then, right? It's what the Sprites have been showing me all this time, so it must be what they wanted!"

"They didn't cause this," Tanik said. "But perhaps Cassandra's fate was inescapable, and the visions you saw were destiny, not foresight. The Sprites may have been showing you in advance to help cushion the blow."

"Fek you, Tanik!" Darius spluttered with tears leaking from his eyes once more.

Tanik held up his hands and took a step back. "Perhaps I should leave you alone."

"Wake her up!"

"If I wake her now, her heart will stop. She won't even be able to say goodbye. She's unconscious. There's nothing we can do for her, but if you want to have a funeral, then I suggest you do it soon. We don't know how long we'll have before Admiral Ventaris finds us here."

Darius lashed out, shoving Tanik back with a kinetic blast; then he mentally picked up Cassandra's cryo-pod and sent it floating ahead of him toward the river. He set the pod down on the riverbank beside the thundering waterfall, and glared up at the sky. "Is this what you wanted?" he roared. "Well you got it! You killed her! Are you happy now?"

Tanik walked up beside him. "Who are you talking to?" he asked quietly.

"The Sprites! You said they're everywhere, right?"

"Yes, but they're not god, or gods. As I said, this isn't their doing. They're not intelligent. They have no will of their own."

"So they can predict the future, but they can't tell us how to stop that future from coming to pass?" Darius demanded.

Tanik shrugged, but offered no reply.

Darius smirked and looked away, staring at the racing rapids before the waterfall. A few moments later, Dyara walked over carrying two handfuls of the red rose-petal leaves from Cratus's trees.

"I thought..." she trailed off uncertainly and hefted the handfuls of leaves. Tears streamed down her cheeks. Her eyes were puffy and red from crying. "Can we open her pod?" Dyara asked.

Darius's mind flashed back to his vision, to seeing Cassandra lying inside her cryo-pod with her head and hair surrounded by red flowers. He'd never related that particular detail to anyone. Maybe this really was *destiny* at work. Darius's lip curled. *Fek destiny.*

Dyara took his nod for permission, and asked Tanik to open Cassandra's pod. He did so, but didn't go through the proper warming cycle first. Frosty white clouds swirled out of the pod as the lid swung open.

Dyara sprinkled the flower petals inside and then stepped back.

Darius's legs shook as he walked up to the side of the pod and peered in. Cassandra looked just as she had in his vision—her face relaxed in sleep, her skin pale and ice cold as he brushed it with his hand. Crimson flower petals lay around her head.

He looked at the horizon, to the thundering waterfall and the scraggly black tree clinging beside it. The sun began to set, splashing the sky with fire.

"They killed her," Tanik said. "She tried to negotiate with them, and they killed her. This just proves that there can be no negotiating with the

Cygnians. The only way we'll ever have peace is to kill them all, or subjugate them, as they subjugated us."

Tanik's words were identical to the ones Darius had heard time and time again in his visions. Looking back to Cassandra's pod, he brushed her cheek once more and slowly shook his head. He opened his mouth to say something, but his mind blanked, so he fell back on his own lines, words he'd foreseen himself speak so many times that he knew them by rote.

"First we're going to slaughter them," Darius said. "Then, when there's only a few of them left, and they're on their knees begging for their lives, we'll show them mercy, but only to prolong their suffering. We'll enslave them just as they enslaved us."

"Yesss," Tanik rasped in an euphoric whisper. "That, would be justice."

There was a bitter irony in giving Destiny its way. So why had he? Why not say something else? Something to prove that this hadn't all been scripted from the start by powers unseen. Something to prove that he could have changed the outcome, or that it might still be changed, and that Cassandra might somehow rise from the dead.

Yet there was no such proof, no stray detail of

his vision left unaccounted for. Darius stepped forward and pressed a button on the side of Cassandra's pod. The lid swung shut, and he extended a hand toward it, sending it floating up over the racing rapids above the waterfall.

He hesitated, blinking hot tears from his eyes, and then dropped his hand to his side. The pod fell with a loud *splash.* It ducked briefly under the water, and bobbed back up a split second later, only to be whisked over the cliff amidst sparkling curtains of spray.

A heavy hand fell on Darius's shoulder. "Come," Tanik said. "Night is falling." That hand left Darius's shoulder as Tanik turned and walked away.

"That's not your line..." Darius whispered.

"I'm so sorry!" Dyara sobbed, not hearing his protest. "I should have listened to you! I thought they were just dreams! I had no idea...."

Darius barely registered her words. A spark of hope bloomed inside of him. He reached out in the ZPF and found Cassandra's cryo-pod bumping and bobbing down the river some eight feet below the plateau where they stood. Thankfully the falls weren't higher, or she might have suffered injury when she went over them.

Darius brought the pod back up to the cliff and

set it down in the field beside that scraggly black tree with a *thump.*

Tanik turned to look, his brow furrowing at the sight of it. "You brought her back up?" he asked.

"That's not your line!" he shouted.

"What are you talking about?" Tanik shouted back.

"*Come, night is falling*—after that you're supposed to say *the Cygnians will be out to hunt soon.* And then I say, *let them come!* But there aren't any Cygnians here, and neither of us said that!"

"Darius..."

"It's different," he insisted. "Something is different. This isn't Cassandra's destiny! This future wasn't cast in stone."

Tanik strode back to Darius. "Maybe not, but how does that change anything? You're not going to be able to bring her back just because the Cygnians aren't here."

"I don't know how it changes anything," Darius admitted. "But Cass has been in Cryo waiting for a cure before, and she can do it again."

Tanik arched an eyebrow at him. "Darius, the Cygnian who stabbed her is gone. He died when the *Nomad* was destroyed."

Darius shook his head. "So? We'll find some other way. You said she's still alive."

"Yes, but we can't wake her without an antidote!"

"So we won't. Not until we find one."

Tanik considered that with a deep frown. "You're in denial. Holding onto an impossible hope isn't going to help her—or you."

Darius ground his teeth. "I'm not giving up on her."

"Very well. Take her with you wherever you decide to go next. It's none of my concern. And where are you going to go next? Have you given that any thought?"

Darius *had* given it plenty of thought. He was planning to go slaughter the Cygnians, just as he'd said while quoting his vision a moment ago. The only problem was, he didn't know how to do it. Dyara appeared beside him, staring at Cassandra's cryo-pod-casket in a daze.

"What about your plan?" Darius asked.

Tanik's eyebrows floated up. "My plan?"

"Yes. Your plan to threaten the Cygnians with ZPF bombs."

"Oh. Well, we can't possibly destroy or threaten all of their planets at once. Not anymore. We've lost the element of surprise."

"Then let's do it one by one," Darius insisted.

"It won't be easy...." Tanik said. "I suppose we

could jump back to Cygnus Prime, but they've got the numbers there to intercept any missiles we shoot long before they reach the surface. There is a sure way, but you won't like it. It's how the Augur delivered ZPFs to Keth worlds."

Darius nodded for him to go on. "How?"

"He'd take control of a Revenant pilot and make them crash their fighter into the planet. The bomb would go off in the explosion."

Darius blinked in shock. "A suicide run? Why kill the pilot?"

"Because it's the only way to shield the bomb. You can't shield something that you aren't physically touching, so the pilot has to remain in his seat, and the bomb in the fighter.

"You could take control of one of the Revenants, even from here, and make them sacrifice themselves for the greater good."

Darius shook his head. "I won't do that. There has to be another way."

Tanik sighed. "We could carry a bomb down ourselves, and leave it somewhere on the surface with a timer set to detonate it after we're gone. But, we'd have to risk our own lives to do it, and the chances of sneaking both ways past the Cygnians' fighters are dismal at best."

"Dismal will have to do," Darius decided.

"Revenge won't fix this," Dyara said quietly. "You won't save Cassandra no matter how many Cygnians you kill."

"Maybe not, but it *will* give them something to think about. Maybe they'll think twice before they prey on innocent children again. Tanik?" Darius turned to him. "Are you coming with me, or do I have to do this alone?"

Tanik appeared to consider the question. He eventually gave in with a nod. "I'll come, but we should take one fighter, not two. Our shields will be stronger if we can combine them."

"Fine, but I'm piloting. Dyara, you stay here with Cass. If we don't make it back, promise me you'll look after her."

Dyara's eyes searched his. "If you promise me you're not going to get yourself killed."

He shook his head. "Not on purpose."

"What about the Revenant fleet? If they come back here—"

"You can explain yourself," Darius said. "You didn't do anything wrong. You can say I had you under my influence the whole time."

"And if the Cygnians come?"

"They won't," Tanik said. "They'll stay close to home for a while."

Darius nodded. "Stay hidden, anyway. If we're

not back in a day, you should probably leave."

"No, what I *should* do, is go with you. You could use a wingmate."

Darius shook his head. "Someone has to stay with Cass. Promise you'll keep her with you until you find a way to bring her back."

Dyara bit her lower lip. "I promise."

Darius flashed a tight smile and pulled her in for a kiss. Her lips moved feebly against his, and he lingered for a few seconds before breaking away.

"Tanik?" he prompted, casting about to find the other man. Tanik stood with his back politely turned, watching the sunset. "Let's go!" Darius said, and began stalking back to his fighter.

It was time for the Cygnians to get a taste of the death and destruction that they so happily dished out to others.

CHAPTER 46

—TWELVE HOURS LATER—

The warp bubble dispersed with a flash of light. Chimes sounded furiously from the contacts panel, and Darius glanced at the nav to get a feel for the disposition of enemy forces around Cygnus Prime.

Surprisingly the Revenant Fleet was still there, locked in a furious battle. Their capital ships were holding off, out of range, while their fighters dealt with vastly superior numbers of Cygnian Blades.

"They're trying to get through to deliver a bomb to the surface..." Tanik said from the co-pilot's seat. "It's not working," he added. "Hopefully we can succeed where they've failed."

Darius sneered and checked the nav to make sure none of the Cygnian fighters were heading their way. They weren't. Darius blew out a breath.

He had the fighter's stealth mode engaged, but that did nothing to diminish the flash of gamma rays that appeared when they'd exited warp. Hopefully no one noticed their arrival.

"Well, we're here," Tanik said. "What's the plan, Darius? How do we get to the surface?"

He considered that. They were cruising at over a hundred kilometers per second, having entered warp at that speed. The planet lay just over forty thousand kilometers away. ETA six minutes. If they cruised the rest of the way in stealth mode and without lighting their engines, the Cygnians wouldn't have much time to spot and intercept them. Yet they had to ignite their thrusters to slow down. If they hit the atmosphere at this speed they'd be vaporized instantly.

Another idea occurred to Darius. "What if we fire a ZPF missile from here? We could dumb fire it. Drop it without lighting its engines. At these speeds, the Cygnians won't have long to detect and intercept it."

"Long enough," Tanik replied. "They'll be watching for something like that, and maximum range for heavy lasers in space is over three thousand kilometers. At our current velocity that will give them at least thirty seconds to react to the threat."

"But if the warheads are as powerful as you say, won't they destroy their own fleet? What's the blast radius on a ZPF?"

"In space? Just a few hundred kilometers. There's no atmosphere to carry the effects."

Darius considered that while staring at the mottled brown and red orb of Cygnus Prime. "How many ZPF warheads do we have?" he asked, wondering if they could afford to spare some as decoys, or to take out enemy capital ships and fighters that got in their way.

"Two," Tanik replied.

Scratch that idea... Darius's veins buzzed with adrenaline, demanding quick action. It was a physical effort to slow himself down and *think.* "Don't *you* have any ideas?" he asked. "You're the one who has all the combat experience."

"I told you how the Augur did it. Take control of a pilot, and force him to make a suicide run."

"If that would work, then we should be able to make it to the surface, too."

"It's one thing racing down at top speed with a bomb ticking in your hold. It's much harder to make a safe landing, leave the bomb on the surface, and then escape."

"I'm not going to kill innocent people!" Darius insisted.

"Innocent?" Tanik scoffed. "The Revenants all have plenty of blood on their hands. None of them are *innocent*. Besides—you'd kill one Revenant to save a thousand. It's excellent math. If you're going to rule the Union someday, you're going to have to learn how to do a little evil to do a lot of good. Famous generals and rulers have been making those kinds of trade offs since the very first wars," Tanik said. "Now it's your turn. Destroy Cygnus Prime, and repeat the process. You could win the war, just like the Augur won his."

"Why don't you do it?" Darius challenged.

"Because my powers cannot affect other Revenants, remember? Only a Luminary like yourself can do that."

Darius scowled. He'd forgotten about that. "I'm lighting our engines and taking us in. We'll fight our way down somehow."

Tanik sighed. "Very well. I just hope for your daughter's sake that your principles don't get us killed and leave her an orphan."

"I thought you said there's no point holding onto hope?"

"In the rare event that you're able to spend the next thousand years looking for a way to revive her, and assuming you don't get yourself killed before then, perhaps you will find a way to bring her back. Who knows? Time is anathema to the impossible."

Darius scowled and shook his head. He lit the engines and flipped the Vulture over. Sailing toward Cygnus Prime tail-first, he engaged the thrusters at five *G*s to slow them down for atmospheric entry.

The Cygnians reacted immediately. Two squadrons of fighters broke off from the main engagement and accelerated toward them.

"We've got incoming!" Tanik warned.

"I see them," Darius replied.

"You're going to get us killed," Tanik insisted.

"Shut up! You didn't have to come, remember?"

Darius eyed the enemy fighters approaching them. He targeted the nearest fighter. Two minutes to firing range.

"I had hoped you would see reason at some point," Tanik said quietly. "If you die, we will lose this war, and the Cygnians will hunt all other species in the Union to death. You're the key to everything, remember? You can't allow yourself to die."

"What does that even mean?!" Darius demanded.

"The choice is yours. I cannot force you to do

what's best."

Darius flipped his fighter back around to face the incoming Cygnian squadrons. "Activate your shield," he said.

"As you wish." All the surfaces inside the cockpit began glowing with a dim white aura. Darius activated his own shield, and the light doubled in brightness.

"How do you propose we shoot back while we're under fire?" Tanik asked. "With two squadrons arrayed against us, we'll be under constant fire. We can't afford to drop our shields for even a second."

"What if we ram them?" Darius asked. "Our shield will protect us, but we'll carve their fighters into pieces."

"Good luck catching up with a Blade fighter to do that! They're much faster than Vultures. Besides, even one collision would weaken our shields enough for their fire to get through, and our shields will do nothing to buffer the inertial effects of a collision. We could be crushed against our harnesses."

"Then we're just going to have to evade their fire and fly past them."

Tanik said nothing to that.

Darius set course for the planet and watched

the seconds counting down to firing range with the enemy fighters. When the count reached five, he began an evasive flight pattern.

The stars spun around their heads in sickening swirls, and Cygnian medium lasers flickered around them in sky-blue streaks. As more and more fighters came into range, the flickering flashes intensified, and soon dozens of lasers hit them with every passing second.

Their shields dimmed with each hit, reducing their glow to a pale aura. Cygnus Prime was a minute and thirty seconds away. Darius checked their approach vector while juking wildly to evade enemy fire. At over eighty kilometers per second, the fighter's velocity flashed urgently, reminding him to slow down before entering the planet's atmosphere. But reversing thrust now or flipping around to decelerate faster, would make him an easier target. If anything, he needed to *speed up*, not slow down.

Tanik was right. They could make a suicide run, but not a slow, measured approach.

Another two lasers tagged them, and this time they drew simulated *crunches* from the simulated feedback system, indicating hull damage. Darius's gaze fell on a damage report. They'd shredded an aileron. That didn't matter in space, but it would definitely matter once they hit atmosphere.

Maybe he could get by with one aileron and compensate with rudder.

More impacts hissed against their shields, and they dimmed to a ghostly glow.

"Darius! We need to get out of here!" Tanik warned. "I can't hold this shield much longer."

"I've seen you shield the Deliverance from an antimatter missile!" Darius objected.

"That was different! I was at full strength! I'm still exhausted from rescuing your daughter, and I haven't slept more than a couple of hours."

"Neither have I!" Darius roared. He couldn't believe they were going to die because of something as mundane as sleep deprivation.

"We have to turn back!" Tanik insisted.

Darius shook his head, and spoke through clenched teeth as he nudged the throttle up. "It's too late! They'll chase us out anyway."

"Not if you break off," Tanik replied. "They're here to defend their world, not to catch strays fleeing the battle! Why do you think they haven't tried to engage Admiral Ventaris's fleet? They're using everything they've got to blockade their own planet and intercept the Revenants' fighters."

Darius warred with himself for a second. The mottled red and brown orb of Cygnus Prime seemed to glare at him, mocking his feeble attempt to reach it. Another *crunch* sounded. This time they'd hit the Alckam drive, but thankfully not the antimatter containment.

"We can't run now," Darius said. "The Alckam drive is offline."

"Yes, we can! Tanik insisted. "I can summon Dyara here to pick us up, but not if we're dead!"

Darius gave in with a scowl, and turned away from the planet. He pushed the throttle up to ten Gs. The thrusters gave a thunderous roar, and Darius's arms were ripped away from the controls. Using his ESC to control the fighter with his thoughts, he engaged an automatic evasive routine, and focused all of his attention and strength on staying conscious and bolstering their shields.

Despite his oxygen mask forcing air down his throat, it was almost impossible to keep breathing. Dark spots swam before his eyes. His ribs ached like they were about to break, and his cheeks were pulled into an involuntary grimace.

The sensation went on for long seconds, and the dazzling blue streaks of Cygnian lasers kept flashing around them, defying Tanik's argument that the Cygnians would break off if they did.

Darius struggled to maintain a shield around their fighter against the repeated assaults of enemy lasers and the unbearable pressure from the Vulture's thrusters. Something had to give.

Darkness gathered at the edges of Darius's vision, leaving nothing but a blurry circle of stars and flashing blue lasers. He fought back, trying to stay conscious, if only for just a little longer....

But it was no use. The darkness swirled in and sucked him under.

CHAPTER 47

Darius came to, gasping for air. His eyes darted around the cockpit looking for obvious damage to his fighter, but saw none. He patted himself down, checking for physical injuries. Again, he was clean.

He had the presence of mind to check his displays next, and saw that the Cygnians had broken off and returned to the main engagement, just as Tanik had said they would. There was plenty of damage to their fighter, but somehow the cockpit was pressurized, the antimatter containment cylinder was intact, and the thrusters were still burning.

Darius noted that Cygnus Prime lay behind them at a range of fifty thousand klicks and counting. They were rocketing away at one hundred and five kilometers per second.

"Tanik?" Darius croaked.

"You're awake. Good. I've contacted Dyara. She's on her way to pick us up."

"You used the ZPF to contact her?" Darius wondered aloud.

"Of course. FTL comms don't exist, remember?"

Darius nodded slowly and his gaze returned to the nav to glare at the Cygnians' home world. The Revenants were struggling to get a fighter through to reach the planet. They'd been trying to do that for half a day with no success.

The only way to break the Cygnians' lines would be to jump in at a velocity even higher than the one Darius had chosen for his approach. A hundred kilometers per second was already a suicidal plunge, but it wasn't fast enough. At two, or three hundred kilometers per second, however... it might be enough. Especially if that ship was a lone Vulture fighter with its reactor and thrusters off, and stealth mode engaged.

The fighter would detonate almost instantly on contact with the planet's atmosphere, but a ZPF warhead could be rigged to blow at the same time. The blast radius would be enough to reach all the way to the ground and do significant damage, if not utterly destroy the planet, as Tanik claimed.

Darius ground his teeth. It might work, but it still required someone to sacrifice their life. Darius couldn't make anyone do that. But he couldn't do it himself, either. His Alckam drive was offline.

"It's a pity that we failed," Tanik said, interrupting his thoughts. "If we could have destroyed their home world, it might have been enough to end the war here. We could have saved trillions of lives."

"Stop trying to guilt me into doing what you want!" Darius snapped. "I have a better idea, and it's considerably less evil than what you suggested."

"Oh? And what idea is that?" Tanik asked. It sounded like he was smiling.

"I'm going to find a pilot willing to make the sacrifice without being forced. I'll send a message to the Revenants over the comms, asking for a volunteer."

"You'd have to find a particularly selfless person, but that could work, I suppose... Make sure you encrypt your message with Revenant codes, not Union ones. The Cygnians will know the Union encryptions already."

"How do I do that?"

"Let me help you," Tanik said. Darius watched

as settings magically appeared on his comms panel. "Done. Go ahead and send your message."

Darius took a deep breath before recording his message. "This is Darius Drake, the Luminary in training, to all Revenant forces in the area. There is a way to reach Cygnus Prime and destroy it, but it will require a sacrifice. Someone needs to give up their own life in the attack. As a Luminary, I'm told that I could *make* one of you do it, but I refuse to do that. Instead, I'm asking for volunteers. If any of you is willing to strike a definitive blow against the enemy, contact me, and I'll share my plan with you."

Darius sent the message and waited anxiously for a reply. It didn't take long before the message light on his comms panel lit red and began to blink at him. Darius saw that the message was from the *Harbinger*. He hit play.

"Darius, you're back," Admiral Ventaris said. "It seems you've developed some scruples since the last time we saw you. What's the matter—you don't mind taking control of me to bring us here, but you won't do it to kill someone? Afraid to get your hands dirty? Let me assure you, we've already lost *hundreds* of people thanks to you sending *my* fleet in a headlong chase after the *Nomad*. And just so that you know, I've already asked for volunteers for what you're suggesting. If no one took me up on it then, they're not going to take you up on it now."

Darius keyed the comms for reply. "You're telling me *no one* was willing to sacrifice themselves for the greater good?"

"Are you?" Admiral Ventaris challenged.

Darius had nothing to say to that. Would make that sacrifice? Even if his Alckam drive was still working, would he really give up his life to take out the Cygnians' home world?

Yes, he decided. The Cygnians had to pay for the millions they'd slaughtered like cattle. The Revenants had grown soft hiding behind the ZPF and their fleets. They'd spent the past few decades fighting *with* the Cygnians against the Keth, not against them to save their loved ones. Darius had been forced to grieve for his daughter time and again because of the Cygnians, and there were millions more grieving parents like him. Yes, he'd sacrifice himself if he could. But, he couldn't.

The admiral went on, speaking into his silence. "Look, Darius, if I were you, and *I* had the power to make someone do it, I would. I'll let you think about that, and what it means to be a *real* leader, rather than an empty title. Meanwhile, I'm going to call a retreat before anyone else has to die."

Darius sat in silence, gaping at his comms panel for long seconds after the admiral's message ended. It seemed that Ventaris and Tanik were cut from the same cloth. To them, the ends justified the means. "One life to save a thousand..." Darius muttered.

"Or trillions, if the Cygnians back down after this," Tanik said.

Darius sucked in a deep breath and let it out slowly. He shut his eyes and cast his mind out, far into space...

It didn't take long to find the Revenant pilots in their fighters, embroiled in a deadly struggle against a hundred times as many of their Cygnian counterparts. Darius probed individual minds at random, trying to find one whose thoughts were conflicted, teetering between self-sacrifice and self-preservation.

He found two, pilot and co-pilot—a couple, if he was reading the emotions between them correctly. They were debating the subject of volunteering even as Darius found them. He thrust his mind into the cockpit with them and listened to their debate.

"There's no other way, Korvin!" the woman in the pilot's seat said.

"There has to be! We'll come back and conduct

a surprise attack some other time. Or we'll lure their fleets away first!"

"They've got hundreds more fleets where this one came from!" the pilot said as her hands flew over the controls.

"It's not worth our lives, Kara!" her copilot snapped. "The Augur forced us to fight the Keth. Then his favorite Luminary took over. And now, some *other* Luminary is asking us to die for his cause, in a new war. He has no right! We deserve a chance to be free, to live our lives for once."

Darius fumed at Korvin's argument. *Cass deserves a life of her own, no one deserves it more. But she didn't get that chance, and no one ever will as long as the Cygnians are around.* Darius had thought this wasn't his war, but he'd been wrong, just as Korvin was wrong.

"We could end the war right here, Korry," Kara said.

"You don't know that. You don't even know that we'll make it to the planet. We could get shot down long before we reach it, and then what? We'll both have died for nothing!"

"I can't do this without you, Korry," the pilot replied. "I can't volunteer on my own and make you die with me."

"You're right, you can't," Korvin replied.

"So that's a no?"

Darius inwardly frowned, hating himself for what he was about to do, but knowing that he had no other choice. He zipped into the man's head, and took over like a ghost, possessing him.

"Fine, let's do it," Darius said, but the voice that came out was Korvin's—not his.

Kara said nothing for a long moment. "The galaxy will remember our sacrifice," she whispered; then her voice rose into a jubilant shout as she added, "They're gonna make fekkin' statues of us!"

"Yeah sure, something for future generations to piss on," Darius said dryly, thinking that's probably how the real Korvin would respond.

"We're going to have to jump out and back in again," Kara said, ignoring that comment. She went on quickly, "We can't accelerate up to attack speed here with them watching us.... They'll see it coming. But if we accelerate before we jump back into the system, our momentum will be preserved and we can use it to make our run on the planet. We'll have to keep the power off and stealth mode on until the last second, but it should work. I'll plot our exit coords as close to the planet as I can. We're going to need some luck not to run into ships or debris along the way, but their fleet is pretty spaced out, so it shouldn't be a problem."

Darius nodded along with that. Kara had obviously given this a lot of thought. She'd come up with the same plan he had. But there was one difficulty he hadn't solved, and he suspected neither had she. Making Korvin speak again, he asked, "What about the radiation signature as we drop out of warp? Won't that reveal us?"

"We could mask it..." Kara suggested. "If we could get someone to fly next to us and sync their jump with ours... no, they'd draw too much attention to us when they fire up their thrusters to peel away."

An idea occurred to Darius with that suggestion, and he made Korvin speak again. "What if someone synced a jump out with our jump *in*? Let's say they jump out just a split second before we jump in. The radiation bursts would overlap and mask each other."

"That's brilliant, Korry! I could kiss you!"

"Don't give a dead man hope," Darius grumbled, feeling like a monster even as he said it.

"Hey, let's not discount the afterlife yet!"

Kara sent a message to the Harbinger explaining their plan and asking for a ship in the fleet to coordinate a jump with theirs.

The Admiral was quick to jump on Kara's

plan, but he pointed out that they'd need hours to accelerate up to the necessary approach velocity, and there was no way just one ship could stick around here to wait for them. Her plan would take a coordinated effort from the entire fleet.

"I'll get a destroyer to wait for you at the exit coordinates," Ventaris went on. "But you'd better time it perfectly, or you're going to collide with them at several hundred kilometers per second."

"Yes, sir," Kara said. "That's what nav computers are for, right?"

"Indeed," Admiral Ventaris replied. "I'll plot and time the jumps just to be sure. You can start spinning up your drive while you wait. Stand by to receive a nav transfer."

"Yes, sir." Kara replied. "That is it, Korry!" she added, as she began spinning up the Alckam drive. "Time for us to make history."

"I've never met someone so enthusiastic to *die* for a cause," Darius said through Korvin. He was genuinely impressed.

"Yeah, well..." Kara trailed off, sounding more sober now. "I guess you can only watch so many of your friends die before you start to wonder where they went."

Darius snorted at that, but decided not to press any further down that line of conversation in case she had a change of heart. Instead he directed his attention to keeping his mental hold on Korvin. That buzzing pressure he'd felt when he'd taken control of the Admiral had returned, but thankfully, it was weaker than before. Korvin was a weaker Revenant than Admiral Ventaris. When Korvin's mental pressure failed to oust Darius, a pleading voice took its place.

Don't do this. I'm begging you, let me go.

Darius grimaced, but said nothing

We're in love! We were going to get married and have kids!

Darius pretended not to hear him.

Haven't you ever had a dream? Something you wanted more than anything? Well, my dream is to live, and to make a life with Kara.

She wants to do this, Darius thought back.

But I don't! Korvin snapped. *And she doesn't know what she's giving up. She hasn't been free to live since she was twelve! Now that she's got her life back, she doesn't know what to do with it, that's all.*

This is bigger than the two of you, Darius thought. *Someone has to do it. The Cygnians are going to kill a lot of people if we don't.*

Yeah, someone has to... so how about you? You're that Luminary, right? So set an example. Lead from the front.

I can't. My fighter is damaged, Darius replied.

How convenient.

"Five seconds to jump," Kara announced.

Tell her you've changed your mind, Korvin demanded.

No.

Tell her, you miserable vagon!

Darius just shook his head. The fighter jumped and the stars disappeared with a bright flash. They reappeared a minute later, and Darius checked Korvin's nav panel to find that they were well outside of the solar system, drifting in deep space.

"This is it!" Kara said. "I'd use a sedative if I were you, Korvin. It's going to take... nine hours at five Gs to reach our exit velocity. Grak! Ventaris must be goffity! Can we even survive that? Can they? Nine hours is a long time to hold off their fleet."

Darius and Tanik had endured eight hours at three and a half Gs while leaving Cratus in order to reach their cruising speed, but five Gs for *nine* hours?

"What's our velocity going to be after that?" he asked.

"A hundred and sixty klicks per second!" Kara whistled. "At that speed a stray speck of dust could wipe us out! You ready with your sedatives?"

"One second." Darius opened a compartment beside Korvin's leg and removed a blue-coded silver injector pen. He screwed the tip into the thigh of his flight suit and depressed the button with a pneumatic *hiss*. The effect was instant. Exhaustion hit him like a wave. "All set," he mumbled sleepily.

"Good," Kara replied. The Vulture whipped back around to line up with the blinking blue arrow of their jump vector, and Darius heard another pen firing. "I've set an alarm to wake us five minutes before we jump back," she said. "That should give us enough time to inject a stim."

Darius nodded. "Gooood," he drawled.

"Throttling up..." Kara said.

Darius watched on the screens as the throttle hit five Gs. The crushing weight on his chest—*Korvin's chest*—was a familiar feeling. Time dragged by, and the pressure remained. Darius gritted his teeth and endured. Korvan's mind was fading fast, so he wouldn't have to endure it for long.

He wondered absently what would happen to him after Korvin was knocked out by the drugs. Would he lose his mental hold on the man, or would Korvin's body drag his consciousness down with it?

Darkness fell, and Darius's mind blanked, giving him his answer.

After what seemed like just a few seconds, he awoke to the sound of a klaxon screaming in his ears.

"Wha..." he mumbled.

"Use your stim," Kara groaned.

Darius fumbled for the utility compartment and found a yellow-coded pen. He injected it, and his eyes flew wide open. "Grak! That's a rush," he said.

"Yeah..." Kara replied in a strained voice.

Darius tried to stretch—

And felt an explosion of pain. The pressure of acceleration was gone, but the damage remained. Even with nanites coursing through their blood to repair injuries as soon as they occurred, tissue damage had accumulated over the last nine hours. They passed the next few minutes in silence, enduring their own private worlds of pain.

"Jumping," Kara wheezed.

"Are you okay?" Darius asked just as a flash of light tore through the cockpit. A minute later the stars returned with another flash of light.

Darius checked the nav for an idea of how the battle had gone in their absence, but the screen was blank. The whole cockpit was dark, and the reassuring hum of the fighter's reactor was dead silent.

"You powered down," Darius whispered.

"Had to," Kara said. "We've got to stay dark to maximize our chances of staying hidden. We're running on battery now. Critical systems only."

"What about shields?" he asked. "Should we..." Darius trailed off in a hacking cough, and he tasted blood. His air hose began rattling with a watery slurping sound. He inhaled some of the blood he'd coughed into the hose, and ended up coughing it back up for the second time. Darius yanked out his air hose and ripped off his helmet.

Korvin's voice intruded on his thoughts just as his coughing subsided. *Motherfekker... you've already gone and gotten me killed, haven't you?*

Darius stared at floating gobs of blood drifting in front of him, and slowly shook his head. "Kara?"

"No shields," she replied belatedly. "Can't risk it."

"What about what you said—about a speck of dust being enough to take us out?"

"I was exaggerating. It'll do some damage, but it'll take more than a speck to do us in. We'll hold off with shields as long as we can."

Darius nodded and peered around the back of

the pilot's seat to watch Cygnus Prime swelling rapidly larger with their approach. Glinting silvery specks appeared, spaced out in front of the planet—*starships?* Darius assumed.

"Not long now..." Kara said.

Tell her you love her, Korvin said.

Darius winced, but did as he was asked.

Kara gave no reply for a long moment, but then she returned the sentiment. "I love you, too, Korry."

I wish we'd had a chance to settle down and have those kids, Korvin went on. Darius relayed that message, too.

"Me, too," Kara said, sniffling audibly. "But this is more important."

"Yes," Darius agreed, and swallowed past a painful lump in his throat.

You're going to burn in hell for this, Korvin said.

I know, Darius thought back. *I'm sorry, Korvin. I really am.*

Cygnus Prime filled their view now, the red and brown surface sweeping up fast, clouds strewn like tattered sheets across it.

"Five seconds to hit the atmosphere!" Kara announced. "Shields up, Korry!"

Darius engaged his ZPF shield, and the cockpit began glowing bright with its aura.

"Three, two, one—"

The Vulture began shuddering violently and glowing bright orange as they hit the upper atmosphere at a hundred and sixty kilometers per second. The air inside the cockpit grew warm, then scalding.

"Launch the missiles!" Darius screamed against the pain.

Kara did, and everything vanished in a blinding flash of light.

CHAPTER 48

Darius woke up crying. He couldn't believe what he'd done. He'd just forced an innocent man to kill himself!

"They did it..." Tanik said.

Darius looked up and watched through a blurry film of tears as a ball of fire went roiling through the darkness of space. For a moment he thought it was a star, but then that ball of fire dimmed and spread, expanding rapidly into a shimmering red cloud of super-heated dust and plasma. A kind of miniature supernova, the result of an exploding planet. Cygnus Prime.

"Look! It's taking out their fleet!" another voice said. It was Dyara. *Dyara?* he wondered.

Pinpricks of light bloomed, speckling the void with fresh bursts of flame as the expanding cloud of dust and gas reached them. She was right.

How was Dyara here? Tanik had been the only one with him in the cockpit of the Vulture.

Blinking in confusion, Darius turned to find her sitting next to him. He wasn't in his cockpit anymore. He sat strapped into a seat in the nonessential crew cabin of a much larger starship.

He remembered spending the last nine hours in Korvin's body, completely unaware of his real surroundings. Dyara had obviously come and rescued him and Tanik.

"Where are we?" Darius asked in a croaking voice.

Dyara turned to look at him, her eyes wide with shock and awe from the event they'd just witnessed. Her gaze softened in sympathy and confusion when she saw his tears.

"Are you okay?" she asked, and grabbed his arm.

He dropped his gaze and shook his head. She obviously didn't know what he'd done.

Dyara's sympathy turned to alarm. She glared over his shoulder. "You said it was just a trance! You said he'd be fine when he woke up!"

"It was," Tanik replied. "And he is fine—physically, anyway."

Dyara frowned. "What's that supposed to

mean?" Her eyes skipped back to Darius.

"I killed him," Darius said.

"What? Killed who?" Dyara asked.

Darius wiped his eyes and made a feeble effort to pull himself together. The least he could do was own up to it. So he explained in a halting voice what he'd done to the Revenant pilot named *Korvin*. By the time he was done with his explanation, Dyara was staring at him in horror.

He nodded and flashed a bitter smile. "Now you know why I'm not fine."

* * *

The Revenants had a raucous celebration that night in honor of the two pilots who'd sacrificed their lives to wipe out the Cygnian fleet and destroy their homeworld.

Darius spent the time in his quarters with Tanik and his daughter's cryo-pod, sharing a bottle of something that Tanik assured him was single malt scotch from Earth. It tasted nothing like single malt, but it was plenty strong, so it was good enough.

"You should be out there celebrating, too," Tanik said as he sucked whiskey through a straw in his flask. He lowered the flask with a grimace.

"Drinking in space leaves something to be desired. Scotch through a straw! Bleh."

Darius nodded. Maybe that was why it didn't taste the same. He peered down at his daughter's cryo-pod and scraped away a layer of frost with his fingernails to get a glimpse of her face. She looked too peaceful to be frozen at the brink of death. Maybe she was sleeping? But no, the *Harbinger's* medics had run scans and performed a tissue biopsy. She'd definitely been poisoned.

"We'll find a way to save her," Tanik whispered, and squeezed his shoulder.

Darius nodded and emptied his flask with a long drag from the straw. "More," he croaked, and wiped his mouth. The action sent tiny golden globules of scotch spinning away to the nearest air intake.

Tanik fetched the half-empty bottle floating behind them. While he re-filled Darius's flask, the door swished open and Dyara walked in. Followed by Admiral Ventaris.

Dyara was frowning, but the admiral beamed brightly. He walked right up to Darius and thrust out his hand.

Darius eyed the hand for a moment. The alcohol had turned his brain to soup.

"May I shake your hand?" Admiral Ventaris

prompted.

Darius scowled. "For what?"

Ventaris dropped his hand to his side. "Dyara told me what you did. It can't have been easy, but I want you to know you did the right thing, although it might not feel like that now."

"You're right, it doesn't," Darius replied.

"All the same."

"I keep trying to tell him," Tanik drawled, and then hiccuped loudly.

Admiral Ventaris stared at him. "Yes... you know, Mr. Gurhain, I'm still not fully satisfied with your explanation for being on board the *Nomad*. You were instrumental in that ship's escape. If not for you—"

"My daughter would be dead," Darius said, cutting the admiral off with a growl. "Blown to bits by your missiles."

Admiral Ventaris turned to him with a thin smile. "Yes, well—" He held Darius's gaze for lack of further justification. "I'll let you get on with your... drinking. I just wanted you to know that someone appreciates what you did. And more to the point, I respect it. When you're ready to formally join this fleet, there'll be a rank waiting for you." The admiral tapped a gleaming black badge with a glowing red outline on his upper left sleeve. Inside of it was a gold triangle with a single star at the top. The insignia of an admiral.

Darius nodded. "I'll keep that in mind... sir."

"Good."

"Cheers to that!" Tanik said, and raised his flask with a lazy grin. It got twisted into an ugly snarl by the scars on his face, and he hiccuped again before he could drink to his own toast. "I think I'd better go lie down... or, or—up, actually, since you can't lie *down* in space." He snickered at his own joke, and turned to leave. "G-night, D-arius," he said, with two more hiccups.

Admiral Ventaris mumbled something under his breath, and Tanik followed him out. The door swished shut behind them, leaving Darius and Dyara alone.

She walked over to him slowly, and he watched her approach with dull, staring eyes.

"I don't know how you could do what you did," she said, stopping in front of him. "But I'm not going to join you in beating yourself up. I don't think you're a bad person. You're a good person with a good heart who was in a bad situation, with the wrong people giving you advice."

"It was my choice," Darius objected, feeling suddenly too sober. "I didn't have to listen to them."

Dyara sighed and grabbed his hands in hers. "No, you didn't have to, so keep that in mind next time. As for right now, you can't let this destroy you. It won't undo what you did. You need to live if you're going to make up for your actions."

Darius nodded slowly. "What if they were right? What if this ended the war?"

"I *hope* they're right," Dyara replied. "That won't make what you did okay, but it would be a start."

"Yeah," Darius agreed and sucked in a shuddery breath. "What about her?" he jerked his chin to Cassandra's pod. "What do I do now?"

Dyara walked over to the pod and peered inside of it with a sad smile. "Nothing yet. Maybe we can find a specialist of some kind—someone with more experience in dealing with Cygnians and their venom. Maybe you'll get a different answer than the one the *Harbinger's* medic gave. Like you said, as long as she's not dead, there's still hope."

Darius swallowed thickly and a broken smile graced his lips. "Hope. That's an empty word if ever there was one."

CHAPTER 49

Tanik walked a suitably drunken line back to his quarters. It was more than enough to fool everyone who passed him in the corridor.

Darius hadn't noticed that he'd only been pretending to drink. He wouldn't have minded getting drunk, but he couldn't afford to lose his wits here, and not yet. He needed a clear head for what he was about to do.

Tanik locked the door to his quarters behind him, and then shut his eyes and raised his hands, drawing on the ZPF with every ounce of strength he had left.

A dazzling light soaked through his eyelids, and when he opened his eyes once more, he saw the source of that light: a dazzling orb hovering in the air, transparent in the center. A window into another world—literally. Through the window he spied a familiar stone edifice. Tanik smiled and stepped through to reach it.

He emerged on the steps of the castle on Ouroboros, having traveled tens of thousands of light years in an instant. Wormholes were mysterious objects. Some took time to cross, while others could take you around the galaxy in the blink of an eye. It all came down to the craftsman, and Tanik was a master like no other. He sucked in a deep breath of Ouroboros's warm air, savoring the scents and flavors of it...

The smell of home. Tanik smiled, and reached into the castle to look for his partner and summon her outside to greet him. Summoning her turned out to be unnecessary. She sat nearby, beside the fire in the entrance hall, and she'd already sensed his arrival.

She came striding down the steps, just as beautiful as ever.

"Tanik!" she said, beaming brightly at him.

"Feyra!" he replied, and ran to greet her with a kiss. As he withdrew, he picked her up and spun her in a circle. She laughed. It was the sweetest sound he'd heard in years.

Tanik set her down and withdrew to an arm's length to look upon her. She was the same as ever:

gaunt cheeks, jutting chin, prominent cheekbones, pointed white teeth, and a sparkling white skin that danced with Sprites. Her eyes were even more crowded with the glowing symbionts, and mesmerizing to look at. Feyra's thin, lanky arms reached for him, and three-fingered hands laced through his.

The Keth were not a beautiful species to most humans, but they were to him. Orphaned by the war, they'd raised him as one of their own. Tanik had come to love their people, even as he'd come to loathe his own. As a child, he'd often wished he could have been born a Keth rather than a human. The Keth hadn't treated him like an outsider, even though he'd often felt like one. His childhood and early adulthood on Ouroboros had been the happiest time of his life—until the Revenants slaughtered his people.

Feyra was one of the few that had survived, and only because the Revenants had mistaken him for the real Tanik Gurhain, a Revenant soldier. Tanik had taken advantage of the mistaken identity and used it to save Feyra's life by claiming that she was his prisoner.

They'd escaped Ouroboros together, and months later, they'd found their way back. Sitting in the ashes of their world, surrounded by the corpses of their people, they'd plotted their revenge. Tanik had planned to use his fake identity to infiltrate the Revenants and find a way to destroy them from within.

The Keth had always said he was destined for greatness. Tanik had never understood why they'd said that until this moment. Now, after twenty years of plotting and striving to tear the Union apart, it was all finally coming together. They'd finally done it.

"Tell me, Tanik," Feyra said in a whispering voice. "Did you succeed?"

"I did. The war has begun. Darius destroyed the Cygnians' homeworld. The Revenants had planned to cripple them in one blow, but I managed to stop them by letting the Cygnian Revenants escape and warn their people."

Feyra's dancing eyes widened and she smiled. "Darius destroyed their world? He has come a long way since you chased him off that cliff. It's a good thing I put him back together again."

Tanik nodded. "Yes, it is."

"But I wonder, why bother? Why him? Why go to so much trouble to make him feel special?"

"Because he *is* special," Tanik said.

Feyra arched an eyebrow—a human gesture, one of many that she'd picked up from him. "But you didn't need him to do any of this. You have the same power to influence other Revenants that he does. You could have done it all on your own."

"Yes, my love, I could have, but then *I* would have to be the one fighting with the Revenants, risking my life to tear them apart from within. This way, I've trained someone else to take up the crusade for me, which means we can be together while the war runs its course. The galaxy will burn, and our people will rebuild."

"Yes..." Feyra replied, smiling blissfully. "It's all happening just as you said it would."

"More or less," Tanik agreed.

"But why lure the girl to her death?"

Tanik smiled. Feyra had always been good at reading his mind. It helped that she was just as gifted with the ZPF as he.

"Darius needs a reason to make this war personal," he explained. "Now he has one. And besides, she's not dead." Tanik reached into his jumpsuit and withdrew a vial of clear liquid.

"What is that?" Feyra asked.

"Antivenin. From a Ghoul's venom sac."

"The one who stabbed her?"

Tanik nodded.

"You extracted it so that you could save her? Why?"

"Insurance. Darius is very powerful. We may need leverage someday."

Feyra looked dubious. "There has never been a Revenant as powerful as you." She rubbed his arm appreciatively and licked her lips with a bright pink tongue. Her sparkling eyes widened, and her mouth parted with a mixture of awe and adoration—or perhaps that was lust. It had been a long time since they'd last seen each other, let alone had time to themselves.

"I am *not* a Revenant," he chided. "Just because I took his name and look somewhat like him, does not mean that I *am* him."

"No, you're right," Feyra replied. "I am sorry. Speaking of your namesake..." She pulled an ancient-looking necklace from a pocket in the loose-fitting white tunic that she wore. It was the heart-shaped locket Darius had seen in his vision. "You're very lucky that no one opened this," Feyra said. She flicked the heart-shaped pendant open with her thumb, and a life-sized hologram of two people wrapped in each other's embrace flickered to life.

"It still works?" Tanik asked, blinking incredulously at the sight of the hologram. One of the two people was Samara—the real Samara, not Nova—while the other was Tanik Gurhain, her husband.

"We do look a lot alike," Tanik mused. "But these scars are a convenient disguise," he said, while running a hand over the raised lines running across his face. "Without them, someone who knew Tanik well might have realized that I'm not him."

"If they had, I'm sure you could have disposed of them quietly. *Did* anyone recognize you?" Feyra asked.

"No. Not even Nova, and I allowed her into my head."

"Yes, it is remarkable that you could hide your true nature from her and still give her some measure of control over you."

Tanik sneered. "She never had any measure of control over me. I was the one controlling her from the moment we met."

Feyra's eyes widened and she grinned. "You are unstoppable, my love."

Tanik smiled and wrapped an arm around her shoulders to draw her in for another kiss. "Yes," he murmured against her lips. "The Augur was the only one who could have stopped me, and we took care of him."

Feyra's eyes sparkled with delight. "Oh! I still have his head mounted on the wall."

Tanik blinked in shock. "In the castle? I thought I told you to get rid of that!"

"I did. I moved it to our cabin in the valley."

Tanik's nose wrinkled. "I find your taste in artwork disturbing..."

Feyra laughed. "Says the one who cut the head off and gave it to me. You shouldn't have done that if you didn't want me to keep it."

Tanik snorted and shook his head. He turned Feyra by her shoulders to look over the forest valley. The sun was setting, lighting the sky on fire. "Beautiful," he murmured.

Feyra laced her fingers through his once more. "Now what?" she asked.

"The other Revenants are still out there," he said. "Trapped on this side of the Eye with us. I think perhaps it's time we re-opened the wormhole so they can go join the war."

"Good idea."

"I wonder whose side the other Luminaries will join? The Cygnians' or their fellow Revenants'?"

"Does it matter?" Feyra asked. "One way or another, they're all going to kill each other."

Tanik laughed at that. "Yes, I suppose they will."

GET THE SEQUEL FREE

The Story Continues With...

Broken Worlds (Book 3): Civil War
(Coming June 18th, 2018)

Pre-order Now for a $2.00 Discount (Kindle)
(http://smarturl.it/brokenworlds2)

OR

Get a Kindle copy for FREE if you post an honest review of this book on Amazon and send it to me here: http://files.jaspertscott.com/bworlds3.htm

Thank you in advance for your feedback!
I read every review and use your comments to improve my work.

KEEP IN TOUCH

SUBSCRIBE to my Mailing List and get two FREE Books (Kindle)!
http://files.jaspertscott.com/mailinglist.html

Follow me on Twitter:
@JasperTscott

Look me up on Facebook:
Jasper T. Scott

Check out my website:
www.JasperTscott.com

Or send me an e-mail:
JasperTscott@gmail.com

OTHER BOOKS BY JASPER SCOTT

Suggested reading order

Broken Worlds
Broken Worlds: The Awakening (Book 1)
Broken Worlds: The Revenants (Book 2)
Broken Worlds: Civil War (Book 3)
Coming June 18th!

New Frontiers Series (Loosely-tied, Standalone Prequels to Dark Space)
Excelsior (Book 1)
Mindscape (Book 2)
Exodus (Book 3)

Dark Space Series
Dark Space
Dark Space 2: The Invisible War
Dark Space 3: Origin
Dark Space 4: Revenge
Dark Space 5: Avilon
Dark Space 6: Armageddon

<u>Dark Space Universe Series (Standalone Follow-up Trilogy to Dark Space)</u>
Dark Space Universe (Book 1)
Dark Space Universe: The Enemy Within (Book 2)
Dark Space Universe: The Last Stand (Book 3)
<u>Early Work</u>
Escape
Mrythdom

ABOUT THE AUTHOR

Jasper Scott is a USA TODAY bestselling science fiction author, known for writing intricate plots with unexpected twists.

His books have been translated into Japanese and German and adapted for audio, with collectively over 500,000 copies purchased.

Jasper was born and raised in Canada by South African parents, with a British cultural heritage on his mother's side and German on his father's, to which he has now added Latin culture with his wonderful wife.

After spending years living as a starving artist, he finally quit his various jobs to become a full-time writer. In his spare time he enjoys reading, traveling, going to the gym, and spending time with his family.

Made in the USA
Columbia, SC
02 November 2018